PENGUIN BOOKS

THE PENGUIN GUIDE TO THE LANDSCAPE OF ENGLAND AND WALES

Paul Coones was born in London in 1955 and was educated at Latymer Upper School and Christ Church, Oxford, where he read Geography. His subsequent doctoral research was concerned with geographical thought in the U.S.S.R. He was appointed to a Departmental Demonstratorship in the School of Geography, University of Oxford, in 1979 and to a College Lectureship at Hertford College in 1980. His principal interests lie within the fields of geographical thought, geopolitics and landscape studies.

John Patten is a Fellow of Hertford College, Oxford, where he taught before entering Parliament in 1979 for the City of Oxford. Now M.P. for Oxford West and Abingdon, he is Minister of State for Housing, Urban Affairs and Construction. The author of a number of papers and books on historical geography, and founder editor of the *Journal of Historical Geography*, he has been interested in the development of landscape since he was an undergraduate at Sidney Sussex College, Cambridge.

PAUL COONES AND JOHN PATTEN

The Penguin Guide to the
Landscape of England and Wales

PENGUIN BOOKS

Penguin Books Ltd, Harmondsworth, Middlesex, England
Viking Penguin Inc., 40 West 23rd Street, New York, New York 10010, U.S.A.
Penguin Books Australia Ltd, Ringwood, Victoria, Australia
Penguin Books Canada Limited, 2801 John Street, Markham, Ontario, Canada L3R 1B4
Penguin Books (N.Z.) Ltd, 182–190 Wairau Road, Auckland 10, New Zealand

First published 1986

Made and printed in Great Britain by
Richard Clay (The Chaucer Press) Ltd,
Bungay, Suffolk
Filmset in Monophoto Times by
Northumberland Press Ltd, Gateshead,
Tyne and Wear

For our parents

CONTENTS

LIST OF ILLUSTRATIONS

PREFACE

Those who attempt an explanatory description of a cultural landscape are confronted with a daunting task. Landscape is in its very essence a totality, composed of a multitude of interrelated elements which cannot easily be separated or divided for analysis without the unity being violated and the overall conception lost. The modern trend towards specialist study in terms of topic, period, district and approach has encouraged the splitting up of the geographical environment for research purposes, to the detriment of the synthesis which comprises the reality. The associated enthusiasm for new theories, while resulting in some penetrating examinations of individual elements or particular groups of phenomena, has tended to sweep aside and dismiss as 'mere description' attempts to account for the nature of particular places. But description, besides being a necessary first step towards explanation, is in truth an extremely difficult and highly skilled operation when the observer is dealing with such a wealth of interpenetrating features as those which make up a landscape. As the great British geographer Sir Halford Mackinder wrote, 'it is the essential limitation of literature that it must make its statements in sequence to the mind's ear, whereas geography presents its map to the mind's eye and states many facts simultaneously'.

A written account must nevertheless start somewhere in its attempt to build up a mental image of the whole, although none of the various available methods is wholly satisfactory. The ultimate need is for a discipline which reflects the unity of the object of study. The present work, rather more modestly, offers an account of the cultural landscape of England and Wales in several broad phases. By this means, as opposed to taking particular elements separately, individual phenomena are at least related in some degree to their geographical contexts and to each other. All too often the analysis of disaggregated systematic themes has in any case led not to a true understanding of process but to the writing of narrative forms of economic or social history. The so-called process sometimes amounts to little more than the flow of time itself, mere sequence being confused with consequence. Landscape is neither a careless jumble of artefacts nor a loose assemblage of necessarily evolving or progressing themes, but a complex entity rooted in a specific time and a particular place.

It is especially difficult to present a portrait of the landscape of England and Wales within the confines of a book of modest proportions, for there are few countries of comparable size in the world which show such diversity in their pattern of landscapes.* The immense variety of natural conditions, the complex history of these islands, and the kaleidoscopic nature of the regional scene make the construction of all-embracing explanatory frameworks hazardous in the extreme. In order to emphasize this condition rather than evade it, this book attempts to furnish for each period a set of remarks which, although generalized, depict the salient aspects upon a broad scale and without, it is hoped, too much over-simplification. Each chapter is followed by descriptions of some highly select sites, chosen to illustrate the principles outlined in the text and to give representative and realistic examples of the richness of the local scene with all its problems, variations and details. It is not intended that these examples should provide an exhaustive chronological, topical or regional gazetteer, but rather a kind of bridge between the general and the specific. The real joy in landscape study comes with the acquisition of a trained eye and mature imagination to visualize the total geographical environment, dynamic in its spatial and temporal associations and suggestive in its internal forces and interrelationships.

With a certain degree of regret, the authors have used the new system of counties introduced in 1974 (on the perhaps appropriate date of 1 April). Precise locations are identified by means of National Grid references, as used on Ordnance Survey maps. A note explaining these references appears on p. 21. Although the book is designed to be largely self-contained, the use of Ordnance Survey maps will enable the relevant features to be readily identified in the field, and facilitate the planning of visits or excursions. Ordinary motoring or touring maps, which concentrate on larger places and on roads and services, are of little help in studying the complexities of the landscape either at home or in the field. The best generally available series of O.S. maps for this purpose is the 1:25,000 scale (approximately $2\frac{1}{2}$ inches to the mile), which displays a wealth of topographical detail, including field boundaries, earthworks, and aspects of physique, vegetation and settlement not depicted on

* Referring in a recent review ('Landscape studies', *The Local Historian* 16 (1984), pp. 172–4) to W. G. Hoskins's seminal *The Making of the English Landscape* (1955), Michael Aston remarks that 'it would now not be possible to write a single volume to cover all aspects of that theme'; the challenge is rendered even more imposing when it is recalled that Hoskins's book, despite its comprehensive title, concentrated upon one principal topic, namely the evolution of human settlement.

smaller-scale maps; but the 1:50,000 ('Metric') sheets are nevertheless useful, though inferior to their 1:63,360 ('One Inch') predecessors. For some of the sites included in this book, examination of 1:25,000 sheets is felt to be especially valuable, and the relevant sheet numbers are therefore given in brackets at the beginning of the description.

ACKNOWLEDGEMENTS

The authors record their debt to all those who have described, investigated and researched the diverse aspects of the landscape of England and Wales, and upon whose writings they have drawn in the production of this book. With regard to the illustrations, they wish to thank Mr P. Masters and Mr A. Lee of the School of Geography, University of Oxford, for their cheerful and enthusiastic assistance concerning photographic equipment and processing respectively, and Mr J. Livingstone of the Department of Geography, University of Aberdeen, for his painstaking and highly professional work in the production of those plates made from original photographs. The text figures were compiled and sketched by Paul Coones, the final versions of Figures 1–3, 5, 12, 15, 18, 20, 22, 25, 28–9, 40, 42, 57, 62, 73–4 and 76 being drawn with exceptional care and expertise by Mrs A. Newman. Figure 8 was drawn by Winifred Coones, to whom the authors are especially grateful: she typed the manuscript meticulously, offering many excellent suggestions for improvement as she did so. Elizabeth Leggatt's wide knowledge of current developments in archaeology and local history proved invaluable in the composition of several passages. Louise Patten undertook a considerable volume of research for the book in the early stages of its preparation, and thanks are also due to Mr and Mrs Leon Brittan, Mr and Mrs John Rowe, and Mr and Mrs Anthony Watson, who were all good enough to make their homes open for lengthy periods for one of us while the volume was being composed. Mr Peter Carson and Mr John Denny of Penguin Books greatly assisted the authors by their flexibility and understanding. The copyediting was performed with outstanding skill and sensitivity by Mrs Judith Wardman. The index was compiled by Mr William Mills.

Photographs and illustrations were supplied by and are reproduced through courteous permission of the following:

Cambridge University Collection: copyright reserved (Figures 4, 30, 31, 39, 45); The Director, British Geological Survey (NERC): Crown Copyright reserved (6); Aerofilms Ltd (10, 11, 13, 17, 23, 24, 26, 27, 41, 46, 51, 67); Society of Antiquaries of London (19); Ministry of Defence: Crown Copyright reserved; print supplied through the kindness of Mr D. J. Bonney and Dr C. C. Taylor of the Royal Commission on Historical Monuments (England) (44); Birmingham Museums and Art Gallery (49); The British Library (50); John Dewar Studios (56); Victoria Art Gallery, Bath (59); The Trustees of the British Museum (63); National Railway Museum, York: copyright (64, 69); Science Museum, London (65); Mary Evans Picture Library (70); Mansell Collection (71); Museum of London (72); The Reference Library, History and Geography Department, Birmingham Public Libraries (75); Gloucestershire County Libraries: Cinderford Branch (77); Mr A. Pope (78); The Photo Source (83).

Figures 9, 16, 21, 32, 33, 34, 35, 36, 37, 38, 43, 47, 48, 52, 53, 54, 55, 58, 60, 61, 66, 68, 79, 80, 81 and 82 were taken by Paul Coones, who would like to thank the National Trust for generously granting him permission to reproduce four of his private photographs of National Trust properties as Figures 35, 36, 52, and 53.

Figures 3 and 73 are based on the 1:1,584,000 Geological Map of the British Islands (5th edition, 1969), and upon information contained in 1:63,360 Sheet 27 and accompanying Memoir respectively, published by the British Geological Survey (Institute of Geological Sciences), NERC, by permission of the Director. Figure 14 is reproduced from 1:10,000 Sheet SW 43 NE, published by the Ordnance Survey: Figures 12, 15, 22, 25, 29, 42, 57, 62, 74, 76 are either based upon or incorporate information derived from maps produced by the Ordnance Survey, Crown Copyright reserved, with the permission of the Controller of Her Majesty's Stationery Office. Figure 18 is based upon Figure 1 and Plate LI of R. E. M. Wheeler and T. V. Wheeler, *Report on the excavation of the prehistoric, Roman, and post-Roman site in Lydney Park, Gloucestershire (Reports of the Research Committee of the Society of Antiquaries of London* No. IX) (1932), by kind permission of the Society of Antiquaries of London. Figure 20 is partly derived from information presented in the map on p. 53 of H. R. Loyn, *Anglo-Saxon England and the Norman Conquest* (1962), and Figure 74 is modelled upon Figure 2.3 in K. J. Hilton (ed.), *The Lower Swansea Valley Project* (1967), both by kind permission of the Longman Group Ltd. Figure 28 includes information contained in N. Neilson, 'The forests', pp. 394–467 of J. F. Willard and W. A. Morris (eds.), *The English Government at Work, 1327–1336*, Volume I: *Central and prerogative administration* (Cambridge, Mass., 1940), Map V, by kind permission of the Medieval Academy of America. Figure 40 is based upon Figure 15 of R. Newton, *The Northumberland Landscape* (1972), by kind permission of Hodder and Stoughton. Figure 57 is based partly upon the plan contained in the Department of the Environment Official Handbook, *The Fortifications of Berwick-upon-Tweed* (4th impression, 1976), by I. MacIvor, through the courtesy of Her Majesty's Stationery Office.

A NOTE ON ORDNANCE SURVEY GRID REFERENCES

The National Grid used by the Ordnance Survey enables the location of any point in Great Britain to be accurately recorded and identified. This is achieved by means of a unique grid reference incorporating a sequence of letters and numbers. The grid comprises a system of intersecting north-south and east-west lines which are drawn so as to produce an arrangement of progressively smaller squares based upon metric units. For the purpose of standard grid reference calculations, the smallest units employed are the kilometre squares, and the largest blocks measure 100 kilometres by 100 kilometres. Each of these blocks is identified by a particular pair of letters, e.g. S W, which covers western Cornwall. These letters, shown in the keys of the individual maps, form a prefix denoting the 100-kilometre square in which the required point falls. The remaining figures (six, in a standard reference) allow the point to be discovered within the block, using the finer divisions. It is important to remember firstly that the construction of the reference is made using the progressive distances eastward and northward from the south-western corner of the block (the point of origin of the whole national system lies off the Isles of Scilly), and secondly that the 'eastings' (north-south lines) are always given *before* the 'northings' (east-west lines). These are numbered along the top and bottom, and along the sides of the map respectively, at one-kilometre intervals from 00 to 99 in each 100-kilometre square.

An example may be given using the O.S. 1:10,000 map of part of Cornwall reproduced as Figure 14 on p. 99. The whole area lies within the 100-kilometre square denoted by the letters S W. The kilometre square in which Amalveor Farm lies is S W 4837, because easting 48 defines the western boundary of the square, and northing 37 the southern. To describe the precise location of Amalveor Farm within the kilometre square, estimate the number of tenths of a kilometre eastward from easting 48 (3), and the number of tenths northward from northing 37 (5). (In effect, an imaginary additional grid comprising lines drawn at 0.1–kilometre intervals is being laid upon the kilometre square.) The intersection of these lines gives the six-figure reference for Amalveor Farm, which is thus S W 483375, giving its location to the nearest 100-metre intersection.

For larger features, or for purposes of general description, the four-figure reference, defining the kilometre square (S W 4837), is often sufficient. Occasionally in this book a degree of precision greater than that afforded by the six-figure reference (S W 483375) has been deemed necessary, and an eight-figure reference constructed, estimating tenths of tenths (i.e. hundredths) of a kilometre square (the location of Amalveor Bungalow being S W 48313755). The use of eight-figure grid references, accurate to 10 metres, is generally practicable only when studying large-scale maps and plans.

To find a point given as a six-figure reference, simply reverse the operation described above. For Amalveor Farm (SW 483375), choose a sheet covering the appropriate portion of the 100-kilometre square SW. Then take the first three figures (483) and insert a decimal point before the last digit: 48.3. Find easting 48, and move beyond it for 0.3 of a kilometre. Take the second three numbers (375), add the decimal point as before (37.5) and find northing 37. Move up beyond it 0.5 of a kilometre. The point where the eastings and northings cross is Amalveor Farm, marked on the map.

Finally, it should be borne in mind that 1:25,000 sheets, the First Series of which each cover a standard area of 10 by 10 kilometres, are denoted individually by the grid reference of their south-west corners to the nearest 10 kilometres. (The Second Series sheets extend over *two* 10-kilometre squares.) Thus Amalveor Farm (SW 483375) will be found on 1:25,000 ('2½ Inch') sheet SW 43, and this is the sheet mentioned at the start of the description of the site entitled 'Zennor, Cornwall'.

A NOTE ON METRIC UNITS

All the measurements in this book are given in imperial units. The metric equivalents are listed below.

1 foot	=	0.3048 metre
1 mile	=	1.6093 kilometres
1 acre	=	0.4047 hectare
1 square mile	=	640 acres = 259 hectares = 2.590 square kilometres
1 metre	=	3.2808 feet
1 kilometre	=	0.6214 mile
1 hectare	=	2.471 acres
1 square kilometre	=	100 hectares = 247.1 acres = 0.3861 square mile

INTRODUCTION

The Nature of Landscape

The term 'landscape' encompasses a bewildering variety of meanings and interpretations, from the subjective impressions of the artist to the designs and creations of the gardener or planner. In one of its most ancient forms the word referred to a tract of land which made up a natural entity or region. This Anglo-Saxon usage has been reflected in the traditional concept of landscape embraced by geographers and pursued as an academic study, although for most people nowadays the term conjures up the idea of a scenic view – a response to its currency among painters. But even, and perhaps especially, in scholastic circles, the idea of landscape is an elusive one. The subject matter and methods of approach are exceedingly diverse, and with numerous disciplines now claiming an interest, it is hardly surprising that the study of landscape has been attacked as too vague and all-inclusive to permit of focused research, logical precision or rigorous explanation. This is a consequence of the inadequacies of prevailing methodological frameworks rather than the nature of the real world, which is not of course neatly divided up along the artificial lines that demarcate the territories of academic specialisms. Several branches of knowledge, particularly those concerned with the unravelling of the past, are occupied with the examination of sets of artefacts preserved in the visual scene. These artefacts are used as clues in the reconstruction of former conditions (archaeology, for example) or the tracing of an aspect of human activity over time (settlement history). Other scholars, notably in geography, have been concerned less with the extraction of individual elements than with attempts to understand the workings of the whole in particular regions or places.

Despite the insistence of some geographers upon a conception of geography which reflects the unity of the 'seamless' geographical environment, landscape research is usually split between the investigation of the natural or physical landscape (rocks, landforms, soils, vegetation, hydrology and climate) and the cultural landscape (the works of man). This is hardly satisfactory in view of the close links between man and nature, which after all make up a great part of the landscape itself. Human societies do not operate in a vacuum, but within a particular *milieu*; thus even when the emphasis is placed upon the works of man (as in this book), the influences of nature and the role played by physical forces and conditions cannot be ignored. Landscape is the visible expression of the altered geographical environment, the tangible product of the operation of natural processes over aeons and the activities of mankind in transforming and using the environment over a much shorter span of time. In many ways the separation of man and environment is itself artificial, for society is not a supranatural category but one inextricably related both in a material and a perceptual sense to natural elements and processes, constraints and resources. Far from being rendered an irrelevance, the environment becomes in certain respects more significant as economic development proceeds. Indeed, some commentators (notably some of the great Russian landscape scholars) have suggested that it is very hard for man to *create* a landscape in the true sense: so-called anthropogenic landscapes generally involve merely the alteration of a natural system and the construction of artefacts within it. (Given sufficient time, most 'man-made' landscapes would revert to their natural state if human interference were to cease.) The real intellectual challenge is presented not by the identification and classification of these artefacts as creations of men and women, or their arrangement into chronological sequences as part of an attempt to use the cultural landscape as proof of society's progressive triumph over nature, but by the investigation of their place within the totality of the geographical environment.

This challenge has only rarely been taken up. But it is still necessary for the student of the cultural landscape to understand the natural environment, or as much of it as varies locally. The physical geography of the British Isles is astonishingly diverse, particularly in terms of geology, landforms and soils, and it is important to know something of these inescapable contributors to the regional scene. It is also imperative to recognize that natural elements are not constant in the face of societal dynamism, as writers of the 'man-made' landscape school sometimes maintain, but change and fluctuate over time. The reconstruction of past environments, notably in terms of climate, soils, vegetation and hydrology, is an important part of the study of historic landscapes and the evolution of the present scene. The contention that the landscape is an artificial commodity fashioned out of 'neutral stuff' by the creative hand of man upon a static and now largely irrelevant physical base rests upon a selective view which ignores the universal use of countless natural elements by society, the environmental foundations of economic functions, and the contribution made by relief, climate and natural resources even in intensely humanized scenes.

In addition to its broad role in geographical inquiry, the study of landscape makes a contribution within several other related fields. As a record of changing man-environment relationships, the landscape constitutes a historical source of very great value, yielding to the eye of the skilled researcher many clues to the past which are absent from written documentary evidence. The remarkable resilience of many ancient shapes or deeply engraved forms testifies to the ability of form to outlast function. Frequently the information is preserved indirectly, the remnants of an early phase being partly removed and partly adopted by a later one. The lines of a town's defences may remain in the street pattern long after the walls themselves have gone; a medieval field system is reflected in the subsequent arrangement of enclosures; a prehistoric trackway survives in the guise of a lane between high banks or hedges. Sometimes whole 'secret landscapes' are discovered, fossilized beneath a succession of imprints. Many features which seem insignificant in themselves, especially boundaries of various kinds, constitute the lineaments of former field systems, settlements or communication routes. Additions to the landscape are often influenced by existing features, so ancient boundaries may be reinforced or given a new expression. Thus the edge of a forest lives on in the landscape of agriculture and settlement centuries after the last trees were removed.

In recent years new techniques have added greatly to our knowledge of former landscapes. One of the most significant has been the development of aerial photography and other forms of remote sensing, which reveal features invisible from ground level. In view of the fact that modern farming can, in just a few seasons, erase countless patterns which had endured for hundreds and thousands of years, it is extremely fortunate that photographs taken from the air in particular conditions of light and at certain times of year can reveal traces of seemingly vanished elements. These 'ghost' forms are often preserved as crop-markings created by the differential growth or colouring of crops raised upon soils which, through spatial variations in their composition or moisture content, carry the former outlines of buildings and other features now gone, or of foundations and ditches buried underneath. Progress has also been made in archaeological methods (ensuring rigorous and thorough excavation), in pollen analysis and related palaeobotanical studies (assisting in the investigation of former vegetation covers), and in dating techniques (providing a tighter relative chronology of events).

It is often remarked that the landscape is a rich historical document of inestimable importance. But it is a very selective, distorted and potentially treacherous source, full of enigmas and interrupted by enormous gaps. In this the cultural landscape is comparable with the stratigraphic record of the geologist, which through its sequence of rocks offers a partial portrait of the evolution of life, and reflects the succession of ancient environmental conditions and the characteristics of now vanished palaeogeographies in a highly incomplete fashion. In both cases some elements are preserved well and others not at all, while particular categories dominate certain spatial or temporal contexts in a grossly unrepresentative way. The oldest parts of the record are among the most difficult to reconstruct, for a great deal is missing and the remnants are often almost unrecognizable as a consequence of alteration, metamorphosis and burial beneath newer layers. Particular areas have undergone intense deformation because of their locations, structures or configurations, which have resulted in their subjection to repeated changes or pressures. It is easy, therefore, in geology and landscape study alike, to draw wrong conclusions from inadequate data, disrupted sequences and unreal distributions, or without due regard for the tendency of contemporary processes and later events to produce a fragmentary and biased picture. For example, an examination of the evidence at face value could suggest that the activities of prehistoric man in southern England were largely confined to the erection of large earthworks upon the higher ground, notably the chalklands; or that the medieval open fields extended only over the English Midlands, until Parliamentary enclosure swept them away; or that the English village was one of the great elements of continuity in the landscape, providing in its layout and buildings a glimpse of original Anglo-Saxon settlement structure and medieval social hierarchy. These and many other beliefs have been undermined since more rigorous scrutiny of the material has shown that they were derived from false premises. Similarly, almost every major period has been proposed at one time or another as the key phase in the creation of the landscape, or, more specifically, the great era of forest clearance, colonization or settlement creation.

These broader issues are of more than mere antiquarian interest. The legacy of the past makes up the landscape of the present, the living environment of modern society, subject to conflicting pressures and events. The landscape is also a repository of values, symbols and images which embody the extraordinarily rich heritage of this country and influence current attitudes and beliefs. It is the nest which society has made for itself, and as such not only recalls the past but also comments eloquently – and often uncompromisingly – on the present.

CHAPTER 1

The Natural Landscape

A study of the natural landscape is indispensable to an understanding of the cultural landscape of England and Wales. Far from providing a featureless surface or *tabula rasa* upon which man has been able to construct a landscape as the unconstrained expression of human ingenuity and free will (if such exists), natural forces have combined to create a highly distinctive environment which continues to influence human societies at every turn. For all his technical skills and sophisticated forms of social organization, man remains a part of his environment. The physical landscape is the intricate product of a variety of elements – location, physiography, geology, climate, soils and vegetation – which if left aside not only render descriptions of the nature and distribution of human activities as embodied in the cultural landscape woefully incomplete and arrogantly anthropocentric, but also violate the essential wholeness of landscape itself. The landscape of England and Wales is a unique synthesis of natural and human elements, inextricably interwoven in a continuous history – a visible record of changing man-environment relations from the earliest times.

The position of Britain

The fundamental geographical attribute of any country is its location on the face of the globe. The British Isles comprise an island group formed from an unsubmerged portion of the continental shelf, separated from Europe by shallow seas but closely related to the continent by merit of the indented coastlines on either side of the narrows. In many respects Britain's position through much of history has been marginal rather than central; the true continent is not Europe, but the great landmass of Eurasia, from which Europe thrusts westwards into the great ocean as a collection of peninsulas and islands. England, 'that utmost corner of the west', has been able to preserve insularity without isolation, her continental connections fashioning her ethnographic development, and her maritime position in turn contributing to the development of overseas trade and eventually to the acquisition of an empire. The lowland angle of Britain, with its estuaries and inlets, faces Europe (where some of

England's geological structures find their continuations), while the highlands are confined to the oceanic border. The history of Britain might
have been quite different if England had been separated from Europe by
a channel rifted through uplands. As a result, the 'envious siege of watery
Neptune' which rendered Britain 'a world by itself' has not prevented
intercourse with neighbouring peoples, a process to which the cultural
landscape bears eloquent testimony.

Climate

A principal function of geographical location is climate, which qualifies
for consideration as the key factor in the creation of natural landscapes.
The balance between heat and moisture in the annual cycle underlies a
host of natural processes and unifies the atmosphere, the surface waters
and the underground reservoirs in the grand conception of the hydrologi-
cal cycle. The nature and type of precipitation and the intensity of
evaporation, the cycles of freezing and thawing, the circulation of the
atmosphere manifested in the movement of pressure systems and the
behaviour of the winds and clouds profoundly influence the processes of
weathering and erosion and the development of soils and vegetation.
While the general characteristics of climate determine much of the general
appearance of a landscape, crucial parameters not reflected in climatic
averages may be equally important. For example, the probability of
extreme events such as droughts and floods, and the likelihood of apparently minor occurrences like early and late frosts can all affect the
pattern of agriculture, which represents man's most widespread visible
manipulation of natural ecosystems.

   The British climate is a distinctive one, although the variety of the day-
to-day weather conditions has often prompted the confused remark that
Britain has no climate, only weather. Such sentiments no doubt serve to
maintain the great British topic of conversation, but it required the eye of
an artist and lover of landscape to rejoice in the diversity. When Ruskin
remarked that there was no such thing as bad weather, only different
varieties of good weather, he was not merely rebuffing those who felt that
nature's prime concern ought to be the suiting of human convenience.
Echoing Constable's fascination with clouds, Ruskin said of himself that
he bottled clouds as carefully as his father (who was a wine merchant)
had bottled sherries, but the immensity of the task proved too great.
Nevertheless the kaleidoscopic pattern of weather conditions in Britain
constitutes the very essence of the climate, which in turn is one of the
principal determinants of the scenery that the landscape painters strove

to capture on canvas. The British landscape, clothed in lush vegetation displaying a multitude of shades of green, illuminated by an ever-changing light and transformed in texture and tone with the subtle passage of the seasons, is the product of Britain's moist, equable, maritime climate.

Air masses from several directions, and therefore of many types, meet or pass over the British Isles, and all have been obliged to travel over a greater or lesser expanse of sea. The proximity of the continent explains the tendency of continental air to extend at times from the east, bringing icy polar weather in winter, sometimes with spectacular results, as in 1947 and 1962–3, while in summer tropical continental air occasionally extends from the south to bring hot and dry weather. 'Blocking' anticyclones of this kind contributed to the droughts of 1975 and 1976. However, most of Britain's weather comes from the west, upon moisture-laden winds which have travelled great distances over the relatively warm ocean. These moderating influences ensure that the British Isles enjoy a mild climate despite their relatively high latitude, keeping the western coasts warm in winter, but also serving to lower temperatures in summer. It is unusual for any single weather type to predominate for very long before giving way to another, but the prevailing westerlies with their frontal systems (formed where the cold air of high latitudes meets the warmer air to the south) themselves bring a sequence of meteorological events with them. The depressions which roll in from the Atlantic produce a pattern of conditions which is predictable in outline, but rarely so in terms of timing and detail: this is what makes weather forecasting in Britain so difficult. It is little wonder that weather records of all kinds are constantly being broken. The monotony of a continental climate, in which maritime influences are excluded, is alien to the British Isles: prolonged extremes of temperature are rare, to the regret of those who claim to prefer the tedious heat and cloudless skies characteristic of other climes. In the summer of 1976, when such conditions were indeed experienced, the landscape began to lose its familiar, well-watered greens, which normally prevail even through the hot spells of summer, and took on instead a parched, brown and distinctly less engaging aspect, with vegetation more reminiscent of a Mediterranean region. If Britain had to endure the kind of summer that many holidaymakers apparently desire, the countryside would probably soon look like something akin to an African savanna. Part of the human dissatisfaction results from the insistence on August as the main holiday month, although climatic records clearly show that it tends to be wet.

Climate interacts with other landscape elements to produce noticeable local variations in the general patterns of temperature and precipitation.

These local climates and, to an even greater extent, society's perception of them are responsible for the location of the holiday towns and health resorts which are such a characteristic feature of the cultural landscape of the British coastline. The principal factor in the creation of regional and local climates is relief, which greatly complicates the climatic pattern by necessitating the adjustment of the fluid circulations of the atmosphere to the solid features of the land surface. The contrast between the wetter west and the drier east is a consequence of the arrangement of uplands, which lie athwart the rain-bearing westerlies. These winds sweep in from the Atlantic, drenching the heads of the mountains with their accumulated moisture, leaving the lowlands as a rain-shadow.

Relief

The uplands and lowlands

The pattern of relief units and the familiar outline formed by the British coasts are the result of the present level of the sea; it is easy to forget that the submarine topography is really only a flooded extension of the land surface, with comparable features and geological structures. Far from being constant, sea levels are transitory and ephemeral, even on the time-scale of human history: Britain was last cut off from Europe a mere 8,000 or so years ago, and portions of land at the coast have been gained or lost in recent centuries. The emergent land surface is constantly battered by the elements, while the submerged regions are preserved by the waters and buried by deposits transported from the shores. The complex balance of forces determines the details of the coastline, with its cliffs, beaches, spits, bars, estuaries, bays, inlets and natural harbours. The movements of the waters, influenced by the configuration of the coastline, give rise to the pattern of the currents and tidal fluctuations, the local characteristics of which have influenced port development (most dramatically in the case of the so-called 'double high tide' at Southampton), Britain's important fishing industry, shipping and trade.

The intricacy of the coastline of the British Isles is demonstrated by the great length of coast (8,617 miles) in relation to the total area of the islands (120,800 square miles). The seas break the continuity of what would otherwise be (and has been in the past) a single compact landmass of Britain. They also reduce the greater island to a long, narrow strip, with a northern portion remote and difficult of access from the south. Throughout a long period of history, racial differences and difficulties of transport served to maintain two separate kingdoms, Scotland and England, and a healthy measure of provincialism survives. The British

Isles consist of three important uplands and three extensive lowlands, the pattern accentuating the triple division indicated by the coastal outlines, since although the Scottish Highlands are placed terminally, the Central Uplands (extending south from the Southern Uplands of Scotland to the Lake District, the Pennines and the Peak District) divide the Scottish from the English Lowland, and the Welsh Upland intervenes between the English Lowland and Ireland. The English Plain fills the continental angle of Britain to the shores of the narrow seas, the direction of consequent drainage being in the same landward direction, facing towards Europe; the Scottish and Irish Plains on the other hand are isolated among the uplands of the oceanic border. The three kingdoms, with their respective capitals, were in essence the three lowlands, separated by march-belts of barren upland and sea-channel.

Wales, the fourth part of the realm, never gained the same independence from England as did Scotland and Ireland. This was largely because of the eastward tilt of her drainage and the transverse lie – east and west – of the chief valleys and coastal routes, which laid Wales open to the English Plain, and enabled the English to drive a wedge between the north and south, using the upper Severn valley. The only extensive fastness of Wales, which formed a last refuge of independence, is that afforded by the natural fortress of Gwynedd, along the shores of the Menai Strait, protected by the mountain ridge which runs from Great Orme's Head south-west to Lleyn, culminating in the peak of Snowdon. The geographical and cultural contrasts between North and South Wales persist to this day. Furthermore, there is no Welsh town whose nodality has been strong enough to raise it to the position of capital of the principality. Indeed, it is said that the principals of the colleges of the University of Wales used to meet in the Great Western Hotel at Paddington.

The English Plain reaches the western seas at only two points. The Bristol and Midland 'Gates' not only admitted the roads from the continental angle into the recesses of the oceanic border, but also severed the western and central uplands of South Britain into Devonian, Welsh and Pennine masses: the Celts were fatally defeated when the Teutonic conquest was thrust through to the Severn and the Dee, dividing them into three separate communities inhabiting three uplands in the ends of the land. The Vale of York and the coastal sill of Durham and Northumberland gave access to Scotland, but the Southern Uplands long prevented the fusion of England with Scotland, as did the St George's Channel in the case of Ireland. In contrast, the physical and historical relations of Wales and England are reflected in the cultural landscape of Wales, which may be suitably considered in connection with that of

England, while the separate histories of Scotland and Ireland have produced landscapes which differ in several key respects from those of England.

Highland and Lowland Britain

This contrast between the uplands and the lowlands is fundamental. The pattern of relief and drainage directed the successive groups of invaders, created the strategic land and water routes upon which towns grew up (to become, in the Midland scarplands, the foci of shires), and largely determined the modes of existence, the distribution and mutual relations of racial groups, and the location of the kingdoms. But it is possible to go further and assert, as did Mackinder, that 'the contrast between the south-east and the north-west of Britain, between the plains and low coasts towards the continent, and the cliff-edged uplands of the oceanic border, with all the resultant differences – agricultural, industrial, racial, and historical – depends on a fundamental distinction in rock structure'. It so happens that the north and west of Britain are formed mainly from geologically old and generally resistant rocks, while the south and east are underlain by younger, softer rocks, contorted or altered to a lesser degree. The boundary, often generalized to follow a line from the Tees to the Exe, separates the Coal Measures and older rocks from those which were laid down more recently (Figure 1).

Highland Britain is the complex product of aeons of time in which great thicknesses of sediment were deposited, consolidated, uplifted and denuded yet again, to be folded, faulted and distorted by great earth movements, a process often accompanied by profound alteration of the rocks. Thus the original sedimentary strata were frequently transformed by heat and pressure into metamorphic rocks, as molten material was thrust upwards from below the earth's surface to cool eventually into igneous rocks. Some of these igneous bodies were intruded into the surface rocks to cool slowly beneath a cover and perhaps be exposed later by denudation. These intrusive igneous rocks, such as granite, differ from volcanic igneous rocks, which were extruded on the surface as lava flows or mixtures of the products of more explosive volcanic activity. Despite prolonged denudation, which reduced the original mountains to mere worn remnants or broken stubs, these rocks still furnish Britain with its upland scenery. The geographical characteristics of Highland Britain derive from its geological structure. The resistant rocks produce poor soils, which have been stripped in places by glacial action, while the exposed nature of the uplands results in a generally harsher climate with high precipitation, much of it falling in the winter as snow. Growing seasons are shorter than elsewhere, and this, combined with the steep

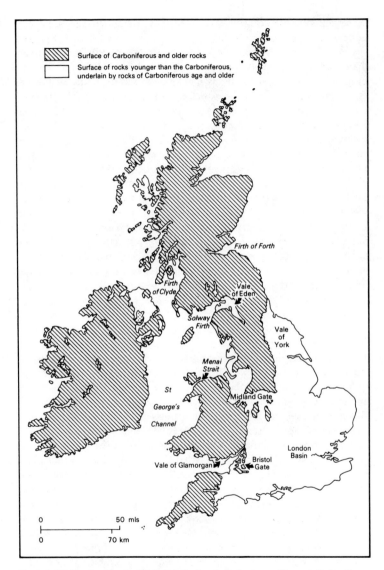

Legend:
- Surface of Carboniferous and older rocks
- Surface of rocks younger than the Carboniferous, underlain by rocks of Carboniferous age and older

Firth of Forth

Firth of Clyde

Vale of Eden

Solway Firth

Vale of York

Menai Strait

St George's Channel

Midland Gate

Vale of Glamorgan

Bristol Gate

London Basin

0   50 mls

0   70 km

Figure 1. Highland and Lowland Britain defined geologically. (NOTE: The post-Carboniferous rocks of Northern Ireland and western Scotland are mainly igneous rocks of Tertiary age)

slopes, infertile and acid soils, has resulted in a predominance of pastoral agriculture.

Lowland Britain, in contrast, is formed almost entirely from relatively young sedimentary rocks composed of sediment derived from the erosion of older landmasses and laid down in lakes or seas before being consolidated and uplifted. These rocks, mainly a series of clays, sandstones and limestones, were gently rather than violently folded, being tilted and eroded to form a sequence of surface outcrops in which older beds are overlapped by successively younger strata. Variations in resistance to erosion have produced a grained surface of escarpments and intervening vales, with basins and plains set amongst them, whose characteristics differ according to geological structure, rock type, the steepness of dip of the beds, and the pattern of drainage. Despite these local variations, the region is one of subdued relief, fertile soils, and a drier climate (with warm summers) than that of Highland Britain, whose uplands serve to shelter much of the lowlands from the prevailing westerly winds. The rich agricultural resources, together with the navigable rivers and general ease of movement and communication, contributed to the growth in Lowland Britain of the traditional concentrations of population.

Geology

Structure and scenery

The broad distinction thus drawn between Highland and Lowland Britain remains valid despite the wealth of detail it embraces. It would be difficult to find a region of the globe of comparable extent that presents such a bewildering variety of rocks of different types and ages as does Britain. Whereas one may travel for hundreds of miles in the continental heartland of Eurasia without observing a fundamental change in geology or structure, it is sometimes difficult to progress more than a few hundred yards, or at most a few miles, in Britain without encountering a new rock type. This complexity is expressed in the scenery at a number of scales, from the role played by major geological units in regional physiography to the effects of individual beds or minor structures manifested in the characteristics of slopes, spring-lines or soils. At the same time, it is important to remember that many relief features do not faithfully reflect the underlying geology. Prolonged erosion has sometimes reduced the highest mountains and toughest rocks to quite unspectacular lowlands, while higher sea levels have truncated and planed down complicated structures, leaving smooth plateaux surfaces. Even huge upfolds of strata (anticlines) may be eroded to a level below that of their neighbouring downfolds (synclines), by virtue of the weaknesses in the anticlinal crest occasioned by tension. Such 'inverted' relief demonstrates in dramatic fashion the efficacy of denudational processes. Snowdon, the highest mountain in England and Wales, is formed not from an original upland, but from the keel of a complex syncline which was once dwarfed by anticlinal heights nearby, now removed to form the Vale of Ffestiniog (Figure 2). At least 20,000 feet of rock have been removed from the anticline, to leave Snowdon upstanding on the syncline; perhaps in the distant future, in the next erosional cycle, the roles will once more be reversed. Such lack of adjustment of relief to structure, or of form to present process, is not uncommon in the physical landscape, and serves to render its appearance all the more intricate and complicated.

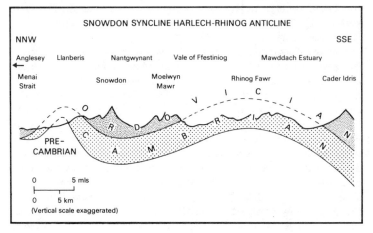

Figure 2. Simplified section depicting the structure of north-west Wales

Geological history and human history

This complexity is the result of a long and involved geological history. The apparently serene modern landscape, undisturbed by volcanoes, severe earthquakes or glaciers, and with catastrophic geomorphological events such as major floods or landslides occurring comparatively rarely during the human lifespan, belies a tumultuous past, the evidence for which is all around us. It is necessary to recall this history in order to reveal the essential relations between natural and human history in Britain. The events of geological evolution are not only inextricably linked to the drama of man's own past, but are visibly manifested and integrated in the landscape itself. Besides influencing the basic relief features and soils of Britain, geology is responsible for the nature, distribution and juxtaposition of the various mineral resources and building materials which have been so important in the evolution of the cultural landscape. For example, the location of the coalfields on the boundary separating Highland from Lowland Britain and the presence of iron ore in certain of the Coal Measures were of enormous significance for the economic and social history of Britain. The events which led to the formation of the Coal Measures and their preservation in a series of basins by means of the earth movements known as the Hercynian Orogeny are not merely the concern of academic geology. As Mackinder concluded, 'Are not the topographical monuments of geological revolution among the causes of analogous revolution in history? ... the Industrial Revolution of English history could not have been accomplished without the Hercynian Revolution of geology, for the coal upon which the one change rested was preserved in the process of the other'.

A survey of geology also helps to place man and his works in perspective. Just as the astronomical revolution reduced him to the size of a microbe in the universe, so the realization that he was the product of a mere moment ago in the history of the earth tempered his feelings of self-importance in the terrestrial scheme. Man's effects upon landscape have undoubtedly been profound, but the natural elements in the scenery of Britain have evolved within a timescale almost beyond his comprehension. In the seventeenth century Archbishop Ussher used Biblical genealogy to date the Creation precisely as the night before Sunday, the twenty-third of October, 4004 B.C. (man, of course, appearing on the following Friday). Thanks to the great discoveries in geology made subsequently, the age of the earth is now estimated to exceed 4,500,000,000 years and the oldest rocks in Britain are at least 2,700,000,000 years in age. Man as *Homo sapiens sapiens* emerged in Britain a mere 35,000 years before the present day. If the time which has elapsed since the appearance of the earliest clearly recorded forms of life is represented, for the sake of illustration, as a single day, the duration of the human species covers, in proportion, less than the last five seconds of the twenty-four hours. Although these fleeting moments are the principal subject of this book, it is only proper to look beyond them, if only briefly, to the geological past. Not only should these pre-human landscapes naturally take their place in a history of the scenery of England and Wales, but the intricate palimpsest of their altered remnants and the rocks created by the processes operating in them constitute the landscape of today.

The geological record

The chronological sequence of the rocks of Britain is expressed in a broad regional succession from Highland to Lowland, with the oldest rocks in the north and west and the youngest in the south and east. Many of the older rocks plunge down towards the south-east, where successively younger strata cover them. This general picture is complicated by regional structures of many types and alignments, and by breaks or 'unconformities' in the sedimentary record where the newer rocks have been deposited upon a denuded surface of older rocks, often with marked discordance. In some areas certain rocks were never laid down in the first place; in others they have been selectively removed by subsequent denudation, the debris eventually being consolidated to form other rocks. As with the cultural landscape as a record of human history, some geological periods are much more clearly evidenced and understood than others. In Highland Britain, which is the product of several periods of earth movements and many erosion cycles, the surface geology can be incredibly complex. This is especially true of Scotland, where Britain's oldest rocks are encountered. Because this survey is restricted to England and Wales, the earliest chapters in Britain's physical history are largely excluded, only a page here and there being represented; nevertheless, England and Wales between them present a wealth of rocks dating from every period except the Miocene.

Geological time is conventionally divided into four categories: eras, periods (each being equivalent to a geological system), epochs and ages (which correspond to a formation, or distinctive stratum or series of strata). The usage of these terms varies among geologists, but the principal subdivisions are given in Figure 3. It is important to remember that the stratigraphic divisions of the geologist, often based upon fossils, are not always those which provide the most meaningful divisions for the student of scenery. Here, the physical, chemical and textural attributes of the rocks embodied in their overall lithological characteristics are of primary importance in accounting for their degree of resistance to weathering and erosion. Furthermore, it is only the sedimentary rocks (and those only slightly altered by metamorphosis) which contain fossils; igneous rocks are frequently much harder to place in stratigraphic sequences.

For most of her geological history, Britain was either part of larger landmasses or was submerged beneath seas which bore no relation to those now lapping her shores. It was only in the last few million years that the present outline of these islands evolved. But the vanished mountain ranges, volcanoes, lakes, rivers, deltas and seas are represented by the

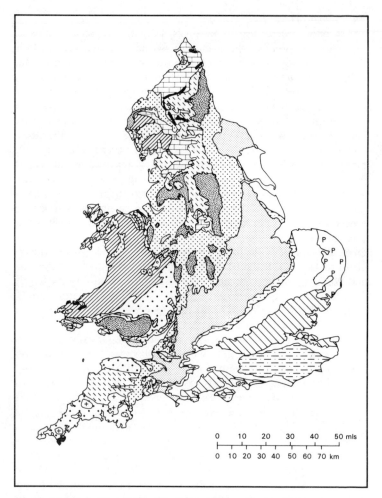

Figure 3. Simplified geological map of England and Wales, with table of strata

rocks which form the Britain of today, and geologists are able to reconstruct former landscapes by studying the deposits derived from them,
together with the fossils they contain. Until recently, descriptive studies
formed the bulk of these environmental reconstructions, but the
'revolution in the earth sciences' has transformed the study of the stratigraphic column. Models of plate tectonics – the spreading of ocean floors

ERA	PERIOD OR SYSTEM		
CAINOZOIC	(Quaternary* (3))	Pleistocene (marine)	
	Tertiary (65)	Pliocene	
		Oligocene Eocene Palaeocene	
MESOZOIC	Cretaceous (135)	*Upper*: Chalk	
		Lower: Hastings Beds, Weald Clay, Lower Greensand, Upper Greensand and Gault	
	Jurassic (195)		
	Triassic (225) Permian (280)		
UPPER PALAEOZOIC	Carboniferous (345)	Coal Measures	
		Millstone Grit Series (Culm Measures in south-west England)	
		Carboniferous Limestone Series	
	Devonian (405)		
LOWER PALAEOZOIC	Silurian (440) Ordovician (530) Cambrian (600)		
PRE-CAMBRIAN	Rocks of Anglesey, Long Mynd, Charnwood etc.		
Igneous rocks (various ages)	Extrusive (volcanics)		
	Intrusive	Basic (mainly dolerites; serpentine in the Lizard complex)	
		Acid (mainly granites)	

NOTES: * See footnote on p. 65.

The beginning of each period in millions of years before the present is given in parentheses.

Glacial and other 'superficial' deposits are not shown.

and the movement and collision of rigid 'plates' of the earth's crust – have provided new, and as yet tentative, explanatory frameworks for the wealth of rock types represented. The behaviour of these plates accounts for patterns of seismic and volcanic activity, the creation of fold mountains, and the distribution of the principal types of sedimentary rock. Furthermore, the position of 'Proto-Britain' with respect to the earth's pole and equator has varied considerably during the last few hundred million years, resulting in a succession of greatly differing climates: tropical, arid, temperate and glacial. For long ages Britain was a region of exotic landscapes, supporting plants and animals subsequently rendered extinct, or whose descendants are now only to be found in countries remote from Europe.

Pre-Cambrian landscapes
The oldest rocks in England and Wales are confined to a limited number of small outcrops. These Pre-Cambrian rocks are the ancient, altered, complex remnants of successive mountain-building cycles, whose dramatic histories span thousands of millions of years. While present as a basement at depth, these rocks appear locally at the surface as a motley collection of igneous, metamorphic and sedimentary types. They are encountered in the Lizard peninsula, north-west Gwynedd (particularly in Anglesey), south-west Dyfed, in Charnwood Forest in Leicestershire, and spectacularly in the Welsh Borderland. The Malvern Hills comprise a distinctive broken ridge of Pre-Cambrian igneous and metamorphic rocks. The upstanding plateau of the Long Mynd in Shropshire is formed from thick Pre-Cambrian silts, grits and conglomerates, while on either side the Uriconian volcanic series outcrop to give rise to Linley and Pontesford Hills on the west, and Caer Caradoc, The Lawley, The Wrekin and other hills along the line of the great Church Stretton Fault on the east (Figure 4). Many of these outcrops take the form of conical hills, but the volcano-like appearance is spurious; the shape is not derived from the original volcano, but from the exhumation of a form created in a later cycle of erosion, preserved under more recent rocks, and subsequently uncovered again. The Roman city of *Uriconium* (Wroxeter), from which the geological name is taken, testifies to the antiquity of parts of the cultural landscape of this district: 'Today the Roman and his trouble / Are ashes under Uricon'. But the real Uriconian ashes are infinitely older than even this distant period of human history, being the product of volcanoes which were probably active more than 650 million years previously.

Figure 4. Structure and scenery: Church Stretton valley, Salop. This aerial photograph, taken with the camera pointing southwards along the Church Stretton valley, affords a magnificent view of a landscape deservedly famous for the striking relationships it displays with respect to geology, relief, soils, land use and settlement. The fault-guided, flat-bottomed valley is floored by generally unresistant rocks, mainly shales: the beautiful patchwork of regular, hedged fields carpeting the lowland as it opens out in the foreground is underlain by Upper Coal Measures (the thin coal seams of which were worked by small pits until almost a century ago). These beds are, however, almost completely concealed by glacial drift. On the right (west), in the middle distance, is the Long Mynd, a dissected mass of varied sedimentary rocks of Pre-Cambrian age. On the left (east) are, firstly, the hog-backed ridges of The Lawley and Caer Caradoc (capped by an impressively sited Iron Age hillfort), formed from Pre-Cambrian volcanic rocks. The outcrop of the Ordovician Hoar Edge Grit is responsible for the escarpment behind, which in turn gives way to another upland of Pre-Cambrian volcanics, grouped around Cardington Hill and Hope Bowdler Hill. In the distance can be seen Wenlock Edge and the associated Silurian limestone escarpments. Thrusting its way confidently and directly through this difficult country is the unmistakable hedged line of the Roman road of Watling Street (West), carefully planned to follow, in a grand curve, the narrow, steep-sided corridor of the Church Stretton valley in order to link Wroxeter on the Severn to Kenchester on the Wye

Lower Palaeozoic landscapes

The succeeding Cambrian, Ordovician and Silurian systems have been traditionally interpreted as elements of one vast tectonic structure, the so-called Lower Palaeozoic Geosyncline. A geosyncline is a huge crustal down-warp which develops through gradual sagging as sediment is worn from landmasses on either side and deposited within it in great thicknesses. Eventually these sediments are compressed, partly metamorphosed, and uplifted to form fold mountains. In the case of the Lower Palaeozoic Geosyncline these earth movements were termed the Caledonian Orogeny, and took place at the close of Silurian times.

Modern theories of plate tectonics, however, maintain that such a scenario is untenable, and propose instead a complicated history of movement of crustal portions and subduction zones involving an ocean which once separated northern from southern Britain. This 'Iapetus Ocean' gradually closed, resulting in the collision of two plates roughly along the line, appropriately enough, of the England-Scotland border. This picture, although speculative and uncertain in detail, has been evoked to account for the pattern of sedimentary and igneous activity in this region.

The Cambrian rocks (called after the Medieval Latin name for Wales) outcrop in north-west Wales and in small areas in the Welsh Borderland and near St David's in Dyfed, where the colourful sequence of beds contributes to the beauty of the coastal scenery. They underlie the desolate tract of the Harlech Dome, a denuded anticline of shales and grits. The beds pass under the Snowdon syncline to reappear at Llanberis, where metamorphism has converted them to excellent slates, with the result that slate quarries dominate the landscape.

In Ordovician times, uniform sedimentation was broken by periods of igneous activity, particularly of a volcanic nature, which have had a considerable effect on the modern landscape. The most spectacular relief features of the Ordovician rocks in Wales are derived from the various igneous bodies, for example the peaks of Carnedd Llewelyn, Glyder Fawr, Snowdon and Cader Idris. Again, the pyramidal form of these mountains is the consequence not of the original volcanic forms but of recent glacial activity. The Ordovician rocks form a broken scarp around the Harlech Dome and give rise to the Berwyn Hills and Plynlimmon before sweeping down through Llanwrtyd Wells to Carmarthen, Cardigan and St David's Head. In Mynydd Presely the Ordovician is responsible for the sill-like intrusions of dolerite (a basic igneous rock) from which were derived the famous 'blue stones' used in the construction of Stonehenge. Similar rocks stand out magnificently at the coast in the masses of Strumble Head and St David's Head, while a volcanic suite underlies Skomer Island on the south side of St Bride's Bay. In Shropshire, Ordovician rocks outcrop as the dolerite intrusions of The Breiddens and Corndon Hill, the volcanic mass of Moel-y-Golfa, and the jagged quartzite crags of the Stiperstones. The lead veins of the Shelve mining district are found in Ordovician strata.

In the Lake District the Ordovician comprises the Skiddaw Slates, which underlie the northern areas, and the Borrowdale Volcanics, which give rise to the mountains of the central region, containing most of the famous peaks. The Skiddaw Slates are not fine, even slates, but slabby and irregular. This is probably a useful deficiency, as they have not been quarried so extensively as the high-quality slates of Wales, and the northern Lake District has consequently been saved from ruination.

The Silurian system, like the Ordovician, takes its name from an ancient Welsh Borderland tribe. It is characterized by a virtual absence of volcanics, and by a contrast between thick sediments laid down in deep water on the one hand, and more varied rocks, particularly limestones, originally deposited in shallow shelf-seas on the other. These lateral changes in lithology (facies) are reflected in the scenery. The former type, the 'basin facies', underlies the smooth, dissected plateaux of Wales, with the harder sandstones such as the Aberystwyth Grits providing impressive coastal scenery. Silurian rocks outcrop over half of Wales, extending from the North Wales coast almost to Carmarthen. In the Borderland the basin facies produces bold, rounded hills, and can be seen in Clun and Radnor Forests, and the synclinal mass of the Long Mountain in Shropshire, which provides a good example of inverted relief. Silurian grits also occupy the southern part of the Lake District. To the south-east of this basin, thinner sediments were laid down in shallow water. This 'shelf facies' is characterized by a varied sequence of shales and limestones, which have subsequently been tilted and etched into a series of escarpments, providing some dramatic scenery in the Welsh Borderland (Figure 4). The richly fossiliferous Wenlock Limestone forms the famous escarpment of Wenlock Edge, while the pattern of scarps in the limestones and vales in the shale beds is repeated on a smaller scale in the Ledbury district west of the Malvern Hills, and in the anticlinal inliers of Woolhope, May Hill and Usk to the south.

The Caledonian Orogeny represented the culmination of a series of earth movements which in plate-tectonics terms were consequent upon the final collision of the two sides of the closing Iapetus Ocean. The palaeogeographical changes were profound. The Lower Palaeozoic rocks were folded, and a chain of mountains, the Caledonides, was created, stretching through northern Britain to Scandinavia. Intense metamorphism in this zone gave way to more gentle alteration of the rocks further south, converting the muds and shales of Wales and the Lake District into slates. These districts were probably foothills lying to the south of the main mountain belt, while in southernmost Britain a new geosyncline was initiated. Thus over most of Britain, land areas replaced the Lower Palaeozoic seas, and terrestrial or continental rocks as opposed to marine deposits began to be laid down. The orogeny also involved phases of intrusive igneous activity, manifested both in sills and dykes (bodies of igneous rock which respectively lie concordantly or discordantly in relation to the bedding of the country rocks into which they were intruded) and in larger masses of granite (the Cheviot granite; and the Skiddaw, Eskdale and Shap granites together with the Ennerdale granophyre, in the Lake District). While these intrusions were only exposed some time later by erosion, extrusive igneous activity also occurred, marked by the volcanic lavas of the Cheviots.

Upper Palaeozoic landscapes: the Devonian
These events took place in the Devonian period, which witnessed the explosive evolution of the land plants and the appearance of the first amphibians. This momentous event – the invasion of the land – terminated a vast span of time during which the landscape had consisted of a barren wilderness devoid of life, the eerie stillness being broken only by the hissing of the wind among the stones, the roar of volcanoes, the rumble of earthquakes, and by the breakdown and removal of rock by the forces of denudation. Age followed age while whole continents were created and gradually but inexorably worn down by rivers which, fed by countless rains witnessed by no living thing, found their way to unite with the waves breaking timelessly upon the seashore.

During the Devonian, most of Britain was part of the Old Red Sandstone Continent, although marine conditions prevailed along a fluctuating shoreline in the south. Consequently, interdigitating marine and continental deposits are encountered in North Devon, separating more fully marine beds to the south from continental beds laid down on alluvial flats in Wales (which was probably an embayment in the southern border of the landmass) and in intermontane basins in Scotland. It is a matter of debate whether the climate was arid, semi-arid or hot-tropical; probably the landscape was reminiscent of the coastal floodplain of the modern Gulf of Mexico. Despite the traditional name of the continental facies of the Devonian, by no means all the beds are composed of sandstone, or coloured red.

The Old Red Sandstone in England and Wales underlies a triangular area extending east and north-east from the South Wales coalfield into Hereford and Worcester and into Salop. The lower beds of the Lower Old Red Sandstone consist predominantly of marls (calcareous mudstones or siltstones) which floor the Plain of Hereford with its red soils, the lowland around the Usk inlier, the Wye valley at Hay, and the vale of Corve Dale in Salop. The upper beds contain some massive sandstones which have been gently tilted to give rise to the erosion scarp of the Black Mountains, the Brecon Beacons, and Fforest Fawr; the Clee Hills of Salop; the undulating upland east of Leominster in Hereford and Worcester; and the imposing outer escarpment on the east side of the Forest of Dean in Gloucestershire. The intermediate beds form low hills in the old county of Herefordshire, and in Gwent give rise to gently rolling country with the occasional ridge. Lower Old Red Sandstone extends beneath later rocks to reappear in anticlinal cores in the Gower, near Pembroke and in the Mendips. The Upper Old Red Sandstone contains a resistant conglomerate which caps the Brecon Beacons and forms an unmistakable line of crags and boulders in the lower Wye valley and Forest of Dean.

In Devon and Cornwall the Devonian rocks have been crumpled and metamorphosed into slates, and folded into an east-west synclinorium (complex syncline) extending across the whole of the South-west peninsula. The Devonian outcrops extensively in the north and south, passing beneath younger rocks which occupy the central axis of the synclinorium. In South Devon the predominantly marine sequence contains volcanics and limestones (which are exposed in the cliffs of Torbay) as well as shales, grits and slates, whose various lithological characteristics are reflected in the relief of the South Hams and Cornwall, with the grits and volcanics forming impressive cliffed headlands. The alternating series of continental and marine beds in North Devon is manifested in a number of ridges and intervening vales on Exmoor, and in the headlands and bays of Barnstaple Bay. To the east the Quantock Hills are composed of an inlier of Devonian rocks.

Upper Palaeozoic landscapes: the Carboniferous
The Carboniferous is probably better known than any other British geological system, because of its economic importance. The environmental conditions prevailing in Britain during the period were very different from those of the preceding Devonian. Britain probably moved to a position north of the equator for the first time, enjoying an equatorial or humid tropical climate. The Caledonides were now worn down, and the pattern of land and sea changed, with landmasses occupying northern Scotland and an area to the south of south-west England, separated by generally shallow seas and a central belt of land extending across Wales (St George's Land) and the Midlands to East Anglia. The characteristics of marine deposition were determined by the changing depth of the sea, the supply of sediment, and by structural controls such as the arrangement of blocks (the Derbyshire Dome, Askrigg and Alston Blocks) and basins (the Craven Lowlands). As a result of these factors, the Carboniferous presents

complex vertical and horizontal changes in lithology, as contrasting sedimentary types were laid down in different places contemporaneously, with individual depositional environments extending to new regions over time. These 'diachronous' facies are responsible for the variety and interest of present-day landscapes on Carboniferous rocks.

The Carboniferous is conventionally divided into three series, the Carboniferous Limestone, the Millstone Grit, and the Coal Measures (in ascending order); but in lithological terms these names indicate only selective generalizations. The Carboniferous Limestone Series contains a variety of rocks besides limestone, while coal seams make up a tiny proportion of the total thickness of the Coal Measures. The Carboniferous rocks which fill the central axis of the great synclinorium of Devon and east Cornwall, known as the Culm Measures after the soft, sooty, impure coal contained in the thick shales, are derived from sediments laid down in all three epochs represented by the conventional series. Although the Lower Culm contains a few impure limestones, the sediments differ markedly from those deposited at the same time in the Mendip, Bristol and South Wales districts a comparatively short distance away. Here, the limestones are much better developed, and are displayed in the famous gorges of Avon and Cheddar, the spectacular cliffs of the lower Wye valley, and in the cliffs of Gower and southern Dyfed.

The Carboniferous or 'Mountain' Limestone contains the classic limestones of England and Wales, which are sufficiently pure and thick to develop some impressive karst features. The peculiar properties of the rock give rise to an assemblage of landforms unique to limestone regions. Limestone consists mainly of calcium carbonate, which is susceptible to the dissolving action of weak carbonic acid. Rainwater, acidulated with carbon dioxide derived from its passage through the atmosphere and the soil, acts as a dilute carbonic acid upon calcareous rocks, dissolving the calcium carbonate and removing it as calcium bicarbonate. Carbonation-solution, which in fact takes place in a number of chemical stages, replaces mechanical erosion (corrasion) as the dominant process in pure limestone terrains. The resistance of limestones to erosion is therefore a consequence less of their inherent strength than of their permeability, which serves to limit fluvial activity. The Carboniferous limestones of Britain are rarely so free of impurities that surface rivers are totally replaced by vertical, underground drainage; but many karst landforms are well displayed and, together with the thin soils, limestone flora and lack of surface water, have helped to create a distinctive landscape.

The limestones were formed in clear, warm seas, the pattern of blocks and basins with their reefs and lagoons affecting the distribution of the various depositional environments. Some of the limestones are composed of the accumulated shells and skeletons of innumerable sea creatures, including the corals, which together with lime-secreting algae, were associated with the building of reefs, while others were chemically precipitated. The original characteristics of the limestones have been reflected in the development of the various landforms consequent upon their subsequent exposure in more recent geological times. The more spectacular karst landforms include dry valleys and gorges; pot-holes, swallow-holes and shafts, down which surface streams disappear; enclosed hollows (dolines), formed by solution or underground collapse; and bare limestone pavements (possibly created in part by glacial stripping), comprising flat-topped ridges or platforms (clints) separated by fissures (grykes). Those who venture underground may follow elaborate systems of passages which open out into caves decorated with a whole range of deposits, the most famous of which are the stalactites and stalagmites, formed by reprecipitation of dissolved calcium carbonate in its crystalline form of calcite. These magnificent subterranean landscapes can be stunningly beautiful, the often brightly coloured limestones and calcareous deposits having been etched into a multitude of shapes.

Some interesting features can be seen in the steeply dipping limestones of the Mendips, on those which outcrop around the South Wales coalfield, and on the thick pure limestone which forms the impressive escarpment of Eglwyseg Mountain north of Llangollen, but the best karst landforms are found in northern England. Four broad types of scenery may be distinguished, based on the original conditions of deposition of the limestone. The blocks of the Derbyshire Dome, Askrigg and Alston Massifs present a range of surface features, with fine cave systems beneath. The Peak District is famous for the gorges of the River Derwent and of Dove Dale, and for the mineral springs which stimulated the growth of spas at Matlock and Buxton. Some of the best limestone pavements, gorges and scars (cliffs of resistant limestone) can be seen on the Askrigg Block – at Ingleborough and Malham, Gordale, and the fault-line scarp of Giggleswick Scar respectively. In contrast, the Craven Lowlands, drained by the River Ribble, are underlain by thick clayey limestones and shales. The third scenic type is that derived from the reef facies, encountered on the edges of the blocks and basins; a good example is the knoll country of Craven, where the original structures can be traced in the relief. Finally, the Northumberland Trough, with its arenaceous (sandy) and argillaceous (clayey) rocks mixed with the limestones, marks an important departure from the dominantly calcareous deposition elsewhere. These rocks, particularly the Fell Sandstone Group and Scremerston Coal Group, are suggestive of the later Millstone Grit and Coal Measures respectively, the Fell Sandstone being responsible for the development of escarpments such as that which sweeps round the eastern side of the Cheviot, and on which several forts and castles have been built.

The Millstone Grit is the result of the spread of these increasingly arenaceous conditions, and of the cyclical sequences of sedimentation which characterize the upper parts of the Carboniferous Limestone Series in northern England generally. Laid down in deltas and shallow offshore environments, more than one facies is represented. Millstone Grit outcrops around the South Wales coalfield, almost surrounds the Peak District, where it forms the 'Dark Peak' of Kinder Scout and Bleaklow, and continues north up the Pennines through Halifax and Keighley to Harrogate, eventually thinning to the east of the Alston Block before passing into the Northumberland Trough. It constitutes the main grit region of the Pennines, underlying the bleak moorlands with their peaty tracts or 'mosses', and capping the limestone uplands of the Askrigg Block at Pen-y-Ghent and Whernside. The Grit country also includes the Lancaster Fells and the Forest of Rossendale, including Pendle Hill. The characteristic scenery of 'edges', and steep valleys or 'cloughs' reflects lithological variations; the grits are responsible for the edges, such as Stanage Edge in Derbyshire and the Roaches in Staffordshire, while valleys such as Hope Dale and Edale in the Dark Peak have been eroded into anticlinal outcrops of the softer shales. The juxtaposition of these contrasting lithologies, particularly where sandstones overlie shales, has created some fine waterfalls and caused some spectacular slope failures, such as those at Mam Tor, the 'Shivering Mountain' near Castleton, Derbyshire. The soft water collected by the streams which flow off the acid moorlands was of considerable significance in the development and location of the textile industry.

The Coal Measures are the most famous rocks of Britain. They are derived from sediments and accumulated organic matter laid down in vast deltaic swamps containing a rich humid tropical flora – an environment similar in some ways to the Dismal Swamps of Virginia today. The Coal Measures display complex patterns of rhythmic sedimentation suggestive of fluctuating sea-levels. They comprise massive sandstones and shales, which make a far greater impact upon relief than the coal seams, although it is the latter which have been responsible for the cultural landscapes of the coalfields. The geological details of structure, particularly dip, folding and faulting, together with the depth and nature of the coal in the seams, and the presence of attendant rocks such as fire clays and sedimentary iron ores, have strongly influenced the mining history and consequently the landscapes of individual coalfields. The most accessible seams were the focus of early mining activity, while the concealed coalfield of Kent (which is a reminder of the presence of Palaeozoic rocks under the younger cover of south-east England) was discovered only in the late nineteenth century. Modern collieries now extract coal from beneath a cover of Permo-Triassic rocks at Selby, south of York, and from under the North Sea off the coast of north-east England, in both instances leaving the older pits (and in some cases the mining villages themselves) abandoned further up the dip to the west. Seams that are horizontal and near to the surface present the possibility of opencast mining, involving the stripping of the overburden and the quarrying of coal from above. The environmental problems and the drastic transformation of the landscape occasioned by opencast mining are the subject of fierce debate, particularly in districts of recognized scenic value such as the Vale of Belvoir and the Forest of Dean.

The coalfields of England and Wales may be separated into three groups on geological grounds (Figure 3). South of St George's Land, Coal Measures are encountered at the surface in Avon and North Somerset, where working of the small basins perhaps dates back to antiquity, and in South Wales and the Forest of Dean. South Wales, despite its awkward structures and faulting, contains valuable seams of anthracite, a hard low-volatile coal with a very high carbon content. The relief of both South Wales and the Forest of Dean coalfields is dominated by the coarse feldspathic sandstones of the Pennant Measures, which form imposing escarpments. Pennant sandstone constitutes the principal building stone of the South Wales coalfield, contributing greatly to the characteristic architecture of the towns and mining villages. The coal seams of the small and isolated Forest of Dean basin outcrop at the surface, and have been worked for hundreds of years by the Free Miners. Although their privileges originally related principally to iron ore (found in the Carboniferous Limestone around the rim of the coalfield), coal was also the prerogative of the Miners, and was extracted by means of small slopes or adits driven into the hillsides. Some of these are still working, but the deep mining which dominated the nineteenth and first half of the twentieth centuries has now ceased. The relics and scars of an impressive industrial past are now largely hidden by the woodlands of this most beautiful coalfield in England.

On the northern flank of St George's Land are the Welsh Border coalfields of Clwyd and Shropshire, including the small but famous field of Coalbrookdale. The Forest of Wyre field was formerly mined by means of shallow pits and open workings, but most of the seams of these coalfields are complex and thin. The group of fields in South Staffordshire, Warwickshire and Leicestershire were, however, important in the early days of ironsmelting.

Finally, the largest and most important coal deposits in England are those found on the Pennine flank. The North Staffordshire field was formerly worked for pottery clays as well as for the 'long-flame' coal used in the manufacture of ceramics; the pottery industry was located largely with respect to these two vital raw materials. Further north on the western side of the Pennines are the Lancashire and badly faulted Cumbrian coalfields; on the east lies the Northumberland and Durham field, which dips east under the North Sea, and to the south is the Yorkshire-Nottinghamshire-Derbyshire field, which contains England's most extensive coal reserves.

The Coal Measures were preserved in these basins as a result of the Hercynian Orogeny, which reached its climax in late Carboniferous times, producing a range of fold mountains extending through central Europe from the Variscan mountains in the east to Armorica (Brittany) in the west. South-west England, being near to the centre of the orogeny, was subjected to complex folding and metamorphism. After the folding, a mass of granite was intruded into the Devonian and Carboniferous rocks, probably in the earliest Permian times. Although the upper surfaces of this granite mass or batholith were not exposed until much later, revealing the cupolas of Dartmoor, Bodmin Moor, St Austell, Carnmenellis, Land's End and the Scilly Isles, the intrusion profoundly affected the country rocks, through processes of baking and mineralization. The quarrying and mining industries of south-west England were founded upon these mineral zones, extracting copper, lead, zinc, arsenic and especially tin, as well as slate and china clay (kaolin). Heated gases rising from the cooling granite were responsible for the process of kaolinization which produced this whitish clay used for pottery, as a filler, and in papermaking. Unfortunately large amounts of waste products derived from decomposed granite (quartz and mica) have to be removed when the clay itself is recovered from the pits, and are amassed to form the huge white spoil-heaps which are such a dominating feature of the country around St Austell and southern Dartmoor.

Further north, the effects of the Hercynian Orogeny were less profound, being restricted to folding with a degree of local mineralization. From the human point of view this was most fortunate, for the comparatively gentle folding of the Coal Measures ensured their selective preservation in basins, with only the anticlinal structures rather than the whole series being subsequently worn away and destroyed. The north-south upwarp of the Pennines was activated, accompanied by mineralization in the Peak District and Alston and Askrigg Blocks. Lead, zinc, barytes and fluorspar were the main minerals, a massive dark blue variety of fluorspar constituting the famous 'Blue John' mined at Castleton in Derbyshire for ornamental purposes. The mining of galena in its 'rakes' and 'flats' (vertical and horizontal masses respectively) has been a major influence in the evolution of the cultural landscape of these districts. Basic igneous activity also occurred locally, and is manifested in the 'toadstones' found in the Carboniferous Limestone of Derbyshire, where the perched water-tables which they create locally amongst the limestones have been important in the siting of villages. Further north, the great quartz-dolerite intrusion known as the Whin Sill extends from the Farne Islands across Northumberland to the Pennine escarpment and Teesdale. It forms the north-facing escarpment upon which Hadrian's Wall is built for part of its length, while on the Northumberland coast it gives rise to scarps and crags which have been commandeered for the sites of castles such as Bamburgh (Figure 34) and Dunstanburgh. The Whin Sill is also responsible for the waterfall of High Force on the River Tees.

Permo-Triassic landscapes
Non-marine conditions predominated after the Hercynian earth movements, as had been the case following the Caledonian Orogeny. This time, however, Britain was not situated in the main mountain zone but lay well to the north of it, and therefore the subsequent deposits created by erosion of the uplands were not so thick or coarse. This contrast between the so-called Old and New Red Sandstones is reflected in present relief patterns. (Because of the inaccurate and imprecise nature of the term 'New Red Sandstone' in relation to the complex facies which these rocks present, the term Permo-Trias is preferable. It also acknowledges the difficulty of separating the two systems lithologically, even though they have been placed in different geological eras on the basis of their fossil faunas. In the present context they are best considered together as the first 'Lowland' rocks of Britain, the important geographical rather than geological boundary being drawn at the top of the Carboniferous, i.e. at the Coal Measures (Figure 1).) Britain was now in the arid trade wind belt, and the depositional environment was one of arid basins, sand dunes, saline lakes and salt-encrusted coastal flats and bays. The rocks are mainly marls, dune-bedded desert sandstones, pebble-beds, breccias and evaporites. These evaporites are rocks composed of salts precipitated from solution in particular sequences from an evaporating sea. The environment may have been comparable with that natural chemical factory, the modern Zaliv Kara-Bogaz-Gol on the eastern shores of the Caspian Sea, an almost isolated gulf in which continuous evaporation was accompanied (until the recent construction of a dyke) by desiccation cycles consequent upon fresh inflows of saline water from the Caspian.

Outcrops of Permian rocks are mainly confined to parts of northern and south-western England. The Magnesian Limestone, a dolomitic limestone containing magnesium carbonate, forms an escarpment overlooking the Durham coalfield and produces cliffs and stacks on the coast between South Shields and Hartlepool. Inland, a narrow outcrop runs southwards from near Richmond, Yorkshire, to Nottingham. On the west side of the country, the Permian is represented by marls, breccias (derived from desert screes) and dune sandstones. The rich soils of 'Red Devon' are developed upon these rocks in east Devon, where the Permian forms beautiful cliff scenery and extends westwards inland as a finger pointing along the axis of the Cornubian synclinorium. Associated with these rocks are the Exeter Volcanics, a varied and sometimes beautiful series of altered lavas, specimens of which may actually be collected from the exhumed vents of the original volcanoes. In north-west England Permian rocks extend along the Eden Valley between the Pennines and the Lake District, from Kirkby Stephen through Appleby and Penrith almost to Carlisle, being downfaulted together with Triassic rocks. Where it has been cemented by silica, the Penrith Sandstone is hard and can form upstanding relief, as at Penrith Beacon.

Triassic rocks occupy a much larger area than the Permian, mantling many older rocks, the structures of which suddenly disappear beneath the cover. This blanket formerly extended even further, and has subsequently been stripped off to reveal fossil landforms created in the Triassic deserts and subsequently buried. The Triassic rocks are important in scenic terms because they lap against and penetrate the uplands of Highland Britain, forming the Lowland Gates of the Midlands and Bristol, and the Vale of York, all of which provide routeways from the English Plain into the uplands of the oceanic border. The Triassic follows a Y-shaped outcrop, with the Pennines separating the two arms and the main limb extending southwards by way of Worcester, along the Severn estuary to the Vale of Glamorgan and the south-west of England. The two arms diverge northwards from the Midlands, the western one passing into the Cheshire-Shropshire Basin and continuing along the coast around Southport, Blackpool, Barrow-in-Furness and St Bees Head in Cumbria before reappearing in the Carlisle Basin, and the eastern one extending through Nottingham and on up to York and the mouth of the Tees. The Vales of Eden and Clwyd are fault-controlled basins of Triassic rocks where, in effect, pieces of the Midland Plain have been literally dropped down into Highland Britain. The scenery of the two Vales is very similar, and highly reminiscent of the Triassic landscapes of lowland England. The Keuper Marl, consisting predominantly of argillaceous rocks which in this instance are less calcareous than the term 'marl' implies, forms heavy, low-lying land in Somerset, Avon, the Trent and Severn valleys, the Vale of Glamorgan, Cheshire and Shropshire, and the Carlisle district (Figure 11). More resistant sandstones and pebble-beds have given rise to the rolling uplands of Cannock Chase, the Forests of Sherwood and Dela-mere, and to the cliffs at St Bees Head, Cumbria. Occasional ridges are also encountered on these beds, such as Alderley Edge in Cheshire, and the ridge to the south of Delamere Forest upon which Beeston Castle stands; other examples include Ness Cliff in Shropshire, Kinver Edge in Staffordshire, Nottingham Castle Rock, and the Budleigh Salterton escarpment in east Devonshire.

The Permo-Triassic rocks are of considerable economic importance. The evaporate sequences have long been a source of salt, which has been recovered by various methods of mining and brine-pumping, a process which is responsible for the dramatic landscapes of subsidence and collapse in certain districts. The 'meres' and 'flashes' of Cheshire are solution-subsidence hollows caused by salt extraction from Triassic rocks covered in most places by glacial drift. The salt deposits stimulated the chemical industries of Merseyside, West Cumbria and Tees-side, while both the Midland brewing industry and the spas of Leamington and Droitwich grew up around sources of mineralized water. The salt domes of the North Sea furnished traps for oil and gas, and the Magnesian Limestone has provided dolomite for furnace linings and for use in the pharmaceutical, glass, tanning and textile industries. Triassic moulding sand was used in the foundry industry of the Birmingham area, while the sand and gravel needs of the construction industry are partly satisfied by Triassic rocks.

Mesozoic landscapes: the Jurassic
The Jurassic system vies with the Carboniferous in terms of complexity. Great lateral and vertical contrasts in depositional conditions were caused when sea levels fluctuated in relation to a series of structural upwarpings. These swells were separated by a number of basins, in Wessex, the Cotswolds, the East Midlands, and in Yorkshire, which serve to divide into sections the great outcrop of Jurassic rocks which extends right across England from Dorset to the North York Moors. The Jurassic comprises a sequence of clays, sandstones and limestones, but it is often difficult to follow any one bed for any distance along the strike, as thickness and lithology can change dramatically. Nevertheless, it remains generally true that the limestones form escarpments and the clays underlie the vales, the Jurassic belt as a whole producing the classic English scarplands. The

rocks and their fossils suggest a warm climate, more humid than that of the Triassic, with the seas supporting coral reefs and a rich fauna, while on land dinosaurs reached their acme and the first birds appeared, amid a landscape of conifers, ferns and many other plants.

It is impossible to describe here the effects of all the various beds upon the landscapes of different portions of the Jurassic belt, so a highly generalized picture must suffice. Broadly speaking, by ascending the Jurassic sequence from the base to the top, a journey is made from the Midland Plain almost to the edges of the chalklands of southern and eastern England.

A thin group of beds provides a transition from the Triassic to the Jurassic. The limestones, shales and marls of the Rhaetic outcrop in the cliffs of the River Severn in Gloucestershire and Avon, and form a very low scarp feature across the Midlands, separating the Triassic plain to the north-west from the first Jurassic clay vale at the foot of the Cotswold escarpment to the south-east. The lower Severn valley and Vale of Evesham are underlain by the Lower Jurassic formation of the Lower Lias, which comprises clays and thin limestones. Further north, the Lower Lias produces the lowland of the Vale of Belvoir, and, at the coast, Robin Hood's Bay in Yorkshire. In Wessex, however, the limestones and shales of the Blue Lias form not only the cliffs around Lyme Regis, famous for their ammonites, but also the Polden Hills in the Somerset Levels. The Middle Lias Marlstone tends to give rise to ridges or occasional hills, such as the ridge encircling the anticlinal Vale of Marshwood in west Dorset, and the outliers of Glastonbury Tor, Brent Knoll and the Pennard Hills to the south of the Mendips. In the Midlands, the Middle Lias outcrops around Grantham and passes east of Leicester to form the scarp at Edge Hill near Banbury. The rich, warm, golden-brown colour of the Middle Lias makes it a notable building stone, seen at its best in the beautiful villages of northern Oxfordshire. The Upper Lias frequently comprises softer sands, which in Dorset produce the distinctive landscape north of Bridport, with its sunken lanes. In the generally calcareous Jurassic sequence of the Cotswolds, the sandy facies of the Upper Lias was important economically for supplying soft water to the woollen industry. In the Yorkshire Basin, the Upper Lias has also been commercially significant, but for quite different reasons, consequent upon the predominance of other facies. The Alum Shales offered alum, and the Jet Rock Series furnished jet (a hard, black form of lignite capable of taking a brilliant polish), which proved attractive to the Romans and Victorians alike as a material for funerary ornaments. Most important of all, the Lias contains workable ironstones at several horizons, notably in north

Oxfordshire, north Lincolnshire (the Frodingham Ironstone), and in the Cleveland Hills of Yorkshire.

The Middle Jurassic contains the most famous members of the Jurassic sequence, the Oolites. These limestones are composed of tiny rounded grains (ooliths), which usually comprise a nucleus of a shell particle covered with calcareous material; the name is derived from the Latin *oolites* ('egg stone'). The Cotswold Basin is distinguished by the massive development of the Great and Inferior Oolites, which produce the best-known, but in many respects atypical, Jurassic relief of the Cotswold escarpment, with its steep scarp face, and associated outliers in the vale beneath. The Inferior Oolite forms the scarp, while the dip-slope (the uplands themselves) is developed upon the Great Oolite, which itself is divided into a number of formations. One of the most interesting of these is the Stonesfield Slate, a fissile, sandy oolite, and not a real slate at all, which was formerly quarried near the village of Stonesfield in Oxfordshire for use as a roofing material. The collapse of the industry, which occurred at the beginning of this century, is lamented, as Stonesfield slate roofs are both durable and attractive, and serve to distinguish thousands of buildings constructed in the region between the seventeenth and nineteenth centuries.

The variety of the Oolite landscapes of the Cotswolds is caused not only by changes in lithology but also by folding and faulting, which influence the pattern of the valleys, and by some interesting slip features, slope failures and valley bulges resulting from the juxtaposition of clays, sandstones and limestones. Despite variations such as these, and differences of soil and vegetation, the Cotswolds evoke an image of smooth outlines, open pastures, stone walls, lush river valleys, and wonderful vernacular buildings constructed from the splendid local stone – an image which has earned the region an accolade as the epitome of 'the English countryside'. It is sobering to recall that this aesthetic adulation (and the related social desirability of Cotswold residences) is a modern preoccupation. At the beginning of the last century Sydney Smith described the Cotswolds as 'one of the most unfortunate, desolate countries under heaven, divided by stone walls, and abandoned to screaming kites and larcenous crows: after travelling really twenty and to appearance ninety miles over this region of stone and sorrow, life begins to be a burden, and you wish to perish'.

In the Wessex Basin, the Middle Jurassic is more subdued, but in Lincolnshire the Lincolnshire Limestone (the local equivalent of the Inferior Oolite) is responsible for the ridge of Lincoln Edge. Ermine Street runs along the eastern side of the Edge, and Lincoln itself is situated on the spur overlooking the only gap of any size. In Yorkshire, the Middle Jurassic uplands of the Cleveland Hills and North York Moors are built upon grits and sandstones rather than limestones, and the relief and vegetation differ accordingly. The Inferior Oolite in Northamptonshire has been an important source of iron ore, particularly near Corby.

The Upper Jurassic sequence of sandy limestones and clays is well represented in the scarps and vales of the Oxford region. The Cornbrash, named after its rubbly, stony, 'brashy' soils, which have proved to be so good for corn-growing, straddles the boundary between the Middle and Upper Jurassic and is revealed as a plateau-like low upland on the Cotswold dip-slope. The Oxford Clay underlies the broad belt of damp, low-lying ground through which flows the River Thames above Oxford, with its flood plain meadows and lines of willows. To the north-east the vale widens to take in the flats of the former county of Huntingdonshire and the Fens to the north, with their vast sombre fields, cut by drainage ditches and traversed by the unrelenting lines of marching pylons. The Oxford Clay of this district provides the raw material for the brick industries of Bedford and Peterborough. To the south-west, in Dorset, where the Middle and Upper Jurassic rocks have been folded into the now eroded anticline of the Weymouth Lowland, the Oxford Clay is encountered in the Vale of Blackmoor and in Weymouth Bay. Above it comes the Corallian, a facies deposit *par excellence*. The calcareous facies is manifested in a broken escarpment, the steep hills of which overlook the city of Oxford and are known collectively as the Oxford Heights. The real change occurs to the north-east, where the calcareous sandstones, grits and rags are replaced by a quite different clay facies, the Ampthill Clay. This floors part of the Fens, but in Yorkshire it in turn gives way to another calcareous facies which is remarkably like that of southern England, the Corallian capping the Hambleton Hills on the edge of the North York Moors, and the Howardian Hills at the western end of the Vale of Pickering. Next in the succession comes the Kimmeridge Clay; together with the Cretaceous Upper Greensand and Gault, it floors the Vale of White Horse in Oxfordshire, a vale which widens to the north-east to flank The Wash and underlie parts of the Cambridgeshire Fens, the Lincolnshire Fens, and the Vale of Pickering. In Dorset, the Kimmeridge Clay is found at the western end of the anticlinal Vale of Wardour, as well as in the Weymouth Lowland, where the steep dips bring Jurassic rocks of contrasting lithologies into close juxtaposition. The scenic effects of these structures are magnificently displayed in the coastal landforms of Dorset, particularly in the vicinity of Lulworth Cove. Finally, the highest Jurassic beds are well developed here also, the Portland Beds forming an impressive scarp in south Dorset as well as appearing in the Isle of Portland, which represents a remnant of the southern limb of the Weymouth anticline. Here the sandy limestone has been quarried extensively for the building stone made famous by Wren, and the landscape of Portland is dominated by the quarries. The more variable Purbeck Beds, also used for building stone, outcrop in the Purbeck district to the east.

Mesozoic landscapes: the Cretaceous

Cretaceous rocks outcrop almost exclusively to the east and south-east of the Jurassic system, which dips underneath them. The pattern of scarps and vales produced by the Cretaceous rocks forms a continuation of the Jurassic scarplands, but it is complicated by some large-scale fold structures which are responsible for the Weald and the London Basin. The sequence is again one of sandstones, clays and limestones, which exhibit considerable lateral variation. This varied collection of rocks, initially folded and then subjected to prolonged denudation, has created an intricate landscape with diverse relief features, vegetation and land-use types. The best example of such scenery is the denuded dome of the Weald, where the in-facing escarpments and central upland impose an overall cohesion, and lend a certain cosiness, to the diversity within (Figure 5).

The lowest Cretaceous series, the Wealden, was laid down in fresh water, on the margins of a delta. The varied sands of the Hastings Beds outcrop in the centre of the dome, in the region variously known as the High Weald, Ashdown Forest, or Forest Ridges, and provide some spectacular slumped cliffs at the coast near Hastings. Some of the iron used in the Wealden iron industry came from these beds. The Weald Clay underlies a horseshoe-shaped lowland around the High Weald, a strip of heavy, wet ground which formerly commanded a certain notoriety on account of its bad roads. In winter it was almost impassable, cutting off the High Weald with its chalybeate spa, Royal Tunbridge Wells – full, in summer, of 'fops, fools, beaus, and the like', according to Defoe – and making the movement of goods, particularly timber and cannon, excessively laborious. Near Lewes, Defoe saw 'an ancient lady, and a lady of very good quality, I assure you, drawn to church in her coach with six oxen; nor was it done in frolic or humour, but meer necessity, the way being so stiff and deep, that no horses could go in it.' Similar beds appear in the Isle of Purbeck in Dorset, producing scenery comparable in some ways to that in the Weald.

The Lower Greensand is a diverse facies of sands and clays, named

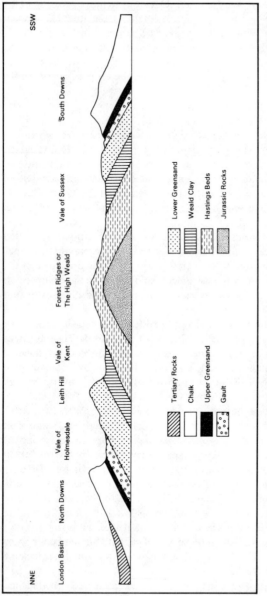

NNE

London Basin · North Downs · Vale of Holmesdale · Leith Hill · Vale of Kent · Forest Ridges or The High Weald · Vale of Sussex · South Downs

SSW

Tertiary Rocks

Chalk

Upper Greensand

Gault

Lower Greensand

Weald Clay

Hastings Beds

Jurassic Rocks

Figure 5. Geological section through the Weald. The section is highly simplified and generalized, with the vertical scale (and consequently the steepness of dip of the strata) exaggerated

after the greenish mineral glauconite, which colours some of the marine formations in the Cretaceous. The sands underlie the acid podzolic heaths of Surrey, although the more fertile, calcareous soils which accompany the Lower Greensand further east support the orchards and hop-fields of Kent. Where the beds contain more resistant material, such as chert, the Lower Greensand can produce an impressive escarpment: Leith Hill south of Dorking rises to nearly 1,000 feet, and is higher than the nearby chalk downs to the north, while St Martha's Hill near Guildford presents the seeming anomaly of a hill composed of soft sand, the relief-former being the ferruginous sandstone or 'carstone' which occurs in the beds of this locality. Further west the Lower Greensand country of the southern Isle of Wight is low and undulating. North of the Weald, the Wealden and the Lower Greensand become hard to separate, as the former is itself a marine series like the Greensand. The Sandringham Sands are covered by heaths in North Norfolk, while a series of clays, sandstones and limestones appear in Lincolnshire, the clays contributing to impressive slumping in the cliffs at Speeton in Yorkshire. The Woburn Sands, the Lower Greensand equivalent in Bedfordshire, offer a small local scarp along the outcrop which extends from Leighton Buzzard to Sandy.

The Upper Greensand and Gault are probably one formation manifested in a sandy and clayey facies respectively; the former produces a minor scarp, often attached to the main Chalk escarpment, and the latter a vale at its foot. In Dorset and Devon the Upper Greensand takes over and, with its grits and siliceous concretions, caps several upland districts such as the Haldon Hills to the east of Dartmoor, and the Blackdown Hills on the eastern borders of Devonshire. It is also exposed in the anticlinal vales of Wardour and Pewsey in Wiltshire, before broadening as a clay contributor to the Vale of White Horse to the east-north-east, and to the vale at the base of the Chiltern Hills.

The most familiar member of the Cretaceous system is of course the Chalk. Chalk is a soft, very pure whitish limestone of problematic origin. It is over 1,500 feet thick in England, and is remarkably homogeneous, although it often contains bands of flint (nodules of dense, fine-grained silica). It appears to be a marine deposit composed of minute calcite plates derived from tiny planktonic algae known as coccoliths, set in a matrix of finely divided calcite. Although almost entirely composed of calcium carbonate, it produces few classic karst features because of its softness and lack of massive jointing. However, dry valleys are common, and dolines may be densely concentrated where the Chalk is covered by a certain thickness of Tertiary beds supporting a highly acid vegetation, as at Puddletown Heath in Dorset. In general the chalklands present an aspect of rolling downlands or undulating plateau surfaces covered with thin soils (often gashed to reveal the white chalk beneath) and a calcicolous flora. The steepness of the dip is a determining factor in the type of scenery developed upon chalk. Near-horizontal dips have produced the wide expanses of Salisbury Plain and the Marlborough Downs (Figure 24); the chalk of East Anglia and the Lincolnshire Wolds is gently dipping, while steeper dips (and hence narrower outcrops) have produced the escarpments of the Dorset and Berkshire Downs, the Chiltern Hills, and the North and South Downs. The steepest dips of all are to be found in the lower escarpments of the Hog's Back on the North Downs near Guildford, the Isle of Wight monocline, and the Purbeck Hills in Dorset. Many of these chalkland structures terminate at the coast in impressive cliffs or stacks, including Flamborough Head, Beachy Head, The Needles, and Beer in Devon.

The human significance of the chalklands has been considerable. Prehistoric peoples took advantage of the natural causeways afforded by the downs to establish a system of routeways, many of which focused on Salisbury Plain. Frequently shunned by later peoples, the chalklands exhibit some impressive prehistoric landscape features. Their margins have been favourite locations for the establishment of spring-line settlements, the attractions including not only the springs thrown out at the junction of the permeable chalk and the underlying impermeable clays, but also the contrasting soils available within a short distance. Flint was a crucial raw material in prehistoric times, being a tough substance capable of carrying a sharp edge on account of its conchoidal fracture. Flint industries used flints produced from mines such as those at Grime's Graves in Norfolk to produce a range of tools and weapons. Later, flint was used as a building material in the chalklands and the nearby vales, contributing to the distinctive regional architectural styles.

Despite its antiquity, the landscape of these districts is currently subject to considerable change. The extensive sheep pastures and downlands which for centuries characterized the delicate chalkland landscape are now increasingly giving way to the plough; more locally, quarries extract chalk for use in the cement industry. Below the surface, the chalk groundwater reservoirs of the London Basin are being depleted through overuse by the large population of south-east England.

Tertiary landscapes

The Tertiary was formerly treated as an era, but it is now usually considered as a system or period, which together with the Pleistocene system constitutes the Cainozoic era (named from the Greek for 'recent life'). It comprises a complex mixture of sands and clays, the result of fluctuating sea levels and alternating marine and continental conditions of deposition. The main regions of Tertiary rocks are the Hampshire and London Basins, where the Reading Beds form an uneven cover at the lower end of the Chalk dip-slope, to be quickly succeeded by the London Clay. In the region west of London, in north Surrey, and in the main area of the Hampshire Basin, the London Clay is covered by a higher formation of the Eocene, the Bagshot Beds. These are responsible for the sandy, acid heathlands of the Camberley district and, together with the highest Eocene formations, the heaths of Hardy's Wessex; both areas have proved to be popular training grounds for the army. Defoe condemned the heaths of Surrey as 'a foil to the beauty of the rest of England . . . a vast tract of land . . . which is not only poor, but even quite steril, given up to barrenness, horrid and frightful to look on, not only good for little, but good for nothing; much of it is a sandy desert . . .' Twentieth-century attitudes to Surrey, at least among the county's inhabitants, are rather different, while outcrops of Bagshot Beds in north London, in the hills of Hampstead, Highgate and Harrow, have influenced the pattern and evolution of residential districts. Where the Reading Beds cover has been removed, the chalk dip-slopes are masked in places by patches of problematical weathering products, partly derived from their degraded remnants, such as the 'clay-with-flints' which has greatly affected the local soils and vegetation. The blocks of hard siliceous sandstone composed of cemented Reading Beds material, known as sarsens or 'greywethers' (on account of a fancied resemblance, from a distance, to grazing sheep), were used by prehistoric peoples in their monuments.

Oligocene deposits underlie the northern part of the Isle of Wight and the southern districts of the New Forest, and also occur in the Bovey Basin at Bovey Tracey in Devon, where ball clays and pipe clays have been quarried since the early eighteenth century, together with a lignite which smelt terrible when burned. The 'crags' or shelly sands of the Pliocene cover large areas of eastern East Anglia, including most of the low coast between Felixstowe in the south and Sheringham in the north.

Between the Oligocene and the Pliocene series of Britain, there is a gap in the sedimentary record: the Miocene is unrepresented by any deposits, being largely a phase of denudation. However, the Miocene epoch was important because it saw the climax of the final phase of major earth movements which have affected the British Isles during their long history. The Alpine Orogeny, as its name suggests, had one of its centres in south central Europe, where the Alps were thrown up at the meeting of the Eurasian and African plates, and was only gently felt in Britain. Nevertheless, it was responsible for several of the country's principal structures, including the Wealden Dome and related London Basin, the folds of south central England (where the folding was most intense), and the strike of the Mesozoic rocks from Dorset to Yorkshire. Further north, the Pennines experienced renewed folding during Alpine times, and the final doming of the Lake District was accomplished, together with the initiation of its superimposed pattern of radial drainage upon a cover of rocks since removed.

The Tertiary period is of great significance for the study of the landscape of England and Wales, because it was at this time that the scenery began to take on its present characteristics. Prolonged periods of denudation resulted in a general lowering of the land surface and in the creation of level surfaces which cut discordantly across geological structures. The distorted and fragmented remains of these planation surfaces are visible in the modern landscape, and reveal themselves on the summits of the uplands as well as in the bevelled forms of the escarpments in the lowlands. They have been preserved by a number of events which have raised them relative to sea level, although these same processes have usually served to complicate and distort them. Tertiary earth movements were prolonged and were not merely caused by Alpine upheavals; a whole series of inclined and intersecting surfaces were developed over many millions of years as a result both of subaerial processes (weathering, mass-movement and erosion by rivers) and of marine action. Exhumation of older surfaces also played a part, while uplifted and warped plains were sometimes trimmed by seas extending to higher levels than today. Upon these surfaces the present drainage system was largely initiated, dissecting and selectively removing them, but often leaving impressive platform remnants and collections of accordant summits (well displayed in the upland plains of Wales). Landforms do not instantly disappear when the processes which created them are no longer operating: the landscape contains many relict elements which have not yet been eliminated, and which will remain for many millions of years. This is especially true with respect to the landscapes of Britain, because of the magnitude and recency of environmental change, which constitutes the final (and in some respects the most dramatic) chapter in the history of evolution of the country's present scenery.

The Pleistocene

The Ice Age
The youngest Tertiary deposit, the Pliocene Coralline Crag of East Anglia, is overlain by similar shelly sands of Lower Pleistocene age. The fossils in

these beds indicate an irregular but progressive cooling of the climate, with arctic flora and fauna gradually replacing the warmer Tertiary species. Although the cold periods were interrupted by warmer phases, the amplitudes became greater, until, in the Middle Pleistocene, full glacial conditions were experienced. A good deal of confusion surrounds the term 'ice age'. Major glacial epochs seem to be widely spaced occurrences in geological history; the last one for which evidence has so far been found took place in Permo-Carboniferous times. Ice ages do not consist of one continuous extension of ice sheets, however, but of several phases of advance separated by warmer periods. The sequence of changes in the Pleistocene ice age is known to be more complex than the terms 'glacial' and 'interglacial' suggest, but it is clear that several periods of glaciation may be identified in the last half million years or so, the most recent of them ending in Britain a mere 11,000 years ago. Climatic changes operate on a variety of superimposed timescales, so that as the present day is approached, it becomes harder to assess the significance of apparent changes in temperature and precipitation, particularly as possible man-made environmental changes must also be considered. But there is no evidence to suggest that the Pleistocene ice age is over, as the terms 'Holocene' or 'post-glacial' (applied to the last 11,000 years) imply; it is much more likely that we are at present living in an interglacial (the 'Flandrian'), and that a new glacial will succeed this temporary warm phase.* Fluctuations upon this scale must not be confused with shorter-term changes of smaller amplitude: a few cold winters do not herald an impending 'new ice age', or even the imminence of a new glacial; they may not in themselves presage any change at all, but simply reflect the variety of conditions experienced from year to year in our climate as a matter of course.

The causes of ice ages are unknown, although various theories have tried to account both for their initiation and for their pulsating nature. Their consequences for landscape, however, are rather more easily appreciated. From a latitude of about 40 degrees north at the beginning of the Tertiary, Britain had continued to drift northwards towards the pole. During the Pleistocene glaciations, the British Isles were subjected to the

* Following the demotion of the Tertiary and Quaternary from the status of eras to that of periods within the Cainozoic era, the Quaternary is conventionally divided into two epochs, the Pleistocene and the Holocene. The case for the elimination of the Holocene, which would make the terms Quaternary and Pleistocene synonymous, together with the argument that the use of 'the Quaternary' implies a distinction from the preceding Tertiary which is unjustified, have led some scholars to give up the term Quaternary altogether. This practice employs the Pleistocene as the name for the latest epoch in the first period of the Cainozoic era, with the present Flandrian stage as the latest age of this epoch (see Figure 3).

spread of ice sheets, some of which merged with those of Scandinavia, while others grew from local centres in the British uplands. The ice extended further south in some glacials than in others. Although the limits are disputed, it seems reasonably certain that southern England was never covered by ice, although at some time an ice sheet probably impinged on the north coast of the South-west peninsula, and, in the south-east, nearly reached London. The most recent glaciation, the Devensian, was less extensive. It is possible to separate and describe these glacials because of the nature and degree of freshness of the landforms created, the types of sediments which were deposited, the floral and faunal remains associated with them, and by the application of a range of dating methods. However, much of this evidence is incomplete, complicated and contradictory, being gathered from various sources and sites, and requires expert assessment: Pleistocene research is a multi-disciplinary field with little to satisfy those who seek simple, unqualified and permanent answers to their inquiries.

Glaciation and the landscape
England and Wales may be divided into five landscape regions on the basis of the pattern of glaciation. In the mountains, freeze-thaw processes active above the valley glaciers led to the growth of screes and initiated the development of steep-walled rock basins known as cirques. A cirque (also called a corrie or cwm) enlarges itself by the action of a cirque-glacier, and where adjacent cirques encroach upon each other a sharp and jagged edge or arête may be formed (for example, Striding Edge, Helvellyn, in the Lake District). Many of the cirques in Wales and the Lake District are now occupied by small lakes. Below the mountain tops, the zone of most spectacular glacial erosion occurred, where the valley glaciers moved outwards from the areas of ice accumulation. By processes of abrasion, quarrying and plucking, the glaciers enlarged the valleys into deep, wide troughs, truncating the spurs and leaving the tributaries as hanging valleys. Some of these troughs, particularly in the Lake District and North Wales, contain finger lakes as a result of glacial erosion along the valley combined with the deposition of morainic dams at their lower ends which have not yet been removed. Much more extensive areas of deposition are to be found in the third landscape zone, that of lowlands situated near the mountains. The extension and final melting of the ice resulted in the eroded material being transported and deposited in a variety of forms which were often reworked by later ice advances. This last set of circumstances may be a contributing factor in the formation of drumlins, those smooth, elongated hummocks of glacial debris which occur in swarms north of the limits of the last glaciation. Irregular spreads of clays, sands

and gravels, often accompanied by erratic blocks, extend over wide areas, often serving to interrupt, complicate or divert the drainage. Sub-glacial streams cut features which were later revealed on the retreat of the ice as distinctive, discordant and often streamless channels, while meltwater streams left a range of erosional and depositional fluvioglacial features.

The lowlands proper constitute the fourth region. Here, spreads of till or boulder clay mask the pre-glacial landscape. Detached masses of ice melted to form kettle-holes, and the land surface is often badly drained. The ultimate extent of the ice can sometimes be traced by the hummocky terminal moraines, which often form impressive features, notably the Cromer Ridge in Norfolk. The moraine upon which York stands has been of considerable importance in the history of that city, the ridge providing a strategic routeway across the marshy lowlands of the Vale of York. Despite the extensive nature of these deposits, which have been of such importance for the development of soils, vegetation and agriculture, the distribution of settlement and of certain economic activities, it should be remembered that glacial activity in the lowlands was not confined to deposition. The rocks of Lowland Britain are of course generally much less resistant than those of the uplands: the chalk escarpment of East Anglia was spectacularly reduced by glacial erosion, massive chalk rafts in the cliffs at Cromer testifying to the ability of glaciers to erode and transport on an impressive scale.

Periglaciation and the landscape
Finally, the regions beyond the limits of the ice sheets were also subjected to intense geomorphological activity. Although glaciers did not directly affect southern England, this area (and others which escaped individual glaciations) experienced a range of processes occasioned by the intense cold near the the ice fronts. These periglacial conditions included freeze-thaw activity, both diurnal and seasonal (the summer melting of the active layer of the permafrost), which was responsible for a range of landforms, sedimentary structures, and deposits. The freezing of calcareous rocks such as the Chalk made them impermeable and therefore susceptible to surface erosion by rapid spring meltwater runoff; the dry valleys may have been formed or at least modified in this way. Periglacial processes of mass wasting were probably responsible for the creation of certain terraces and slope forms upon the uplands of England and Wales, particularly those in the south-west, which were never glaciated. In the case of Dartmoor it is probable that periglacial activity, acting upon the rotted granite produced, it is thought, by deep weathering under warm, humid conditions during the Tertiary, played an important role in the

final fashioning of the present landscape. The Dartmoor granite, with its pattern of joints, has given rise to the famous tors, which were supposedly exhumed and left upstanding by the removal of weathered material; but whether they are primarily the product of the Tertiary or the Pleistocene (or, most likely, both) remains a matter of debate. The efficacy of periglacial slope processes, particularly solifluction (the downhill flow of thawed surface deposits), as evidenced by the slope forms, deposits, and the huge fields of granite boulders (clitter) which must have been derived from further upslope, suggests that the present landscape owes a good deal to the Pleistocene, although planation surfaces of presumed Tertiary age are much in evidence (Figure 9).

Periglacial structures may be seen in unconsolidated deposits in many parts of southern England, involving frost-heaving and contortion of the surface layers. Surface stones have sometimes been arranged into lines or polygons, and striped vegetation patterns reflect differential sorting of the surface materials: they are well seen in the Breckland of East Anglia. Former mounds, or pingos, raised as blisters of frozen earth and water by hydrostatic pressure, have left chaotic terrains of hummocks and craters following their collapse: one of the best fossil pingo landscapes can be examined at Walton Common, Norfolk (T F 7316). More generally, the choking of valleys with slope debris and gravel, followed by periods of reworking and incision by streams, has left an impressive legacy of river terraces. These level spreads of gravel have provided important dry-point sites for settlements, from small villages to towns like Oxford, whose social geography was influenced by the pattern formed by the flight of Thames terraces which rise above the damp floodplain. Some of the villages and their surrounding fields are currently at the mercy of the rapacious appetite of the sand and gravel industry, which threatens, by the creation of vast flooded gravel workings, to transform the Thames valley above Oxford into a single huge trout farm.

Sea-level changes
These changes in the river valleys of Britain were intimately related to a complex set of fluctuations in the relative levels of the sea and land. During the glacials, sea levels fell as a consequence of the amount of water locked up in the ice caps. Such glacio-eustatic changes depressed sea levels worldwide by a substantial amount (possibly more than 300 feet in some glacials), a fall which was more than sufficient to join Britain to Europe and to expose large areas of the surrounding continental shelves. When the ice melted in the interglacials, sea levels rose again: the early Flandrian transgression was rapid, particularly during the period before 5,000 B.C.,

resulting in the final flooding of the land bridge between Britain and Europe in the second half of the seventh millennium B.C. This general picture was complicated by a number of other processes, most notably the local, temporary depression of the land surface caused by the weight of the ice caps. The melting of the ice was accompanied by isostatic rebound, the uneven nature of which was largely responsible for the formation of warped raised beaches, particularly in Scotland, where the thickness of the ice was greatest.

The combined effect of these base-level changes is clearly evidenced in the present landscape, although it is extremely difficult to differentiate between the various forces at work. Sea levels higher in relation to the land than those of today have created raised beaches and more extensive coastal marine planation surfaces, while the rise of the sea from lower levels has submerged forests and drowned river valleys (the 'rias' of southwest Britain). Involved series of fluctuations have continued into historic times, producing sedimentary sequences in the Somerset Levels and the Fens of East Anglia which have been of great significance for the settlement and human use of those districts. Coastal changes involving the development and movement of dunes, the silting of harbours, the growth of spits and bars, and the erosion of shorelines have all had implications for human activity, so that man has taken a hand in attempting, with mixed success, to gain some control over them.

Natural vegetation
The climatic and sea-level changes of the Pleistocene are largely responsible for the composition of the natural vegetation of Britain. The early Tertiary flora, reconstructed from fossils in the London Clay, suggests a type of tropical forest (Figure 6). During the Tertiary the tropical elements gradually disappeared, and the increasingly cold phases recorded in the Plio-Pleistocene Crags began the progressive elimination of frost-sensitive species. In the first glacial, tundra vegetation characterized the British landscape, and it was to return with every full glacial thereafter. The interglacials, on the other hand, witnessed the replacement of the open steppe tundra with birch-pine and then mixed deciduous forest in the mid-interglacial stage, before the onset of the new glacial completed the cycle with a regression to a second coniferous forest and eventually to the treeless tundra. This picture is complicated by the occurrence, within glacials, of brief warmer periods called interstadials, which served to replace tundra with coniferous forest, but which were not sufficiently warm or long enough to witness a return to full deciduous forest.

These vegetation cycles, reconstructed from the pollen record, were

Figure 6. South-east England 50 million years ago: an idealized reconstruction of the landscape in London Clay times. This reproduction of an oil painting by M. Wilson in the Geological Museum, London, shows an imaginary scene near an estuary on the shores of the sea in which the London Clay was being laid down as sediment. The vegetation (note the palms, and the mangroves in the swamp) displays strong affinities with the modern tropical lowland evergreen forests of Indo-Malaysia. A secondary element comprises equally exotic warm-temperate woody plants such as *Magnolia*, seen in flower on the left. The animals in the picture appear very strange to modern eyes, although in truth the mammals were already developing rapidly from primitive forms as a consequence of the demise of the carnivorous reptiles. Of the species depicted here, only the crocodiles are essentially similar to living species (which themselves display a decidedly 'primitive' and sinister air!); the animals in the centre are a bit like hippopotamuses with feet reminiscent of an elephant's, while the graceful little creatures under the *Magnolia* are early ancestors of the horse, and were about the size of a fox terrier

accompanied by faunal developments, although generalizations are hard to make, on account of evolutionary and adaptive changes. The vertebrate lists for the Pleistocene in Britain are certainly exotic enough to catch the imagination. Remains of reindeer and woolly mammoths have been recovered from glacial deposits; elephants, hyenas, rhinoceroses and hippopotamuses lived here during interglacials, with bison, wolves, giant deer and arctic foxes in addition to some of the above being found in interstadials. Many of these animals had great significance for the early human societies.

The changing British flora was also profoundly influenced by the ability of various species to return north after each glacial. It has been suggested that the comparative poverty of the British flora reflects the widespread extinction of plants in glacials, and the limited period available for plants (and animals) to return from the continent before the rising interglacial sea level cut them off. The thorny problem of what is meant by a 'native' species may be resolved by including as native only those plants which were growing in Britain between the end of the most recent (Devensian) glaciation and *c.* 6,250 B.C., when Britain was last cut off from Europe.

Most of the plants which had not reached Britain by this date but are now to be found here have been introduced by man, either accidentally or deliberately. Some plants only just failed to get back, while others are known to have been in Britain in earlier interglacials, but failed to establish themselves in the present one. Indeed, several of our most familiar plants and trees, which many like to think of as thoroughly British, such as the horse chestnut, are not native at all, although some of them, like the allegedly alien conifers which some people love to hate, have been here before.

It has been suggested by some that the warmest part of the Flandrian interglacial occurred between 6,000 and 4,000 B.C., and that the climate is now gradually reverting to colder conditions as a new glacial approaches. Others, referring to the complex variety of small-scale climatic fluctuations in the Flandrian for which there is evidence, do not support this view. However, it seems that at about this time, England and Wales were covered by mixed deciduous forest up to a height of perhaps 2,500 feet, except where the wetlands were occupied by fen communities, and the flatter, badly drained uplands by peat. In the generalized model of vegetational changes which occur during an interglacial, the descent from the climatic optimum is accompanied by progressive soil deterioration and the replacement of the 'climax' deciduous forest by more open vegetation. This model may well apply to the last few thousand years in England and Wales, but the natural sequence of events has been obscured and complicated by the activities of man. These have greatly influenced the nature of the vegetation, so that it can no longer be described as 'natural'.

At this point a survey of the natural landscape of England and Wales takes on a new dimension, because from the moment when human societies appear it becomes extremely difficult to separate natural from man-made environmental changes, and consequently to differentiate between natural and cultural landscapes. But this does not imply that nature is banished to a passive background role, or that natural history comes to a full stop, allowing the scholars of human history to begin their own study independently. Environmental changes of all sorts are still occurring, and it should never be forgotten that mankind's brief spell of existence is set within an extraordinary period of geological time – a period of great changes in climate, landforms, sea levels, soils, vegetation, and animal populations – in the midst of which the cultural landscape has been fashioned.

CHAPTER 2

Prehistoric and Roman Landscapes

The origins of man extend back well into the Pleistocene, if not before, but the effects of our primitive ancestors upon the natural landscape were probably restricted except at the local scale, and most of the evidence has in any case been swept away, in higher latitudes at least, by the environmental changes which followed. It is a nice question when man ceased to be a purely 'natural' animal element in the environment and became separable as 'man the toolmaker', imposing the first 'cultural' changes upon the landscape. Since our knowledge of early man's activities was at first derived largely from studies of his tools, it is not surprising that the conventional divisions of prehistory were based upon a classification of artefacts. The classic 'Three Age System' comprises the Stone Age (divided into Palaeolithic, Mesolithic and Neolithic) – much the longest of the three – the Bronze Age, and the Iron Age (Figure 7). But for a study of the changing landscape, the focus of attention must be the nature and chronology of natural and man-made environmental change. (Nevertheless, although the Three Age System is under heavy attack for its simplicity and rigidity, its familiarity as a framework has served to prolong its usage.) The rapid evolution of the genus *Homo* through the Pleistocene culminated in the emergence, in the Upper Palaeolithic, of our own subspecies, *Homo sapiens sapiens*, which appeared in Britain approximately 35,000 years ago, during the Devensian glacial period. (There has been much speculation about the relationship between climatic change, and the challenge it presented, and the spectacularly speedy evolution of man.) The great environmental changes which terminated the Devensian and ushered in the present Flandrian stage, and the initiation soon afterwards, in the Mesolithic period, of the first really major alterations to the landscape by *Homo sapiens sapiens*, make the withdrawal of the ice sheets a suitable starting point for a history of the cultural landscape of England and Wales.

This event was not, however, the unqualified relief for man that one might imagine. The growth and spread of forests, which accompanied the amelioration of the climate, probably necessitated a drastic change of life style. The open tundra of the Late Glacial supported herds of herbivorous mammals which had constituted the basis of the specialized Upper

Years B.C.	Stage	Principal environmental events	Vegetation	Conventional divisions of prehistory
— 0	F	Climatic		I R O N A G E (BRONZE AGE)
— 1,000	L	deterioration	Renewed growth of peat ↑ Accelerated forest clearance ↑ Soil leaching and podzolization ↑	BRONZE AGE
— 2,000	A			NEOLITHIC AGE
— 3,000	N		Increase of 'cultural pollens' ↑	
— 4,000	D	Climatic	Elm decline	MESOLITHIC
— 5,000	R	'optimum'	Growth of peat ↑ Mixed oak 'climax' forest, with alder, elm and lime:	
— 6,000	I	Britain severed from Europe	few open communities Decline of pine; increase of elm and oak	
— 7,000	A	Rapidly rising		UPPER PALAEOLITHIC
— 8,000	N	sea levels Climatic amelioration	Hazel-birch-pine forest Birch-pine forest	
— 9,000	D E V E N S I A N	Withdrawal of the ice Late Glacial period	Grass-sedge heath Tundra Open plant communities	EPI PALAEOLITHIC

Figure 7. Generalized outline of the prehistory of England and Wales

Palaeolithic economy, and as the habitat retreated, so did the animals. The Upper Palaeolithic culture, represented in its full glory in the cave art of France (but, alas, leaving no such legacy in Britain), passed gradually away. The ecological history of prehistoric man became a history of adaptation to, and increasingly of effects upon, the spreading Flandrian forests. These were gradually cleared or substantially altered as agriculture developed, population numbers increased and technology advanced. But the Flandrian climate has not been stable: superimposed upon the general post-glacial warming have been a number of intricate and incompletely understood subsidiary climatic fluctuations, varying in scale and duration. These were of considerable importance, particularly in marginal environments, and the activities of prehistoric man must be viewed in relation to them.

Mesolithic landscapes

The Devensian ended about eleven thousand years ago, and the late glacial heath vegetation of grasses and sedges with scattered juniper and willow bushes was gradually replaced by birch and then, in southern Britain, by pine forest. As the climate became milder, warmth-demanding trees like the elm, oak and then the lime arrived from Europe, so that in the later Mesolithic, by which time the land bridge had been breached, most of Britain was covered with mixed-oak 'climax' forest (p. 71). It is possible to gain an impression of this forest, whose composition varied regionally and locally, by studying fossil pollen assemblages preserved in certain kinds of deposits, together with 'macroscopic' plant remains recovered from bogs and lakes, and (most dramatically, in visual terms) the submerged forests drowned by the rise in sea level.

Mesolithic man had not been idle in the face of these developments. Although he commanded only a simple technology, and lived a nomadic existence, occupying primitive huts too flimsy to have survived, his use of fire enabled him to alter his environment in a purposeful, partially managed fashion. Some kind of control which fell short of full domestication appears to have been achieved over selected elements of the native fauna. Deliberate burning of the vegetation improved the grazing potential of the forest land and assisted in the expansion of the animal populations. This interference is reflected in the changing structure of the forest itself, apparent particularly in the increasing dominance of the fire-resistant hazel. Some of these early clearances initiated irreversible soil changes: it is likely, for example, that the acidification of certain soils and the formation of blanket bog on the uplands, while theoretically attributable in some cases to a trend towards a wetter climate, are the result of human interference, which at the very least accelerated processes that were occurring naturally. Such pedological changes have been of great significance subsequently, influencing the appearance of later landscapes to a considerable degree. Some of the formerly wooded uplands, for example, marginal and probably fragile ecologically, deteriorated into heaths or moorlands upon which trees have never been able to re-establish themselves to this day.

Neolithic landscapes

During the Neolithic the scale and character of forest clearance underwent significant changes. Modern experiments have demonstrated the surprising efficacy of Neolithic stone axes in felling substantial areas of woodland, and while a form of shifting cultivation permitted forest regeneration in some areas, it seems likely that semi-permanent clearings were also maintained. Perhaps the removal of the forest from some of the light soiled lands in southern England occurred at this time, particularly the Breckland and the chalklands, which have been maintained in their open state by the grazing of sheep and rabbits in historical times (p. 106). The pollen evidence suggests that true agricultural economies, involving domestic herds and the cultivation of fields, began to replace the natural mixed oak woodland with a range of man-influenced vegetation types. Pollen records show an increase in cereals and grasses, the so-called 'cultural' pollens derived from plants which were associated with human activities. The controversial 'elm decline' which took place in the early fourth millennium B.C. is generally deemed to have been anthropogenic in nature, related to Neolithic agricultural activities, perhaps involving the stripping of the trees for fodder. Hazel was deliberately coppiced for wood and browse. These changes opened up the 'climax' forest locally to create a secondary woodland of oak, ash and birch, with some alder. Modern woods which today show the least evidence of disturbance, particularly those in the uplands, are probably comparable with this secondary type encountered in the Neolithic. Finally, the processes of soil acidification begun in the Mesolithic may have been further accelerated. Burning and ploughing could well have contributed to the development of hardpans which, by impeding drainage, encouraged the growth of blanket peat. In Ireland and west Wales Neolithic fields and occupation sites have actually been found buried under peat. Woodland clearance, by interrupting nutrient cycles and reducing transpiration rates, would tend to increase the amount of soil water, again leading to waterlogging.

These advances in agriculture were closely related to concomitant developments in social organization. Sedentary agriculture came to be associated with more sophisticated social practices, changes in forms of territorial organization, new trading links between groups (based upon specialization, surplus and exchange), and with the evolution of new patterns of permanent or semi-permanent settlement. Groups of immigrants arrived from Europe, and a complex process of cultural contact, set against a background of local and regional societies and economies which were themselves advancing in distinctive ways, was reflected in the earliest cultural landscapes generally identifiable in England and Wales today.

The best known of the new cultures has come to be called the Windmill Hill culture, after the Neolithic settlement at Windmill Hill in Wiltshire (p. 94). The inhabitants grew primitive species of wheat and barley, made simple pots, and used a variety of flint implements, obtaining the raw material from mines in the chalklands (p. 105). As the Neolithic period progressed, the style of the artefacts underwent certain changes, which varied between groups and between regions. The chief visible legacy of these peoples in the landscape is the impressive earthworks and enigmatic monuments which have survived the ravages of time to puzzle subsequent generations.

The most characteristic large-scale settlement features of the Neolithic farming peoples are the causewayed camps. These circular or oval enclosures are surrounded by one or more rings of banks and ditches, with undug sections of the latter furnishing access causeways. Examples include Windmill Hill itself, Knap Hill (also in Wiltshire, SU 121636), Hembury Hill, Devon (ST 113031), and Hambledon Hill, Dorset (ST 849122), where the filled ditches of the Neolithic camp (next to the dominating Iron Age hillfort) yielded extensive skeletal remains mixed up with organic material, pottery and flintwork. It seems that the camps were not primarily defensive in function, but were motivated by economic and social needs, perhaps serving as rallying points for trade and ceremony; it has been suggested that the apparent funerary practices centred upon Hambledon Hill imply that the site was used extensively for religious ritual. All those mentioned here were probably constructed in the fourth millennium B.C. Few Neolithic settlements other than the camps have survived, and indeed their nature remains largely a matter for speculation.

There is, however, a wide selection of monuments designed for purposes other than habitation. Funerary monuments belong to two broad types: earthen long barrows and megalithic chambered tombs. The long barrows (Figure 8) generally represent the earlier type, and are found in the

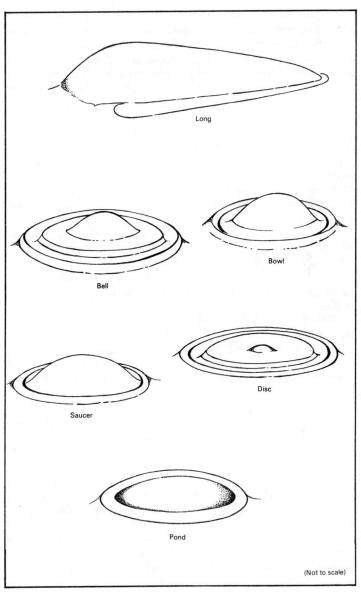

Long

Bell

Bowl

Saucer

Disc

Pond

(Not to scale)

Figure 8. The principal types of barrow

chalklands, while the chambered tombs are characteristic of the western peninsulas. The two are probably closely related; indeed, the long barrow may simply be a kind of megalithic tomb, whose design reflects its use of chalk as a construction material rather than the tougher rocks of Highland Britain. Long barrows essentially comprise elongated mounds of earth and chalk up to 300 feet long, 100 feet wide, and 11 feet high. The generally larger eastern end contains the burials, which are multiple, but the actual process of interment remains obscure. The barrows were built near to, or actually on top of, 'mortuary enclosures' in which bodies were accumulated until they disintegrated. Eventually the area was closed and the bones were placed in a hut which in turn was covered with earth to form the mound seen today. (It was an ancient belief that once the bones were dry it was permissible to move them, as by that time the soul had left the body.) No doubt the mortuary hut inside the mound soon collapsed, making re-entry into the barrow difficult. Such a chronology is suggested by the excavation Wor Barrow in Dorset (p. 102) and others of the two hundred or so which remain. Mention should also be made of a special, very long type of Neolithic barrow, called a bank barrow; that at Maiden Castle (p. 103) is nearly 1,800 feet long. At the opposite extreme are the 'short' long barrows, such as the oval barrow on Thickthorn Down, Dorset (p. 102).

Although there is a case for considering the megalithic tomb as a regional variant of the long barrow, it differs in that the mound does not simply represent the final covering of a mortuary: rather, the chamber functioned as a vault and was deliberately and often massively constructed to admit successive interments. A few have remained relatively intact, such as the chambered long barrows at West Kennett in Wiltshire (p. 95), and Stoney Littleton, Avon (ST 735572). Some developed over time (in the manner of medieval churches), and represent huge expenditures of effort. There are several regional types. Passage graves (where the chamber is linked to the exterior of the mound by a passage) are concentrated in north-west Wales (Barclodiad y Gawres, SH 328708, and Bryn Celli Ddu, SH 508702, both on Anglesey). Gallery graves (consisting of an internal chamber, sometimes subdivided or connected to side chambers) are represented by the so-called Cotswold-Severn group (Belas Knap, Gloucestershire, SP 021254). A separate class, found in the Scillies and Cornwall, possesses a portal but no passage; these entrance graves probably represent the remnants of passage graves (Brane or Chapel Euny Entrance Grave, Cornwall, SW 402282). Simple megalithic tombs which have lost their covering mounds are known as 'dolmens', 'cromlechs', or in Cornwall 'quoits' (Trethevy Quoit, St Cleer, SX 259688); most of these consist of a few massive stones with or without a capstone.

Finally, the most problematic class of Neolithic monuments comprises the cursūs (plural of cursus), henges, early stone circles, and unique imponderables like Silbury Hill (p. 95). It is assumed that they were sacred places of some sort, but most of the vaguely defined functions which scholars have imparted to them derive from little more than guesswork. The cursūs, of which the longest is the Dorset Cursus (p. 102 and Figure 15), are long sets of two parallel banks and outer ditches, with square or curved terminations. The henges, which may occupy a place in later Neolithic culture comparable to that of the causewayed camps earlier on, comprise stone or wood circles set inside a circular earth bank with an internal ditch. Unique to the British Isles, they are most common in southern England, the best-known being Avebury (p. 96 and Figure 13) and Stonehenge; examples further north include Arbor Low, high up in the Peak District of Derbyshire (SK 161636), and the set of three principal henges at Thornborough in North Yorkshire (SE 2879 etc.). Some, despite their size, are now very indistinct: Durrington Walls in Wiltshire (SU 150437) is almost a third of a mile in diameter. Woodhenge Timber Circle nearby (SU 151434) may have supported a roofed building, or may just have been a ring of posts.

Some of the larger stone circles erected by prehistoric peoples are probably, like the first round barrows, late Neolithic in date, for example those at Stanton Drew in Avon (ST 601633). But the majority are considered to have originated in the Bronze Age, which in the conventional sequence succeeded the Neolithic.

Bronze Age landscapes

The passing of the Neolithic into the Bronze Age was not accompanied by marked environmental changes or by any immediate alterations to the landscape. The use of metal tools (which inspired the term Bronze Age) was in any case long delayed in Highland Britain, where the pattern of small, temporary clearances connected with pastoral activities continued basically unchanged through most if not all of the period. Lowland Britain was more densely settled and, in the light soil districts at least, exhibited a discontinuous pattern of altered or partially cleared woodland, reflecting a mixed farming economy which involved the cultivation of cereals. Although the damp vale soils of the lowlands were still densely wooded, true agricultural landscapes had been created in several regions of England and Wales by the start of the first millennium B.C. However, the Highland-Lowland dichotomy should not be pushed too far: there were enclaves of grain farming in the uplands, and as the Bronze Age progressed, large areas of forest clearance emerged in the Lake District (especially in the vicinity of the Neolithic 'axe-factories' at the head of Langdale), on the North York Moors, the Pennines, in Wales and on Dartmoor, where the process was related to the creation of a Bronze Age landscape rich in field monuments (p. 97). The Bronze Age was apparently slightly warmer than today, enjoying higher summer temperatures, and as a consequence the treeline probably lay at a substantially higher altitude. This made the marginal lands on the edges of the uplands more attractive to settlement than they have been at any time since, and the 'high-water mark' of agricultural and related activities which was reached during the Bronze Age is evidenced in the landscape. Towards the end of the period, cyclical climatic deterioration, with a trend towards cooler and wetter conditions, crucially affected these marginal districts, and the frontier of settlement retreated. Soil changes initiated by a combination of natural and man-made influences were accompanied by the conversion of the cleared uplands to a variety of heath and bog communities which have generally been maintained to this day.

These extensive areas of soil deterioration and vegetation change which accompanied the later, large-scale clearances were thus created as a consequence both of the favourable climate and of the new technology of the Bronze Age, centred upon the bronze axe, a much more effective tool than the polished stone axe of the Neolithic. These new Bronze Age clearances also demonstrate the important role played by pastoralism in landscape evolution, for although arable agriculture left a greater archaeological legacy, the effects of woodland removal upon the total upland environment were profound.

Prehistoric field systems are in any case notoriously difficult to date, and sometimes almost as hard to see, except on aerial photographs. Where visible on the ground, they consist of small, usually rectangular enclosures surrounded by earth banks, stone walls or hedges. The fields are squarish, possibly because they were worked with a light plough known as an ard, which cut a furrow but could not turn the sod; ploughing was therefore done 'along and across' in order to break up the soil more thoroughly. These ancient fields were formerly widespread, being part of deliberately planned extensive systems, but can now only be seen in any number in a few localities, for example in parts of the chalklands (Thickthorn, Dorset; Marlborough Downs, Wiltshire). In some instances they can be dated by means of their field relations (with respect to barrows, settlements and trackways), or by objects found within their boundaries, as in the case of the Bronze Age hoard found at Amalveor in Cornwall (p. 100). Some of the clearest remains of Bronze Age agriculture can be seen on Dartmoor, where the use of resistant granite, rather than fragile timber, and the absence of later settlement have aided the survival of the cattle pens and enclosures constructed by the pastoralists who lived at sites like Grimspound (SX 701809). This late Bronze Age settlement comprises a pound and the remains of various huts, now set amid the glorious isolation of the moor at a height of 1,500 feet.

Many of the most impressive Bronze Age landscape features are associated with the rich and powerful Wessex Culture, which, succeeding and probably assimilating the earlier Beaker peoples, flourished on the chalklands of central southern England (whence it spread) in the middle of the second millennium B.C. This period witnessed significant developments in technology, social organization and trading patterns. Stonehenge was remodelled, the sarsen and bluestones being placed in their modern positions.

Of the thousands of round barrows (formerly called 'tumuli') constructed in the Bronze Age, the Wessex types in particular recall complex rituals and vast expenditures of labour. Round barrows compare with the Neolithic unchambered long barrows in that the mounds represent the terminal covering of a sacred area, and not tombs in the strict sense; but they usually (though by no means exclusively) contain only single burials. There are many variants, but a handful of principal types have been identified, their style and contents apparently reflecting the prevailing social hierarchy (Figure 8). The vast majority are 'bowl' barrows, which look like upturned basins, ranging from a few feet across to over a hundred, and sometimes reaching twenty feet in height. Wessex alone boasts several thousand bowl barrows, but specializes also in the less common 'bell' and 'disc' types, named after the shapes created by the presence of a berm or platform (narrow and wide respectively) between the central mound and the encircling ditch. Bell barrows have large mounds, the sides of which have partially slumped into the ditch to form a bell shape; disc barrows have much smaller mounds, and contain cremations rather than inhumations. Among the best round barrow cemeteries, displaying the different kinds, are Oakley Down (SU 018172; p. 102) and Poor Lot (SY 589907) in Dorset; Normanton Barrows (SU 118413) and Winterbourne Stoke (SU 101417) near Stonehenge in Wiltshire; Lambourn Seven Barrows (SU 328828) in Berkshire; Therfield Heath (around TL 341403) in Hertfordshire; Five Knolls (TL 007210) in Bedfordshire; and Salthouse Heath (TG 069421 to 077423) in Norfolk. Many barrows have regrettably been destroyed and are now preserved only as crop-markings.

Finally, a large proportion of the country's standing stones (not to be confused with glacial erratics or weathering forms) are Bronze Age in date, such as the Devil's Arrows, Boroughbridge (SE 391665), in North Yorkshire. Stone rows and circles are particularly common in the Highland zone (Challacombe Stone Rows, Devon, SX 690809, and many others on Dartmoor: see Figure 9), but there are examples also in lowland England (the Rollright Stones, Oxfordshire, SP 296308). Some of the circles seem to have been deliberately sited in especially dramatic positions (Bryn Cader Faner, Llandecwyn, Gwynedd, SH 648353) or beautiful settings (Castlerigg, near Keswick in Cumbria, NY 292236).

Figure 9. Brisworthy stone circle, Devon: a heavily restored early Bronze Age monument on the edge of Dartmoor

Iron Age landscapes

Much of the period embraced by the Iron Age was stormy both climatically and politically. The cool, wet spell which began in the late Bronze Age probably continued until the fifth century B.C., when it was replaced by a trend towards warmer, drier conditions. Climatic fluctuations such as these may have contributed not only to the retreat of the upland margin of agriculture and settlement but also, in the wider European context, to the complex patterns of migrations and cultural assimilations which, judging from the archaeological evidence, characterize Britain in the Iron Age. It is undoubtedly true that the Iron Age landscapes reflect an increasing intricacy and regional diversity of man-environment relations.

Several developments were significant, although it must be remembered that in many respects the conditions of life differed little from those which had prevailed in the Bronze Age, and several of the changes were of degree rather than of kind.

Further areas of woodland were removed, but a great deal still remained by the end of the Iron Age, diversified by altitude, aspect, soil type and the effects of human interference. But on the wetter upland surfaces of Highland Britain the open vegetation associations of heath and bog developed in those places where irreversible soil changes broke the cycle of regeneration. Many of the most scenically popular districts of our modern National Parks (all of which are situated in the Highland zone) are in reality derived from late prehistoric 'landscapes of dereliction' (Figure 9). It is important to acknowledge the scale and ecological effects of these clearances, since the archaeological record is frequently unrepresentative or incomplete, particularly in those upland regions where the acid soils have destroyed most of the artefacts.

If the mass-produced iron axe represented a significant technological advance for tree felling, then so did the heavy plough in the cultivation of the lowland soils. Although the evidence for the timber buildings of the Iron Age settlements is scanty, grain storage pits have been found, associated with permanent farms based on mixed agriculture. As with the Bronze Age pattern of settlement, the marginal districts contain some of the best-preserved elements in landscape terms, notably in districts of resistant building stone such as Cornwall, where hut clusters and field boundaries occur in several places (Figure 14). Extensive areas of Iron Age fields survive on the chalklands. One of the finest collections covers Fyfield Down and Overton Down (SU 142710) in Wiltshire, and includes splendid examples of Iron Age lynchets up to ten feet in height. Lynchets are secondary features produced by the downslope build-up of soil against the boundary of an arable field (positive lynchet) and the removal of material below the obstacle (negative lynchet). The terrace-like features seen today under the pasture which has preserved them result from a combination of the two types, and their presence neatly demonstrates the continuity and stability of Iron Age agriculture, based upon fields laid out with permanence in mind.

However, much of the direct evidence relating to agriculture and settlement is hidden, particularly in the wetlands: the remains of late Iron Age lake villages at Glastonbury and Meare in Somerset, with their wooden trackways and systems of infield-outfield cultivation, were strikingly preserved but invisible to the eye beneath the meads and willows of the Levels. Fascinating as the late prehistoric developments in agriculture are, there is, in the final analysis, little for the student of the visible landscape to examine. It is becoming increasingly apparent, however, that the Iron Age witnessed rising levels of economic and social sophistication, which in landscape terms was expressed in hierarchical systems of land organization and settlement. Many of the patterns produced by land boundaries, lanes and trackways which were formerly believed to be medieval, or, at the earliest, Anglo-Saxon, are now thought to derive from pre-Roman times. The Iron Age field systems and settlements to be seen today, such as those at Gussage Hill in Dorset (p. 102), are the isolated remains of a much more extensive and integrated cultural landscape.

These developing social structures, coupled with population increase and the emergence of new political relationships between and within the various tribes, provide the background to the history of the most conspicuous Iron Age landscape feature, the hillfort. Hillforts developed from Bronze Age prototypes to embrace a range of sites, sizes and degrees of fortification, reflecting their differing functions and histories of occupation. By no means all were primarily forts in the literal sense (nor were they all built upon hills); they were probably used as places of refuge, temporary or permanent settlement, elements of a system of transhumance involving the use of summer pastures, or as meeting places and territorial headquarters of tribes or chieftains, anxious to secure themselves amid growing political tension. Hillforts are common in some regions (Dorset is particularly rich), while there are hardly any in eastern England. They became progressively more elaborate with time, and often display several phases of construction, the methods of which have been partially reconstructed by archaeologists, using the unfinished hillfort of Ladle Hill in Hampshire (SU 479568).

Five basic types have been identified. Contour hillforts were built to exploit the natural shape of the hilltop, and to capitalize upon the advantages of height. Some possess only one set of ramparts: such univallate hillforts include Penbury Knoll, Dorset (p. 102), Old Winchester Hill, Hampshire (SU 641206), and Sutton Walls in Herefordshire (SO 525464), one of a large number of hillforts in the Lugg and Wye valleys, following the line of a major strategic routeway. Hod Hill (ST 857106) and Poundbury (SY 683912), both in Dorset, are examples of bivallate hillforts, while multivallate types in the same county include Eggardon (SY 541948), Badbury Rings (ST 964030; Figure 10) and Maiden Castle (p. 103 and Figure 16), the entrances of which are particularly cleverly constructed. Herefordshire Beacon (SO 760399), like many contour forts, is splendidly situated, with magnificent views. South Cadbury (ST 628252) in Somerset was rebuilt several times, as was Old Oswestry in Salop (SJ 296310), which in places exhibits as many as seven ramparts.

Figure 10. Badbury Rings and Ackling Dyke. The multivallate Iron Age hillfort of Badbury Rings crowns a low spur (capped with Reading Beds) upon the dip-slope of the Dorset Downs between Wimborne Minster and Blandford Forum. This aerial photograph was taken from a point south of the hillfort, facing just east of north. Ackling Dyke, approaching from the north-north-east on its way from Old Sarum, is revealed as a line of hedges stretching to the horizon. Instead of continuing straight through the eastern (right-hand) side of the fortifications, it abruptly changes direction just before reaching the Rings, altering course by 40 degrees to the west. It crosses the light-coloured field directly above the fort, touches the outer rampart on the north-west and leaves the photograph on the left-hand side, being most clearly visible in the vicinity of the western entrance of the hillfort. It is probable that the initial line of Ackling Dyke was indeed originally continued to the eastern edge of the fort, there joining the road to Hamworthy, but that shortly afterwards the new road between Badbury and Dorchester was completed and the Dyke became the main route to south-west England, adopting a new alignment which eventually took it all the way to Exeter

The second group consists of promontory forts. These were sited upon spurs, with banks and ditches cutting off the neck. One of the most beautifully positioned is that on Bredon Hill, Hereford and Worcester (SO 958402), while Hengistbury Head (SZ 165910) in Dorset, although greatly eroded by the sea, is an extremely interesting and important site, having been a major port and market during the Iron Age. The third type, the cliff-castle, followed the same principle as the promontory fort, but embraced coastal headlands rather than ordinary spurs; Trevelgue Head, Cornwall (SW 827630), is guarded by six lines of ramparts and ditches. Where the territory was too gentle to offer an eminence suitable for a hillfort, plateau forts like Yarnbury Castle (SU 035404) in Wiltshire were built. Finally, hillslope forts were constructed primarily for cattle ranching or the penning of sheep. They are common in south-west England, examples being Clovelly Dykes in Devon (SS 311235) and Buzbury Rings in Dorset (ST 919060).

As there was little formal burial in the Iron Age, there are few funerary sites to compare with those of the earlier prehistoric periods.

Roman landscapes

After the Roman invasion of A.D. 43 some striking new elements entered the landscape of England and Wales. The incorporation of Britain into the Empire was accompanied by the imposition of an advanced alien culture, which for its own wider purposes introduced a sophisticated system of military installations, a new transport network, and a standardized hierarchy of settlements, based upon models devised far away from the British scene. In these three principal respects the impact upon the landscape was, in terms of what had gone before, sudden, profound and, above all, highly planned and organized.

The conquest progressed by stages. In the first few years the lowlands were secured as far as the line of the Fosse Way, which ran between Exeter and Lincoln. Most of this 'civil zone' soon settled down to an ordered pattern of life, the Romans building upon some of the institutions they found there, including the territorial organization of the tribes. The Highland or 'military zone', although penetrated by Roman troops, was never brought under the same degree of control, and the Romans had to be content with maintaining a secure frontier on the edges of the upland masses. In these regions their military genius was reflected in the various installations which not only dominated the landscape but exploited to the full the physical opportunities provided by the scenery.

The ruins of several kinds of fortification can be seen today, ranging in size from large forts to signal stations and watchtowers. The legionary fortresses were constructed to a standard symmetrical plan, the whole being shaped like a playing card (rectangular with rounded corners). One of the finest surviving examples, showing the various buildings, is that at Caerleon (ST 340907), known to the Romans as Isca, which was founded *c.* A.D. 75 after the conquest of South Wales. Smaller auxiliary forts were designed for more mobile troops. Practice camps were used for training in military and engineering techniques; there are several clusters to be seen in Wales, for example on Llandrindod Common, Powys (SO 054601). A special class of forts was built on the south-east coasts of England from the early third century onwards, as a protection against Saxon raiders. These 'Saxon Shore' forts may have been part of a wider defensive system designed to cover the north-west frontier of the Empire. Some of the best, probably dating from the late third century, include Portchester, Hampshire (SU 625046), Pevensey, East Sussex (TQ 644048) – where the Roman masonry so impressed the Normans that they retained it for the outer bailey wall of their castle – and Richborough (TR 324602) in Kent. This last was built upon an earlier Roman site which began life as the base camp for the invasion of Britain, and it is one of the most interesting sets of Roman remains in the country.

The most impressive military monument of all is of course Hadrian's Wall. Begun at the instigation of the Emperor Hadrian in A.D. 122, it utilized the physical advantages of the fault-guided northern perimeter of the Alston Block to link by the shortest route (the Tyne-Solway gap) the two coastal gateways into Scotland. Agricola, that shrewd and intelligent governor of Britain, had, in A.D. 79–80, already constructed a military road, the Stanegate, between Corbridge and Carlisle, and Hadrian decided to construct a permanent boundary with a threefold function: as an obstacle of strength, an elevated patrol line, and a fortified base from which to mount encircling sorties against the barbarians. The fifteen-foot-high Wall was protected by a deep ditch, while at the rear, behind the lateral communications route of the Stanegate, lay a boundary dyke (the *Vallum*) which controlled access to the military zone from the south. Garrisoned by sixteen large forts (Figure 17), the Wall was patrolled by milecastles set one Roman mile (4,860 feet) apart, and smaller signal turrets were set between them at intervals of 1,620 feet.

The completion of the Wall, coupled with a desire to ease the pressure on the closed frontier, inspired the Romans to reoccupy the territory to the north and refortify, in A.D. 142, the Forth-Clyde line originally established by Agricola. At this time the Wall was thrown open, but soon resumed its military function following a series of reverses which culminated in the abandonment of the Antonine Wall *c.* A.D. 180. The Wall also suffered from the activities of Roman military leaders pursuing their own ambitions in the Empire. The 'forgotten army', stuck out on this distant frontier on the very edge of the civilized world, was depleted more than once for personal use elsewhere, with disastrous consequences:

the barbarians seized their opportunities to overrun and smash the wretched thing, necessitating the rebuilding of certain stretches (notably by the Emperor Severus after the debacle of A.D. 197). A good deal of the Wall remains today, particularly in the remote middle section (p. 106), where plundering for stone in later centuries was less thorough than elsewhere. Here the Wall rises and plunges like a switchback over the crags of the Whin Sill, affording magnificent views of the wild landscapes of Northumberland, which in Roman times would have displayed more bog, scrub and woodland than today, but no Forestry Commission plantations.

The Romans required, and soon built, their own road network, geared to their administrative, military and economic purposes. The straightness of these cleverly designed roads is well known, but in fact it is generally not the overall course which is straight, but only the individual sections between set points such as fords, passes and other physical features. Substantially built to a basic model and resting on a raised bank or *agger*, the original roads survive only in a few places, because so many modern routes (notably those converging on Lincoln and Cirencester) have followed their course. However, original stretches survive of Ackling Dyke in Dorset (p. 102), of Stane Street in West Sussex (SU 940105 to 970128), and of the road which passes steeply over Blackstone Edge, on the boundary of West Yorkshire and Greater Manchester (SD 975172). Elsewhere, the lines of Roman roads may be traced for miles across country in lanes, footpaths, hedgerows and parish boundaries (Figures 4 and 11).

The settlement pattern too was, generally speaking, imposed. Of the villas, there is little to be seen, except at certain excavated sites like Chedworth, Gloucestershire (SP 053134). They were much more common in some regions of the civil zone (for example, around Ilchester) than others such as the Fens or Wessex, where large imperial estates were devoted to the production of corn and wool for the army. It is important to remember that the villa, although representing in the popular view the archetypal Roman settlement form, was, in the case of the larger examples at least, exclusive and specialized. In certain respects the villa constituted the contemporary equivalent of the eighteenth-century country house, set in its own estate and occupied by the upper classes (or, increasingly, one suspects, by social climbers and *nouveaux riches* who busied themselves, as in every age, with rivalling the fashions of their neighbours and devising ever more devious ways to avoid paying tax).

A variety of other settlements appeared, related to military needs (the supply depot of Corstopitum, NY 983648, behind Hadrian's Wall),

Figure 11. The Fosse Way in Leicestershire, at the junction with Watling Street. The subdued terrain of drift-covered Triassic mudstones is typical of the Midland Plain

economic activities such as mining (Charterhouse-on-Mendip lead mining settlement, Somerset, ST 5056), transport (posting-stations like God-manchester, Cambridgeshire, T L 2470), spas (Buxton and Bath) or ports (Rochester). Some of these grew into fully-fledged towns, which were among the most imposing features of the new landscape. The Romans appreciated a good site – many towns, as may be guessed from the place-name elements *castor* or *chester*, were preceded by military forts – and the remains of the new settlements, as a consequence, are now usually hidden beneath modern urban centres. The *coloniae* (Lincoln, Gloucester, Colchester and later, by promotion, York) were intended for retired soldiers, who were given plots of land as a pension; cantonal capitals, on the other hand, were principally administrative and market centres. Only in certain towns was there a recognizable degree of grid planning, and in only a few cases, such as Gloucester, do any elements survive. Indeed, apart from indirect survivals such as alignments, boundaries and religious traditions embodied in the sites of later churches built on pagan sites, there is little of the Roman towns left to see in the landscape, at least from the ground. Substantial remains like the extremely solid town walls and bastions at Caerwent, Gwent (ST 469905), are very much the exception.

Nevertheless, the few isolated fragments of Roman buildings and engineering works in existence give a glimpse of the effect that Roman culture had on the contemporary landscape. The standard Roman institutions make their appearances, including baths (notably at Bath itself), theatres (Verulamium, Hertfordshire, TL 134074) and amphitheatres, both large (Caerleon, Gwent, ST 33859035) and small (Charterhouse-on-Mendip, ST 499565). Perhaps the best example of an amphitheatre is that known as Maumbury Rings (SY 690899) at Dorchester, Dorset, where the Romans adapted a Neolithic henge monument. (Maumbury Rings furnishes a macabre instance of a lingering tradition, for in 1705 it was the scene of the strangling and burning of a young woman shabbily convicted of murder, an event which, having been preceded by a couple of hangings as a 'warm-up' item, was witnessed by an assembled audience of 10,000.) Funeral monuments are rare, for the Romans buried their dead in cemeteries, but a few conical round barrows were erected for important citizens (Bartlow Hills, Essex, TL 586449).

A notable feat of Roman engineering was the Fenland canal known as the Car Dyke, probably designed principally for purposes of flood control. That it was also used for the transport of grain is possible, although its potential for long-distance haulage may have been limited. Stretches can still be seen in the Cambridgeshire Fens between TL 461713 and 496642. Roman Dorchester was supplied with water taken from the River Frome at Notton by a remarkable twelve-mile-long aqueduct, the line of which can still be seen west-north-west of Poundbury hillfort (SY 681912 to 671917). No less arresting as an example of Roman ingenuity is the *pharos* or lighthouse at Dover (TR 326418), which would have been visible from the French coast.

Beyond the influence of the direct machinery of colonial organization – the military installations, roads and towns – the effects of Roman rule upon the rural landscape were less tangible. Large areas were set aside for grain production, in order to supply the customary diet to those troops occupied in the pastoral upland regions. In the Fens it seems likely that the Romans seized the opportunity provided by a slight regression of the sea after *c.* A.D. 80 to drain the emerged land and establish with a free hand, unconstrained by patterns of native ownership, a new landscape of colonization and settlement. (The rebellious Iceni, formerly led by Boudicca, were invited to perform the hard work.) This landscape can really be appreciated only from the air, and elsewhere the evidence is much more confused and even less well preserved. The diversity of regional farming practices and economies may account for the many forms taken by Roman fields, even where they have been identified with relative certainty amid their successors. Some regular layouts exist, notably the 'long fields' on Martin Down, Hampshire (SU 044198), and elsewhere – perhaps associated with the use of the new and much more effective heavy plough – but widespread planning was infrequent.

This state of affairs no doubt reflects the general conclusion that at the grass roots, certainly in the military zone, traditional ways of life persisted. In the native settlements (such as Din Lligwy on Anglesey, SH 496862), connected not by Roman roads but by the ancient prehistoric tracks, which continued to serve basic needs, agricultural practices and social patterns continued much as before. This assertion assumes considerable significance when it comes to assessing the long-term contribution of the Romans to the landscape of England and Wales. Except in certain major respects, related to the imposition of colonial rule by powerful conquerors, this contribution may be more limited than the important place occupied by the Romans in the history of Europe might suggest.

Once the machinery was withdrawn and the will which inspired the Empire with momentum and purpose collapsed, the administration and transport systems geared to it became largely superfluous. The Romanization of at least parts of Britain was shown to be a veneer, and this crumbled. In Wales the departure of the legions signalled a Celtic revival. Elsewhere the Romano-British culture which had evolved during the occupation came under increasing Germanic influence. Britain had never been a central participant in the destiny of the Empire: she was indeed highly peripheral, and as a province was added late and abandoned early when the decay set in. The Dark Ages into which she passed obscured and in many cases severed the threads which Roman rule had woven into the landscape.

Conclusion

Thoughts such as these prompt further questions about the overall significance of the various phases of antiquity for the evolution of the landscape. It is clear that in several respects this early period was of great importance. The processes of natural and man-made environmental change profoundly influenced the plant cover and the development of soils. Pedological changes in turn were often crucial to the creation of subsequent patterns of vegetation, for in several regions, even when clearances ceased, trees did not return, or if they did, the composition of the woodland differed markedly from the original cover. Prehistoric man indulged in more than merely temporary clearances for purposes of casual farming: agriculture achieved, in places, a permanent basis, accompanied by the establishment of a settlement hierarchy, the lineaments of a network of routeways, territorial divisions representing a nascent political structure, and a basic regional pattern of cultural groupings. Elements of all these developments are preserved, albeit indistinctly and often indirectly, in the landscape.

This picture stems from a reassessment of prehistoric man himself. While one should not be seduced into exaggerating his level of sophistication (conferring on him the precocious ability, not to speak of the desire, to construct early computers from arrangements of sarsen stones), we have come a long way from the once popular image of the hairy dwarf-like savages who, over seemingly interminable aeons, spent their time tinkering with bits of flint and making countless pots, apparently in order to scatter the fragments liberally over the countryside for modern archaeologists to gather up with exaggerated respect and classify. Prehistoric man looked and often behaved much like modern man, who may have advanced in terms of technology and knowledge but little if at all, it is often remarked, in terms of wisdom.

The conception of prehistoric Britain as a peripheral backwater of more advanced cultures centred in Europe, the Mediterranean and the Near East, coupled with the inherent selectivity of the archaeological record, in turn encouraged other misconceptions. Several of these revolved around the 'hyperdiffusionist' school, which in effect suggested that everything came from somewhere else, and that Britain was the last staging post for a whole sequence of invading culture groups, each with its own sort of pot. More detailed study of the landscape as a totality, rather than its separate aspects, has modified this picture, as have the substantially revised chronologies produced by the realization that dates collected by radiocarbon (^{14}C) methods diverged significantly from 'real' dates, and had to be recalibrated accordingly. It is now suggested that many of the 'diffused' elements in fact *pre*-date their supposed European equivalents, and much more stress is being laid upon local development, cultural contact and ethnic intermixture.

In view of all this, a decent measure of academic humility is desirable.

The purposes of most of the prehistoric monuments described in this chapter remain a complete mystery, and this should be more freely admitted. Both the vaguely defined 'religious' or 'ritual' functions ascribed to them and the more extravagant astronomical theories (stone rows must point in one direction or another, after all) often obscure more than they reveal. Defoe realized this when he wrote of Stonehenge, that most famous yet almost equally misunderstood monument:

'Tis indeed a reverend peice of antiquity, and 'tis a great loss that the true history of it is not known; But since it is not, I think the making so many conjectures at the reality, when they know they can but guess at it, and above all the insisting so long, and warmly on their private opinions, is but amusing themselves and us with a doubt, which perhaps lyes the deeper for their search into it.

The monuments themselves assume a disproportionate significance because they have survived better than the other elements of the prehistoric landscape. The factor of selective preservation means that what we see today is in some ways neither typical nor representative, and many of the individual remains are set in surroundings which have changed out of all recognition. It is all too easy to let the selection of artefacts, whether pots, coins, or tools, important as they are, distract attention from, rather than contribute to, the answering of the major question of what the landscape actually looked like. The remains of a Roman sandal add a little more to our knowledge of, say, life on Hadrian's Wall, but the student of landscape wishes to know what the soldier who wore it *saw* when he gazed out over the scenery stretching away in front of him.

Furthermore, the distribution of archaeological sites may also be artificial. A large proportion of the prehistoric landscape features which have survived are concentrated in certain districts, especially the upland margins and the chalklands. Is this a true distribution, reflecting a preference for these areas, perhaps deriving from an inability to clear the woods or plough the heavy soils of the lowland vales? It seems more likely that the prehistoric peoples also colonized parts of the lowlands, the sites of their activities lying concealed or obliterated beneath subsequent settlements. The later settlers could have been attracted either by the existence of the prehistoric settlements themselves, or by the same physical advantages which had inspired the original, but by then vanished, site. If this is true, then many of the prehistoric sites of today are even less representative than was thought, occupying environments which were marginal then as now, and displaying in their forms and contents a degree of cultural conservatism.

Much of our knowledge of the landscapes of antiquity is therefore indirect, as the visual elements which have survived constitute only a small part of the picture. But these ancient landscapes are there nevertheless, not so much in visible forms, but in the shapes inherent in the landscape – in boundaries, routeways, settlement patterns and field systems. These shapes are deeply ingrained and resistant to change, being subject to the forces of inertia. It is in these features that the 'secret' prehistoric landscape should be sought – even the motorist cannot fail to notice the line of a Roman road – rather than in the frequently disappointing prehistoric 'sites' *per se*. So often in the landscape of England and Wales comparatively recent materials conceal ancient foundations.

Sites

The Neolithic landscape of the Avebury district, Wiltshire

The field monuments in the vicinity of Avebury constitute the most impressive (but in terms of scale and splendour to a large degree unrepresentative) Neolithic landscape in the country. They are situated by the headwaters of the River Kennet, near the inner margin of the wide Lower Chalk shelf where the ground begins to rise at the outcrop of the overlying Middle Chalk to form the Upper Chalk-capped western escarpment of the Marlborough Downs. That this region was of considerable importance in prehistoric times, when it supported relatively dense populations, is clear both from the convergence here of several ancient routeways and from the wealth and diversity of the monuments, many of which employ the local sarsens (p. 63) in their construction. The complexity of the man-made landscape, the high level of technical accomplishment embodied in its more prominent features, and the sheer effort required for their construction banish conceptions of our Neolithic ancestors as animal savages lacking cultural, technological, social and artistic sophistication. Modern archaeological investigation at Avebury has revealed the capabilities of Neolithic man; but the purpose of his creations still eludes us.

The principal Avebury monuments are six in number (Figure 12). Windmill Hill causewayed camp (SU 087714) is the type site of the middle Neolithic cultures identified in southern England. Constructed upon a Middle Chalk outlier, it comprises three rings of banks and ditches, the outer ditch being 1,200 feet in diameter. The 21-acre site, dated to *c.* 3250 B.C., has yielded axes which, to judge from the materials used – flint and certain distinctive igneous rocks – were imported from various regions of England. Deposits in the ditches suggest an economy based upon wild food, mixed grain agriculture, and domestic animals, mainly cattle.

The West Kennett Long Barrow (104677) was built at about the same

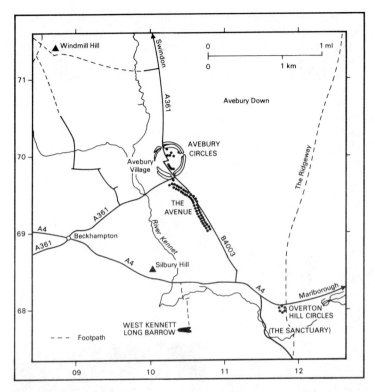

Figure 12. The Avebury district

time, but the collection of bones and pots recovered suggests that it remained in use for more than a thousand years. Recently restored, it is the largest stone-chambered collective tomb in England and Wales. It consists of a trapezoid-shaped mound 330 feet in length. The broader east end conceals, behind a façade of sarsen boulders, five internal burial chambers which open on to a roofed axial passage that the visitor may enter without stooping, as the height of the ceiling reaches eight feet. The class of the barrow's clientele, the circumstances of their decease, and the ceremony of their entombment are unknown.

The consummate enigma of the group is Silbury Hill (100685), a huge flat-topped eminence 130 feet high. It is composed of twelve and a half million cubic feet of material, and represents a remarkable feat of engineering, being very cleverly built in stages as a kind of stepped cone.

With Overton Hill Circles (118679), known as 'The Sanctuary' but in fact consisting of a series of concentric rings of posts and stones which were arranged through several phases, it is even unclear what the original structure looked like, let alone what its function was. It seems likely that a building evolved on the site, but it is possible that only timber circles existed.

The centrepiece of the complex is the great henge monument of Avebury itself, which was linked to 'The Sanctuary' by a line of a hundred pairs of sarsen stones, a mile and a half long, known as the West Kennett Avenue. (Most of these stones have gone, but the stretch of the avenue which leads up to the southern entrance of Avebury has been restored.) The circle of Avebury (103699) covers twenty-eight and a half acres and comprises an outer bank 1,400 feet in diameter and between fourteen and eighteen feet high, with a ditch inside, the original height difference between the two being at least fifty feet. There are four causewayed entrances, still used by roads converging upon the village of Avebury, the eastern part of which lies within the bank and ditch (Figure 13). Inside the ditch is a stone circle of (originally) nearly a hundred stones; within this, there are two much smaller stone circles arranged non-concentrically. With the setting of a third at the northern entrance, these originally formed a row which continued the line of the Avenue. The use of the site continued into the

Figure 13. Avebury: an aerial view from the east

Bronze Age, and there are many round barrows in the locality, for example at Overton Hill (119682).

It is an arresting thought that the active life of the Avebury complex probably spans a period of human occupancy and moulding of the landscape which in temporal terms exceeds the years separating the Norman Conquest from the present day by two and a half times. Despite its location close to modern roads and settlements, Avebury is very much a place for the visitor with imagination; and informed, intuitive imagination of the right kind remains an important tool in present approaches to the mystery of Avebury, which has so far withheld its ultimate secrets under the assaults of modern inductive science.

The moorland Plym, Devon (O.S. 1:25,000 Sheet SX 56)

The 1:25,000 map is indispensable for tracing the wealth of prehistoric monuments scattered across the open moorland in the basin of the Dartmoor Plym above Cadover Bridge (SX 555646). They must be sought on foot by setting out from a starting point such as Brisworthy (560652), Ditsworthy Warren House (584663) or Trowlesworthy Warren House (567648), paying careful attention to available landmarks.

Despite detailed and comprehensive research in recent years, many questions about this extremely important Bronze Age landscape are still unanswered. Nevertheless, three phases in its evolution have been identified. In the early Bronze Age, at the beginning of the second millennium B.C, a 'funerary landscape' was laid out here, in association with a degree of deforestation. The monuments include cairns (for example at Drizzlecombe, 591672 etc.), cists or stone burial chambers (often associated with cairns), stone rows (Drizzlecombe, 591669 etc.) and stone circles. The circles may be freestanding, as at Brisworthy (565655, Figure 9), or, particularly if they surround a burial, they are sometimes connected to stone rows (Ringmoor Down cairn circle and row, 563658).

The second chapter was set in the middle of the second millennium B.C., when forest clearances accompanied the establishment of settlements. Although a system of transhumance probably operated, it is likely that some at least of the occupation was permanent, with the self-sufficiency of the communities probably founded upon dominantly pastoral agriculture combined with a certain amount of alluvial tinning. The larger groups of pounds and hut circles, especially between Legis Tor (570653) and Drizzlecombe (594671 etc.), are close to the river's edge and overlook areas which were heavily tinned in medieval times. It is tempting to suggest that a pattern of exchange existed, involving the 'export' of tin for the 'import' of other commodities.

The final period occupied the second half of the second millennium B.C. The pollen evidence suggests that overgrazing occurred, and it is possible that the low stone banks known as 'reaves', which marked contemporary land boundaries, were part of an attempt to regulate the livestock. A climatic deterioration involving increased rainfall and cooling of a degree or two, together with the clearing and overgrazing, led to podzolization and the development of blanket bog. The moorland Plym shows how important limited environmental changes can be in marginal districts, for even if the impact was not direct, the shrinkage of the areas of good land would only have exacerbated the deleterious effects of grazing. Whatever the cause, depopulation in the early part of the first millennium was sufficient to allow shrub recolonization in the Iron Age, and to create a gap in the record of human settlement which lasted until the medieval period. This desertion helped to preserve the prehistoric landscape.

It was not until the thirteenth century A.D. that the valleyside benches of the Plym were again occupied in anything but a casual fashion. This era of colonization was to transform the moorland edge of Dartmoor, producing features which, superimposed upon the prehistoric landscape, must be carefully distinguished from it. One of the most interesting activities in the Plym basin at this time was rabbit warrening, which took its place in the local economy together with agriculture and tinning. Near the Bronze Age monuments at Ditsworthy and Trowlesworthy are some remains of the warrens, where rabbits were bred for profit. The long banks or 'pillow mounds' have been equated with the 'buries' where the rabbits lived, and are the most distinctive relics of the second main period of human activity in this beautiful valley on the edge of Dartmoor.

Zennor, Cornwall (O.S. 1:25,000 Sheet SW 43)
The coastal platform which runs along the northern edge of the granite peninsula of Penwith in Cornwall presents a remarkable concentration of Bronze Age and Iron Age landscape features. The Zennor district is especially noteworthy for its prehistoric field systems, settlements and chambered tombs. In western Cornwall Saxon influence was weak, belated and selective, and the ancient Celtic landscape of this part of Penwith shows little sign of having been affected by it. It is still composed of dispersed farms, hamlets and small, intricate fields.

The term 'Celtic fields' is deliberately vague. It is generally applied to the small, regular, approximately rectangular fields, surrounded by banks or walls, which were created anything up to a thousand years before the Saxon occupation. Separated by walls of granite boulders, these fields were resistant to change and survive magnificently around Boswednack (SW 443378) and Zennor (455385) (Figure 14). They are thought to date

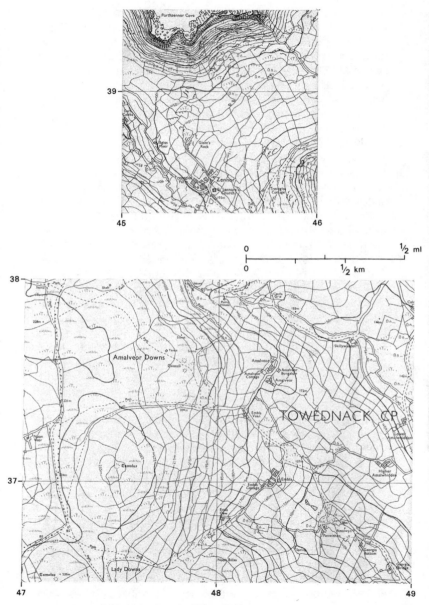

Figure 14. Prehistoric field patterns, Zennor and Towednack

from the Iron Age and may have been laid out by peoples who migrated to Cornwall in search of tin. (The Penwith peninsula is separated from the rest of Cornwall by a lowland passage which is believed to have functioned as part of a route connecting the Atlantic peninsulas of Ireland, Britain and Europe.) Some sections of the coastal bench are underlain by basic igneous intrusions of greenstone which flank the Penwith granite. Together with local solifluction deposits, these provided slightly better soils than those on the exposed uplands, and perhaps encouraged the development of the distinctive terraced fields at Boswednack. On the Amalveor and Lady Downs south of Towednack (4736–4737), above the plateau, there is evidence of an early infield-outfield system. The infield referred to the superior land which lay near the farm buildings. It was manured and held in continuous cropping, in contrast to the more distant outfield, which was cropped and then left in fallow. The edges of the outfield are marked by wide, curved boundaries (for example that which trends westwards and then northwards from 47503675 to 47353720), while the infield (478368 to 477371) is elaborately subdivided (Figure 14).

Associated with these field systems are a number of Iron Age 'villages'. The most famous in Penwith is that at Chysauster (472350), where eight oval houses with courtyards are arranged in pairs on either side of a 'street', with additional huts nearby. Each of these formerly thatched houses had a garden plot, and one has a ruined 'fogou', an underground chamber or passage, whose purpose is uncertain. The occupation of Chysauster is thought to have begun *c.* 100 B.C., but some scholars believe that, despite its late prehistoric appearance, the settlement actually dates from Roman times, testifying to the limited impact of Roman culture upon the periphery. Similar settlements near Zennor, originating in the first century A.D., include Upper Treen (438372) and Porthmeor (434371), the latter displaying two pounds, the first containing seven huts and two courtyard houses and the second a courtyard house and fogou. The local working of tin may also date from this time.

This essentially Iron Age landscape has roots which stretch back even further. What we see at Bodrifty Iron Age village (445354) is a number of huts enclosed by a pound wall probably dating from the late second century B.C., but the original settlement, of which traces survive, was constructed in the late Bronze Age. Actual Bronze Age villages have been traced on the edge of the Penwith summit plateau behind the coastal bench, on Trewey Common (465370) and Trendrine Hill (474385). Some of the field boundaries also date from this period. A late Bronze Age hoard was found in a hedgebank at Amalveor, demonstrating the antiquity of the landscape. The prehistoric routeway from St Just to St Ives, which is preserved in lanes, footpaths and the lines of parish boundaries, passes through Amalveor Farm and is associated with a number of Bronze Age monuments, including the Nine Maidens stone circle (434351).

The upland platform preserves a yet more distant phase of occupation, the Neolithic. A fine example of a quoit (p. 78) can be seen above Zennor (469380). The mound which formerly covered the tomb has gone, and the capstone has collapsed. The condition of the quoit was not improved by the activities of a local farmer who blew up part of the antechamber in 1881 in search of treasure. He was disappointed.

The Dorset Cursus and Ackling Dyke, Dorset and Hampshire

Dorset is a county rich in prehistoric monuments. One of the most complete prehistoric landscapes to survive can be explored in the north of the county where the enigmatic Dorset Cursus is crossed by Ackling Dyke Roman road. Numerous public footpaths crisscross the area, and a perusal of the O.S. map will reveal paths to most of the field monuments depicted on the sketch-map (Figure 15).

Figure 15. The Dorset Cursus and Ackling Dyke

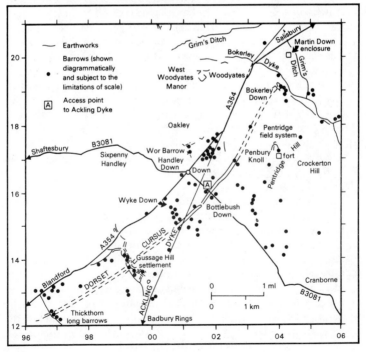

The best starting point is on Bottlebush Down at SU 016163, where the B3081 cuts through the raised causeway of Ackling Dyke (point *A* on the map). This fine Roman *aggar* ran from Old Sarum (p. 200) to Badbury Rings (Figure 10); the road is unmistakable on the map, variously taking the form of a track, bridlepath, minor road, parish boundary, raised causeway and the A354 itself. The most impressive sections on the ground are those which extend for a mile in both directions from the above-mentioned location. They can easily be walked using the public footpath on top of the rampart. To the north-north-east Ackling Dyke soon passes Oakley Down round barrows (SU 018172). The bowl, bell and disc varieties are all represented, and together they form one of the finest Bronze Age cemeteries in southern England. Proceeding in the opposite direction (south-south-west) from the B3081 intersection, a comparable walk carries one past the much ploughed Wyke Down barrows to the Dorset Cursus (SU 011152).

This is the longest Neolithic cursus so far known in this country and consists of two parallel banks with external ditches set 300 feet apart. Although its six-mile course incorporates or passes close to several long barrows, and is closed at each end by transverse banks and ditches, much of the Cursus is indistinct, and it is not a public right of way. Nevertheless, it can be clearly seen here at the junction with Ackling Dyke; it is also worth examining at the point where it is cut by the B3081 (SU 019160), a quarter of a mile south-east of that road's intersection with the Dyke. The purpose of the Cursus remains a mystery: it is assumed rather lamely that it played some role, perhaps that of a processional way, in Neolithic necrolatry. Near its north-eastern termination lie Grim's Ditch and Martin Down Enclosure (SU 043201), a Bronze Age animal pound furnishing evidence of large-scale cattle ranching in the district *c.* 1,000 B.C. At the other end of the Cursus can be seen the two Thickthorn long barrows (ST 971123), one of which yielded Windmill Hill pottery indicating a date of *c.* 3,500 B.C.

Later monuments are also encountered along the line of the Dorset Cursus. Gussage Hill is the site of a large Iron Age settlement, with fields, dykes and an enclosure (ST 993141); these have been largely destroyed by ploughing. Back again towards the north-eastern end, the Cursus is overlooked by the univallate Iron Age fort of Penbury Knoll (SU 039171), constructed upon a gravel-capped hill and consequently almost ruined by modern gravel extraction. Still, Penbury gives a good view westwards of Ackling Dyke, Oakley Down and, in the distance, Wor Barrow. To the north may be seen Iron Age fields, and further off, at the end of the Cursus, Bokerley Dyke. This is the most recent part of the assemblage, being a late Roman-British defensive earthwork thrown up across the downland saddle in the fourth century in order to block the main route into Dorset from the north and protect the Durotriges. It may originally have been built to guard the estate of which the settlement of Woodyates was an outpost; it was later used as a line of defence for Dorset against the Saxons (see p. 138).

Maiden Castle, Dorset

The 'whole stupendous ruin', wrote Thomas Hardy, 'may indeed be likened to an enormous many-limbed organism of an antediluvian time ... lying lifeless, and covered with a thin green cloth, which hides its substance, while revealing its contour'. Maiden Castle has been hailed as the greatest of the English hillforts; following Sir Mortimer Wheeler's famous excavation in the 1930s, it is undoubtedly the best-known (Figure 16).

Figure 16. Maiden Castle hillfort: the southern ramparts

The history of the saddle-backed chalk ridge with its two hilltops consists of three main periods: Neolithic, Iron Age and Roman. The Windmill Hill peoples of the Neolithic built a causewayed camp on the eastern knoll, over which was later constructed a lengthy bank-barrow along the ridge: little of these structures can now be seen. The huge ramparts which so impress the visitor are the legacy of four phases of Iron Age development, which began *c.* 350 B.C with a simple fort on the eastern knoll. This was enlarged a century later to take in the western hill with a single rampart and ditch. The fortifications were rebuilt *c.* 150 B.C. at twice the original scale, with the addition of further ramparts on the north and south, and barbicans at the eastern and western entrances. Finally, in the early first century B.C., complex entrances were contrived and the ramparts and ditches strengthened. By this time Maiden Castle, unlike many other hillforts, which were used only for refuge in times of trouble, was an important permanent settlement with a sizeable population engaged in agriculture and various forms of manufacture. It was probably the political centre of the Durotriges, and by Iron Age standards embodied a relatively secure military stronghold protected by elaborate earthworks and defended by slingers – the excavations revealed huge ammunition dumps of pebbles transported from Chesil Beach. However, when the fort was attacked in A.D. 43 or 44 by the Second Legion under Vespasian, the Roman artillery overwhelmed the defenders in a bloody battle. The 'war cemetery' found by Mortimer Wheeler contained the moving sight of a skeleton with the iron head of a Roman dart lodged in the spine. Once the Roman town of Durnovaria (Dorchester) was established nearby, the remaining inhabitants of Maiden Castle probably drifted away.

Nevertheless, a third and final phase in the site's history was enacted some time later, in about A.D. 367, when a Romano-Celtic temple was built in the eastern part of the hillfort. This temple, together with others of apparently similar date, has been interpreted as evidence of a late pagan revival, but it is important to recall that the temple at Lydney, Gloucestershire (p. 111), also excavated by Wheeler and given a date of A.D. 364–7 largely on coin evidence, is now thought by other scholars to represent a refurbishment of an earlier Roman building. The reasons behind the siting of these Roman temples in Iron Age hillforts remain a matter for conjecture. The tempestuous story of Maiden Castle thus comes to a quiet and enigmatic end, although it has been suggested that it was refortified in the late- or sub-Roman period.

Chanctonbury and Cissbury Rings, West Sussex

These two Iron Age hillforts are splendidly situated on the South Downs north of Worthing. Chanctonbury Ring (TQ 139121) crowns the Chalk escarpment near Washington and is a familiar landmark because of the beech trees planted within the enclosure in 1760. Two associated cross-dykes lie about 400 yards away on the scarp crest to the west and south-east, while inside the Ring are the foundations of two Roman buildings, one of which has been identified as a Romano-Celtic temple. The strategic advantages of the site can be appreciated if one approaches Chanctonbury from the north-west, climbing the steep scarp-slope by means of footpaths from Washington or Lock's Farm (131127).

Cissbury (140082), although occupying a position down the dip-slope of the escarpment two and a half miles to the south, is also situated upon an eminence. In this part of the South Downs there appears to be a kind of discontinuous 'second escarpment' upon the dip-slope of the main one. It may have formed as a result of lithological contrasts within the various zones of the Chalk which have been selectively exploited by the forces of erosion. The footpath from Chanctonbury to Cissbury runs from the scarp crest (780 feet) down the upper section of the deeply dissected dip-slope with its dry valleys or 'bottoms', to reach the second escarpment at Cissbury, where a new ascent is made from a height of 430 feet to 600 feet in the Ring itself. The builders of the hillfort at Cissbury used these natural advantages to the full, enclosing an area of sixty-four acres with a large rampart, ditch and counterscarp bank. These features date from the middle of the fourth century B.C., but the site was first occupied more than three thousand years earlier, when a Neolithic flint mining industry second only to Grime's Graves in Norfolk flourished here. On the south-western side of the fort over two hundred mounds and depressions survive, which mark the dumps and filled-in shafts of an extensive system of mines (137079). Some of these vertical shafts were forty feet deep, and several sets of radiating galleries ran off them at various depths, where the bands of flint were encountered. The highest beds of the Chalk, which form the secondary escarpment on the Downs, are a rich source of superior flint.

This activity had long ceased when the Iron Age fort was constructed, and another seemingly quiet spell followed the second eventful chapter of Cissbury's history. Lying in the territory of the Atrebates, who were friendly to the Romans, Cissbury was not maintained as a fort in Roman times. During the occupation the interior was in fact ploughed, and the lynchets to be seen in the south-east portion (13950795) may date from this time. But at the end of the Roman period the fort, then no doubt somewhat decayed, was quickly refortified, presumably in response to the growing Saxon threat. The defensive function of this ancient site was briefly revived on one further occasion in English history, when a seaborne attack again threatened: in 1587 beacons were placed upon Cissbury in readiness for the impending arrival of the Spanish Armada.

Many features of this prehistoric landscape have vanished as a consequence of the great changes which have taken place on the South Downs in the intervening centuries. Especially drastic has been the recent ploughing up of the Chalk downland, in association with the new technology and financial inducements which characterize modern farming, to produce a prairie landscape of large arable fields. The walker on the Downs can no longer enjoy the once familiar expanses of springy turf and downland flora, which now tend to be confined to slopes too steep for agricultural machinery. Few people applaud the change in terms of landscape aesthetics or ecological diversity; the chalk downland vegetation was a singularly beautiful plant community, containing as many as forty-five species of flowering plants and mosses per square yard. It was not, however, a 'natural' vegetation association, or one which the prehistoric peoples would have recognized; rather, it evolved in close relationship to the phases of settlement evidenced in the landscape. Until the Neolithic, Bronze Age and Iron Age clearances removed much if not most of the woodland, the Downs were covered with mixed oak-hazel forest on the deeper soils of the gentle slopes, and elm-lime forest on the scarps. (The beech, ash and yew woods of today constitute quite different secondary associations.)

'Celtic' fields of assumed Bronze Age and later dates survive on the hillside at Park Brow (153086), nearly a mile east-north-east of Cissbury, from where they can be clearly seen. Early farming activities, which initiated important soil changes on the chalklands, declined in the Saxon period. The arable cultivation of Roman times was succeeded by the conversion of the Downs into a vast sheep walk. This use, together with moderate grazing by rabbits, determined the distinctive aspect of the grassland. It continued for centuries, until the diminution in sheep numbers, the drive to arable in the last war, and the decimation of the rabbit population by myxomatosis in the 1950s drastically reduced the area of sheep-adapted chalk grassland. It is a mere tenth of what it was half a century ago, and much of the now ungrazed remainder has entered upon the succession to less diverse tall-grass meadow, scrub and secondary woodland. But the loss of this very special anthropogenic (or at best semi-natural) grassland of the Downs, dominated by the interlacing lateral shoots of the fine-leaved sheep's fescue (*Festuca ovina*) and red fescue (*Festuca rubra*), is no less lamentable for its not being wholly 'natural' in origin.

Housesteads Roman Fort, Northumberland
The Roman fort of Housesteads (NY 790688) is magnificently positioned amid some of the finest scenery in the vicinity of Hadrian's Wall. The walk along the section of the Wall which lies to the west of Housesteads gives an unequalled conspectus of its natural setting, highlighting the brilliant use made of the Whin Sill. It also brings the visitor to the nearby milecastle 37, which is one of the most interesting of its type remaining. This central stretch of the Wall remained remote and dangerous until recent times: in the late sixteenth century the antiquary William Camden was afraid to visit it because of the mosstroopers, and a hundred years later Housesteads itself was used as a headquarters by an infamous gang of robbers and thugs. These activities served a useful purpose, however,

in restricting those practices which elsewhere had already turned the Wall into a convenient quarry for building stone.

Housesteads guards the gap created by the Knag Burn as it passes through the Whin Sill escarpment. Several Roman roads converged on this point, which also marked a route for advance into the country north of the Wall. These strategic considerations led the Romans to favour the spot for the construction of a fort although the restricted site made the actual building more difficult than elsewhere. The Roman name of the fort is uncertain; modern scholars refer to it either as *Vercovicium* or *Borcovicium* (the name given in the *Notitia Dignitatum*). Housesteads superseded the fort at Chesterholm, which had been built two miles away on the Stanegate. During the building of the Wall, it was realized that both tactical advantage and valuable time could be gained if the forts were sited on the Wall itself rather than behind it, thus allowing the encircling sorties to be released more quickly and decisively (see p. 87). The fort was rebuilt after each of the disasters which overwhelmed the Wall, in A.D. 197, 296 and 367, before being finally destroyed in the closing years of the fourth century. The most interesting feature of Housesteads is the development there of a large settlement comprising not only houses for women, children and retired soldiers, but a kind of market for trade with the natives themselves. A gateway was actually made in the Wall for purposes of commerce – the only example to be found along the whole length of the Wall. The third and early fourth centuries witnessed the extensive growth, outside the walls, of this undefended settlement, which even acquired a measure of self-government. Its presence testifies to the generally peaceful life enjoyed on the Wall; it was not abandoned until the catastrophe of 367.

In Roman times, the site of Housesteads was covered with buildings. The fort itself occupied a rectangular site of five acres and was manned by a 1,000-strong infantry battalion. It comprised a headquarters building, granaries (with raised floors), commandant's house, hospital, barracks and latrines. The buildings were arranged on a set plan divided by a regular pattern of streets, and the whole was enclosed by a massive wall surmounted by angle-towers and (later) interval-towers, and pierced by gateways on each of the four sides (Figure 17). The fort boasted an impressive drainage system, but the bath-house was constructed on the left bank of the Knag Burn, outside the walls, following the usual practice. The section of the *Vallum* near the fort was filled in (in Roman times) and the hillside was covered by the shops and taverns of the civil settlement, beyond which lay the temples, shrines and cemeteries. A series of problematic terraces overlie the line of the *Vallum*; they may be cultivation terraces and in their original form date possibly from the second century, although

Figure 17. Housesteads from the south-east, showing the Roman fort, the infilled *Vallum*, the cultivation terraces, and the platforms of the civil settlement

they were reused subsequently. It was the ruins of this settlement which inspired the name Housesteads, but any suggestion of domestic cosiness is misleading: in one of the shops were found the skeletons of a man and a woman, brutally murdered, their remains having been hidden under the floor. The visitor is left to ponder on the nature of the motive and the identity of those involved in this long-concealed crime, which took place so long ago on this desolate frontier.

Lydney Park Roman temple complex, Gloucestershire
One of the most atmospheric Roman sites in Britain lies within Lydney Park, on the southern edge of the Forest of Dean in west Gloucestershire. Camp Hill (SO 616027) is a steep-sided southward-facing spur bounded on three sides by deeply incised streams, while woods clothe the rising interfluve to the north. The flattened summit of the spur offers splendid views across the Park to the wide flats of the River Severn a couple of miles away to the south and south-east. It had been appreciated in the eighteenth century that The Dwarf's Hill was the site of an ancient settlement of some kind – indeed, the stone walls which crowned it were then still quite high – but it was not until Dr and Mrs R. E. M. Wheeler carried out a major excavation in 1928–9 that the nature and significance of the remains emerged. The Wheelers' report, from which the site plan (Figure 18) and drawing (Figure 19) are taken, proposed the following four-phase chronology for Lydney.

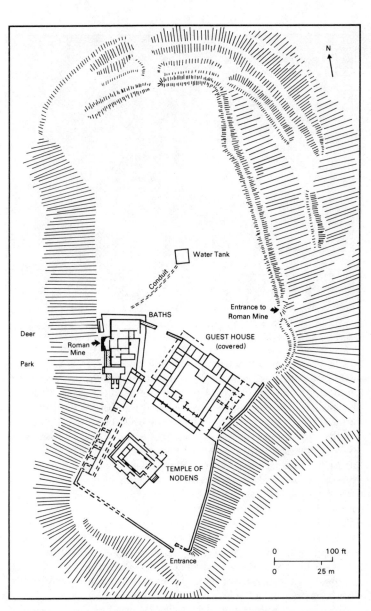

N

Water Tank

Conduit

BATHS

Entrance to
Roman Mine

Deer

GUEST HOUSE
(covered)

Roman
Mine

Park

TEMPLE OF
NODENS

Entrance

0   100 ft

0   25 m

Figure 18. Plan of Lydney Park hillfort and Roman temple complex

Figure 19. Lydney Park Roman temple complex: a reconstruction drawing of the buildings as viewed from the south-south-east (Wheeler, 1932)

The earliest known inhabitants of the hilltop were the Iron Age peoples of the first century B.C., who built a promontory fort of five acres, bounded on the north and east by a bank with an external ditch which cut across the spur. The original ramparts were five feet in height, but they were raised at a later date (see below), and are still ten feet high today. The later history of this community is uncertain, for the evidence has been obscured by later developments. The second period of activity was initiated in the early Roman period. It was centred upon a population housed in rectangular huts and engaged in the manufacture of barrel-shaped pots ('flower pots') and the mining of iron ore. Pockets of haematite are encountered locally in certain lithological divisions of the Carboniferous Limestone Series, which underlies, and outcrops around the edge of the main basin of the Forest of Dean coalfield. Evidence of the exploitation of these deposits in the third century A.D. was found in the form of two mines situated within the confines of the fort. One of these reaches a depth of fifteen feet and extends underground for a distance of fifty feet, displaying original pick-marks on the wall of the tunnel.

The third phase, according to the Wheelers, took place in the later part of the fourth century, when Camp Hill became a religious centre of some wealth and importance. A complex of four principal buildings was erected, the whole being enclosed by a *temenos* wall (Figures 18 and 19). The most striking of these was a temple, 85 feet by 67 feet, consisting of an arcaded *cella* surrounded by an ambulatory corridor with five alcoves or 'chapels'. The triple sanctuary lay at the north-west end of the *cella*, and the entrance, situated above a flight of steps, was positioned on the opposite (south-east) side of the building. Alterations were carried out soon after the initial construction, however, following the collapse of one of the *cella* arcade piers into a subsurface cavity in the limestone beneath. The temple was dedicated to the native British god Nodens, a local deity; judging from the mosaic found in the *cella*, depicting fishes and sea-monsters, and the fragments of bronze images of fishermen and mermen, the cult may have been partially connected with nature, hunting, water, or the Severn itself. The Wheelers pointed out that complex dedications were typical of Mithraic and other transported oriental cults, but the finds included several small figures of dogs (now housed in the small private museum by the house), which, together with the famous Lydney 'curse', exhorting Nodens to withhold good health from the thief of a ring, suggest that the principal cult was one of healing. The belief that the licking of sores by dogs aided recovery is found elsewhere in the ancient world (cf. Luke xvi:21), and dogs were often kept at healing shrines. A long, narrow building (*abaton*) north-west of the temple may have been used by patients, perhaps seeking magical and prophetic dreams; alternatively it could represent a series of shops selling souvenirs and votive offerings. Northeast of the temple lay the guest house (now covered), which was a hall with a central courtyard, and west of this are the foundations of a conspicuously large (possibly ritual) bath-house, with a hypocaust.

The whole is suggestive of a place of pilgrimage, for purposes of healing and contemplation. Mortimer Wheeler, largely on numismatic evidence, dated the construction of the temple to A.D. 364–7, and as a consequence Lydney has been taken as the classic example of the late resurgence of paganism in a Roman Empire which was by that time nominally Christian. However, recent research suggests that this view is not tenable. Firstly, the Roman naval officer who donated the mosaic described above probably lived during the third century, not the fourth; secondly, the general composition of the coin collection suggests a date earlier than the 360s; thirdly, it has been shown that Wheeler's mosaics cover earlier floors and are in fact secondary features; and fourthly, the known sequence of changes made to the buildings is hard to compress into the remaining years of the Roman occupation. It is therefore concluded that the complex dates from the late third or early fourth centuries, and that its origins may stretch even further back.

Despite the apparent collapse of the 'late pagan revival' theory, the intrinsic interest of Lydney remains, and several important questions still await an answer. Whatever the date of its construction, why was the temple complex built in such a remote spot? What was the 'catchment area' of the pilgrims or patients who travelled here? What was the pattern of life for the residents? It is especially tantalizing to speculate on the nature of the demise of the Roman settlement, after the legions withdrew from Britain and left those inhabitants of the wild and isolated Forest of Dean which existed at that early time to resume their traditional mode of life, if indeed they had ever been obliged to relinquish it. (They have, after all, successfully resisted ever greater external challenges to their independence during the subsequent centuries!) The information provided by the landscape in answer to these problems is scanty. The prehistoric defences were remodelled, but by the sixth century it is likely that nature was reclaiming her own. It is perhaps worth noting in this context that when the Normans came to build their motte-and-bailey castle here in the twelfth century they decided to place it upon the adjoining spur across the brook to the south-east (61750245), fortuitously leaving the Roman site untouched. Although the landscape has changed greatly over the last millennium and a half, Lydney still retains a touch of magic. One may stand amid the ruins of the temple of Nodens and in the mind's eye restore the dense woods to the Vale below, and try to picture the Roman buildings which once crowned this lonely spur above the great sweep of the untamed Severn.

(Lydney Park is open to visitors on certain days of the year, and the camp and museum may be viewed at other times by appointment. Applications should be made to Lydney Park Estate Office, which will also advise on access.)

CHAPTER 3

Dark Ages Landscapes

In A.D. 410 the Emperor Honorius informed the Britons, in response to their appeal for help against the marauding barbarians, that henceforth they must look to their own defence. Assistance from Rome was indeed at an end. Thus began a long, turbulent and obscure period which continued until the Norman Conquest. But even this, the most truly 'memorable' date in English history, lay in what was in many respects an age of transition, one which lacked a clear beginning as well as a definite end. Through and beyond the vaguely defined Dark Ages or Anglo-Saxon epoch there were many elements of continuity as well as of change, and the intricate patterns of movement, mixture and assimilation of migrating peoples complicated the regional geography of Britain to a degree which makes generalization extremely difficult, and would continue to do so even if all the facts were available, which they most emphatically are not.

Nevertheless, the eventful political history of these times, involving the arrival and spread of successive groups of immigrants, rendered this long span of over six centuries a formative period for several reasons. The cultural legacy, in terms of language, institutions, religion, customs, law, local government by shires and the evolution of regional identities, was very considerable. The image of an age characterized by ravaging and pillaging Teutons who laid waste with fire and sword, living in primitive wattle and daub huts and bequeathing to posterity nothing of value save their beer, does no justice to the truth. The settlers progressed greatly in terms of social organization, sophistication and civilization as the years went by. The artistic achievements of these centuries, viewed in the broader European context, have rarely been equalled and perhaps never surpassed in this country. The contribution in landscape terms was also significant, although it was more involved and less easy to understand, particularly in view of the great regional differences, than the traditional account would have one believe. Recent suggestions that it is no longer realistic to envisage the early Saxon period as witnessing the implantation of the immutable nucleated English village in no way diminish the importance of the era for the history of rural settlement, since scholars do not yet understand the processes which stimulated the emergence, from the ninth century onwards, of new elements in the settlement landscape. These elements embodied the germs of the more familiar arrangements of hamlets and villages which appeared later, after further upheavals in the medieval period.

Much of the uncertainty which relates to such intriguing questions stems from the nature of the evidence. The visible shapes and forms, and the place-names which were the mainstays of the older interpretations, are now known to be incomplete and often misleading sources of information. Much of the most important material concerning Saxon landscapes is in fact hidden, or only indirectly reflected in the visible scene. For example, the dominant building material was wood, which has generally failed to survive, so that only with the latest advances of modern archaeology has it been possible, in a few places only, to gain a fair assessment of the location and type of settlement, the architectural styles, and the ways of life of the inhabitants. The study of boundaries, land units and estates has proved to be far more important than the description of present village layouts, and research is now concentrating upon the uncovering and reading of this 'secret' landscape.

This pursuit does not merely offer an adjunct to the formal compilation of written history, but represents a major source for the period. Documentary evidence is in general so scarce and limited, and in some cases so coloured by particular ethnocentric standpoints, that the landscape provides a great deal of the information, limited as it is, relating not only to agriculture or settlement but to the political events and economic forces which initiated and influenced the moulding of the face of the country. The routes taken by the new arrivals, their diffusion and interaction, and the changing political geography of Britain, have all left their mark in the landscape.

Saxons and Vikings

During the sub-Roman period barbaric raids increased in severity, and after the mid-fifth century major incursions took place. For some time during the later stages of the Empire, Germanic troops had been used by the Romans, and it has been suggested that the revolt of these communities triggered off the greater disturbances which followed. But the relationship between these mercenaries and their untamed kinsfolk, if that is what they were, in northern Germany and Denmark is uncertain, as is the precise identity of the Angles, Saxons and Jutes who came to Britain in a more general period of unrest consequent upon demographic changes and the shifts in political power resulting from the waning of the Empire. There is evidence to suggest that, once having arrived in England, they all called themselves Angles, while the Romano-Britons and the Celts (who were fighting not only the invaders but also each other) called them Saxons, much as the Scots of today refer to the English as Sassenachs. Of these early confused stages of the Saxon immigration, little can be said. In places there was bloodshed and violence, the resistance of the legendary King Arthur holding up the Saxon advance. Some of the numerous ditches and dykes to be seen in parts of England (p. 138) may date from this time. Elsewhere the picture was probably less dramatic, particularly after the initial groups had established themselves relatively securely. By the end of the sixth century much of lowland England had been colonized, and the new families were no doubt eventually assimilated peaceably enough. If it is true that the Saxons were seeking permanent settlement in order to cultivate the fruits of civilization, then decent relations were likely to have been observed wherever possible. In Wales and Cornwall the Celtic kingdoms carried on as before, preserving their links with the past. They were discouraged by such boundaries as Offa's Dyke (p. 135) from interfering with the Saxon kingdoms of the Lowland zone, which emerged as the early territorial groupings became consolidated into larger blocs.

These political units remained the fluctuating amalgams of smaller spheres of influence, but four major kingdoms may be identified: East Anglia, Northumbria, Mercia and Wessex (Figure 20). The relations between them and the relative waxing and waning of their power were conditioned by their racial composition, cultural and social development and by geographical position. Tension between them may have prompted the building or refurbishment of some of the peculiar linear earthworks referred to earlier. In Northumbria, where Celtic influence lingered, traditional British styles were combined with those of the Mediterranean to produce a new level of artistic achievement in literature, metalwork, sculpture and architecture. This development was closely linked with the activities of the Christian Church, which through the monasteries and churches kept the flame of civilization burning. The mixture of Latin and Celtic cultural traditions apparent in Northumbria (where the old Christianity had been preserved) was directly related to the two prevailing factions in the Church, and the spread of religious establishments after the triumph of the Latin party at the Synod of Whitby in A.D. 664 had profound consequences. Indeed, many of the visible landscape features of this period which have survived in England, albeit in altered and often battered forms, are associated with the churches themselves. Thus the break with Christianity occasioned by the Saxon invasion was repaired when St Augustine arrived in Kent at the very end of the sixth century. The civilizing impetus which this event heralded is hard to overestimate.

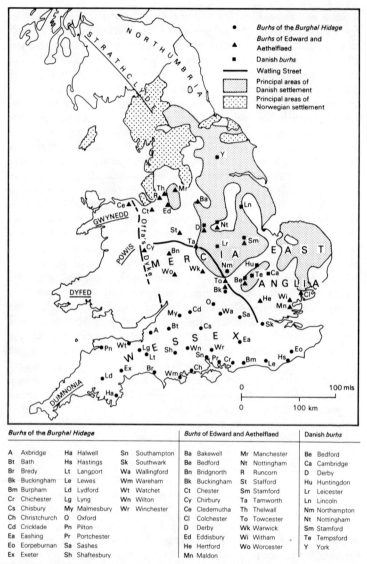

	Burhs of the Burghal Hidage			Burhs of Edward and Aethelflaed		Danish burhs	

Burhs of the *Burghal Hidage*

A	Axbridge	Ha	Halwell	Sn	Southampton
Bt	Bath	Hs	Hastings	Sk	Southwark
Br	Bredy	Lt	Langport	Wa	Wallingford
Bk	Buckingham	Le	Lewes	Wm	Wareham
Bm	Burpham	Ld	Lydford	Wt	Watchet
Cr	Chichester	Lg	Lyng	Wn	Wilton
Cs	Chisbury	My	Malmesbury	Wr	Winchester
Ch	Christchurch	O	Oxford		
Cd	Cricklade	Pn	Pilton		
Ea	Eashing	Pr	Portchester		
Eo	Eorpeburnan	Sa	Sashes		
Ex	Exeter	Sh	Shaftesbury		

Burhs of Edward and Aethelflaed

Ba	Bakewell	Mr	Manchester
Be	Bedford	Nt	Nottingham
Bn	Bridgnorth	R	Runcorn
Bk	Buckingham	St	Stafford
Ct	Chester	Sm	Stamford
Cy	Chirbury	Ta	Tamworth
Ce	Cledemutha	Th	Thelwall
Cl	Colchester	To	Towcester
D	Derby	Wk	Warwick
Ed	Eddisbury	Wi	Witham
He	Hertford	Wo	Worcester
Mn	Maldon		

Danish *burhs*

Be	Bedford
Ca	Cambridge
D	Derby
Hu	Huntingdon
Lr	Leicester
Ln	Lincoln
Nm	Northampton
Nt	Nottingham
Sm	Stamford
Te	Tempsford
Y	York

Figure 20. England and Wales in the early tenth century. The map depicts the state of southern Britain at the time of the Anglo-Danish struggle. It shows the principal kingdoms (the Celtic kingdoms are underlined), the pattern of Scandinavian settlement, and the three groups of *burhs*. Some details of the map are conjectural

In the eighth century Mercia reached its peak of power under Aethelbald and Offa. Mercia itself lay in the west Midlands but at this time was able to dominate the whole of southern England. In the ninth century, however, it was forced to give way to Wessex, which under the rule of Alfred and his successors resisted the Danes and became the principal kingdom in the land.

Eastern England bore the brunt of this new wave of conquest. The Danes, like the Saxons, began as raiders and later, after *c.* A.D. 865, came in larger numbers as settlers and farmers. Although Alfred was able to counter them, he was obliged to recognize that portion of the east of England which lay beyond the line of Watling Street to the Thames-Lea confluence as Danish territory, the 'Danelaw' (Figure 20). However, the Danes were made loyal to Wessex in the tenth century, during a period when Wessex was again in the ascendancy, and although in the early eleventh century a Dane fought his way to the throne in the personage of Cnut, Danish hegemony was short-lived. Meanwhile, in the tenth century the Norsemen had sailed round Scotland and left their mark in north-western England.

The Vikings' chief imprint upon the landscape was recorded in the form and distribution of settlements, and their presence is remembered in a series of basic place-name elements. But these names, together with the fragments of art which have come down to us, suggest that their culture soon became blended with that of the existing inhabitants. In church sculpture, for example, pagan Viking symbols are discovered intertwined with Saxon Christian motifs, which were themselves artistic mixtures derived from several sources. Close study of Viking place-names reveals that the various threads are not so pure and obvious as first appearances might suggest. It is surely tempting to conclude that in spite of the struggles indulged in by monarchs and rulers, and the changes in the racial composition of the population caused by the influx of foreign peoples, the lives of ordinary men and women continued in many respects largely unchanged. Important figures who resisted the invasions were no doubt prime targets for violent persuasion, and the educated clerics who compiled the documents which have come down to us clearly had axes to grind, but lower down the social scale new customs and habits were selected, altered and assimilated into the cultural melting pot. Proof of this is found in the survival, in certain regions, of traditions which stretched back even to prehistoric times, while much of England could still be described as 'Saxon' for many years after the Domesday Book was compiled.

Rural landscapes

The interpretation placed upon these events is of the utmost significance when it comes to assessing the landscapes of the period. Not so long ago it was believed that the Saxons and to a lesser extent the Vikings arrived to find a more or less virgin territory on which to inscribe, as upon a clean slate, the basic elements of the cultural landscape of England. According to this view, the essential pattern of rural settlement was laid out by immigrants who brought with them from their homelands certain ready-made models which they proceeded to implant in this country. Having established a network of nucleated villages they moved on to clear the 'primeval' forests, particularly in the clay vales, which they then cultivated using their special heavy ploughs. The various primary and daughter settlements thus created could be recognized by their post-medieval morphological characteristics as depicted on maps, by their present appearances, and through the identification of a few key place-name elements. The different 'waves' of immigrants, it was suggested, displayed their own linguistic traits and forms of social organization. For example, the Jutish custom of partible inheritance – the equal division of land among heirs – could be used to account for the more dispersed settlement pattern apparent in Kent. In a similar fashion the names of villages enabled the phases of colonization to be distinguished, using the occurrence of such elements as *ham* (homestead or village) and *tun* (farm or estate). Often the personal name of the founding father was incorporated, *ingas* referring to '*x*'s followers'. Thus Reading began life as a settlement inhabited by the followers of *Read*, while Whittington was concluded to represent the estate of a man named *Hwit*. A village incorporating *ham* was presumably one of the innumerable primary settlements or *hams* distinguished by this most familiar of lowland place-name ingredients. (Woodland clearings, especially those dating from the second phase of colonization in the forest, were indicated by incorporation of *leah* into the name.) In the districts of Scandinavian settlement, the Viking components *by* and *thorpe* were interpreted in similar fashion. In short, the newcomers established a kind of pioneer frontier of settlement which represented the first large-scale creation of a cultural landscape in England.

In recent years this simple picture has been challenged from practically every angle. It is no longer possible to maintain that the Saxons were obliged to tackle essentially virgin forest and make the first great clearances, for the achievement of the prehistoric peoples in this respect is now acknowledged. It also seems unlikely that the sub-Roman period witnessed a return of secondary forest so great that the Saxons were everywhere forced, in effect, to start all over again. True, much of the claylands would still have been thickly wooded, and the abandoned chalk uplands reverted to scrub, a process possibly accompanied by the establishment there of the beech, which is such a familiar chalkland tree today. No doubt the area covered by cultivation in Roman times was extended by forest clearance during these centuries. But the fact remains that the landscape which greeted the Saxons was not an untamed wilderness giving them *carte blanche* to lay the foundations of what people like to think of as the quintessence of rural England.

Field systems

The Saxon colonists who arrived after the invasion probably found the Britons farming much as they had done for centuries, and, being considerably and probably greatly outnumbered in most areas by the indigenous population, only adapted and absorbed the old practices and did not see the need to replace them with any home-grown package of their own. It has been shown that the boundaries of some Saxon estates were not carved out of the waste but were derived from existing Roman and prehistoric land divisions. Furthermore, there is no reason to suppose that the early Saxons possessed in their homelands a system of agriculture radically different from that which they found in England. It was certainly not a fully-fledged open field system, as some scholars once supposed, and the evolution of the open field agriculture which established itself by the end of the period was a more complex business. Indeed, its origins are currently the subject of an involved debate from which few clear conclusions can be drawn. The question is of considerable importance, however, not least because fields of proven Saxon date are almost non-existent in the English landscape, but also because we cannot expect to understand the pattern of settlement if the nature and organization of rural society and economy elude us. The problem is compounded by our ignorance, despite prolonged research, about the working of open fields, the causes of their regional variations, or the time and manner of the inauguration of common grazing rights over the holdings.

Some scholars have traced the beginnings of the open fields back to the Roman long fields. Others see little evidence for this, pointing firstly to the dissimilarity between open field furlongs (strip parcels) and the shapes of Roman fields such as the cattle paddocks by the Fen Causeway near March in Cambridgeshire, and secondly to the apparent absence of furlongs in early Saxon field systems. The open fields seem to have developed in the middle Saxon period, possibly as a result of increasing pressure on the land. This could have caused the infield-outfield system, if such may be identified at this time, to break down through the extension of the intensively farmed infield at the expense of the outfield. The subdivision of the fields, a process related perhaps to piecemeal colonization and to customs of partible inheritance, may have taken the form of intermixed, strip-like holdings. One solution to the problem presented by the reduction of outfield grazing, or by the loss of pasture consequent upon the detachment of lordships from the waste as multiple estates were split up, was to pasture the stock on the cultivated infield instead. This, however, would have required a measure of communal agreement, which perhaps led in turn to the establishment of common field rights. In this need to regulate land use, with respect to both arable and pasture, to ensure subsistence for all the members of the community one may be able to trace the genesis of the open fields. Whatever the explanation, the result was a replanned landscape, particularly in cases where heavy ploughs permitted cultivation of the claylands on colonizing sites.

Settlement

There are very few clues in the visible landscape with which to test this and other hypotheses relating to the agrarian changes of the Anglo-Saxon era, but the controversy carries considerable implications for related features, particularly settlements. It is extremely probable that the process of nucleation was intimately related to the evolution of the new patterns of land tenure and agricultural practice. It is clearly tempting to connect the necessity for a centralized and hierarchically structured community to work and co-operate over the successful management of an open field system with the evolution of a central settlement, and indeed with the development of the feudal system itself, which grew out of the accompanying social relations. The ethnic explanation for nucleation has in this manner been discredited: the nucleated village was not a cultural type, stamped on to the landscape by the early Saxons. Apart from the matter of its gradual rather than sudden appearance on the English scene, it is important to recognize that neither nucleation nor the open fields characterized all non-Celtic parts of the country; and no satisfactory answer has been given to the question *why* Saxon settlements should of necessity be nucleated. The belief was that they were, and historians were happy to go out into the landscape to identify and classify them.

This operation was frequently based upon the assumption that the recent or present forms of the villages as depicted upon old maps or examined in the field preserved the basic structures of the original Saxon settlements. Thus, although the buildings themselves were of more recent date, encompassing everything from medieval to modern, the plans were judged to have remained resistant to change. For example, the 'green' villages of parts of eastern England, with their buildings arranged around a central open space, were held to represent a scheme of defence combined with provision of temporary pasture for livestock gathered in the middle. The more loosely arranged 'fragmented' village form, on the other hand, could be interpreted as a settlement created by individual squatting on common pasture, or the establishment of a woodland clearing. The founding communities of such loosely knit settlements were less rigidly organized than those where the place-name supposedly indicated that a 'leader' and his people had inaugurated the village.

While this kind of interpretation is no doubt valid in certain cases the procedure is a dangerous one. Archaeological evidence shows that some nicely structured villages with Saxon names bear almost no relation to the original Saxon settlements, which often existed near to the modern site but not on it. Sometimes there were several antecedents, both the site and the plan undergoing changes and even fresh starts, as at Longham (TF 9415) and North Elmham (TF 9820) in Norfolk. Groups of farmsteads could be replaced by tighter collections of buildings only to scatter again later, perhaps in medieval times. Appearances can therefore be deceptive, and it is dangerous to conclude that the plan of a village, even if it seems to fit one of the handy stereotypes, is derived from a Saxon original. A good deal of the Saxon period was in fact characterized not by the solemn implantation of immutable villages, but by settlement mobility and change; one suspects that many of the classic features of so-called pioneer Saxon villages, including the nucleated pattern itself, date from later Saxon times. In terms of the landscape, the presence of many original Saxon settlements can be detected only by means of the fragments of pottery scattered around isolated churches, notably in East Anglia. The modern villages lie elsewhere.

Even in those instances where the modern plans can be shown to have incorporated their originals, the morphological classifications applied to them leave much to be desired. This is particularly evident with respect to those schemes based upon selected 'key' features, whose significance seems more or less to have been decided at the start. The variety of villages to be observed in the landscape makes such brief typological labels as 'linear' or 'square' highly questionable, especially when the villages differ so much within the categories and are long and thin or clustered round a central area for any one of a hundred reasons. Furthermore, the various categories are not mutually exclusive. Such objections can be made to any classificatory exercise, but the functional connotations placed upon the essentially formal typology have been responsible for several rather simplistic generalizations.

Take for example the functions of the village green cited earlier. Firstly, contrary to popular opinion, greens are not a standard feature of the English village. In many regions they are rare, and in quite a few instances they were inserted later to create a market area, to fill the space left by decayed holdings, or even to provide, as a calculated effect, a traditional touch in a planned village. The defensive hypothesis applied to them seems a little far-fetched, as villages were rarely designed to resist attack by beast or man. In north-east England, however, the villages did contain fortified buildings, and the threat of marauders from across the Scottish border was a major theme in the landscape of the region for many hundreds of years. Green villages are indeed characteristic of the area, but the defensive argument cannot be applied in the same way to all the others, especially where the arrangement of the buildings was not consistent with such a requirement. Similarly, many greens are so small that the suggestion of pasturing is unrealistic. No doubt there are lots of possible explanations, which may be applied to different cases.

The same can be said of place-names, the analysis and derivation of which is a potentially valuable but extremely hazardous operation. Even the experts rarely agree, and the pitfalls are so numerous that the validity of the whole exercise might well be called into question by the layman as a far-fetched linguistic indulgence. The use made of place-names in the study of Saxon and Viking settlement exemplifies the problems involved. For a start, an Old English name is of itself no guarantee that the settlement was founded by the Saxons, who frequently gave their own names to older places. Similarly, apparently Scandinavian place-names often turn out to be hybrids, formed when the Vikings encountered settlements already in existence; this is especially serious because in some areas place-names constitute about the only available evidence for Scandinavian colonization. Furthermore, Scandinavian languages persisted in England until at least the eleventh century, so the presence of *by* and *thorpe* names cannot be taken to prove Viking occupation of virgin sites. This is a possibility even with respect to supposedly classic Scandinavian colonists' landscapes, such as Borrowdale in Cumbria. Finally, in the west of England particularly, a good number of Celtic names survived, mainly those relating to physical features.

General observations such as these, together with more detailed reassessments of particular names, have necessitated a fresh look at the older models of Saxon settlement. The invocation of personal affiliations in place-names has probably been overdone: other readings are equally probable. Recalling the example of Whittington cited above, the *tun* may not have been associated with a man called *Hwit* at all, but could have been inspired instead by a 'topographical' characteristic giving a '*tun* at

Hwiting (the white place)'. This second reading gains support from the fact that there are several Whittingtons in England, which renders the personal appellation less likely. Similarly, *ingas* was added to topographical terms as well as to personal names, as in Nazeing, Essex, 'the people of the spur of land'. A further element of doubt comes from the difficulty of separating *ingas* ('people of') from the singular suffix *ing*, which was also used in the formation of place-names but without any connotation of familial or social relationship. Clavering, Essex, is a formation composed of *ing* and the Old English *clæfre* ('clover'), to give 'a place where clover grows'. Thus Clavering is a totally different phenomenon from Reading ('the place inhabited by the followers of *Read*'), and it is important to differentiate between them, especially as there is some evidence to suggest that the Clavering type may actually pre-date the Reading class.

Careful examination of the earliest versions of the place-names available can sometimes prevent these kinds of errors. The apparently straightforward *ham* ('village') can easily be confused with *hamm*, a quite separate component covering a range of physical situations, such as dry-points and meander cores, where the place in question is hemmed in by some geomorphological feature. Even the Old English versions, where available, do not always help, for a clear distinction was not made between the two. Only by a detailed assessment of the various spellings of a particular name with respect to their date (*hamm* continued to be used as an active element referring to a 'river meadow' until modern times), together with the physical geography and archaeological history of the site, can any degree of certainty be attained. Such an analysis of Hanham, on the outskirts of Bristol, led to the rejection of both *ham* and *hamm* in favour of a reading derived from the Old English *hanum*, 'at the rocks', appropriate to a site above the sombre and rocky Pennant Sandstone section of the Avon gorge.

The study of the Scandinavian settlement is also plagued by uncertainties. Particularly thorny problems are posed by the considerable measure of interpenetration and amalgamation of existing place-names that occurred. The interpretation placed upon the pattern carries great implications for any overall picture of Viking migration and colonization. Was the movement an overwhelming one of intensive settlement, or does the high percentage of linguistically mixed and altered place-names suggest a more complex process? Detailed research using geological maps depicting superficial deposits as well as the 'solid' geology has led some experts to conclude that many of the best village sites in eastern England had already been taken by English inhabitants when the Danish armies struck in the ninth century, and that the body of civilian colonists, arriving in the wake of the contingents of warriors, had to be satisfied with filling in the gaps where they could. Their settlements tend to be smaller, and occupy restricted gravel islands or even sites in the claylands. Many of these Viking hamlets and villages were located in tracts which had been cleared by the Romano-Britons or even by the earliest Saxons, but had been neglected since; so remains from all these periods are sometimes encountered in close proximity, the sequence of colonization and settlement creating intricate and complicated patterns in the landscape.

Leaving aside the involved and often specialized detective work which the unravelling of the 'secret' landscape requires, more tangible reminders of the Saxon and Viking colonizations survive in the rural landscape. Although the precise sites and present plans of villages must be carefully assessed before making a judgement, this caution should not become obsessive. The position of villages and the shapes of their territories (sometimes reflected in parish boundary patterns) often display interesting relationships with physical features, particularly those which influenced the distribution of resources such as water, arable land and pasture. The 'strip-parishes' associated with spring-line villages are the most popular example of this kind of approach. These settlements are particularly common on escarpments, where the junction of adjacent rock types often produces a line of springs. The territory of each village was delineated so as to include portions of several soil types from the top of the scarp slope to the base. The lines of Saxon land boundaries, carefully described in contemporary documents, can sometimes be traced on the ground as lanes, banks or ditches. Especially suggestive are the presence of ancient hedges, tracks which appear to be unrelated to other elements of the present landscape, or the deep sunken lanes with double hedgebanks which are characteristic of parts of the West Country. Many of these thought-provoking linear survivals (some of which may even be prehistoric in origin) are concealed in the deepest parts of the countryside.

The most obvious single features are the parish churches. The use of stone in their construction has aided their survival, although the timber nave of the Saxon church at Greensted in Essex (TL 539030) provides a remarkable addition to the list. The full appreciation of these churches is properly a subject for the architectural historian, but their distribution, dates and styles offer valuable clues to the student of landscape, and afford rare opportunities to sample actual Saxon work. Some, like St Lawrence, Bradford-on-Avon, Wiltshire; Odda's Chapel, Deerhurst, Gloucestershire (SO 869298); and St Cedd, Bradwell-juxta-Mare, Essex (p. 133), were 'lost' for many years, being given over to other uses which disguised their true identity. Other splendid examples are those of St Mary, Deerhurst, Gloucestershire (SO 870300); All Saints, Brixworth, Northamptonshire (SP 747712); and St John, Escomb, County Durham

(NZ 189301). Early Saxon work such as that embodied in these churches is of course less plentiful than that dating from the later years of the period, when, after the end of the Danish raids, church building enjoyed a revival. This phase contributed a great deal to the development of the external appearance of churches. Of particular interest are the towers. The style of the characteristic 'round towers' of East Anglia (Haddiscoe, Norfolk, TM 439969), which were perhaps originally designed as watch-towers, may partly reflect the shortage of building stone and the limitations imposed by the use of flints in place of freestone. Elsewhere, quoining and stripwork can be quite elaborate, as at Barton-upon-Humber, Humber-side (TA 035219), and Barnack, Cambridgeshire (TF 079050); the patterns may record a degree of Danish influence. The 'Rhenish helm' tower at Sompting, West Sussex (TQ 161056), occupies a class of its own.

Finally, if any doubt still prevails about the artistic achievement of these centuries, a visit should be made to the remote and windswept Roman fort at Bewcastle, Cumbria (NY 565746), north of Hadrian's Wall. (The place-name is made up of an old Norse element added to *ceaster*, to denote 'the dwelling within the Roman camp'. The existence here of a medieval castle probably accounts for the development of the name into *Bewcastle* rather than the more regular form of *Bewcaster*.) Here within the confines of the Roman site stands the church of St Cuthbert, the oldest portion of which was built *c.* 1200 using stones from the fort itself. The churchyard contains an extraordinary treasure for what is now such an out-of-the-way spot, a richly decorated cross dating from the late seventh or early eighth centuries, depicting sacred figures and foliage and inscribed with runic lettering. This product of the 'golden age' of Northumbria, blending Celtic and Saxon cultures, is remarkable proof of how the creations of this region could achieve not only national but European significance.

Towns

There were few towns in England and Wales between the sixth and ninth centuries, and those that there were generally amounted to little more than loose gatherings of population in what had formerly been Roman settlements. The reoccupation of Roman sites is often apparent from place-names, such as the occurrence of the element *ceaster* (as in Towces-ter), but it would be unwise to accept this as proof of an unbroken sequence of habitation. Urban traits had probably not persisted to any marked degree, and the Roman aspect of these towns was by this time greatly diminished, even where a measure of continuity had prevailed. Cambridge was described at the end of the seventh century as an empty ruin of Roman buildings, although in this case the dismal nature of the picture may be exaggerated, reflecting a particularly violent phase in the wars between East Anglia and Mercia. Nevertheless, although the early Anglo-Saxons often chose Roman sites for their settlements, particularly for the establishment of ecclesiastical centres (pp. 131 and 133), it is doubtful whether these centuries were conducive to the evolution of economic and social structures which would encourage the development of a vigorous or integrated urban hierarchy.

Nevertheless, the origins of Anglo-Saxon towns were more complex than this simple picture suggests, and certainly more diverse. Apart from the Roman towns, of which London and York formed a class apart, followed by a handful of other important ecclesiastical centres, a range of new sites was also developed. The place-name element *wic* (as in Norwich or Ipswich) was applied to a broad category of settlements. Some were early trading posts, linked to royal or religious centres. One of these was Hamwih (Hamwich), an unfortified market centre near the mouth of the Itchen in Southampton Water. It enjoyed connections with Winchester, but declined in the tenth century, to be superseded by the nearby fortified town of Hampton, the precursor of modern Southampton, the prefix having been given in order to distinguish it from Northampton.

The major phase of urban revival came in the ninth century, partly through the effects of Viking raids. In response to the Danish threat, Alfred of Wessex initiated, in the late ninth century, a major programme of *burh* construction, which was continued by his son Edward the Elder. A *burh* was a fortified place of one kind or another, and the term had been used in relation to towns for some time before Alfred decided to build a chain of strongpoints as a principal element in his reorganization of the defences of Wessex. The system was carefully formulated, and a good deal is known about it because the plan was laid out and the *burhs* listed in the *Burghal Hidage*, a document dating from A.D. 911–19 or before (pre-886). This recorded the number of hides associated with each *burh*, a hide being a unit of land supporting one free family. Every hide was to contribute one man for the defence of the *burh*, the garrison being provided on the basis of calculations relating to the length of the defences and the numbers needed to man them.

Some of the *burhs* were established upon ancient sites, including Iron Age hillforts such as Chisbury, Wiltshire (SU 279660), although the most famous examples (Old Sarum, Wiltshire; Cissbury, West Sussex; South Cadbury, Somerset) were probably refortified later, in the early eleventh century, when the defensive factor became paramount. For the *burhs* were not simply military posts, but incorporated commercial functions as well. Shrewdly located and regularly spaced with respect to routeways and potential hinterlands, many of the new settlements enjoyed considerable economic prosperity, and subsequently grew to become important centres, often county towns. Some of these, like Winchester, were built upon Roman foundations, but many of the *burhs* which were successful in the long term were true Saxon towns such as Oxford.

Although most of the Saxon evidence has been obliterated as a consequence of the very success of these towns, elements of the plans have occasionally survived in the landscape (p. 141). The building of ramparts was accompanied by a degree of internal planning, often apparent as a grid pattern of streets. The overall impression was not unlike the layout of Roman forts. Markets were held not in true market places, but in wider portions of particular streets; and churches, possibly partly defensive in function, were frequently sited near the gates (Figure 21). Although some

Figure 21. The Saxon tower of St Michael's, Oxford. Now set amidst a busy shopping centre, this eleventh-century tower stands next to the site of the former north gate of the *burh*. The tower is made from tough Coral Rag random rubble. This impure oolitic limestone, quarried locally from the Corallian (Upper Jurassic), has enabled the tower to survive the ravages of time much more successfully than many more recent buildings of the nearby colleges, which were constructed from easily weathered stone taken from stratigraphically adjacent members of the same formation. The quoins at the base of the tower and the parapet at the top are not original. On the right of the picture can be seen part of the oversailing half-timbered upper storey of No. 28, Cornmarket (probably dating in its essentials from the fifteenth century), one of the very few notable buildings managing to survive the wave of modern commercial abominations which have all but ruined this street

of the *burhs* were short-lived, others represented an acceleration in urban growth the like of which was not seen again until much later. Indeed, the larger ones may have had populations reaching one or two thousand, a huge total for the period and greater than that contained in many medieval towns. Life in such settlements was no doubt crowded and unhealthy.

The Wessex *burhs* were copied elsewhere in England, notably by Queen

Aethelflaed of the Mercians, sister of Edward the Elder of Wessex, who continued the campaign after her death. (The kingdom of Mercia had effectively ceased to exist some time before, the north-eastern part having been conquered by the Danes, the rest passing under the sway of Wessex.) A series of *burhs* was built across Mercia in the early tenth century, concentrated in a zone along the line of Watling Street, the Danish frontier. Others were established in the east Midlands as Danish territory was progressively won back (Figure 20, p. 116). Some display the favoured promontory position (Bridgnorth, Salop), and the larger ones became the centres of counties bearing their names. Only one Saxon *burh* was established in Wales, at Cledemutha (Rhuddlan, Clwyd) in A.D. 921.

The effects of the Viking incursions upon urban growth were not, however, restricted merely to the creation of fortified places as a response to the military threat of the invasions. The Vikings were keen to promote trade – albeit heavily based on slavery and piracy – and in setting up the boroughs of the Danelaw (Figure 20) they exerted a positive influence of their own. The stimulus given to places like York and Cambridge by the development of commerce was very considerable. Extensive excavations in Viking York have revealed the extent of commercial prosperity in the ninth-century city, but few clues to this period of activity are evident in the landscape today, apart from the frequency of 'gate' street names in the Danelaw towns, derived from a Scandinavian word for 'street'. Finally, the destruction of the monasteries which took place during these years was succeeded by a late Saxon religious resurgence, a movement closely connected with the establishment and growth of towns. The new towns which grew up next to the monasteries at places like St Albans and Ely differed from the *burhs* in having spacious and open market places. A fashion had been initiated which had great consequences for the development of the medieval town, which in this and in other respects owes more to the days before the Norman Conquest than might at first appear.

Sites

Dorchester-on-Thames, Oxfordshire

Despite its apparent total lack of visible Saxon survivals, the landscape of Dorchester-on-Thames is an excellent example of the problems associated with the study of early Saxon settlement, in particular the vexed question of continuity with the Roman period.

Dorchester is situated upon a gravel terrace near the confluence of the Rivers Thame and Thames, in the Kimmeridge Clay-Gault Vale between the Oxford Heights to the north and the Chalk escarpment of the Berkshire Downs and Chilterns to the south and east. Just across the Thames to the south lie the Lower Chalk outliers of the Sinodun Hills. The location of Dorchester has proved attractive for settlement over an extended period. Strategically placed in a regional context, the defensive advantages of a dry point upon the gravel terrace, surrounded on three sides by water yet next to a river crossing, were already appreciated and exploited in prehistoric times. From the archaeological point of view, the apparent concentration of activity in the gravel areas has been extremely useful, for gravel subsoils preserve artefacts and display crop-marks particularly well. (The accompanying disadvantage is that extensive gravel terraces attract commercial gravel-digging enterprises, and many sites of interest have been quarried completely away.) Given of course that the pattern of these erased or 'ghost' landscape features may be an artificial one, determined by the distribution of the gravels themselves, the Dorchester district boasts a rich concentration of crop-markings, engraved as it were one upon another, and so constituting a complex palimpsest. The elements do not appear to be random or unrelated but, on the contrary, make up a unique assemblage, whose internal relationships nevertheless still pose many questions.

Prehistoric remains are – or were – impressive (Figure 22). To the north-north-west of Dorchester once lay (before gravel extraction ruined the site) a Neolithic and Bronze Age complex consisting primarily of a henge and cursus. Circles of the same period exist to the east across the Thame near Overy. To the south-west lies the Iron Age promontory fort of Dyke Hills, an *oppidum* covering 114 acres of once densely settled land between the River Thames on two sides, the River Thame on a third, and a massive double bank on the fourth or northern side. Across the Thames, accessible from Dorchester by public footpaths via Dyke Hills and Little Wittenham Bridge, is the univallate Iron Age hillfort of Sinodun Camp (SU 569924), while half a mile to the south-east is another Chalk outlier, Brightwell Barrow (576919), which has yielded Iron Age pottery. At Northfield Farm (559951) is the site of an Iron Age/Romano-British village. It is likely that Dyke Hills sheltered a native settlement which was transferred to Dorchester after the Roman occupation. Taken together, these remains create a magnificent prehistoric landscape.

The next phase occurred during the Roman period, when a Roman town was established at Dorchester, probably developing from a conquest-period fort. Roman Dorchester was a regional centre, situated between the Atrebates to the south, the Dobunni to the north-west, and the Catuvellauni to the north-east, exploiting the river crossing and set within

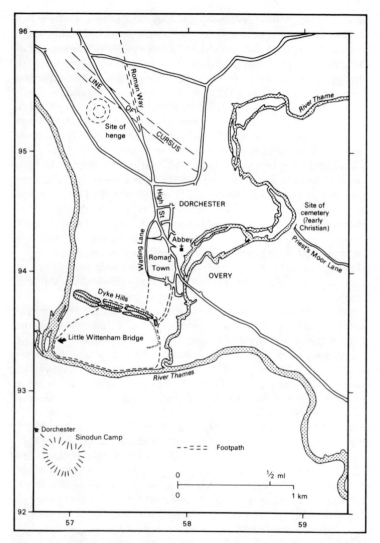

Figure 22. Dorchester-on-Thames, Oxfordshire. (NOTE: The recently opened bypass is not shown)

an important grain-producing district. It was linked to the Roman town of Alchester by a road which now runs northwards out of Dorchester as a bridleway (575952). The walled town seems to have covered an area of only thirteen and a half acres, but the location of the ramparts on the eastern side is uncertain, and it is known that the settlement extended beyond the lines of the defences. Today there is very little to see of Roman Dorchester, which lies mainly to the west of the High Street and is covered by houses and allotments, but traces of the bank and ditch are visible on the south-west, inside the angle formed by Watling Lane. The plan was quite unrelated to the present layout.

In Saxon times Dorchester became a place of national importance when in A.D. 634 or 635 St Birinus, the first bishop of Wessex, chose it as his seat and centre of missionary activity. Later in the century the district was threatened by the Mercians to the north, and the see was moved to Winchester. Although Dorchester again became a cathedral city, this time the seat of a Mercian bishopric, its secular importance was declining. It was not fortified as a *burh* and was superseded by the nearby towns of Oxford and Wallingford. After the Norman Conquest the see was again transferred, this time to Lincoln, and in the early twelfth century Dorchester was described by William of Malmesbury as 'a small and unfrequented town, yet the beauty and state of its churches very remarkable'. The general lack of later developments has meant that, in archaeological terms at least, the Saxon settlement is probably largely undisturbed.

What was the relationship between Saxon Dorchester and its Roman predecessor? What did the Saxons find when they arrived here? The establishment of the bishopric might suggest that Dorchester was a place of some importance still, even one which enjoyed royal connections, as it is unlikely that a major centre of English Christianity would be located upon a Roman site purely for antiquarian reasons. The archaeological evidence gathered so far implies that although Dorchester ceased to be a Roman town proper in the fifth century, it was still occupied. The inhabitants, judging from early Saxon burials, possessed late Roman and early German objects, including Germanic-style belts, and some scholars have therefore concluded that the link between Roman and Saxon Dorchester was provided by Germanic mercenaries. In view of the general lack of fifth-century finds, however, the presence of a more dispersed and amorphous Romano-British community which had discarded a manifestly Roman life style is equally possible (cf. p. 125). No definite signs of the main Saxon settlement appear until the sixth century, when sunken huts were constructed inside the limits of the Roman town, so if there was any continuity it must have been indirect. The Saxon settlement appears to have ignored the Roman plan, so it seems reasonable to conclude that Romano-British Dorchester did not survive into the sixth century.

This lack of coincidence lends support to an alternative hypothesis, which proposes that there was in fact little continuity as such – it has already been hinted that this concept is itself a loaded and complex one – and that Dorchester attracted successive peoples independently, for the same essentially geographical reasons. In the case of the Saxons, the site – on the very edge of the diocese – may have been chosen in order to strengthen the claim of Wessex to the Upper Thames valley, a claim which was relinquished in the face of opposition from Mercia, only to be superseded later by a counter-claim on the part of the Mercians themselves. These questions can only be answered by continued examination of the hidden landscape, a source of evidence which is all the more important because of the lack of detailed documentary sources for the Saxon period, and the loss of records relating to abbeys occasioned by the Dissolution. No doubt the Saxon cathedral lies underneath the present Abbey of St Peter and St Paul, and the location is significant because the site appears to be outside the line of the Roman walls, despite the apparent predilection of seventh-century Saxon churches for the interiors of late Roman towns and forts (p. 133). Perhaps the defences had been enlarged in the later Roman period, or were ignored by the post-Roman community. On the other hand, there are also several examples of early churches situated just outside the walls of Roman towns upon the sites of cemeteries which either were or became Christian in the late Roman period. It is conceivable that a Roman building existed on the Abbey site, and that some echo of Roman Christianity survived to attract St Birinus. Across the River Thame to the east lies a group of crop-marks which appear to represent a cemetery, possibly one connected with the seventh-century bishopric. It is interesting that the adjoining field has long been known as Priest's Moor.

Dorchester reveals clues to its former identity even in its relatively modern visible landscape. The street plan is probably medieval – a small triangular market place west of the abbey may recall an abortive attempt to found a borough – and this, together with the presence of an abbey (Figure 68) in a settlement which is too small for a modern town but has unusual features for a village, is enough to awaken the curiosity of the observant visitor. The landscape is slow to lose even its most ancient lineaments; and the cob walls (made from clay and straw) which can still be seen represent the survival of an age-old tradition, for the material has been used in Dorchester since prehistoric times, good building stone being unavailable locally. The best example is the boundary wall just north of Willoughby House, near the northern end of the High Street opposite the junction with Martin's Lane (57709455).

Bradwell-juxta-Mare, Essex, and Reculver, Kent
The overwhelming of the Roman 'Saxon Shore' forts (p. 87) by those against whom they had been constructed did not signal the end of their existence: indeed, as resilient features of the coastal landscape, they had many changes of fortune yet to come. There is evidence that in certain cases the Romano-British inhabitants met a bloody end. The *Anglo-Saxon Chronicle* records that Pevensey (identified with the *Anderida* listed in the *Notitia Dignitatum*, a late Roman survey of the Empire's military arrangements) was captured by Aelle of the South Saxons in A.D. 491, and that no one inside was left alive. Whether or not such violence was typical of the initial Saxon take-over of these run-down or abandoned installations is unclear, but in some cases the Saxons settled on the sites and put them to their own uses. Sporadic settlement during the Saxon period occurred at Portchester, possibly initiated by Germanic mercenaries in the obscure period of transition embracing the late fifth and sixth centuries. However, it is worth noting that much of the evidence for these mercenaries derives from archaeological finds, made at several sites, of material objects such as Germanic-style belt fittings. These were also used by barbarians in the Roman army, as well as by the Romano-Britons, so the case remains unproven. It seems likely that a good deal of cultural interchange took place between the Romano-Britons and the Germanic barbarians, and that the Saxon invasions were the culmination of a more gradual and complex process of intermixture and assimilation. At Portchester a community of farmers occupied the site, cultivating their smallholdings and living in sunken huts, but the identity of the inhabitants and the degree of actual continuity are uncertain.

The chronology is far clearer in the case of the most notable Saxon use of the forts, which involved the establishment, in three of them, of early Christian monasteries in the years following St Augustine's arrival at Canterbury in A.D. 597. In the mid-seventh century the Roman fort of Burgh Castle (*Gariannonum*) in Norfolk (TG 475046) was given to the Irish missionary St Fursa by King Sigeberht of East Anglia. It is probable that the site was destroyed, along with other religious houses in East Anglia, by the Danes *c*. A.D. 869, and there is little to see today. Archaeological excavation has revealed a series of oval huts, possibly the monks' cells, and a few plaster fragments from the monastic church which St Fursa built. More rewarding visually are the churches at Bradwell-juxta-

Mare (Bradwell-on-Sea), Essex (TM 031082), generally held to be the Roman *Othona*, and Reculver (*Regulbium*), Kent (TR 227693).

At Bradwell, the church of St Peter-on-the-Wall straddles the line of the west wall of the Roman fort, of which only fragments survive, much of the site having been eroded by the sea. The tiny church, built largely of Roman material, represents the nave of what was almost certainly the original building erected by St Cedd *c*. A.D. 654. St Cedd, Bishop of the East Saxons, was a Celtic churchman from Lindisfarne, but he accepted Roman ways following the Synod of Whitby. That Roman influence was already being felt is shown by the style of the post-Augustine Kentish churches (the earliest group of surviving Christian churches in England), with which Bradwell has strong affinities. Thus, despite the apparent cultural break caused by the arrival of the Saxons, the Roman connection persisted, albeit in a religious and artistic form rather than a military one. Bradwell is a remarkable survival, especially when one remembers that it was probably sacked by the Vikings at the time of the Battle of Maldon, fought nearby in A.D. 991, and that during the period before 1920 the church was used as a barn. (The huge patched sections in the walls represent the entrances made for farm wagons.)

St Peter-on-the-Wall once boasted an apse at the east end, two *porticus* or 'chapels', one each on the north and south (overlapping the nave and the chancel), and possibly a west porch. These features can be appreciated more clearly, albeit only in plan, at St Mary's, Reculver (Figure 23). The Roman fort originally lay three quarters of a mile inland, but the sea has encroached so much that half of the site has disappeared. King Egbert of Kent gave Reculver to the priest Bassa in A.D. 669. The defences of the fort were readily adapted to form precinct walls for the enclosed community of monks, and the fort furnished a handy supply of building stone for the church. The original minster comprised a nave, apsidal chancel and two flanking *porticus* (used in this instance not for burials but for a vestry and an altar for offerings). A west porch was added in the eighth century, but monastic life ceased in the tenth century at the time of the Viking raids. The building was extended in the twelfth century with the construction of two Transitional Norman west towers, and in the thirteenth a square-ended chancel replaced the apse. That the Saxon work now comprises merely low walls and foundations is a result not of gradual decay but of an extraordinary act of vandalism by a clergyman of the parish who, in the first years of the last century, used the threat of the advancing sea as an excuse to demolish the church! Only the two west towers were left, as an aid to navigation. The parish clerk recorded, with feeling:

Figure 23. The remains of the originally Saxon church of St Mary, Reculver

Mr. C.C. nailor been Vicar of the parish, his mother fancied that the church was kept for a poppet show, and she persuaded har son to take it down, so he took it in consideration and named it to the farmers in the parish about taking it down; sum was for it and sum against it, than Mr nailor wrote to the Bishop to know if he might have the church took down, and is answer was it must be dun by a majority of the people in the parish, so hafter a long time he got the majority of one, so down come the Church . . .

The last tax that Mr nailor took was these words, Let your ways be the ways of rightness, and your path the peace, and down come the church, and whot wos is thoats about is flock that day no one knows.

Offa's Dyke

With regard to the landscape, if not indeed in other respects, Offa's Dyke must rank as the most remarkable single achievement of middle Saxon England. It represents the culmination of the efforts made by the powerful rulers of Mercia during the eighth century to settle and demarcate the political border with the Welsh. An earlier structure, Wat's Dyke, which extended from Basingwerk on the Dee to the Morda Brook south of Oswestry, is thought to have been built by King Aethelbald of Mercia. In A.D. 757 he was succeeded by his cousin Offa, an able, civilized and outward-looking ruler who corresponded with no less a personage than Charlemagne, and who was king of Mercia for almost forty years. In the latter part of his reign he ordered (and probably masterminded) the construction of an immense earthwork designed to stabilize the frontier along its whole length from coast to coast.

In view of the lack of evidence for the existence of Offa's Dyke in the far north, it is likely that Wat's Dyke served as the frontier line at this end. Once thought to have embodied the concept of an agreed frontier on account of the respect for certain Welsh settlements apparently shown by its course, Offa's Dyke is now concluded to represent a successful attempt to end Welsh penetration eastwards. In at least three places (the Severn valley around Welshpool, the Vale of Radnor, and west of the Wye in Gwent) English salients beyond the line of the Dyke seem to have been overrun by the Welsh, leaving traces of their presence in the place-names.

The border landscape speaks eloquently of the fundamental facts of British geography and the subtle and intricate connections between Highland and Lowland on the one hand and Celt and Saxon on the other. Mention has already been made (p. 33) of the significance of the pattern of relief and drainage for the historical geography of the region. The hopes of the Welsh were shattered once the English had separated Wales firstly from the Celts of Dumnonia (the South-west peninsula) after the Battle of Dyrham in Gloucestershire in A.D. 577, and secondly, in the early seventh century, from the kingdom of Strathclyde to the north (Figure 20). They also drove wedges up certain of the Welsh river valleys which gave out, fatally for the Welsh, eastwards on to the English Plain. Now, by means of a superbly engineered boundary which, although man-made, used the disposition of physical features in a masterly fashion wherever political considerations allowed, this achievement was consolidated.

For the greater part of its length Offa's Dyke consists of a bank with a ditch on the western side. The scale varies: occasionally the bank reaches heights exceeding ten feet, and the ditch plunges to similar depths, but on average the bank rises to about six feet above the old surface, while the mean width across the bank and ditch is about sixty feet. Where possible the earthwork follows westward-facing slopes, and it concentrates especially on controlling the valleys of the eastward-flowing rivers. In places its course is uncertain, and in others the Dyke is absent altogether. Many of the gaps may not be original. Their presence does not, therefore, lend support to the interpretation of the Dyke as a symbol of peace; nor, as has been suggested, do they denote areas of former forest so thick that the builders of the Dyke, unable to penetrate the contemporary woodland, incorporated it into the defensive system. To appreciate these points it is necessary to explore Offa's Dyke in the field, a study rendered a great deal easier in recent years by the opening of Offa's Dyke Path. Although the Path does not follow the whole length of the Dyke, it incorporates the greater part of it into a longer route which runs through much of the finest scenery of the borderland. (Three of the best sections of the Dyke have been singled out in the brief description below. They are followed for much, but not all, of their length by the Path itself; other rights of way cross it or run nearby where this is not the case.)

The various portions of the Dyke reflect differences in the balance of forces involved. Starting in the north, the stretch between Treuddyn and Llanymynech lies right on the edge of the uplands, penning and splitting the Welsh by truncating the valleys. Some excellent sections, illustrating these principles, can be followed between a point within the grounds of Chirk Castle, Clwyd (SJ 267383), southwards to Baker's Hill in Shropshire (254311). For much of the way the Dyke marks the actual boundary between England and Wales, before passing into Salop near Orseddwen.

Between Llanymynech and Mellington Hall, Powys (three and a half miles south-east of Montgomery), the Dyke crosses lowlands, using the River Severn as part of its course. The military position is much weaker here and the line of the Dyke may suggest a compromise.

The next part crosses the remote uplands of Clun Forest in south-west Shropshire, where the aim of the Dyke was clearly to restrict ridgetop movement. The fine portion between Bryndrinog Farm (SO 257826) and Garbett Hall (264770) via Spoad Hill and Llanfair Hill includes the Dyke's highest point, at over 1,400 feet.

Next comes the Vale of Radnor, which was largely left to the Welsh, and then a part, between Rushock Hill north of Kington and Bridge Sollers on the Wye, where only short stretches are encountered across the river valleys. Between Bridge Sollers and Redbrook in west Gloucestershire the Wye itself probably operated as the frontier for nearly all the way.

The final part of Offa's Dyke, between Redbrook and Chepstow, and across the little Beachley peninsula to the Severn at Sedbury Cliffs, is discontinuous, using the great cliffs of the Wye gorge. No proper answer has been given to the question why the river itself was not used here as it was elsewhere. Some maintain, rather improbably, that the Welsh were granted the whole river to themselves for purposes of fishing and navigation, while the particularly massive appearance of the Dyke along the left bank may reflect a showy display of strength or a less than subtle hint on the part of the Forest of Dean inhabitants who no doubt had a hand in building it. The best bit, with superb views of the Wye valley, can be followed from Modesgate (SO 545006) to the Devil's Pulpit (ST 543995) via Lippets Grove (Figure 37).

There are practically no documentary sources relating to *Offediche*. The landscape itself provides most of the available information both for the earthwork itself and for the regional political geography of the eighth century. Once established, the Dyke continued to influence the development of the landscape. It still functions as a variety of boundaries, from national to parish level; lanes and footpaths follow it; woodland limits respect it. Settlements have been affected by its presence: the Dyke made a promontory fort out of the site of Knighton, Powys; the main street of Llanymynech is aligned along the ditch, and numerous farms lie directly upon it.

Bokerley Dyke, Hampshire and Dorset; Wansdyke, Avon and Wiltshire; the Devil's Dyke, Cambridgeshire

Offa's Dyke is by far the longest and best-known Saxon linear earthwork, but several other sizeable ones exist. By and large they remain complete mysteries, and one can hazard little more than guesses at their dates of origin, their purpose, and the identity of those who instigated and built them.

The early history of Bokerley Dyke as an earthwork thrown up across the Roman road from Old Sarum to Badbury Rings has already been alluded to (p. 102). Part of the Dyke may date from *c.* A.D. 367, a year in which several parts of England suffered from Saxon raids. Bokerley Dyke appears to end rather abruptly, but it must be remembered that it seems to have been built to block the chalk gap flanked by the woods of Cranborne Chase on one side and the heaths of north-east Dorset on the other, and perhaps the Dyke was terminated as soon as it reached these districts. After a spell of abandonment Bokerley Dyke was refurbished, probably during the late fifth or early sixth centuries, thereafter functioning as a barrier against the Saxons. However, the general conclusion is that it was finally breached in the late sixth century, and that the Romano-British population withdrew to a second defensive line some fifteen miles in the rear. The line of Combs Ditch can be traced south and south-west of Blandford Forum for about three miles, between ST 851021 and 886000. Eventually this position too was overwhelmed (possibly in the mid-seventh century) and the Romano-Britons retreated again, to be finally vanquished in the heaths of south-east Dorset, an episode perhaps related to the Battery Banks west of Wareham (SY 886876 etc).

Wansdyke extends across Wessex for a distance not far short of fifty miles, but its course is broken, and in fact the earthwork consists of two separate main portions. West Wansdyke can be seen south of the River Avon between Bristol and Bath, while East Wansdyke follows the southern edge of the Marlborough Downs. The gap between them, stretching from near Bath to Morgan's Hill (S U 030670) north-north-east of Devizes, is filled by a section of the Roman road between Bath and Silchester. Judging from the Saxon charters, the name *Wodnes Dic* (Woden's Dyke) may have been derived from *Wodnesbeorge* ('Woden's Barrow', identified as Adam's Grave chambered barrow, S U 112634, near Alton Priors) during the ninth century; alternatively, Wansdyke may have been so called as early as the late sixth century. The ditch is on the north side of the Dyke, so the structure was designed to resist attacks from that direction. It has been proposed that Wansdyke was built in the late fifth century to block the Saxon advance south, but, like Bokerley Dyke, it probably has a more complex history, having been made for one purpose and reinforced for another. Its west and east sections may represent attempts by Wessex to counter Mercian and Anglian expansion in the late sixth and early seventh centuries respectively, but if the truth be told all suggestions are almost pure guesswork. The earthwork is as striking as it is mysterious (Figure 24). One of the finest stretches, particularly for the walker, is that

Figure 24. Wansdyke, Wiltshire

on the Marlborough Downs between S U 018672 and 196665; at 127652 the Dyke is cut by the minor road to Alton Priors, which turns south off the A4 at Fyfield at 146687.

The Devil's Dyke in Cambridgeshire presents a very similar enigma. This huge dyke stretches for over seven miles across the chalkland routeway of the Icknield Way south-west of Newmarket, linking the fen edge at Reach on the north-west (TL 568661) to the once forested clay lands near Woodditton on the south-east (653583). (The whole length can be walked along a public footpath.) The intention thus seems to have been the blocking of the route into East Anglia from the south-west, for the ditch is positioned on the south-west side of the bank. Three similarly aligned lesser earthworks have been identified in front of the Devil's Dyke: the Fleam Dyke, or 'dyke of the fugitives' (TL 537556 to 558532), extending south-east from Cambridge; and beyond this, the poorly preserved Brent and Bran (Heydon) Ditches. The Brent Ditch, incidentally, has its ditch on the north-eastern side.

Some scholars believe that the dykes were constructed in the fifth century as part of the struggle between the Britons and the Saxons, but which side was responsible for building them is not known. Alternatively, they could date from the sixth or seventh centuries as an element in the frontier disputes between Mercia and East Anglia. It is not impossible that some parts of the system were involved in both periods, having been initially created at the earlier time but undergoing reconstruction subsequently. All that can be said is that the Devil's Dyke is later than the third century, while the Heydon Ditch adopted its present appearance between the early fifth and sixth centuries. Some of the struggles during this confused era were dramatic and bloody: the hacked skeletons left by one violent encounter were found in the Bran Ditch.

In conclusion, these linear earthworks, taken together, may date from one or several periods during the sub-Roman and Anglo-Saxon eras. They may have been constructed in order to reinforce or exploit natural defences such as marshes or woods, thereby to control lines of communication. The ditches were dug on one side only, presumably that from which the assault was expected. They were apparently surveyed and planned by eye, the more sophisticated techniques of the Romans having already passed out of use. Some coincide with the lines of parish boundaries, and it has been suggested that certain of them follow the boundaries of late prehistoric estates. It is very unclear how the dykes actually worked. They could hardly have functioned as infantry defences, since the available manpower would have been insufficient to cover their great lengths. Mounted troops might have found them to be a more serious obstacle.

The disposition of the dykes strongly suggests that they were designed to obstruct and focus movement along key routeways, and this, together with the immense labour involved in their construction, militates against a role as frontier works intended merely to impress. But in this last respect they are undeniably successful, even when viewed by modern eyes.

Wareham, Dorset, and Wallingford, Oxfordshire

Wareham and Wallingford are two of the finest surviving examples of Saxon town planning. Both were essentially products of Alfred's scheme of *burh* plantation (p. 126). The physical advantages of the two sites permitted the full flowering and near complete development of the Saxon pattern of defences and internal streets, to a degree which was usually impracticable elsewhere. Enjoying commercial success as market centres and considerable status as strategic strong points, Wareham and Wallingford were thriving towns in the Saxon and early medieval periods but declined thereafter, leaving many of their original features more or less intact (Figure 25).

Wareham (SY 9287) was cleverly sited at the narrowest point between the Rivers Piddle and Frome, which come within half a mile of each other just before they reach the head of Poole Harbour. Alfred's biographer Asser described it as a 'most secure situation, except on its western side where it is joined to the mainland'. The ninth-century *burh* was not the first settlement on the site. Iron Age and especially Roman finds are numerous, and there are signs that the Romano-Britons lived on in relative harmony with the Saxon immigrants. A remarkably instructive series of early Christian inscriptions preserved in the church of Lady St Mary, thought to have been cut between the seventh and ninth centuries, includes two which are British in style and epigraphy. Furthermore, until it was reconstructed in 1841–2, Lady St Mary's gave the appearance of an eighth-century Saxon church which may indeed have been a rebuilding of an even earlier Celtic monastery or shrine, whose presence might explain the persistence of British traditions. It is probable that by the time of Alfred the settlement was already a port of some importance, containing a religious establishment of note, a king of Wessex having been buried there in A.D. 802.

The massive rampart and ditch enclose the *burh* on three sides, the frontage on to the River Frome completing the rectangle on the south. The gridiron street pattern, based on two main intersecting streets with four gates set in the sides of the defences at the cardinal points, probably also dates from the ninth century, although, given the initial geometrical layout of the basic structure, the grid could have evolved more gradually.

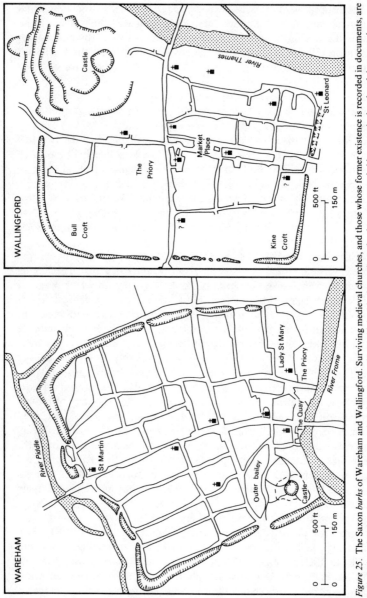

Figure 25. The Saxon *burhs* of Wareham and Wallingford. Surviving medieval churches, and those whose former existence is recorded in documents, are indicated on the plans by crosses; these symbols have a question mark beside them where the site once occupied by a particular church is uncertain.

Wareham capitalized upon its advantages and prospered. In the late tenth or early eleventh centuries the church of St Martin was built by the north gate (cf. St Michael, Oxford, Figure 21), and in the twelfth a priory was founded and a motte-and-bailey castle came to occupy the south-west quarter of the town, not far from the busy quay. Gradually, however, Wareham declined as the upper reaches of Poole Harbour silted up, and the new town of Poole diverted trade away. Wareham became a small market town, whose present Georgian appearance resulted from the destruction of many of the older buildings in a fire in 1762. The defences are still most impressive, particularly on the west, where they were pressed into service in 1940 as an anti-tank barricade. Although the recutting which was done is no doubt regrettable archaeologically, the result gives a good idea of the original defensive potential of the system.

Wallingford (SU 6089) is similar to Wareham in several respects. Sited upon a gravel terrace, it occupied a strategic fording and later bridging point of the River Thames a little above the Goring Gap. Like Wareham it was already an important place in Roman times and probably even earlier, in the Iron Age. An early Saxon cemetery has been discovered on the south-west side, and there are hints of later Saxon activity here before the establishment of Alfred's *burh* in the late ninth century. Again the defences (which were probably restored several times) surround the town on all sides except that of the river, although it is possible that the boundary on this fourth side actually extended to the opposite bank of the Thames in the form of an outwork, designed to prevent the bridge from being rushed. (The civil parish boundary does in fact extend eastwards in a loop across the river.) The ramparts, best seen on the south-west side, by the recreation ground, are very like those at Wareham, and it seems that the grid plan was contemporary with them. However, Wallingford was sacked by the Danes in 1006, and the regular street plan may have originated then, influenced by the shape of the defences.

In early medieval times Wallingford was a bustling little town, boasting a diversity of trades and occupations. A castle was built in the north-east quarter, near the river (as at Wareham), and the north-west sector contained Wallingford Priory. Most of the rest of the area within the defences was occupied by houses, workshops and inns, and by the market place. But as other Thames crossings came to be established, this prosperity was gradually surrendered to new growth points which had the advantage of superior locations. Modern Wallingford has, like Wareham, some good Georgian houses, but there are earlier buildings too. Some of the gaps left by the medieval decline are now being filled with modern developments, which have also sprawled beyond the defences; at Wareham this process has been somewhat restricted by the expanses of ill-drained land surrounding the town.

Some interesting questions are raised by a study of certain boundaries and alignments in Wallingford. The boundaries of the four parishes (created by the amalgamation of the eleven churches existing here in the Middle Ages) do not conform to the street plan, nor are they confined by the defences. Perhaps they originate from the community which existed here before the *burh* was established. The alignment of the Norman church of St Leonard bears no relationship to that of the other churches or to the defences, which suggests that the positioning of the church was influenced by earlier features, possibly dating from the same pre-*burh* period. (Linear elements in the landscape frequently influence the orientation of churches so that the east-west setting is distorted.) Only detailed archaeological investigation would confirm these suggestions.

CHAPTER 4

Medieval Landscapes

The Norman Conquest has been variously assessed by historians as marking the true beginning of English political history or as a somewhat vulgar interruption of an essential continuity by an unpleasant but largely irrelevant group of people who represented the closest equivalent in western Europe to the continental Barbarians. Of course, it is easy to say that no doubt the truth lies somewhere in the middle; but the actual conclusion will vary depending on the questions asked and the evidence consulted. From the point of view of landscape study, the argument which has already been presented in this book with regard to major political events is underlined even more forcibly by a consideration of the state of England in the second half of the eleventh century. For some time after 1066, especially in certain regions, everyday life at the lower end of the social scale, bound up with customs, institutions and practices which had evolved slowly from ancient origins, continued in many respects much as before. The Normans constituted a new elite – a particularly energetic, ruthless and highly organized one – but they did not represent a folk movement in the way the Saxons or Vikings had done. In gathering the reins of power, they modified some aspects of English life and accelerated changes in others, but their activities were not marked by any noticeable break in the archaeological record or by any great technological innovations. The social and economic changes which occurred under the Normans – the last Norman king died less than a century after the Conquest, and the Normans soon ceased to form a separate group in English society – were often indirect. They were set within a much older framework, in which Anglo-Saxon patterns of administration, settlement and agriculture figured prominently.

Domesday England

Much of the importance credited to the Normans in the popular mind derives from the extraordinary document for which William I himself was responsible, the volumes known as the Domesday Book. But although this was compiled twenty years after the Conquest, the England which it describes is Saxon, not Norman. Far from signalling widespread change, it reveals the extent to which the landscape of England was already taking on certain of its basic lineaments. The country which the Normans conquered was far from empty: large areas were occupied, managed, cultivated and settled. However, before any conclusions can be drawn from the Domesday Book, it is essential to appreciate its limitations as a historical source.

Like most documentary materials used by historical geographers, the Domesday Book was not drawn up with regard to the purposes for which modern scholars require it. William's intention was not to gather material for a geographical description of England in 1086, and various techniques and interpretative structures – some more legitimate than others – have been employed in order to render the information of use in this context. Despite prolonged and detailed attempts to construct such a geography, based upon the mapping, comparison and analysis of Domesday data, a full interpretation has not yet emerged. The reasons for this are several. Firstly, it is not entirely clear what the original purpose of the survey was, or precisely how the contents were gathered. On one level the Domesday Book clearly involves some kind of taxation assessment, an inventory of the kingdom's wealth, assets and landownership structure. What it was ultimately used for, or indeed whether in fact it turned out to be a great bureaucratic white elephant, we do not know. Secondly, the taxation entries are given in a confusing variety of forms which are difficult to match up or interpret with certainty. The holdings of landowners and the units of taxation are often recorded as territorial amalgamations, concealing under a single heading what in reality were several distinct settlements. Classifications are seen to change from one district to another, as do units of measurement. Many terms are far from clear: the misinterpretation of the word 'manor' – the holding of a feudal lord – has resulted in completely false distributions of various categories of land use being employed as a basis for interpretation because the modern reader failed to appreciate that some manors were not compact and centred upon a single nucleated settlement, but were extensive and even fragmented. For example, a number of convoluted reasons were put forward to account for the apparent absence of woodland from the High Weald before it was realized that this woodland had been entered under the names of places situated around the edge. Much of the woodland was probably not recorded at all. A final major drawback of the Domesday Book is that it omits the four northern counties and Wales. Nevertheless, despite all these deficiencies it gives a general picture of the state of England in 1086, and can be used in conjunction with other sources to provide more detailed local reconstructions.

In certain respects Domesday England would not have seemed so unfamiliar to modern eyes as one might imagine. It was certainly not covered in impenetrable forest, awaiting those great phases of medieval clearance and colonization which at one time were thought to have been chiefly responsible for moulding the English landscape as a whole. Many districts were relatively open, while others supported secondary and often managed woodland. It was areas such as these which were cleared in medieval times to leave a legacy of woodland-related place-names. The Domesday record is confusing because several different methods of recording and assessing woodland were used, ranging from length-breadth measurements to the ability of the wood to support a certain number of swine or provide fuel. Royal forests were not included (except the New Forest), as they lay outside the common law and were kept specially for the royal chase. The word forest was a technical term for a hunting reserve which was not by definition wooded, although the extensive uncultivated tracts set aside by the king obviously embraced large numbers of trees.

The Domesday Book contains many references to 'waste', but these applied less to 'natural' wastes such as heaths, moors and marshes (which incidentally were far from virgin by this time) than to the lands devastated by warfare. This destruction was caused by raiding by the Scots, Welsh and Irish, and above all by William's ruthless suppression of opposition, exemplified by his famous 'harrying of the north' between 1068 and 1070. Certain aspects of the distribution of this waste are perplexing, because much of it lies on the uplands, apparently leaving the lowlands relatively untouched. This pattern is the opposite of what might be expected. Perhaps the Normans organized forced migrations to repopulate the ravaged lowland sites, leaving the uplands deserted as an indirect consequence of the desolation below.

While the proportion of wild and waste land recorded in the Domesday Book seems on the high side, it was probably considerably less than in other European countries at the time. The arable acreages suggested by the survey are considerable, as far as one can tell from the pitfall-laden information relating to plough-lands and plough-teams. Much of the land on the better soils was already under cultivation, while the floodplains of the rivers provided valuable meadows for hay. References to pasture are much more irregular, and there are only a few incidental indications of the arrangements governing its use. Domesday is of very little assistance concerning agrarian organization, telling us almost nothing about the distribution and structure of the open fields, let alone shedding any light on the vexed question of their origins.

As indicated earlier, the Domesday Book's entries were organized around taxable estates rather than individual settlements, so the listing of a particular manor does not of itself prove that there was a village there, nor does an omission necessarily imply that the place was created as a result of early medieval expansion. Much settlement was actually dispersed, although the nucleations which had yet to appear were the products of a long process of development which originated in mid- and late Saxon times. The evolving hierarchy of rural settlement was a complex phenomenon, both temporally and spatially, forming a kaleidoscopic pattern which militates against large-scale generalizations. Nevertheless, the basic distribution of population emerges clearly, with concentrations in the fertile regions of southern and eastern England, and lower densities occurring on the lowland sandy heaths such as the Breckland, and in wide thinly populated tracts extending across the north. The population of England may have amounted to about one and a half million, although some estimates approach two million. The Domesday Book specifically mentions only about 275,000 people, drawn from every level of society but all presumably heads of households, so some form of multiplier must be used to obtain an idea of the true number. The total produced in this way is so far removed from the original figure that it cannot but be an extremely rough estimate. But it is certain that only a small percentage of the population lived in towns, which, except for a handful of important foci, were small, vulnerable, impermanent and lacking in qualities the modern observer would associate with urban life. The survey says very little about them, hardly mentioning London, the largest borough of all, or Winchester, which formed the headquarters of the whole Domesday enterprise. But town life, especially its commercial aspect, was undoubtedly gaining momentum.

Finally, the collection of small-scale craft and manufacturing concerns scattered across the country were described in the Domesday Book only in a very partial and incomplete fashion. Ironworks are occasionally mentioned, and lead works appear under the Peak District entries. Quarries do not receive the attention which might be expected in view of the undoubted contemporary expansion of building activities, and the only enterprise dealt with in any detail is the production of salt, which was an essential item in the medieval economy, being the only known preservative for meat and fish. Rock salt was not worked until the later seventeenth century, so salt was obtained from brine springs in the Keuper Marl districts of Worcestershire and Cheshire (p. 55) or by the evaporation of seawater in pans situated at the coast.

The Normans and Wales

The Domesday Book is a unique but tantalizing source, and it would be unwise to regard it as the ultimate authority on the early medieval landscape, even for those regions where its selective and idiosyncratic entries appear to be relatively reliable. But what of the north, and Wales? These can hardly be discounted as incidental omissions of areas on the margins of the main theatre of events. There is a strong case for maintaining that the Norman impact upon Wales was considerably greater than that experienced in England. Wales, particularly its more remote uplands, had remained peripheral to the social and economic developments taking place in Saxon England. The Saxons were obliged to be satisfied with penning up the inhabitants of Wales rather than overcoming them, even though they had succeeded in splitting the Welsh territories into three parts, colonizing much of one of them (the South-west peninsula), while Scandinavian settlers had imposed a Viking character on Lancashire and Cumbria, part of the former Celtic kingdom of Strathclyde (Figure 20). For this reason the Normans' policy towards the remaining, central Celtic stronghold in Wales was much more clear-cut than the process by which they assumed authority and wielded power in England. The transition comprised a violent struggle of conquest in which they were almost certain to prevail once they had successfully exploited the physique of Wales in order to divide and rule, taking advantage of the persistent tendency of the loose collection of kingdoms and principalities to disintegrate in the absence of a powerful ruler. Nevertheless, the military domination was not accompanied or superseded by cultural assimilation, at least in *Pura Wallia*, which managed to resist external pressure and the forces of internal tribal fragmentation (occasioned by the physical geography of upland Wales) until Gwynedd finally fell to Edward I in 1282–4. Wales proved to be a tougher nut for the Normans to crack than Brittany, which was also a Celtic peninsula but one more subdued in terms of relief, being somewhat akin to Cornwall. The glaciated Welsh massif was larger, higher and more rugged; moreover its inhabitants were fiercely independent.

The lowlands of 'Outer Wales', in the south and east, were relatively easily penetrated, however, and the physical and cultural duality began to be clearly reflected in the landscapes of the two regions. The Anglo-Normans imposed completely new forms of social organization, and the rule of the powerful, semi-independent marcher barons was maintained through the imported institutions of castle, manor and borough. The distinctive patterns of agrarian practice, land tenure, trade and town growth all contributed to major changes in the *Marchia Wallie*, the March of Wales, more especially in the Englishries, those parts of the marcher lordships which were administered according to English laws and customs. In the Welshries, which generally extended over the higher ground of the lordships, the Welsh adhered to their own life styles but paid tribute to the Anglo-Norman lords. These essential divisions were fundamental to the evolution of the Welsh landscape, both in the medieval period and later.

Although the Domesday Book did not deal with Wales, some indications of the appearance of the country can be gleaned from the few entries which describe the border districts. The scattered references suggest a pattern of thinly populated territories clothed in trees, a picture which tallies with that afforded by certain studies of Offa's Dyke (p. 136), and by the documentary evidence detailing the exploitation of the Welsh forests by the Normans. But it is unlikely that the mixed oak woods were characteristic of other parts of Wales, particularly on the higher ground, where more open birch-hazel woods gave way to heathland and various anthropogenic forms of grassland, maintained by grazing. Nor was the settlement pattern simply one of dispersal, based upon tribalism and pastoralism. The systems of transhumance, involving the seasonal migration of herds and flocks from the winter *hendre* to the temporary summer dwelling or *hafod* in the grazing lands above, embraced the cultivation of arable plots. In the lowlands, particularly the Englishries, there was probably a good deal of nucleated settlement, surrounded by arable fields. Here the bondmen of the lord or chief lived together in clusters of homesteads, operating varieties of open field systems involving strips and common rights. On the margins of the arable the freemen occupied their more scattered holdings. In this way a pre-Conquest basis existed for the establishment and spread of the Norman manorial system. The landscape was already an old one, but in certain of her regions Wales shared with England a sequence of changes related both to the new culture and to the significant economic expansion which characterized the period between the late eleventh and early fourteenth centuries.

The economic background to the medieval landscape

The developments in the landscape which occurred between the late eleventh and late fifteenth centuries took place within a framework of profound economic change. The early medieval period, taken as a whole, was one of demographic growth and economic advance. By about 1300 the Domesday population of England had probably trebled, reaching 4 or $4\frac{1}{2}$ million, although the increases varied considerably from place to place. In landscape terms this was reflected in the extension of the limits of cultivation in the potentially fertile fenlands, upon the margins of the uplands and the poorer soils of the lowlands, into the peripheral regions – the north, south-west and Welsh border – and at the expense of the forests by a process of clearing or 'assarting'. New settlements were founded, including self-governing towns or boroughs, whose privileges were enshrined in royal or seigneurial charters. Often they grew up around the barons' new castles, or outside the gates of religious houses, which at this time were in the ascendancy. Large areas were given over to forests, parks and chases, for the pleasure of the nobility.

Nevertheless, the medieval economy was still relatively unsophisticated and unstable. The failure of the harvest or the ravages of disease could have disastrous consequences for settlements of all sizes, based as they were almost wholly upon agriculture and vulnerable to the effects of famine and pestilence. The economic progress of the early medieval period was abruptly and savagely terminated by the bubonic plague or Black Death outbreak of 1348–50, which is estimated to have killed between 30 and 45 per cent of the population. Some demographers, identifying the Black Death as a crisis of public health which spread to Europe from Asia, reject the view of those who regard it not as a random biological event but as a kind of sudden Malthusian nemesis. It is certainly true that by the time the Black Death struck, the subsistence crisis had already been reached, and had manifested itself in the great European famine of 1315–17, but it was the Black Death which decimated an already unsteady population. During the first half of the fourteenth century demographic growth had given way to a static or even a declining population which had exhibited a diminished resilience in the face of food shortages and disease. The Great Pestilence may, technically speaking, have indeed been simply a disease, but it remains unclear why it attacked the population with such overwhelming violence. The retreats and reversals evident in the fourteenth-century landscape resulted from a complex set of circumstances influencing demographic cycles at various scales, in which the effects of the Black Death, if not its origins, were closely bound up with social and economic factors.

Other elements contributed to the slump. The frequency of poor harvests may well have been related to some form of climatic deterioration which was part of a secular trend towards cooler, wetter summers and increased storminess. Even minor changes in climatic parameters significant to agricultural practice and crop growth could have profound consequences for cultivation in marginal areas. During the early medieval period, when the country enjoyed a period of milder winters and slightly higher summer temperatures, the limits of cultivation had been pushed too far into the uplands to be sustained. With the recession the agricultural margin retreated, a movement to which climatic change seems to have been a real contributor, although it is impossible to be certain. For example, the decline of the vineyards which had flourished in southern England in the twelfth and thirteenth centuries has been interpreted as an indication of climatic change; but the decay of the monasteries in which many of them were situated may also have been important.

Whatever the precise nature of the causes, the effects of the economic setback were profound. The population did not recover until the late fifteenth and early sixteenth centuries. The resulting scarcity of labour caused the decline of demesne farming (the cultivation by villeins of the lord's land for the latter's profit). As wages and costs rose, landowners increasingly leased for rent, which in turn led to a growth in peasant farming. The demand for wool and the lower costs of labour associated with sheep farming prompted the conversion of arable to pasture, a process manifested in the enclosure of the open fields and the fossilization of ridge-and-furrow under grass. This transition was also related to the eviction of tenants and the abandonment of villages, although it was by no means the only cause of depopulation. Most susceptible were those settlements which were not marginal but which lay in districts where the economic balance between arable and pasture was finely balanced and therefore easily tilted.

However, not all the consequences were negative. The groundswell of activity in the spheres of reclamation and enclosure by agreement carried prosperity with it. There are always some people who will turn a crisis to their advantage: later medieval England witnessed the rise both of small farmers profiting from the lease of demesne lands, and of increasingly wealthy merchants based upon the cloth trade and displaying their wealth in a range of fine late medieval domestic buildings and churches. The manufacture and trading of cloth also stimulated the growth of certain towns, which in their economic relations were closely tied to rural hinterlands. All these developments left their mark on the landscape.

Medieval agrarian landscapes

The popular image of the medieval agrarian landscape usually entails a nucleated village surrounded by two or three open fields divided into strips, individually owned but worked under a common system. The true picture is much more diverse and involved, and despite a vast amount of research many features of open field agriculture remain poorly understood.

It is important to distinguish right at the start between the formal aspects of open fields (a term which can be applied generally to those fields in existence prior to enclosure) and the functional arrangements which governed their use and underlay agrarian practice. The remnants of the open fields which have survived in the landscape can provide a good deal of information regarding the former category – the appearance, physical extent and boundaries of the fields – but much less about the latter, particularly the agreements, rotations and systems of tenure which were in operation. Thus the term common field is a functional term which should be used only in cases where it is known that common rules governed cultivation and grazing. This involved the co-operation of all the owners of the strips, who agreed (and enforced) the rotations to be employed in the fields, and participated in throwing the whole field open after harvest and in fallow years for the common pasturing of the stock. This arrangement did not apply on all open fields, and similar agreements sometimes governed enclosed fields; so the terms open field and common field are not interchangeable.

Other factors complicate the issue still further. Many open fields were not in fact completely open: the units formed by the intermixed strips or parcels could be marked by hedges, fences or walls. Far from being rigidly inflexible, stifling those initiatives and innovations which were supposedly delayed until the coming of Parliamentary enclosure (formerly hailed as the spearhead of the agricultural revolution), the open fields encompassed great regional and local variations in style and practice. They varied with soils, drainage, climate, the balance of different types of land and the proximity and amounts of waste at their edges, with prevailing inheritance customs, settlement patterns and the influence of nearby market towns. The open fields were diversified by a variety of techniques such as the cultivation of fodder crops upon the best part of the field ('hitching'). Indeed, the whole scene, far from being visually monotonous, was capable of exhibiting considerable variety and must often have been a pleasing patchwork of colour. One only has to picture the pattern of strips, the contrasting unploughed balks or headlands, which no doubt sported some gay wild flowers, the pasture around and sometimes within the field, and, further off, the woodland or marsh. It is certain that the open field landscape would have looked quite different from the vast open 'prairie landscapes' created by modern farming, which some people try to justify aesthetically by suggesting that this is, after all, what England looked like before enclosure. Nothing could be further from the truth, not least because neither were the soils poisoned and the fallow eliminated, nor was the wasteland – all too valuable for the medieval farmer – removed to produce a bare and featureless landscape of huge fields full of the same crop.

The key unit of the open field was not the strip (a unit of tenure) but the selion (a unit of ploughing). The selion was a width of land which could either be ridged or ploughed flat. The parallel selions were grouped into strips, and a parcel of strips of varying sizes which ran in the same direction was called a furlong. A tenant held a number of strips of varying sizes in separate furlongs; as a result, his strips ran in a number of directions and were located in different parts of the open field. Despite what is sometimes written about two or three field systems, the basic unit of rotation was not the field but the furlong, and the rotations were carried on quite independently of the actual number of fields.

The ridged selions were created by a particular method of ploughing using a certain type of plough. The 'heavy' plough cut through the soil and turned the furrow-slice to the right. Consequently, if the field were simply ploughed up and down by working progressively across it from one side to the other, each double run would merely produce a tiny ridge overlying an unploughed ribbon of ground, the soil being thrown inwards from the two furrows on either side. This would have been a pointless exercise, so instead the field was ploughed as a number of separate units, each with its own central axis. Ploughing started along the centre line and worked gradually away from it, turning the soil inwards from both edges as the plough went along one side and back down the other. Every sod on each side was therefore turned the same way and laid against the previous one. It has been suggested that once the plough team had progressed to a point a certain distance from the original centre line, the distance it was obliged to walk along the headland to the other side for the return run was such that it was easier to start a new circuit, based upon the axis of an adjacent unit. Repeated ploughing of exactly the same units year after year gradually led to the formation of adjacent ridges, separated from each other by furrows produced where the furrow-slices were turned away from each other. This practice created the familiar pattern of ridge-and-furrow which can still be seen preserved under pasture in many regions (Figures 26 and 45). The C-shaped or reversed-S curve apparent in the plan of ridge-and-furrow is thought to have resulted from the technique of turning the team on the narrow unploughed headland at the margin of the furlong so as not to damage neighbouring strips. The headlands often survive in the landscape as long sinuous ridges lying at right angles to the ridge-and-furrow. It is probable that these are the balks referred to in medieval documents as features separating the land of different farmers, a description which has often been interpreted

Figure 26. Ridge-and-furrow at Napton on the Hill, Warwickshire. This aerial photograph was taken in favourable conditions of low sunlight, looking north-eastwards across grid square SP 4560 towards the village. The post-medieval features, such as enclosure boundaries and the Oxford Canal (which enters the picture at the top left-hand corner), mainly disregard the pattern formed by the furlongs of the former open field system (see also Figure 45)

as signifying their presence between the parallel strips (see p. 183). However, the furrows themselves were probably regarded as sufficient demarcation lines.

Enough has already been said to indicate the problematic nature of open field landscapes. Some of the difficulties are inherent, reflecting our ignorance of agrarian practice; others stem from the often puzzling remains of open fields surviving in the modern landscape. The fundamental purpose of ridge-and-furrow is itself unclear. If the persistent and deliberate ploughing of precisely the same unit was carried on in order to create a ridge to assist the drainage, as is often suggested, then why was it the custom in some areas, such as parts of Devonshire, to employ a different method and plough flat? Drainage after all is a local question, not one to apply to whole districts. Patently well-drained sites carry ridge-and-furrow. It is not improbable that its purpose was quite other. Some scholars consider that digging actually played a part in its formation, while others have proposed that the practice of ploughing in ridges, once begun, became near-universal. The differences observable from place to place in the form of ridge-and-furrow may well result from the net effect of a whole set of variables, including local land measurements and tenurial arrangements, soil type and the depth and frequency of ploughing. Of course, ridge-and-furrow, being caused simply by the action of a plough, need not have been restricted to the open fields, nor be medieval in origin. Some examples have been conclusively dated to medieval times (such as those at Bentley Grange, West Yorkshire, SE 267131, which are overlain by medieval iron pits), but others are much more recent, having taken on their present appearance only when the last ploughing occurred. This emphasizes the general point that the few surviving open fields, even those at the classic site of Laxton, Nottinghamshire (SK 7267), are by no means unaltered or representative, having experienced, among other things, a variable measure of consolidation of holdings (p. 181). Similarly, it is dangerous to use post-medieval maps to study them, as such sources do not necessarily give an accurate representation of open fields in their original state.

Nevertheless, some of the more straightforward aspects of the open fields may profitably be studied in relation to other elements in the landscape. The pattern of the furlongs prompts interesting thoughts on the history of colonization in particular districts. In some cases the irregular arrangement of furlongs reflects the sequence of blocks of land carved from the waste and then subdivided by the community, although in other instances the furlongs themselves appear to be subdividing features created after the establishment of early, large-scale strips. Strangely indented parish boundaries or kinks in lanes may represent the interlocking of furlongs belonging to adjacent parishes, where cultivation had been pushed right to the limits. The distribution of ridge-and-furrow in marginal areas can indicate the farthest extent reached by agriculture under the pressure of land hunger. The ploughing of steep slopes resulted in the creation of long terraces known as strip lynchets (not to be confused with prehistoric or Roman lynchets), and their precarious location can speak volumes about the desperation experienced in certain periods of the Middle Ages to press every acre into service.

The open fields, although extending beyond the classic region of the English Midlands, were by no means universal. In certain districts, enclosed fields replaced them at an early date, while newly cleared marginal areas displayed a variety of field types. In the far west and in the uplands of Wales the field systems were often derived from Celtic models, and were accompanied by distinctive settlement patterns and tenurial arrangements. In the Englishries of the Welsh marches, modified open field systems prevailed, smaller and more fragmented than those in England, while in the Welshries the manorial institutions were imposed more superficially and the traditional agrarian landscape tended to keep its identity. In *Pura Wallia* the degree of preservation was even greater. The complicated patterns of loose clusters and single farms were related to particular systems of tenure (especially partible inheritance), and diverse local landholding arrangements applied to the waste, pasture and limited arable. Only after the Edwardian conquest did the old order change, the lands of rebels and defaulters passing to the king by the principle of escheat. This weakened the traditions of reallocation and communal organization, and with the upheavals of the later medieval period many of the former tribal lands passed to the free market and were taken up by ambitious individuals who rationalized and consolidated the holdings with an eye to developing estates. The open sharelands and pastures underwent enclosure, leaving single farms set within their own territories of irregular fields and located with reference both to physical factors and to the related availability of different types of land.

Early enclosure of various kinds characterized many parts of England, especially the west and the north. It resulted less from the activities of rapacious landlords or the conversion to pasture than from the desire of groups of small farmers to come to a mutually beneficial arrangement, especially in regions of decreased population, by continuing the process of subdivision of the open fields in order to produce their own enclosures. So smooth, gradual and complete was this largely unrecorded process that it has led some scholars to the erroneous conclusion that open fields never existed at all in these regions. The evidence in the landscape to the contrary is slight, but can on occasion be most revealing, especially where the new boundaries clearly respect the former divisions of the open fields, producing distinctively curved hedges or walls which follow the edges of the old strips (Figure 27). Good examples may be seen on the eastern outskirts of Castleton (SK 155829), and south-west of Brassington (SK 2253), both in Derbyshire. At Combe Martin in Devon (SS 5846) tiny rectangular plots now occupy the strips of the open fields.

Elsewhere new enclosed fields were being created by the early medieval onslaught on the woodlands, marshes and upland margins. This process may have been going on for some time; the abundance of documentation

Figure 27. Piecemeal enclosure of strips at Cosheston, Dyfed. The long, narrow hedged fields on the flanks of the village were created by the piecemeal enclosure of bundles of strips from the former open fields. The strips were grouped under such revealing names as Headland, Upper Furlong and Lower Furlong. By contrast, larger and more regular enclosures can be seen in the middle distance towards Carew River

from the twelfth and thirteenth centuries should not be taken to imply that such activity was confined to those years. Forest clearings or assarts (p. 163) can sometimes be distinguished using three kinds of evidence, which are especially suggestive if they occur together. The first embraces place- and field-names involving certain woodland-related elements such as *stocking* or *rydding*, which refer to clearings of stumps and to land 'rid of trees' respectively. There are many similar terms. Secondly, these areas frequently display parcels of remaining woodland (often greatly altered), together with thick hedges which are particularly rich botanically. The presence of certain species such as dog's mercury (*Mercurialis perennis*), bluebell (*Endymion non-scriptus*) and wood anemone (*Anemone nemo-rosa*), which are slow colonizers, may indicate that the hedge represents a portion of relict woodland. The number of shrub and tree species in a hedge, under certain conditions, has also been shown to reflect its age, allowing a rough estimate to be made of its date. Finally, the pattern of fields produced by assarting is characteristically irregular, incorporating narrow winding lanes and scattered settlements. Landscapes of this kind are especially characteristic of the edges of uplands such as Dartmoor, where the laborious clearance of boulder-strewn moorland produced a mosaic of tiny fields. These enclosures are defined by banks, often built up with clitter and crowned by scrubby trees, for example those to be seen around the isolated farms of Cholwich Town (SX 587619) and Cudlipptown (521791). Many of these upland margin fields were subsequently deserted, and now serve to indicate the 'high-water mark' of cultivation reached by the farmers of the Middle Ages.

A particular kind of woodland clearance has given a highly individual appearance to parts of south-east England. A speciality of the Wealden landscape of Kent and Sussex is the network of narrow strips of scrub or trees bounding the fields cleared from the waste during early medieval times. These 'shaws', which take the place of hedges, probably recall the piecemeal nature of the colonization of the Wealden forests and remain as a clear reminder of the activities of the pioneering medieval farmers. Their plentiful standing trees and rich ground floras combine with the small size of many of the fields to confer upon the present landscape a distinctive, seemingly densely wooded aspect. The feel of a landscape of medieval assarts can still be sampled by exploring the sheltered lanes, shaws, and tiny fields around the hill-top village of Mayfield (TQ 5826) in East Sussex, where the names of many of the scattered farms incorporate the element *ryd* (Woodreed Farm, 553258) or *stocc* (Stockland Farm, 529248).

Some of the most spectacular feats of colonization took place in the marshes, where the land had first to be reclaimed before its latent fertility could be exploited. But the marshlands, like the other forms of waste which lay beyond the arable, were, despite their designation, far from wasted. Complicated rights and practices governed their exploitation for fish, eels, fowl for food, rushes and sedges for thatching, and peat for fuel, in addition to their use as grazing land. Some of these practices produced their own landscapes, most notably the cutting of peat in the 'turbaries'. The Norfolk Broads, once regarded as natural lakes, are now known to represent huge medieval peat workings from which millions of cubic feet of material were removed before some positive movement of base-level (a rise in the level of the sea relative to that of the land) drowned them, probably in the late thirteenth or early fourteenth centuries. Careful study of the Broads revealed that, unlike natural bodies of water, they have steep-sided margins and straight boundaries, as well as actual balks of uncut peat.

Large-scale reclamation and enclosure of the wetlands was prompted by the value of the land produced by drainage, both arable, as in the dramatic case of the East Anglian Fens, and meadow, which was a more suitable form of land use in the Somerset Levels (p. 185). In eastern England a landscape of sea banks, dykes and ditches interwoven with irregular fields developed stage by stage as more land was taken in. The task, carried out by groups of small freeholders and later by the large landowners, especially the religious houses, was an immense undertaking, and was accompanied by new forms of social organization, distinctive regional economies, local population increases, and the creation of some striking landscapes. It is all the more depressing therefore to record the retreat which took place in the wetlands after the early fourteenth century, when many hard-won areas suffered from neglect and a lack of maintenance of their drainage works. But a start had been made, not only in the two principal regions but also in other coastal marshlands of southern and eastern England. The results of medieval activity are evident in the modern landscape even in those districts where later reclamations have tended to obscure these modest but important beginnings (p. 239). For not only have the drainage operations and the subsequent cultivation of the reclaimed lands left a direct imprint, but the changes effected in local and regional economies are also clearly evident. During the Middle Ages the Norfolk marshlands were transformed from a poor and sparsely populated district to one of the richest areas of England, and the profits derived from sheep-rearing on the newly reclaimed fens were reflected in the building of some of the grandest churches in all England.

Forests, chases and parks

Despite the drive for the reclamation and colonization of certain areas, extensive tracts of land were deliberately kept out of agricultural use during the Middle Ages and maintained as uncultivated districts given over to the chase. Special systems of law and administration were applied to them, and rules were laid down governing land use, economic exploitation and habitation. As a result, particular kinds of landscape were produced which differed greatly from those of the adjoining agricultural districts.

Royal forests were game preserves owned by the Crown, subject to their own regulations and run by forest courts and officials. Although some of them were in existence before the Conquest, the forests were formalized by the Normans, and at their greatest extent in the early medieval period may have covered up to 30 per cent of England. This estimate, however, refers to the extent of their legal jurisdiction, intended to embrace those areas around the actual uncultivated core over which the deer might stray. The forests proper accounted for a smaller but still sizeable proportion of the country, whose significance was increased by the severe regulations excluding any use prejudicial to the existence of the protected animals (boar as well as deer), thereby effectively preventing the extension of agriculture into them (Figure 28).

Figure 28. The royal forests of England, 1327–36

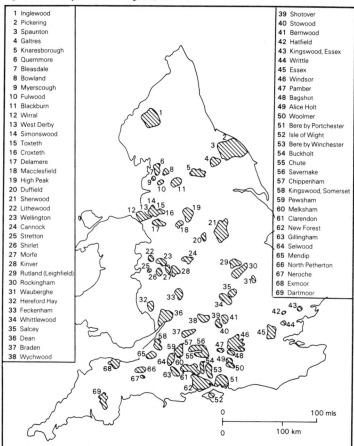

1	Inglewood	39	Shotover
2	Pickering	40	Stowood
3	Spaunton	41	Bernwood
4	Galtres	42	Hatfield
5	Knaresborough	43	Kingswood, Essex
6	Quernmore	44	Writtle
7	Bleasdale	45	Essex
8	Bowland	46	Windsor
9	Myerscough	47	Pamber
10	Fulwood	48	Bagshot
11	Blackburn	49	Alice Holt
12	Wirral	50	Woolmer
13	West Derby	51	Bere by Portchester
14	Simonswood	52	Isle of Wight
15	Toxteth	53	Bere by Winchester
16	Croxteth	54	Buckholt
17	Delamere	55	Chute
18	Macclesfield	56	Savernake
19	High Peak	57	Chippenham
20	Duffield	58	Kingswood, Somerset
21	Sherwood	59	Pewsham
22	Lithewood	60	Melksham
23	Wellington	61	Clarendon
24	Cannock	62	New Forest
25	Stretton	63	Gillingham
26	Shirlet	64	Selwood
27	Morfe	65	Mendip
28	Kinver	66	North Petherton
29	Rutland (Leighfield)	67	Neroche
30	Rockingham	68	Exmoor
31	Wauberghe	69	Dartmoor
32	Hereford Hay		
33	Feckenham		
34	Whittlewood		
35	Salcey		
36	Dean		
37	Braden		
38	Wychwood		

0   100 mls

0   100 km

Nevertheless, the forests served a useful purpose in conserving large areas of woodland, many of which were in any case probably unsuitable for cultivation. Furthermore, they were not by any means kept free from exploitation. Despite the love of the chase which posterity has imputed to the Norman kings, the royal forests were not only, and perhaps not principally, kept for the pleasures of hunting. The king was always on the move with his retinue, and the forests conveniently furnished the large quantities of game demanded by the itinerant royal court for its sustenance. Also, through a series of concessions made to favoured persons, the forests proved to be a useful source of income for the Crown. Woodland resources included the products of the trees themselves – timber, coppice wood, bark and charcoal – together with tracts of land for cattle farms, grazing and pannage, some of which also contained deposits of valuable minerals such as iron, lead and tin. These assets were realized through the grants made to nobles, forest officials and monasteries, so that the woods constituted distinctive but not entirely sealed elements in the medieval economy.

Although they were progressively cut into by assarting and encroachment as the administrative structure lapsed – or was deliberately ignored (p. 230) – the peculiar customs, privileges and economies of the royal forests have left a deep impression on the landscape. Some were indeed thickly wooded and awesome: of the Forest of Dean, William Camden wrote: 'this was a wonderfull thicke Forrest, and in former ages so darke and terrible, by reason of crooked and winding wayes, as also the grisly shade therein, that it made the inhabitants more fierce, and bolder to commit robberies'. Even at the edges of the forest, upon parcels of land granted by the king to private owners (especially monasteries) to exploit selectively on the understanding that they preserved the woods for the deer, the trees could still be closely set in an imposing tangle of vegetation. In about 1280 the Abbot of the Benedictine Abbey of St Peter's, Gloucester, was licensed to cut down and dispose of the underwood (the smaller trees or the poles produced by cutting coppice, pollards, or young suckers) of his wood at Hope Mansell on the northern edge of the Forest of Dean. Permission was granted as the underwood was considered 'unfit to support the King's deer, and because wolves and malefactors frequently repair to it and stay there, by reason of its density'. But at the same time the Abbot was instructed to enclose the wood by means of a low hedge, with free ingress and egress for the deer.

The various royal forests have either changed greatly or vanished altogether since the Middle Ages, but certain medieval activities and patterns of ownership can still be traced in the landscape. The trees themselves, when subjected to specialist botanical analysis, can reveal something of former practices of woodland management and the history of the forest in question. It is often possible, using field evidence and old maps and documents, to trace the medieval boundaries and the pattern of enclosures derived from the assarts. Many ancient forest terms and names survive. Common place-name elements in the Forest of Dean, of mixed origin, include *lawn, glade* and *grove* (signifying various types of clearing or enclosure); *meend* (a piece of waste or open ground in the forest); *eaves* (the edge of a wood); *tuft* (a clump of trees); *vallet* (a knot of felled trees); *brake* (a thicket); *haie* or *hay* (an enclosure, or area fenced off for hunting); and *purlieu* (the outskirts of a forest). A large and varied group employ individual tree species names. Others afford some clue to the former owners, as in the case of Abbots Wood on the eastern side of the Forest of Dean, which was given to the Abbot of Flaxley by Henry III in 1258 in place of the right to take two oaks a week from anywhere in the Forest for use in the abbey's forge.

Many similar place-name elements can be used to identify the sites of chases. In essence, chases were private forests owned by nobles or ecclesiastics rather than by the king, and were subject to common as opposed to forest law, unless they lay within the confines of a royal forest. Nevertheless, they were maintained and exploited in a fashion similar to the forests. During the Middle Ages nearly thirty chases were created, some of which owed their existence to the apportioning of part of a royal forest, such as Tidenham Chase on the edge of the Forest of Dean.

A far more common means of keeping deer and symbolizing the status of a noble was the medieval park. Nearly 2,000 are known to have existed at one time or another, the highest number being recorded during the years before the Black Death. There were probably many more which have left no trace. Unlike those parks which the wealthy members of later societies were to lay out for themselves, the medieval parks were designed not for ornament but to provide hunting and a source of wood products and meat. Some also contained fishponds. Naturally enough, they were especially plentiful in areas of infertile soils, and their numbers seem to have been greatest in the wooded or unimproved districts of the west Midlands and Home Counties. The Crown too owned parks, often in association with royal forests, as at Woodstock in the Forest of Wychwood (Oxfordshire), while the greater landowners each held several, distributed between their various manors. The medieval parks usually encompassed areas of less than a couple of hundred acres. Unlike the forests or chases they were securely enclosed by means of a ditch and bank, with a fence, hedge or wall on top which the deer were unable to clear. Sometimes the earth banks can still be traced, or the curved hedges of the park boundary identified. Elsewhere only the field- or place-names furnish a clue: Old Park, Park Lodge, Park Farm or Park Wood are relatively common in the vicinities of medieval parks.

Finally, brief mention should be made of a fourth category of game preserve, the warrens, which were enclosures for the breeding of rabbits for meat and skin. Rabbits (coneys) were introduced into this country in the twelfth century, and some warrens, notably those on Dartmoor (p. 98), may be almost as old as this, although the buries and other features visible at these sites today are almost certainly post-medieval in origin. However, as the rabbit population of the country grew, so these artificial warrens fell out of use. The term 'free warren' conveyed a different meaning, being applied to areas set aside for the hunting of small game, originally those species considered harmful to crops or – ironically perhaps – to deer. Later they were used as a source of animals to be hunted purely for sport.

Castles, fortified houses and moated settlements

The various kinds of fortified residence which characterized the medieval landscape were created as a consequence of the need felt by the upper echelons of a hierarchical society to furnish themselves with a degree of protection in an age when social instability and violence were endemic. But as time went on, the purely military function was blended with other considerations which eventually superseded it altogether. Fortified buildings were conceived not just as strongholds but as administrative centres, agents of colonization and the spread of cultivation, and as private residences from which to organize hunting in adjacent forests, chases and parks. Finally, in their imposing and massive appearance, they acted as symbols of status and power, and came to be regarded as the very embodiment of the feudal system itself. Today, even in their state of grand ruination, they possess great popular appeal. Stimulating the imagination and exciting the fancy, they probably colour many people's image of the Middle Ages more than any other surviving element of the medieval landscape.

This is especially true of the castles, which differed from the fortified places and systems of strongholds constructed before or after the medieval period by merit of their creation as essentially private establishments. They developed considerably in their architectural and military aspects during these centuries, but with respect to their role in the landscape several broad phases may be distinguished. Castles appeared with the coming of the Normans, and a vigorous period of construction followed the Conquest. (A very few, such as Ewyas Harold in Hereford and Worcester, SO 385288, were built *c*. 1050 by Norman favourites of Edward the Confessor.) The early motte-and-bailey castles were constructed of earth and timber, the motte or mound being surrounded by a ditch and capped by a wooden tower which looked down upon a fortified courtyard or bailey enclosed by a bank or palisade, coupled with a ditch. These castles were used as a means of controlling the newly conquered country and were erected in both England (particularly on the south-east coasts) and Anglo-Norman Wales. All the timberwork has gone, but many of the mottes remain. The castles which can be seen today mostly date from the twelfth century and later, when massive stone keeps and walls replaced the earlier timbers (Figures 33, 34 and 35). Several hundred were in existence by 1150, their distribution reflecting the general pattern of landownership, while the precise site of each was carefully chosen in order to make the most of the strategic and tactical advantages offered by the surrounding physical and cultural landscapes.

The most elaborate and magnificent castles were built in the late thirteenth and early fourteenth centuries, in a monumental style exemplified by Dunstanburgh in Northumberland, with its great gatehouse (p. 194), and by the castles built by Edward I after the final conquest of *Pura Wallia*. These castles are the most perfect specimens of medieval fortification in Britain, and in many cases a fortified town was included in the overall design of the site. At Conwy, Gwynedd, the whole system, including the walls, forms a remarkable assemblage; other impressive castles and related features dominate the scene at Caernarvon, Beaumaris and Harlech in Gwynedd, and at Flint and Rhuddlan in Clwyd.

By the late fourteenth century the great age of the castle was over. The wane of feudalism, the financial problems facing the Crown, and the increasing expense of meeting both the demands of warfare and the follies of fashion in stone all contributed to this decline. The aristocracy began to be drawn by the attractions of greater comfort, while the rising gentry, who had never lived in castles, flaunted their new-found wealth by erecting more modest fortified manor houses. Buildings of this type had in fact been in existence for some time, one of the earliest being Stokesay in Salop (SO 436817), but it was in the fourteenth century that they really came into their own. Permission had to be obtained from the Crown before the house could be fortified with battlements. Almost five hundred 'licences to crenellate' were granted, but given that some people, then as now, did not care to apply for planning permission, the true number was probably in excess of this figure.

The term 'moated settlement' embraces a wealth of forms, and it is only the presence of the encircling moat which confers a common identity upon these diverse habitations. Most of them, however, were manor houses or farms owned by the smaller landowners. About 5,500 have been identified, some two thirds of which were constructed between 1200 and 1325, but this is a conservative estimate: some sites are difficult to detect because the moats have been filled in, converted into ornamental bodies of water, or put to various other uses. Moats can be confused with fishponds, and many were indeed employed as such. Since the degree of protection afforded was generally more psychological than material, it is not unreasonable to conclude that considerations other than defence also inspired the digging of the moats. They served to protect the farm's livestock against wild animals, and if the settlement lay on the edge of a royal forest, the moat excluded the protected deer, which could not by law be restrained from feeding as they pleased if they gained access to stores and crops. Moats may have been useful as a source of water for livestock and in case of fire. Finally, they conferred a measure of prestige upon the owner of the house, and were sometimes part of an integrated plan designed to show off the manor to its best advantage, as at Kirby Muxloe in Leicestershire (SK 524046).

The distribution of moated settlements is an interesting one, but its underlying reasons are complex and incompletely understood. Since the list of sites so far compiled no doubt falls short of the real total, the distribution maps produced reflect the uneven pattern of research activity across the country. More than five hundred sites have been identified in each of the counties of Essex and Suffolk alone, but only a handful are known to exist in certain other counties, notably Northumberland, Cumbria, Devon and Cornwall. The current figure for the whole of Wales is less than 150, which might be explained in terms of a need for more substantial defences, although in its history of fortified buildings Wales is much more akin to England than to Scotland and Ireland. In these unsettled kingdoms defensive structures continued to be built long after the age of the castle had passed, but in Wales more peaceful conditions prevailed and tower-houses, like the Old Rectory at Angle, Dyfed (SM 866030), were much rarer than in Ireland, Scotland or the northern border counties of England, where the scarcity of moated settlements may indeed relate to a continued necessity for stronger residences manifested in pele towers, barmkins and bastles (p. 192).

Consequently, with respect to south-east Britain it is necessary to consider other, non-military factors which played a part in influencing the distribution of moated settlements. Particularly significant were the nature and pattern of regional agricultural colonization and the prevailing social and tenurial structures. In both Wales and England moats are most common in the lowland districts. One of the best-known Welsh examples is Hen Gwrt at Llantilio Crossenny in Gwent (SO 396151), the manor house of the bishops of Llandaff. In spite of its defences this building was overwhelmed during Glyndŵr's rebellion, to be rebuilt in the sixteenth century as a hunting lodge in Raglan Castle Red Deer Park. In England, moats are most common in lowland clay areas, especially eastern England and the west Midlands. A clay subsoil and bedrock naturally assisted moat construction. Furthermore, the distribution of moated sites is similar to that of medieval parks, particular concentrations being apparent in districts of poor soils which had only recently been cleared of trees and colonized. For example, there are many moated sites upon those infertile, heavy or ill-drained soils of Worcestershire and Warwickshire where the face of the country had remained well wooded until medieval assarting within former royal forests and other woodland areas allowed a pattern of late settlement to develop. Where the system of land tenure was based upon freemen, and large manors were either rare or had been broken up, conditions were similarly conducive to the establishment of individual farms, many of which acquired a moat. Such was the case in Lincolnshire, where some three hundred moated settlements have been identified.

Rural settlement

It is difficult, for several reasons, to write briefly but accurately about medieval rural settlement. The older models and generalizations based upon over-simplified classifications of form and presumed origin have recently been challenged by a wealth of immensely detailed local studies whose wider significance has yet to be assessed. Few attempts have been made to bridge the gap with truly integrated regional works recognizing the essential diversity, dynamism and complexity of rural settlement, treating it within the context of natural features, land use, social organization, tenurial arrangements, demographic and cultural evolution, and prevailing patterns of colonization. The subject is indeed kaleidoscopic, involving as it does so many aspects of the physical and human environments, unified within the regional *milieux* which confer distinction upon particular places and give character to individual landscapes.

The conception of the English village as a solid, unchanging, familiar and, by implication, more or less thoroughly understood element of the traditional scene is almost embarrassingly inadequate. In many villages the church clock does indeed appear to be stuck at ten to three, and although the immemorial elms are alas no more, and the manor house conceals its ancient core behind more modern and often less engaging accretions, a sense of timelessness seems to permeate the scene. But in most cases the occupants of the medieval settlement, if they could return, would recognize few if any of the buildings, not even the odd surviving medieval house, prettified by an adventitious population in accordance with eclectic modern visions of rurality. These medieval inhabitants, visiting once again the place of their birth, would as often as not be in grave danger of losing themselves in a street plan alien to them, and in certain instances they might even fail to find the site of the village at all. All these elements were liable to change in response to evolving physical, social and economic circumstances. Some villages moved, shrank or wasted away, never to recover; others continued in various ways the intricate process of development which had begun in Saxon times or even before, perhaps incorporating planned elements, or expanding into towns or being engulfed by them.

It is equally hazardous to draw conclusions from the village plan, for which no really satisfactory descriptive – let alone explanatory – classifications have been devised. Street plans are a classic case of 'equifinality', where comparable structures have evolved in different districts at widely separated periods for radically contrasting reasons. Nor is it easy to describe the settlement patterns of the various regions of England and Wales using such terms as nucleated or dispersed, primary or secondary settlement, which incorporate necessarily arbitrary divisions between village, hamlet and farm. The whole field of rural settlement geography still awaits the construction of a theoretical basis. To be successful, such challenging research will have to take account of all these problems and examine rural settlement in a truly integrated fashion, taking account of all these factors at an appropriate spatial scale.

What then remains of the landscape of medieval rural settlement? The visible survivals are inevitably a mere fraction of the hidden landscape, which can often be revealed only by meticulous analysis of documents, maps and aerial photographs, and ultimately by the use of archaeological techniques. The vast majority of medieval villages were not created at a particular time and preserved unchanged in the visible landscape there-after; rather, the Middle Ages contributed to a continuous process of settlement change still going on today. The identification and assessment of this contribution are made even more difficult because we know so little about the appearance of medieval villages. By and large only the more elaborate buildings, constructed of stone, such as churches, manor houses and the occasional barn (for example the magnificent tithe barn at Bradford-on-Avon, Wiltshire), have survived. The peasant hovels of mud, timber and thatch had to be rebuilt at short intervals because they decayed and collapsed, so it is hardly surprising that they have failed to last through the centuries in the same way.

In spite of these problems, sufficient fragments of the landscape of medieval settlement can be retrieved and assembled by those with the necessary skill and patience. It would be wrong to give the impression that the lineaments of medieval settlement have been irretrievably lost in the flux and change of intervening centuries. One of the most remarkable themes in the landscape of England and Wales is that of continuity; but this quality is often manifested most strongly not in those features which are generally considered (often for aesthetic or emotional reasons) to represent the unshakeable roots of our heritage, but rather in seemingly insignificant, indirect and perhaps unexpected ways. Time and again it is the ordinary as opposed to the exceptional or illustrious which speaks most eloquently of the past, both in terms of people and places, and which weaves the really telling threads into the fabric of the landscape.

The reconstruction of the medieval rural landscape requires careful attention to detail, both in the field and in the record office, and a high degree of versatility in assessing the evidence. As a brief illustration, five complementary approaches to the study of rural settlement may be mentioned.

The first source of information is provided by those settlements which were either created or significantly altered during the Middle Ages, although the sequence of the changes is in many instances very uncertain. Recent research has challenged the belief that the process of nucleation was largely restricted to earlier Saxon times except in those districts where new villages were formed as part of the medieval colonization movement (as along the fenland margin in Lincolnshire), or that dispersed patterns were either very ancient (as in south-west England) or a phenomenon ('secondary dispersal') which followed the earlier creation of villages. Rather, many villages may themselves date from the Middle Ages, when a dispersed pattern (which, far from being a late addition, could have emerged in mid-Saxon times) gave way in the face of new nucleations, while in other regions this dispersion continued as the predominant form. One region is well known for having undergone a major phase of reconstruction, exhibiting to this day a marked degree of planned organization in its villages, and that was the North. It is likely that this development was related to the devastation wrought there by William I in 1068–70, which necessitated a deliberate regrouping and recolonization if the area was to enjoy any measure of prosperity ever again, and provide revenues for the Crown. Here it seems that a policy was adopted of attracting free tenants through the replacement of bondage obligations by a system of rentals, in order to promote the desired recolonization. Within settlements, the scheme produced regular landholding units arranged in partially or wholly organized plans. Some of the apparently planned villages of Durham and Northumberland may date from this time, including some of the 'green' villages, as well as the classic linear villages with ordered patterns of parallel plots arranged on both sides of the street and terminating in back lanes. This form is exemplified by Appleton-le-Moors in North Yorkshire (SE 7387). But it is also possible that the structure of Appleton-le-Moors was the product of a different set of influences, involving some kind of social and tenurial reorganization necessitated by increasing population pressure upon meagre land resources. Such extreme regularity is the exception rather than the rule, but the pattern of narrow strips of individually owned enclosures called tofts (or crofts when they did not incorporate a building plot), separated from the surrounding open fields by the back lane, can be seen elsewhere, for example at Braunston in Northamptonshire (SP 5366), and at Warkworth, Northumberland (p. 205, Figure 40), where the village developed into a borough.

The layout can also be detected, albeit in ghost form, upon the sites of deserted medieval villages, which constitute a second source of knowledge about medieval settlement. The study of abandoned sites might seem strange, since there is rarely anything visible above ground except an isolated church, manor or farm, but the plans preserved in earthworks or crop-marks and visible on aerial photographs are, like the subsurface remains studied by archaeologists, frequently unaltered, since they have not been overlain or disturbed by subsequent developments. The term deserted medieval village is misleading; many of the settlements in question are not deserted. Some are merely shrunken, while others are completely non-existent as visible structures; a good number are not medieval at all, either in origin or in terms of the period of their decline. Finally, there are those which cannot even be labelled as villages. There are probably several thousand sites in England and Wales, many still awaiting discovery, and they should not be automatically regarded as exceptions, or members of a special category; they are common elements in the eventful history of rural settlement.

In spite of these qualifications, it is undoubtedly true that the later Middle Ages were particularly significant for the fortunes of a large number of settlements. The downturn in the medieval economy referred to earlier in this chapter is the general context within which to consider the adversities which beset so many of them at this time. In explaining their demise, the changing relationships between the elements of population, agricultural productivity, agrarian structure and land use, viewed in conjunction with local factors such as the policy of the landowner, come closer to the heart of the matter than dramatic single causes such as the Black Death. The few sites which have been subjected to detailed archaeological research, such as the striking deserted village of Wharram Percy in North Yorkshire (SE 858643), have sufficiently demonstrated that their overall history is far from simple.

The sites of deserted villages have been identified using several types of evidence. Even the seemingly naïve technique of searching out blank areas upon maps of otherwise evenly settled districts can sometimes initiate a profitable line of inquiry. Suggestive field-names, such as 'Town Field', and particular quirks and oddities in the configurations of roads, fields and boundaries may arouse suspicions. But such discoveries are rarely conclusive in themselves. The presence of isolated churches constitutes stronger evidence. In parts of East Anglia, for example, churches which lack attendant villages are not uncommon, having survived depopulation by reason both of their strong fabric and of the desire to maintain the living in order to serve the dispersed community and gather the tithes due to the rector. (Even so, many East Anglian churches seem to have stood alone since they were constructed.) In some cases the old village church has been turned into a chapel serving a nearby manor house, the group being surrounded by the earthworks of the former settlement, as at Statfold in Staffordshire (SK 238071). Examination of the area around the church can often help in the discovery of a deserted settlement by revealing the presence of trackways, ridge-and-furrow, or a pattern of fields reminiscent of the crofts and piecemeal enclosures associated with villages. The immediate vicinity of the church at Kilpeck in Hereford and Worcester (SO 445305) displays a good selection of these features. The existence of substantial earthworks may render the exercise comparatively simple, but in many instances only indistinct traces of occupation can be seen. Village desertion associated with emparking often resulted in the total clearance of the medieval settlement except for the church, which was left on its own in the newly created park. In some cases the village was abandoned in medieval times while in others it was finally demolished by an eighteenth- or nineteenth-century landlord who wished to landscape his estate (pp. 245 and 247). Many of the most important clues are discernible only from the air, as aerial photography can pick out surface irregularities, ridge-and-furrow, soil-marks and crop-marks which are invisible from the ground (Figure 31). Analysis of the various superimposed elements may help to establish a chronology for the evolution and desertion of the settlement. Detailed examination of the components from ground level is also necessary in order to explore their interrelationships and to piece together the village plan. But even where it is possible to study all these aspects, the actual cause and timing of the desertion may remain a mystery unless documentary research and archaeological investigation are also carried out.

The creation and subsequent expansion of villages or their contraction to the point of total disappearance represent only the extremes of fortune which settlements experienced. More subtle changes also occurred, and a third line of attack with respect to medieval settlements is to study the qualitative metamorphoses they underwent. This can be attempted by examining the changing form and arrangement of the individual components in the overall structure. Generalization is difficult and often dangerous owing to lack of knowledge of the medieval morphology and to the problem of equifinality; but repeated elements do occur, relating to different periods, and particular formations can be recognized which reveal something of the history of the village. The pattern of buildings, tofts, open spaces and streets developed in relation to such factors as demographic history, economic basis, tenurial organization and the influence and intentions of the lord. Villages often preserve the remnants of several past episodes, or of one dominant trend. For example, the plans of some villages reflect dispersal from an original centre to a common-edge, while others are composed of an amalgamation of several sub-units, perhaps associated with a process of subinfeudation. This may go some way to account for certain features of rural settlement which are noticeably common in parts of East Anglia. Here, large villages frequently contain a number of foci rather than a single core, and incorporate moated sites and more than one church, as at Icklingham in Suffolk (TL 7772). At Swaffham Prior in Cambridgeshire (TL 568639) two churches actually share the same churchyard, but the reasons for this are not known: perhaps rivalry between local lords played a part. The churches of the adjacent parishes of Alvingham and North Cockerington in Lincolnshire also stand together in a single churchyard (TF 368913).

In these and other respects the buildings themselves, especially parish churches, offer a fourth avenue of research. The church is frequently the oldest building in the village, and its position in terms of site and situation, the shape and arrangement of the churchyard, the history of the building expressed in its archaeology and architecture, and the wealth of detail which informed study reveals can all help to unravel the complexities of the surrounding landscape. Particularly important are such considerations as the dedication (which can sometimes be used to ascertain the time of foundation), and the original status of the church (some began as chapels connected to a mother church), which can assist in the elucidation of the origins and development of the local settlement pattern. The position of the church in the village and the relationship of the churchyard to property boundaries may give some indication of the respective dates of origin of church and settlement, or indicate a territorial shift of one or the other in association with a reorganization of the village at some period in its history. Since the principal entrance to the church was made on the south side, the presence of a main door elsewhere, especially on the north, should be investigated. Often this alteration was made as a result of a change in the location of the village.

Most churches are of course singular landscape features in themselves, reflecting local geology, regional cultures, the diffusion of architectural styles and the location and accessibility of a district with reference to prevailing social fashions and artistic taste. Whether one lingers among the stately structures of the Jurassic stone belt, admires the Perpendicular towers of Somerset, enjoys the homely spires of Kent or Sussex, wonders at the stupendous 'wool' churches of the Cotswolds and East Anglia or experiences with awe the chill of the granite edifices of Dartmoor, the thrill of the English parish church – each one is unique and has something of special interest – is such that once caught, few enthusiasts can pass any church without taking a look. Others are discouraged by the plethora of architectural terms, but these are only one aspect of church study, and for the purposes of understanding the landscape are a means rather than an end. A basic understanding of the elements of church architecture, combined with an eye for significant detail and the interrelationship of different forms within a regional context, can sometimes reveal the changing fortunes of a parish in a way which is impossible to convey in clinical technical terminology. The stories of individual churches express countless variations upon a familiar theme: the replacement of the Saxon building – erected perhaps on an ancient pagan site – by the Norman church, the addition of the aisles in the twelfth or thirteenth centuries; the chancel rebuilt in the fourteenth century and the west tower added, together with a west door; the remodelling during the fifteenth century (reflecting local prosperity), involving an extra stage to the tower and new Perpendicular windows; the appearance of a Jacobean pulpit, elaborate monuments or a special chapel to the family of the lord of the manor; the west gallery for the village orchestra: these and many other elements enshrine the history of continuity and change in a tiny corner of England, and remind us of the artistic capabilities and imagination of people who lived during centuries we are sometimes tempted to dismiss as backward and unenlightened. Such achievements cannot be equalled today, for all our apparent advancement and sophistication; and modern communities are hard pressed to maintain their churches. Those who rail against the Victorian restorers should remember that the nineteenth-century campaign, whether to modern taste or not, was necessitated by negligence in the seventeenth and eighteenth centuries, and without it many churches would have ceased to exist.

The importance of the regional context needs stressing, not only for churches but with respect to the whole rural landscape, and a fifth approach to settlement is provided by the integrated regional portrait, synthesizing the various components of society and environment within particular geographical frameworks and relating them to each other and the wider world. Such studies can lend colour, depth and meaning to the bewildering diversity of settlement forms, gathering together individual cases and qualifying generalizations. Take for example western Dyfed, the old county of Pembrokeshire, in south-west Wales. Despite the intricacy of the landscape occasioned by complex geological structures (exploited to great scenic effect at the coast), by erosional history and cultural evolution, there is a broad distinction between the northern and southern districts. The northern part of the peninsula lies at the end of the huge sweep of Lower Palaeozoic rocks which comes down from North Wales, giving rise to Mynydd Presely and the surrounding uplands, now greatly eroded to form undulating plateaux. The more prominent features are associated with igneous masses. In contrast, the gentle terrain of the south is composed of folded Upper Palaeozoic rocks, denuded and cut by a series of planation surfaces. The high angles of dip encountered in the Hercynian structures and the narrow outcrops produced as a result concertina the sequences which, further east, surround the South Wales coalfield and flank the coastal route from the southern borderland.

The cultural landscapes of the two districts reflect this contrast (Figure 29). The Welshry of the more rugged north displays an essentially dispersed pattern of settlement, though not so scattered as in other Welsh districts, the small hamlets of adjacent farms reflecting the tendency of the free clansmen, cultivating an infield-outfield system, to live close to each other in small nucleations. The churches are small and simple, with bellcotes rather than towers, and the place-names are dominantly Welsh. The south, on the other hand, less windswept and more fertile, looks so reminiscent of lowland England in its settlement patterns and field systems that it has long been referred to as 'Little England beyond Wales'. The beginnings of this split could well lie in the earliest times, but the crucial

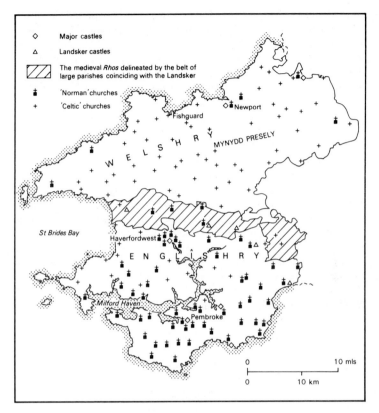

Figure 29. Medieval Pembrokeshire

phase of cultural differentiation occurred in the twelfth century. At this time the Anglo-Normans penetrated south Pembrokeshire, having thrust their way along the coastal lowland from the east. The military conquerors exploited the opportunities afforded by the physique of southern Dyfed, notably the ria of Milford Haven, to consolidate their hold. The quality of the land facilitated the creation of a lowland agricultural economy. The Norman lords undoubtedly took many Anglo-Saxons with them into Pembrokeshire, and Flemish settlers were also brought in to provide labour. Over a hundred villages and hamlets were established in the Englishry, in association with motte-and-bailey castles and a wealth of English place-name elements. The churches acquired large towers, suggesting a defensive function; and a range of other strongholds featured in this militarized landscape. The manorial system prevailed, and was reflected in the arrangement of villages and surrounding fields, but an important role was played by individual colonization. Consequently, in addition to nucleated villages, surrounded in some cases by patterns of enclosures based on the strips of former open fields (Robeston Wathen, SN 0815; Cosheston, SN 0003, Figure 27), there are offshoots such as Carew Newton (SN 046046), settled from the castle village of Carew nearby, as well as single farmsteads on freehold estates granted in return for military service (Flemington, SN 054020). There is also evidence for a generation of later assarts (Moor Farms, near Manorbier, SS 0498).

The boundary between the Welshry and the Englishry was demarcated by a line known as the *Landsker*, a word of Norse origin meaning a frontier (Figure 29). Its precise course in medieval times is not fully known, but its significance for the cultural landscape of Pembrokeshire was considerable, for it functioned as a distinct linguistic and cultural divide. A number of castles were built along it, but they were never integrated into an overall strategy against the Welsh, and they ceased to mark the military front line after the Anglo-Normans, assisted by Flemish immigrants, succeeded in colonizing districts to the north of the Landsker. The zone of debatable country (*Rhos*) which stretched across central Pembrokeshire as a kind of no-man's-land remained for many years the scene of border warfare, which militated against secure inhabitation and peaceful cultivation. Perhaps the belt of unusually large parishes which accompanies the route of the Landsker is a reflection of this.

Many other elements of the patterns established at this time have survived to the present day. Of particular interest are those features of the landscape which recall the newcomers' attempts to impose their own forms of organization upon the indigenous culture. In the district around Pembroke it is possible to identify a special kind of Anglo-Norman landscape which adapted and incorporated original Welsh features that were never fully eliminated. The Flemish immigrants also left their mark on the social character of the region. These curious mixtures, together with the sense of frontier and the visible evidence for the various phases of colonization, help to bring the landscape of the Anglo-Normans to life in a way unrivalled in those parts of England where later developments have obscured the original picture.

Towns

The towns of medieval England and Wales, except for a handful of places at the very top of the urban hierarchy, like London, Bristol, Norwich and York, were small settlements with populations numbered in hundreds rather than thousands. They were intimately related to their rural hinterlands, performing generally unspecialized functions based upon marketing, trade and the provision of services. With the economic growth of the twelfth and thirteenth centuries, many of them came to enjoy considerable prosperity, but their essential vulnerability was revealed, often ruthlessly, in the later medieval period. Commercial decline, competition from neighbouring centres, depopulation, fire or physical changes involving the courses of rivers or the erosion of coastlines could all adversely affect the life of a town, or even kill it completely. But in the early Middle Ages the threat of such misfortunes did little to diminish the optimism and confidence of those who sought to promote urban growth or to benefit from the wealth associated with towns.

While acknowledging the value of the generalizations made about medieval townscapes, studies at the individual level have revealed a considerable diversity in the origins, structures, plans and development of towns. Several classes have been identified, such as planted or new towns, planned urban settlements, and towns created from expanded villages. But such types do not make up the mutually exclusive categories of an all-embracing classification, and in practice the labels are sometimes hard to apply. Most towns displayed some element of planning, if the term is taken to imply the existence of regular structures or layouts, particularly those which were deliberately created. Even if they were not consciously promoted, regular patterns could still evolve under the influence of social or economic forces operating upon particular sites. A large number of additions to the fabric of towns initiated by individuals or institutions assumed a distinctive appearance stemming from a degree of co-ordination which fell short of full-scale planning. Many of these projects could be considered as plantations, since, although the sites were not virgin, the existing settlements were insignificant in absolute or relative terms. On the other hand, not all planted towns possessed layouts which were created *in toto* at birth, and few in fact exhibited the gridiron plans popularly associated with them. Finally, much of the planning actually dated back to Saxon and even Roman times, the medieval features being derived from pre-existing frameworks, particularly those which guided later developments through the presence of symmetrical patterns of defences, gates and streets.

In spite of these and other complications relating to the use of the terms 'planned' and 'planted', a considerable number of towns were indeed started from scratch or promoted from humble origins during the early Middle Ages. Some were laid out at the gates of religious houses, capitalizing on the presence of a shrine: examples include Bury St Edmunds, St Albans, and the appropriately named Newton Abbot. Others were founded by the Crown, the most notable being the towns linked to Edward I's castles in North Wales. Here the commercial and military functions were closely intertwined, the opportunities for trade being stressed as part of a campaign to persuade the Welsh to tolerate the military garrisons in such places as Flint, where the main street of a gridiron town runs directly to the castle. Edward was influenced in the style of his town building by the *bastide* towns of Gascony; and in addition to the Welsh castle towns he played a principal role in the foundation of Kingston upon Hull, Berwick-upon-Tweed (p. 251) and New Winchelsea, which remains the classic example of the gridiron plan.

New Winchelsea owed its creation to the destruction of the old town by marine erosion, and it is ironic that the new settlement decayed later in its turn when the Brede estuary silted up and spoilt its harbour. The layout can be traced in the streets of the part of the town which retains its buildings, and in the pattern of hedges and hollow ways in the deserted section beyond. Defoe reported that 'the ruins are so bury'd, that they have made good corn fields of the streets', Winchelsea being 'rather the skeleton of an ancient city than a real town'. But the history of Winchelsea illustrates the eagerness of town planters to capitalize on the coastwise and export trade by establishing urban settlements upon estuarine and coastal sites. Remains of medieval ports can be seen at several other places, including The Quay at Poole, Dorset, and the waterfront at King's Lynn in Norfolk, with their warehouses and alleys. Inland, river crossings offered similarly promising locations. Those towns which commanded a good site with respect to both trading routes and rival centres profited handsomely from the trade carried on along their bustling wharves and in the markets and inns. Stratford-upon-Avon and comparably placed river towns were particularly successful in filling their burgage plots. Some of the most spectacular developments in urban morphology and fabric took place in towns associated with the cloth trade. Totnes in Devon preserves many features from its heyday, the clear line of the medieval walls enclosing a Norman motte with its shell-keep, surrounded by some interesting medieval buildings. The church was completely rebuilt in the fifteenth century, recalling the years when Totnes blossomed into a flourishing woollen-manufacturing town. One of the most splendid late medieval townscapes of all is that of the cloth town of Lavenham, Suffolk.

Many of the landscape features of medieval towns were related to the social structures and territorial organization associated with borough status. A borough was a settlement which had been afforded privileges in self-government, trade and landholding. These jealously guarded rights were either traditional, having been enjoyed 'time out of mind', or enshrined in a charter granted by the king or a lord (lay or ecclesiastical). Among the most important aspects of borough status were the burgage rights, under which burgesses held urban plots on payment of fixed money rents as a contribution to the communal borough tax. Since the burgesses paid for their privileges in this way, and because these towns were often busy trading and commercial centres, with markets and fairs, boroughs constituted potentially rich sources of profits derived from rents and tolls. The burgages generally took the form of long, narrow strips of land (garths) which extended back from restricted street frontages to form gardens or plots for livestock before terminating in back lanes or other boundaries (p. 205). Successful towns had all their burgage plots taken up, and the gridiron plans are often found to date from the confident years of the early twelfth century when the founders anticipated little difficulty in achieving this objective. New Sarum (Salisbury) was one of these (p. 202). Even when the medieval buildings have been replaced, or hidden behind later façades, the property boundaries of the burgages tend to persist, clearly recognizable in the modern townscape (p. 205). In some towns, such as Thame, the plots extended out over the nearby open fields and took on the reversed-S shape of the selions.

A second important influence on the town plan was the market. A market town was granted a charter which provided for a weekly market and an annual fair. Frequently the acquisition of a charter marked the first stage in the development from purely rural status to that of a full borough, and in the course of the thirteenth century some 2,500 market charters were conferred upon communities throughout England. The principal buildings of these growing settlements were the market cross, the market house or guildhall, and the shops and shambles, which were stalls hired out on market days for the sale of fish and meat. Markets were held not only in market places but in other open spaces such as churchyards, particularly on saints' days. (Indeed, all sorts of activities, including church ales and other high-spirited celebrations and festivals, took place in and around churches during medieval times which would horrify many modern churchgoers.) The shape of the principal market place was partly determined by the origin and early form of the town itself, and the market in its turn often influenced the pattern of later development. Triangular market areas frequently grew up near the gates of abbeys, as at Dorchester-on-Thames (p. 132). Some derived their configurations from the patterns created by the convergence of routeways. Others were laid out beyond the outer walls of castles: the market place at Devizes, for example, grew in two stages, extending from its initial site into the bailey of the castle, whose outlines are reflected in the plan.

Market places were often comparatively late additions to towns, and new areas had to be cleared to accommodate them. This process produced the bulged, cigar-shaped main street so characteristic of the many linear town plans produced in the Middle Ages. The desirability of a market location frequently prompted the encroachment of buildings on to the market place itself, creating a block in the middle of the street, or obscuring the area altogether, as in the case of Hereford. Churches also appeared in market places, particularly in new towns where the demand for additional places of worship at some distance from the original parish church upset established parish patterns. These new churches therefore tended to be mere chapels of ease, identifiable not only by their position but also by their lack of a graveyard.

Town defences, although generally in a fragmentary state today, are sometimes very ancient. Medieval builders often incorporated Roman walls or used material from them, and Roman masonry can still be seen in the medieval walls of several towns, notably Exeter. Judging from records of murage grants, a good deal of wall building took place during the thirteenth century, but this activity declined as improved methods of attack rendered such defences of limited use. Some of the finest medieval urban defences are those at York, Southampton, Chester, and the Welsh castle towns such as Caernarvon and Conwy. Even when the walls no longer exist, their former presence can sometimes be detected in the town plan, or in boundaries and street-names. The gates were often the most elaborate parts of the defences (Bargate, Southampton) but have suffered from being widened in deference to modern traffic, which has not always prevented heavy lorries from ploughing into and partly demolishing them. Occasionally the gates were actually detached from the main line of the defences and placed on a bridge, as at Warkworth, Northumberland (p. 202), and Monmouth, Gwent (p. 261 and Figure 61). The clergy often took particular care to protect themselves, not so much from the threat of outsiders, but more directly from the hostility of the adjacent populace; the palace of the Bishop of Bath and Wells was moated, walled and castellated. Such a state of organized security contrasted sharply with those poorer communities who lived in mean extra-mural suburbs positioned outside the defences of many towns. These districts were the setting for a motley collection of undesirable or unpleasant trades and functions such as tanning and fulling which were excluded from the town by the intra-mural dwellers.

Sites

Braunton Great Field, Devon

The Great Field at Braunton is well known as a rare survival of the once widespread open field landscape, preserving for posterity the pattern of curved arable strips which accord with the popular image of medieval agricultural practice. Of course, the presence of former open fields can be detected in many parts of the country by drawing upon a range of evidence, both field and documentary (p. 153ff.). Only at a handful of places, however, can such fields be directly examined, having weathered subsequent alterations well enough to bear some resemblance to their original state. Braunton Great Field, still unenclosed, claims a place in this highly exclusive category. The presence of narrow hedged fields on its north side (next to the road to Saunton) suggests that the process of enclosure of the strips was indeed begun here at an early date but was never completed. Braunton is all the more interesting because at one time it was thought that open fields never existed in this region of England, the Great Field being explained away as a relatively recent reclamation from the estuary of the River Taw.

But if Braunton Great Field is famous on these grounds, it should be equally well known as an example of the uncertainties and misunderstandings which pervade the study of the open fields, and the hazards which surround their reconstruction when, as is usual, documentary evidence is scanty and present appearances deceptive.

The Great Field occupies an area of about 350 acres on the south-west side of Braunton, once a large and prosperous nucleated village founded upon agriculture and looking quite different from the visual manifestations of retirement, recreation and road traffic which characterize it today. The Great Field (Figure 30), which is crossed by public footpaths from Braunton, is made up of strips (with the curved edges which are generally taken as proof of medieval origin), grouped into shotts or furlongs, and separated by balks (or, in local terminology, *landsherds*; cf. the *landscars* or *landskers* in the open fields of Laugharne, Dyfed, and the *lawnsheds* of the Isle of Portland). The Close Rolls for 1324 record the existence in the Great Field of strips held in an intermixed, scattered pattern of ownership. Although the twentieth century has witnessed a considerable degree of amalgamation of the strips, reducing the number of individual farmers, the Great Field was still so fragmented in the 1930s that the Air Ministry withdrew a plan to turn it into an aerodrome, deterred by the spectre of a legal nightmare. It is now the only vestige of the open fields which, judging by local enclosure boundaries, once covered

Figure 30. Braunton Great Field in the summer of 1953, looking north-east

much larger areas of the district, particularly to the east on Braunton Down.

A number of problems make it difficult to interpret this strange remnant, the very survival of which is to some extent suspicious. The modern form of the Great Field, together with the recent practices and modes of organization relating to it, are not reliable guides to its use in medieval times. Indeed, it would not be surprising if our medieval forebears – for whom, incidentally, the very word 'strip' was unknown (having been invented by historians) – found the appearance of today's field decidedly unfamiliar. One only needs to consider the degree of strip consolidation, the types of crops grown, and the changing natures of agricultural techniques, organization and ownership to appreciate this. Furthermore, the rules and conventions for the working of particular open fields are often far from clear, and cannot necessarily be discovered merely by examining the landscape. As explained on p. 153, the internal fragmentation of open (subdivided) fields into strips does not of itself prove the former existence of rules of common cultivation (including enforced, agreed rotations) and rights of common grazing. In the late nineteenth century, according to local people, the Great Field was thrown open to common gleaning and grazing after the harvest; but the nature of the medieval arrangements, particularly regarding the existence of rotations, remains obscure.

Even the formal landscape is plagued by uncertainties. For example, it is often assumed that the balks are original medieval features marking the boundaries between strip-parcels. (The term *landsherd* has been derived from the Old English *landscearu*, boundary.) In view of the custom which prevailed in parts of Devon of ploughing the strips flat, it is certainly tempting to assume that here the balks took the place of double furrows as boundaries, but this raises two further unresolved questions, namely the age of the balks themselves – some scholars believe them to be relatively modern, not medieval at all – and the origin, function and regional distribution of ridge-and-furrow (see pp. 155–6). It has been claimed that since balks as strip boundaries would have been excessively wasteful, they were either headlands, common ways giving access to the strips, or simply lengths of grass used for grazing: certainly they could not have been beneficial to the arable, as they harboured weeds and rats.

In short, it is dangerous to assume that what we see at Braunton Great Field today is anything other than an eroded and rather eccentric portion of an open (subdivided) field, which in terms of form gives us a tantalizing glimpse of a medieval landscape, but cannot be taken as a reliable record of medieval agriculture in a functional sense. Nevertheless, one direct and in some respects more immediate question can be posed: why was the Great Field never enclosed?

The Somerset Levels: the medieval landscape
The extensive low-lying tract of the Somerset Levels is the greatest marshland region of the west of England. Until medieval times, the Levels were generally regarded as a place to be avoided, although a range of traditional economic activities were based upon the resources of fish, fowl, rushes, reeds, turf, brushwood, timber and pasture lands. The early inhabitants had responded to the adversities of the fen either through sensitive adjustment to the prevailing conditions, most notably in the case of the Iron Age lake villages of Glastonbury and Meare, or by confining settlement to the dry-points, a strategy adopted by the Anglo-Saxon colonists (reflected in the occurrence of place-names ending in *-ey*, derived from the Old English for 'island', especially in the sense of an island in a marsh or floodplain) and by the early Christian monks, who found the Levels highly suitable for their desired life of solitude and isolation. In these ways adaptation, adjustment and toleration served to define the human response: there was no real attempt to *change* the natural landscape.

The Levels are underlain by a complex sequence of deposits through which protrude a number of 'islands' (at one time literally so in times of flood). These are composed of outcrops of Keuper, Rhaetic and Liassic rocks (Brent Knoll, Glastonbury, and the Pennard and Polden Hills), some of the lower islands such as Chedzoy and Sowy being capped by the problematic sands and gravels known as the Burtle Beds, which are believed to be estuarine or marine deposits dating from the last (pre-Devensian) interglacial. The present aspect of the Levels, however, has been conditioned largely by the Flandrian rise in sea level. The pattern of freshwater peats, alluvial deposits and marine clays was determined by the rates of sedimentation in the river valleys in relation to sea-level rise. The development of peat has been especially pronounced since the initially rapid pace of post-glacial sea-level change levelled off and was overtaken by the accumulation of sediment. Fluvial deposition in the sluggish streams led to the raising of river beds and to the formation of levées, natural banks built up along the edges of the channels. Finally, a combination of processes during the late stages of the transgression created a belt of thicker marine clays near the present coast. It is important to remember that the position of the modern coastline is to a great extent the result of human activity: at the time when the Bronze Age wooden trackways were being constructed amid the regenerating peat in an attempt to combat flooding and maintain the routes between the dry-points, the coastline lay up to several miles further inland than today. This was not because contemporary sea level was higher (indeed, it had not quite reached its present position) but because subsequent reclamation has succeeded in pushing the sea back.

These physical characteristics, in association with certain climatic factors, have given rise to the environmental problem confronting man in the Levels. The surrounding uplands are susceptible to intense rainstorms, which in turn produce sudden increases in stream discharge. The rivers in their natural state, characterized by extremely gentle gradients, were unable to contain and transport the large volumes of water produced by such events in the upper parts of their catchments; furthermore, deposition at their mouths and the raising of bank-full levels in connection with the construction of the levées increased the magnitude of the flooding once the banks were overtopped, since the surrounding floodplains were actually lower than the river channels themselves. The barrier of the coastal clay belt served to exacerbate the problem, as did the frequency of high tides and adverse winds in the Bristol Channel, sea and river water literally colliding at the coast to transform the Levels into a vast lake.

There have been three major phases of drainage and reclamation activity in the Levels, the most recent embracing the period since the Second World War, when it was at last appreciated that improvement of the main rivers held the solution to the problem. But the first assault took place in the Middle Ages, when the great ecclesiastical landowners attempted to regain their grip on lands which were fragmented through encroachment and abused by a combination of overstocking, ill-defined intercommoning arrangements and administrative laxity. The key to the physical transformation lay in the upgrading of ordinary pastures into profitable meadowland capable of producing a hay crop, which in the medieval economy was a valuable source of winter fodder. Especially suitable were the potentially rich alluvial areas surrounding the already prosperous dry-points such as Sowy 'island', on which stand Westonzoyland (ST 3535), Middlezoy and Othery. The flats stretching away to the south and west of Sowy were reclaimed by Glastonbury Abbey in the thirteenth century. The new meadows were protected by walls and crossed by causeways, of which the lines – and some actual sections – survive in the landscape, for example the Burrow Wall (next to the A361 between Othery and the Keuper Marl eminence of Burrow Mump, ST 359305) and Southlake Wall from Burrow Bridge to Pathe (which follows the right bank of the River Parrett upstream before turning north at 375295 as part of a footpath from Stathe to Pathe). At the coast, walls were being built at an even earlier date to keep out the sea and turn areas of the claybelt into protected grazing lands called warths. In Bleadon Level (ST 3256), near the estuary of the River Axe, the 'Old Wall' encloses an area of intricately bounded reclaimed pastures, divided by the drainage ditches known throughout the Levels as rhynes (pronounced 'reens'). Such irregular enclosures and winding ditches distinguish the areas of medieval drainage activity.

Although it would be hard to describe this first phase in the alteration of the Levels as anything more than piecemeal and small-scale, a significant start had been made, and its benefits provided an incentive to further improvement later. The interval, however, was of several centuries, and the assault was not renewed with any conviction until the classic 'age of the improver' arrived, when the landscape of the Somerset Levels underwent another stage in its transformation.

Hampton Gay, Oxfordshire

Many deserted villages leave few traces in the landscape, and the reasons for their failure are often obscure. Sometimes, however, the remains of the settlement are clearly evident not just from aerial photographs but on the ground as well, and in certain cases documentary sources have enabled the causes and chronology of depopulation to be established.

Hampton Gay (SP 486165) lies in the Cherwell valley north of Oxford, situated upon the edge of a gravel terrace within a meander loop of the river. It is a forlorn place in winter, and even the lushness of the summer vegetation is tinged with melancholy. The site is best approached from Shipton-on-Cherwell on a public footpath by the church. This crosses the canal, the river and then the railway to reach the church, ruined manor house and, to the east, the three cottages which are all that is left of Hampton Gay. Manor Farm can be seen a mile away across the fields to the south-east. The mounds, ridges and depressions visible in the pasture field by the church indicate that the village was formerly more extensive, and the pattern of streets, tofts and crofts can be made out (Figure 31).

Figure 31. Hampton Gay. The site of the deserted village viewed from the east. Cows graze among the earthworks which lie between the ruined manor (bottom) and the church (centre). At the top of the picture, beyond the railway line and the River Cherwell, stands Shipton-on-Cherwell church, next to the Oxford Canal

The demographic history of Hampton Gay can be partly reconstructed from documents, mainly taxation surveys, although the incomplete chronology makes the period of the depopulation uncertain. It may have begun before the early fifteenth century, and seems to have continued through the next two hundred years. The manor was held by Osney Abbey, which procured lands and properties from the freeholders, converting the arable into pasture for sheep and cattle, and utilizing the meadows by the river. After the Dissolution, the manor was sold to a local woolgrower, John Barry of Eynsham. During the second half of the sixteenth century the Barry family, living in their Elizabethan mansion at Hampton Gay, continued and indeed accelerated the policies the monks had pursued. Their drive to enclose and engross (i.e. amalgamate farms in order to create larger pastures) prompted riots in 1596, and by the early seventeenth century Hampton Gay was at its lowest ebb. To what extent these enclosures were directly responsible for the depopulation is unclear. A resurgence occurred during the eighteenth and nineteenth centuries, related to changes in agriculture and the working of a paper mill. A map of 1797 shows about ten houses in the main part of the village, and in 1821 there were 86 inhabitants. It might seem reasonable to attribute the perhaps unexpected architectural appearance of the church to this revival, for instead of being medieval, or in a state of decay, the building dates almost entirely from 1767–72; further alterations took place in 1859–60, when it was gothicized. In fact the money for the rebuilding was donated by a minister, and neither the history of the church nor its relationship with the local community is straightforward. Its ecclesiastical status was uncertain, and it operated as an extra-parochial free chapel used in earlier times by the lords of the manor, who paid the minister. But in 1887 the sixteenth-century manor house was abandoned after a fire, the paper mill went bankrupt, and the fortunes of Hampton Gay resumed their downward path. Nevertheless, even today the village has not quite disappeared, so it ought strictly to be termed 'very shrunken' rather than 'deserted'. The irregular pattern of its decline emphasizes the complex phases of waxing and waning often experienced by those settlements which are too simply termed 'D M Vs'.

Newland, Gloucestershire: the church of All Saints

In the most westerly part of Gloucestershire, between the Rivers Severn and Wye, lies the Forest of Dean, a complex syncline of Upper Palaeozoic rocks in the centre of which nestles a small wooded coalfield. The visitor is immediately struck by the dearth, in the core of this district, of medieval churches, and by the general absence of historic settlement of any description. This state of affairs is a direct consequence of the setting aside of Dean, since Saxon times, as a royal forest. The Forest of Dean, with its own laws and customs, was effectively isolated from many of the forces which fashioned the landscape elsewhere. Only in the manors on the edge of this exclusive royal playground, deliberately maintained as waste, did nucleated settlements grow up around medieval churches in anything approaching a conventional fashion. The Church did not gain a foothold in the Forest proper until much later, when squatting led to the establishment of encroachments with growing populations (Figure 48). Then, except for a handful of nineteenth-century churches, this 'desolate, extra-parochial tract of land', where no house of worship '*was* EVER *known*', came to be dominated, as was the South Wales coalfield, by 'Chapel' rather than 'Church'. But even in the peripheral villages, the distinctive legal system, culture and economy of Dean have left their mark. This is particularly noticeable where the exploitation of timber, iron and coal took place in those parts of the Forest adjacent to the unnaturally truncated hinterlands of the surrounding settlements. Indeed, some of these villages maintained close connections with the divisions of the Forest made for purposes of administration and the enforcement of Forest Law. The physical locations, composition and style of buildings, and the former dual economies of the villages reflect these influences, as do many of the churches, which are mostly ancient.

One of the most rewarding of these, although somewhat atypical on account of its architectural richness and later date of foundation, is the 'Cathedral of the Forest', the church of All Saints at Newland (SO 553095). Newland is situated on the western side of the Forest, a mile from the River Wye. It originated in the early thirteenth century in an assart upon land granted by King John to Robert de Wakering, the rector of nearby Clearwell (571080), then called Wellinton, the oldest settlement in the district. The early rectors of the new church were all men of status, which may partly account for the scale and high quality of the building. Also, Newland soon became a place of importance in its own right, empowered after 1283 to draw tithes from all the new assarts in Dean, unless these lay in other parishes. Its name, curiously enough, is still pronounced with the stress on the second syllable. The church lies in a large square churchyard, which, being surrounded by buildings, forms a sort of close; this arrangement prompts the thought that perhaps the founder had ideas of creating some kind of planned borough here. To the north-west is a large and irregular field which may be derived from one of the original clearings. The church itself is a spacious one, with wide aisles separated from the nave by dignified Early English arcades; two chapels were added to the basic plan *c.* 1300, and a third, in the Perpendicular style, about a century later. This chantry was founded to support the 'morrow mass' priest, who was bound 'to goe from oone Smythe to an other & from oon mynyng pitte to an other ... twise every weke to saye theym gospells.' The glorious pinnacled upper stage of the tower is late Decorated work of considerable distinction (Figure 32).

Figure 32. The church of All Saints, Newland

The church's collection of monuments reflects the historical geography both of Newland itself and of the Forest of Dean in general. It includes a thirteenth-century effigy of a priest, believed to be Robert de Wakering himself, and the striking tomb of Jenkin Wyrall (d. 1457), one of the foresters-of-fee who were charged to protect the Vert and the Venison. He is dressed in contemporary hunting costume. A flat slab in the south aisle is incised with the figure of a bowbearer attired in the manner of the early seventeenth century; it was the bowbearers' duty to attend upon the king when he hunted in the Forest. The most famous monument, however, is the uniquely interesting 'miner's brass', which depicts a medieval Free Miner in traditional garb, equipped for the winning of ore. He carries a hod and pick, and apparently holds between his teeth a stick with a candle attached to it. In the churchyard are some good 'Forest' headstones, embellished with stylized emblems and quaintly expressive carved faces, but they are now alas largely cleared away and stacked up against the wall.

Corfe Castle, Dorset

Corfe Castle looms spectacularly upon one of the finest natural defensive sites in England. The Corfe River, flowing north to Poole Harbour, has cut a deep gap in the east-west ridge of the Purbeck Hills. The place-name

'Corfe', like so many in this district, has a topographical meaning; it embodies the Anglo-Saxon word *corf* (a pass), derived from *ceorfan* (to cut). Closer inspection of the cleft shows that the Corfe River actually consists of two streams which join just to the north of the castle, having created *two* valleys, with part of the ridge remaining between them as a conical hill in the middle of the pass. Thus Corfe Castle occupies a remarkable seat, crowning a residual mass of chalk which falls away sharply to the Steeple Brook on the west, the Byle Brook on the east, and their confluence as the Corfe River on the north. The castle was virtually impregnable except on the south side, where the ground slopes more gently towards the village, and it was secure from attack so long as no artillery could reach it from the escarpment to the east and west. Situated in this commanding position, it could dominate the Isle of Purbeck, from 'Egdon Heath', north of the Purbeck Hills, to the fertile valley and coastlands on the south.

Corfe provides an excellent example of Norman castle design, although it was built in several stages, possibly developing from a pre-Conquest fortress. The Domesday Book's 'Wareham Castle in the Manor of Kingston' is usually understood to refer to Corfe, and of William I's castle the wall of the inner bailey remains. The keep and part of the outer bailey quickly followed, *c*. 1100, and a century later King John strengthened the defences, walled the separate, second bailey beyond the inner ward, and built an unfortified courtyard house for himself to the east of the keep. The thirteenth century witnessed the consolidation of the potentially vulnerable village side, the digging of a ditch south of the inner ward, and the surrounding of the outer bailey by a boundary wall. The fortifications were thereby completed. The castle, following the lie of the land, is boot-shaped, with the leg (first ward) extending from the village and the toe (second ward) pointing westwards; the ankle and heel contain the inner bailey. The present chaotic ruination is mainly the consequence of a deliberate attempt to blow the castle up when it offered resistance to Parliamentary forces during the Civil War (Figure 33).

The village has also declined in its fortunes. In its heyday it was the centre of the Purbeck marble industry, producing a decorative stone which became fashionable in the thirteenth century, particularly as material for Early English shafts and piers in churches and cathedrals. The roofs of Corfe village are still covered with the beautiful grey Purbeck slates, also quarried locally – the sunken lanes of the locality bear witness to the labours of the stone hauliers. (Two misnomers should be noted here. Purbeck marble is not true marble – a metamorphic rock – but a shelly limestone which could carry a high polish. Similarly, Purbeck slate is not

Figure 33. Corfe Castle from the village

real metamorphic slate, but a fissile sedimentary rock, mainly a slabby limestone, which could be split by exposing it to frost.) Although Corfe was incorporated as a town in the sixteenth century and returned two M.P.s until 1832, it lost much of its importance with the passing of the stone trade. Clues to the settlement's former status can be traced among the buildings, but Corfe is now an unpretentious village, albeit a highly picturesque one.

Bamburgh Castle, Northumberland

The key strategic gateway from England into Scotland is the coastal corridor which lies to the east of the Cheviots, in the zone where the modern boundary descends from the central watershed to follow the River Tweed. The natural and cultural landscapes of Northumberland are in many respects transitional between the two countries. The Carboniferous Limestone Series of Northumberland differs from that found elsewhere in England and displays certain affinities with the Scottish Lower Carboniferous. Differential erosion of these beds has produced a more complex pattern of relief in the region of the 'gate' than might at first appear, particularly where the resistant Fell Sandstone forms a double escarpment as a result of strike faulting, or where the crags of the Whin Sill (p. 53) and its associated dolerite intrusions interrupt the rough green and brown pastures of the eastern lowland. The use of these rocks, particularly the current-bedded sandstones, in buildings whose architectural styles incorporate a number of distinctly Scottish motifs further enhances the sense of marchland.

The historic significance of this long-disputed region as a fusion of cultural influences consequent upon its strategic role is most clearly appreciated in its magnificent heritage of fortifications of several types. The pattern created by these and the various battle sites is closely related to the arrangement of the ridges, vales and river gaps. The coastal sill offers perhaps the finest militarized landscape in Britain, the beautiful coast, with its sudden dolerite cliffs, lines of dunes and stunted trees, contributing a grand melancholy to the scene. The visual evidence for centuries of insecurity, violence and war is everywhere. Although Northumberland contains one of the earliest examples of the change from castles to fortified houses (Aydon), strongholds continued to be built long after other parts of England had relaxed into the more leisurely construction of manor houses. Keep-like buildings known as pele (or peel) towers were being designed in the thirteenth century and were still deemed necessary in the seventeenth. By the late Middle Ages the term was being used in connection with a wide range of defensible constructions. Barmkins (or barmekins) consisted of a ward or walled place of refuge associated with a stronghold. Bastles were fortified farmhouses which incorporated the function of a barmkin by providing accommodation for both people (on the upper floor) and livestock (below). The upper storey was reached by an external stone stairway (which probably superseded the earlier device of a movable ladder); the lower room was often covered by a barrel-vault (Hole, near Bellingham, NY 867846) and guarded by a small, strong door. Some larger houses were also referred to as bastles.

Bastles are found in areas of predominantly dispersed upland settlement in the frontier zone. Their construction characterized the late sixteenth and early seventeenth centuries, when the power of the marcher lords had waned and a degree of lawlessness still prevailed in this remote and sparsely populated region where Crown influence was weak. There was thus a need for those who could afford it to provide themselves with a measure of security, but by this time the threat came not from armies but from casual raiders and cattle rustlers. After the Union of 1603 even these disturbances diminished, but as rents remained low the farmers used their increased incomes to provide against any resumption of hostilities. These buildings were the final expression of an age-old tradition of fortification which embraced not only villages and farms but monasteries, churches and towns (Warkworth even has a fortified bridge).

The crowning glories of this landscape of strife are of course the medieval castles. Belsay, Dunstanburgh, Norham and Warkworth are particularly impressive, as are Alnwick, Bamburgh, Chillingham, Chipchase and Ford, although those in the latter group were substantially altered or remodelled in later centuries according to contemporary taste. Bamburgh (Figure 34) was drastically and controversially restored in the years around 1900 by Lord Armstrong, but is still a magnificent prospect, largely on account of its position upon a precipitous outcrop of the Whin Sill. The narrow site is ideal, and has been developed to enclose three baileys and a twelfth-century keep, and a ruined chapel of the same date, surrounded by partly medieval curtain walls. An exceedingly rare feature of the keep is its ground-floor entrance, a nice illustration of the degree of security enjoyed on this near impregnable rock. The remainder of the buildings are Lord Armstrong's.

Figure 34. Bamburgh Castle and the Whin Sill

Bamburgh was the ancient capital of the Anglian kingdom of Bernicia, the northern part of the realm of Northumbria which also included the kingdom of Deira, centred upon York, and which stretched from the Humber to the Forth. Superbly placed on the undulating ledge of the coastal sill, Bamburgh was chosen as capital in recognition both of the physical unity of the frontier region and of the strategic importance of the gateway to the later kingdom of Scotland.

Dunstanburgh Castle, Northumberland

Despite its state of grand decay, Dunstanburgh – unlike Bamburgh – remains unadulterated by later 'improvements'. It is also relatively unspoiled in other respects, since intending visitors cannot drive to it but are obliged to walk along the coast path from nearby Craster or Embleton, $1\frac{1}{4}$ and 2 miles away respectively. The shattered castle stands in splendid isolation upon a rocky headland formed from the Whin Sill, where the bold dolerite escarpment reaches the coast and suddenly transforms the generally low shoreline (developed upon the gentle dip-slope of the Sill) into high cliffs. The geological details of the Sill and its relation to the country rocks are responsible for some of the defensive advantages of the extensive eleven-acre site. Near the north-east end of the sheer, hundred-foot-high dolerite cliff which protects the castle on the north is the Rumble Churn, probably formed from differential erosion of a sedimentary inclusion; during storms the waves crash on to the rocks with such force that spray is propelled even to the height of the battlements. At the south-east end of the castle, below the Egyncleugh Tower, is the deep, narrow chasm known as Egyn Cleugh or Queen Margaret's Cove, which was probably excavated by erosion along a north-west-trending fault. A similar structural weakness is encountered at Cushat Stiel, a third of a mile to the south; here, where a fault shifts the Whin Sill scarp a quarter of a mile westwards, away from the shore, lies an inlet now cut off by a dyke, blocked by shingle and backed by a marshy gap. Despite its small size, it is assumed that this constituted the harbour mentioned in historic accounts of Dunstanburgh. A ditch ran from the end of the harbour, around the western side of the castle, to Embleton Bay, thus converting the peninsula to an island.

The castle was built by Thomas, second Earl of Lancaster and chief councillor and commander against the Scots in the years after the English defeat at Bannockburn in 1314. It is important to remember, however, that the construction of Dunstanburgh was motivated principally by Thomas's personal intrigues against his cousin Edward II, not by the demands of border warfare as such. Nevertheless, Dunstanburgh assumed a role in frontier strategy after Thomas's execution in 1322, and was altered considerably in the 1380s by John of Gaunt as Lieutenant of the Scottish Marches, when Embleton was suffering severely from Scottish raids. In the fifteenth century the castle was involved in the confused struggles of the Wars of the Roses, after which it fell rapidly into disrepair.

The visitor approaching Dunstanburgh from Craster confronts the castle from its most vulnerable side. It is strange that these gentle southern slopes should lead up to the main living quarters of the castle, and that the final defensive retreat seems to be so prominently exposed. John of Gaunt appreciated the weakness of the arrangement. He blocked the central passage of the original gatehouse and turned it into a keep (Figure 35), constructed a new and ingenious entrance on the west side, and created the inner ward. (The original passage of the gatehouse was reopened in 1885.) To the east of the keep, the south curtain wall continues towards the sea, encompassing first the Constable's Tower and then an unnamed turret, and terminates in the Egyncleugh Tower, which overlooks the inlet mentioned above. On the western side is the Lilburn Tower.

Figure 35. Dunstanburgh Castle: the keep (originally the gatehouse), with the corner turrets of the Lilburn Tower visible through the entrance passage

If one is using Embleton as a starting point for the walk to Dunstanburgh, it is worth visiting the village's excellent 'vicar's pele', built in 1395 after a particularly destructive Scottish raid. Such towers were special pele towers (see p. 192) designed for country vicars, who were prone to being carried off by the Scots. Other pele towers in the Dunstanburgh district include Craster, and Proctors Stead near Dunstan.

Lower Brockhampton House, Hereford and Worcester
Lower Brockhampton (SO 687560) is beautifully positioned among the orchards and woods of the dissected Old Red Sandstone country to the

west of the River Teme. The half-timbered late fourteenth-century manor house is faced by a superb detached timber-framed gatehouse built about a century later. The group, viewed from beside the moat, is very engaging (Figure 36). While it is natural to assume, when considering moated sites, that the building and the moat which surrounds it are contemporary, this need not be so. At Lower Brockhampton, the presence of a nearby ruined twelfth-century chapel (exhibiting Norman and later features) and various earthworks suggests that a larger settlement once existed here. It is always a possibility that moats, particularly those encountered on the sites of deserted or shrunken villages, were dug some time after the construction of the building they encircle. It may be that here the moat is dated not by the house itself but by the late fifteenth-century gatehouse which lies over it.

Figure 36. Lower Brockhampton House

Tintern Abbey, Gwent
The densely wooded gorge of the lower Wye offered a splendidly wild and remote setting for the establishment of a Cistercian religious house. The Cistercians favoured such places for the pursuit of their life of seclusion, simplicity and manual labour, and the thinly populated and uncultivated regions of Wales and northern England proved particularly attractive to Cistercian communities. Several of the ruined abbeys are set amid magnificent scenery, notably Fountains and Rievaulx in North Yorkshire, Valle Crucis in Clwyd, and Tintern in Gwent (Figure 37).

Figure 37. Tintern Abbey from the west-south-west. Offa's Dyke runs along the highest section of the skyline beyond, hidden by trees

Tintern (SO 533000) was founded in 1131, three years after the first Cistercian house in England was inaugurated at Waverley, Surrey. The site, a virgin one, lies upon an alluvial flat on the right (west) bank of the Wye, enclosed by the steep valleyside slopes and cliffs which rise above the entrenched meanders of the river. The valley is still clothed by lush woods, and it is not too difficult to picture the landscape which surrounded the abbey in medieval times. The original twelfth-century church was rebuilt in the late thirteenth century, its graceful vaulting and the fine tracery of its windows marking a departure from the austerity which originally distinguished the Order. By the early 1300s Tintern had reached its zenith, the abbey and monastic buildings being set within an extensive area of 27 acres which was enclosed by a precinct wall.

The influence of the abbey extended far beyond its walls. Tintern, like other religious houses, was an important agent of landscape change in medieval times, exploiting a variety of local resources, clearing woods, draining marshes and initiating settlements upon new agricultural lands. The outlying estates can be identified today by their 'grange' place-names, such as Rogerstone Grange (ST 506966) to the south-west and Trelleck Grange (SO 492016) to the west-north-west, upon the dissected plateau above the valley. Others were situated further afield: Moor (Lower)

Grange (ST 428855) lies in Caldicot Level by the Severn, a district reclaimed partly through the efforts of the Cistercians. Extensions such as these suggest that the farming activities of the Order not only fitted neatly into but also rejuvenated the traditional agricultural economy of south-east Wales, adapting prevailing agrarian practices and extending them to new districts. In the late thirteenth century Tintern was recorded as owning over three thousand sheep, and soon afterwards the monks were busy creating a new settlement on their manor of Plataland, the clearance of woodland being suggested by the modern name of Newchurch (ST 454976).

The cultivation of the estates and the management of the buildings were the responsibility of the lay brothers, who took the vows of poverty, chastity and obedience but concentrated upon the practical side of the abbey's life. In the early days, when the monasteries were colonizing new lands, they tended to outnumber the monks, but as the years progressed they gradually declined in importance. This was one sign of the changing times. The Black Death and its related economic changes not only reduced the numbers of both lay brothers and monks but occasioned a labour shortage which made the running of the granges increasingly burdensome. The attraction of the monastic image faded, the secular element gained at the expense of the religious, the weight of taxation increased, wars with France severed links with the mother houses, and in Wales (although not at Tintern) Owen Glyndŵr's rebellion in the first years of the fifteenth century caused considerable damage to the abbey buildings. Nevertheless, it was the monasteries' continued wealth rather than their growing weakness which prompted Henry VIII to suppress them and expropriate their funds. Ironically, although Henry intended to retain the majority of the monastic lands as a permanent income-producing endowment, the Crown's continual need for ready money resulted in a failure to realize the full potential of the properties.

Soon after the Dissolution of 1536, the lead was stripped from Tintern Abbey and later sold to the Earl of Worcester. Despite losing the whole of its roof in this sordid fashion, the abbey has survived the ravages of the elements remarkably well. There was no settlement of any size nearby to exploit Tintern as a convenient source of building stone, and it was only slightly affected by the iron, wire and brass works founded there soon after the Dissolution. Indeed, the condition of the fabric remained such that during the late eighteenth century, when the Wye valley became a fashionable attraction for visitors indulging in the cult of the picturesque, William Gilpin suggested that the abbey could be 'improved' by a little judicious demolition to soften some of the lines and enhance the perspective!

The church is more or less complete except for parts of the walls, the north arcade and of course the vault. It consisted of an aisled presbytery, north and south transepts with eastern aisles, crossing, and aisled nave. The monks' choir occupied the crossing and the easternmost bay of the nave, separated by a stone screen or pulpitum from the lay brothers' choir in the main part of the nave. The west window, of seven lights, has nearly all its geometrical tracery intact. The famous east window, originally of eight lights, still retains its central mullion and circle over. The much admired glimpse of the wooded valleyside which it affords from the interior is a result of accident rather than design, for this beautiful window, which covers nearly the whole east wall of the church, would originally have been filled with tracery and glass (Figure 38).

Figure 38. Tintern Abbey: the crossing, presbytery and east window

The monastic buildings, occupying three sides of the cloister, were here placed not on the south side of the church, as was usual, but on the north, possibly on account of drainage to the river. The claustral buildings, which were altered or rebuilt during the thirteenth century, comprised the various domestic quarters of the monastery. Apart from the kitchen and the infirmary (a separate set of buildings with its own cloister, located to the north-east of the main cloister), the only building in which a fire was permitted was the warming house.

Tintern's fame as a place of great romantic beauty is fully deserved. The setting is breathtaking and the visual quality of the ruins outstanding. An exquisite pattern of light and shade is created when the sunbeams fall upon the arches and clustered shafts and accentuate the differences in colour, bedding and texture apparent in the stone. The chief building material was Tintern Sandstone, quarried locally from the Upper Old Red, but for intricate details other rock types were used. Tufa was employed in the construction of the vault, on account of its lightness. The architectural detail, particularly the surviving window tracery, displays that special beauty characteristic of the subtle change at the end of the thirteenth century from Early English to the earliest Decorated. But academic descriptions cannot convey the haunting atmosphere of Tintern, which great artists and poets alike have striven to capture. The great masses of ivy which clothed the ruins in the days of Turner and Wordsworth have been removed out of concern for the fabric, and careful restoration has prevented further decay. Whether this renders the abbey more or less 'romantic' is a matter of taste and aesthetic preference. What is remarkable is that the spell of Tintern, cast most powerfully perhaps on a moonlit night, is by no means dispelled by the hordes of summer tourists who come to visit the souvenir shop and café next door.

Old Sarum, Wiltshire

This impressive monument boasts a long and distinguished history, although the fame of Old Sarum derives chiefly from its spectacular failure as a settlement. A classic 'rotten borough', Old Sarum returned two M.P.s until 1832, despite the fact that the town was already in ruins when Leland described it *c.* 1540, having probably been abandoned during the previous century.

Four major phases in Old Sarum's development have been identified. The earliest period, that of the Iron Age, is clearly represented in the earthworks of the univallate hillfort. It seems probable that either Old Sarum itself or Stratford-sub-Castle (SU 133323), beyond the defences to the south-west, was the Roman town of *Sorviodunum*, and the lines of several Roman roads may be seen converging on the site. The fortress was abandoned for several centuries during the Dark Ages, but a Saxon town with a mint existed here from at least the ninth century. It was the Norman Conquest, however, which ushered in the fourth and most important period of building. Superimposed upon the basic structure of the hillfort, the early medieval programme of construction gave Old Sarum the features which characterize it today. The natural defensive strengths of the site were enhanced by a redigging of the Iron Age ramparts, and a motte and royal castle were erected on the hill-top in the centre. Finally, the transference of the see from Sherborne in 1075 inaugurated the great years of Old Sarum as an ecclesiastical centre and town with cathedral, castle, walls and houses.

All this is hard to imagine today. None of the houses remains, and the cathedral is visible only as a ground plan preserved to the north-west of the inner bailey. The first cathedral was completed by Bishop St Osmund in the late eleventh century, but it was greatly extended and largely rebuilt by his successor, Bishop Roger, in the early twelfth. Roger was also responsible for much of the building within the inner bailey. This is reached by a modern wooden bridge on the east which crosses the deep ditch at the same point as did the former drawbridge. The castle itself occupied the northern portion of the inner bailey (to the right as one enters through the gatehouse). Comprising a set of buildings arranged around an open, square courtyard, it was more like a bishop's palace than a castle, except for a small but strong tower at the north-eastern corner. The dominant feature today, however, is the keep or postern tower (lying almost straight ahead and due west from the gatehouse), which dates from the late twelfth century, being of the same age as the renewed curtain wall and the gatehouse itself (Figure 39).

Figure 39. Old Sarum, looking westwards

Despite this energy, the faults of the site were by this time clearly apparent. In the early 1200s the clergy petitioned the pope to move the cathedral to the fertile valley below, protesting that the wind prevented them from hearing Mass, that water was expensive, and even that the whiteness of the chalk caused blindness! Moreover, relations with the military garrison were poor, and the congregation was dwindling. Authority to transfer the see to Salisbury was granted in 1219; the cathedral was finally razed in 1331, and the materials were used in New Sarum's cathedral close. Old Sarum declined as a town with the growth of its offspring and the diversion of its trade; its physical disadvantages had from the start militated against its future as a cathedral city. It is noteworthy not only as an example of Norman failure in town planting, but also as an upland site which survived far longer as the ancient precursor of a modern town than was usual. (The Iron Age hillfort on St Catherine's Hill, Hampshire, thought to be the forerunner of nearby Winchester, was deserted in the first century B.C.)

Old Sarum is perhaps best appreciated in stormy weather, with a strong wind and dark clouds – the kind of day chosen by Constable for his painting.

Warkworth, Northumberland, and Appleby, Cumbria

Warkworth is a classic example of a planned medieval borough. Situated inside the last meander loop of the River Coquet, where the river finally emerges from its tortuous passage through the Carboniferous gritstone escarpments east of the Cheviot to broaden into the estuary at Amble, Warkworth offers a compelling assemblage of landscape features. The meander core consists of a low spur overlooking the river's lowest crossing point (Figures 40 and 41). The settlement is best approached from the north, using the bridge which carried the ancient track linking the Anglian coastal settlements of Northumbria. (The line of this old routeway is continued to the south of Warkworth as a footpath to Broomhill, where it joins the modern A1068 to Widdrington, which was part of the Anglian royal estate of Warkworth.)

The fortified bridge was built in 1379 but has since been widened. Once across, the visitor passes along the short stretch of Bridge Street and joins Castle Street, which in turn rises to the castle sited in the meander neck. It now becomes clear why the fortification on the bridge was necessary, for once an assailant was across the river he was faced directly with a keep unprotected by any curtain wall. The castle was cut off by the river only on the east and west; the south was without natural defences, and the medieval town itself filled the rest of the meander core on the north. This

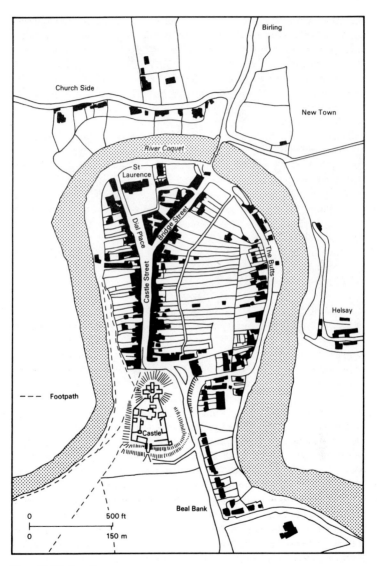

Figure 40. Warkworth

Figure 41. Warkworth, looking north-north-east

arrangement suggests that the settlement pre-dated the castle. Additional evidence comes from the Norman church at the north end of the town, just west of the bridge, which was probably built on the site of an eighth-century church. The existence of a settlement of any size here would have precluded the construction of a large bailey on the north side of the castle, and the visitor encounters the keep instead, with the bailey to the rear. The castle was begun in the twelfth century, but its main features date from the activities of the Percy family in the late fourteenth and early fifteenth centuries. The keep, a bevelled square with polygonal turrets, combined utility, comfort and beauty within the confines of a formal composition to a unique degree.

The medieval borough, founded *c.* 1200, also embodied a formal plan, involving the main street between the castle and the church. Although the townscape which confronts the modern visitor is dominantly eighteenth-century – a reminder of the time when Northumberland at last became less violent and more prosperous – the medieval scheme is still very much in evidence. The burgages are best preserved on the eastern sides of Castle Street and Bridge Street. The modern gardens retain the shapes of the garths, and the boundaries or 'butts' in the district down near the river are known to this day as The Butts.

The planned medieval borough of Appleby in Cumbria bears a remarkable resemblance to Warkworth: the layout of the two settlements is nearly identical. Appleby is situated in a meander of the River Eden, with a castle and church in corresponding positions. The single large street of Boroughgate with its burgages runs between them, its eighteenth- and early nineteenth-century appearance failing to obliterate the distinctive shapes created by the old plots. Beyond the much altered but originally Norman church of St Lawrence (cf. St Laurence at Warkworth), at the north end of Boroughgate are The Butts, again situated down by the river. The borough charter was granted in 1179, and the town continued to suffer from Scottish raids which ravaged this western part of the march as they did Northumberland. But in one important (and useful) respect Appleby provides a more complete picture than Warkworth: there is much more visible evidence for the pre-Norman settlement, largely because its location differed from that of the new town. 'Old Appleby' nearby, with its own church of St Michael, Bongate (traditionally 'senior' to St Lawrence), preserves the plan of a green village, while the church has a Saxon hogback gravestone built into the north doorway. That which is hidden at Warkworth may be more clearly seen at Appleby.

Failed new towns of the Middle Ages

By no means all the towns founded during the three centuries following the Norman Conquest prospered. A substantial number were partial or complete failures, and the reasons for this are not always clear. In general terms, the demographic and economic relapse of the fourteenth century exposed the less viable urban enterprises to competition and prompted the essential collapse of the new town movement. When the pace of regional economic change quickened once more, towns were considered in some respects to be restrictive, cramped, conservative and guild-ridden; for these and other reasons the principal manufactures of pre-industrial England and Wales, far from being exclusively urban in location, spirit or affiliation, displayed strong connections with agrarian activities and hence with the countryside. Towns were, in the main, small, unspecialized and vulnerable, and it was not until the onset of industrialization that they began to take on the aspect and functions associated with modern large-scale urban development. Change rather than growth was the characteristic feature of pre-industrial towns; many of those which suffered decline disappeared almost completely from the landscape, while others shrank to become almost unrecognizable as settlements which had once displayed pretensions to urban status.

The individual causes of failure were various. Natural environmental changes accounted for the demise of Ravenserodd in Humberside, founded by the Earl of Aumâle soon after 1230; sited upon a sandbank at the mouth of the Humber, the town now lies under the sea near the present spit of Spurn Head. Undermined by a shift in the spit, Ravenserodd had, by the middle of the fourteenth century, been 'swiftly swallowed up and irreparably destroyed by the merciless floods and tempests'. Other settlements were adversely affected by the silting up or movement of rivers; Hedon in Humberside (TA 1828), also founded by the Earl of Aumâle, may have failed as an indirect result of such factors, for difficulties of navigation along Hedon Haven disadvantaged the town in competition with rival ports. Such rivalry was keen and often cut-throat: Prince Llewelyn's new market town of 1273, which he planned to build next to the new castle at Dolforwyn, Powys (SO 152951), was besieged and destroyed by the English. The jealousy of nearby Montgomery ensured that all traces of Dolforwyn, on its narrow hill-top site, were already gone by 1330: today it consists only of mounds in the grass.

Even royal patronage was no guarantee of success. Newton, founded in 1286 by Edward I on the shores of Poole Harbour in Dorset (SZ 005851), may well have been still-born. The site is so uncertain that historians searching for it were for many years misled by remains of buildings nearby which are now thought to be of quite different origin, not connected with the town at all. Queenborough, on the Isle of Sheppey in Kent (TQ 9072), a very late royal plantation dating from the 1360s, never consisted of more than a single main street; despite its intended role as a defensive post on the Medway, competition from Rochester crippled it from the outset and by Defoe's time it was a 'miserable, dirty, decay'd, poor, pitiful, fishing town; yet vested with corporation priviledges'.

A further group comprises towns which despite their failure made a second attempt by establishing a new borough next to the original one. (For a different reason, Warkworth (p. 202) also sported a 'new town' intended for mariners and fishermen, but it proved abortive and the original town retained its dominance.) Montacute in Somerset (ST 4916) developed from *two* planned boroughs: the first, established round a priory of the Abbey of Cluny *c.* 1102, apparently failed to provide sufficient income, so a new town was laid out to the east *c.* 1240, centred upon the square thereafter known as The Borough. Montacute underwent decline in the sixteenth century, possibly through competition from Ilminster and Yeovil, but the dignified houses of Ham Hill Stone (Upper Lias), although relatively recent in terms of external appearances, provide visual evidence of the town's former status.

Most of these shrunken boroughs reveal their origins on close inspection, although some are so decayed that the landscape offers few clues. Rackley in Somerset (ST 395548), set up in the 1180s under papal and royal charters as a port and borough on the River Axe, now comprises only a few farm buildings and cottages, together with bits of wharves near a much altered and no longer navigable Axe. Newtown (Francheville) on the Isle of Wight (SZ 4290), a mid-thirteenth-century planted borough, was adversely affected not only by competition from nearby towns but also by French raids during the fourteenth century. Today the silted creek, grassy remains of streets, empty burgage plots, a suggestive pattern of hedges and, rather eccentrically, a dominantly eighteenth-century town hall accompany the handful of buildings which are all that remain of the once busy harbour and town. Stogursey (ST 203429), in a remote part of Somerset – its isolation no doubt contributing to its failure – reveals its origins in a rather different way. The place-name itself is interesting; it is derived from *Stoke Courcy* and reflects the fact that the town was promoted by the de Courcy family, supporters of William I. In the first years of the twelfth century, a priory was founded there by the Benedictine abbey of Lonlay in Normandy, and this event explains a number of singular features which confront the observant visitor to the decidedly spacious parish church of St Andrew, originally the priory church. The details of the fine Norman crossing, and the original scheme of three apses attached to the east sides of the two transepts and the east end of the chancel, all suggest continental practice.

In general, however, failed medieval boroughs betray their identities more obviously in the overall pattern of their streets (even if these are mere lanes today), and the arrangement of their buildings. New Radnor, Powys (SO 2160), is a clear example of a fortified town with a grid pattern of streets, which never developed sufficiently to take up its burgage plots, fill the area within its walls and eventually to overrun and consume its defensive boundaries, which instead simply decayed with time. Neither military necessities, religious connections, manorial energy, nor even royal patronage could guarantee demographic and economic success for the medieval planted town in the face of the vicissitudes of fate which conspired to destroy the weaker enterprises.

Burford, Oxfordshire

In the Middle Ages Burford was a thriving market town and borough on the River Windrush. It was situated at the junction of the route from London to Northleach and Cheltenham with the road from Lechlade, which ran through the town before sending branches off to Stow-on-the-Wold and Chipping Norton. Much of its interest today stems from the striking survival of many medieval features, both in the town plan and in the buildings.

Burford, the *'burh* by the ford', became a seigneurial borough in the years around 1200, and was run by an alderman and burgesses until the early seventeenth century, when the manor was bought by a resident lord who successfully challenged the corporation's rights and privileges. A seigneur's borough had its charter granted through a lord, in this case Robert Fitzhamon, Earl of Gloucester, and not by the king. The lack of a royal charter tended to place the self-governing townspeople in a potentially weak position in respect to a lord who chose to exercise his rights. During the medieval period this legal flaw did not manifest itself at Burford, and the borough flourished, with its merchant guild, market and fairs. Dealings in hides and livestock, butter and wine, timber and charcoal (from nearby Wychwood) took place in Burford, but the chief fountain of its prosperity was, in common with other Cotswold towns, the wool trade. Economic decline set in during the post-medieval era, although the coaching trade was of considerable importance in the eighteenth century. But in 1812 the new turnpike road to Gloucester, in order to avoid the steep valleyside, abandoned the former route through the centre of Burford (along Witney Street and Sheep Street) and bypassed the town to the south, its line being followed by the modern A40.

This decay in fortunes has greatly assisted the preservation of the medieval town (Figure 42). The core of Burford lay near the church of St John the Baptist, which stands at the lower (northern) end by the river. The ford was soon superseded by a bridge (the present structure dates from the fourteenth and fifteenth centuries), and a broad street ran southwards up the hill. This street was used as the market place, and burgage plots were laid out on either side, running back to end in the usual lanes. Although the town was not walled, the compact plan has persisted remarkably well, providing a framework for later development. The long High Street was not wide enough to accommodate buildings such as those which often grew up in the middle of medieval market places, so development took place up The Hill instead, thereby extending the built-up portion of the main street beyond the line of Witney Street and Sheep Street.

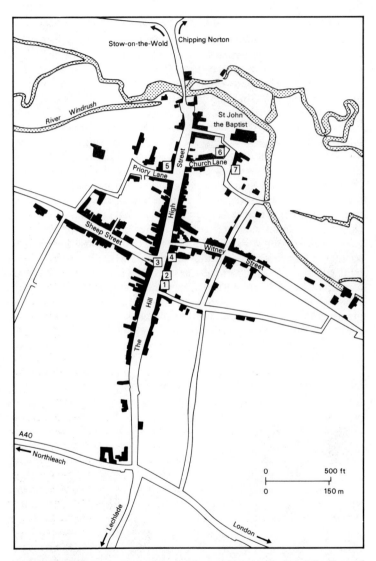

Figure 42. Burford. The numbers refer to buildings mentioned in the text: 1. the House of Simon; 2. Wysdomes; 3. the Tolsey; 4. the Crypt; 5. Falkland Hall; 6. the Grammar School; 7. the Great Almshouses

There are a considerable number of medieval buildings left to complement the plan. Some of them were subsequently refronted, notably during the eighteenth century when the coaching inns flourished. Wysdomes (seen on the right in Figure 43) is a half-timbered house of *c.* 1500 with a late eighteenth-century shopfront, and incorporates various internal modifications. In many instances the medieval cores of the houses are not visible from the street. Nevertheless, several excellent originals can be seen, particularly in the High Street, which presents an enjoyable sequence of buildings succeeding each other with delightful irregularity. The Crypt is fifteenth-century, timber-framed; Falkland Hall, on the corner of Priory Lane, is a mid-sixteenth-century stone building, the house of a wealthy clothier. After the opening of the local Great Oolite quarries, many houses were rebuilt in stone, but sometimes the timber-framed upper storeys might be retained. The House of Simon (Simon Wisdom the clothier), visible on the extreme right of Figure 43, and the Tolsey or Court House, both of the sixteenth century, have half-timbered upper sections resting on stone bases, although the original work once displayed by the Tolsey (market court building) has been stuccoed. Off the High Street, in Church Lane, are the Grammar School (1571, but altered in 1868) and the Great Almshouses of the mid-fifteenth century. Finally, the imposing but architecturally complex church with its elaborate porch derives its Perpendicular appearance from the almost complete remodelling which took place in the fifteenth century at the peak of the wool trade's prosperity.

Figure 43. Burford, looking north down the High Street from The Hill

CHAPTER 5

Pre-industrial Landscapes

The span of time covered by the sixteenth, seventeenth and part of the eighteenth centuries has come to be known among economic historians and historical geographers as the pre-industrial period. In some respects the term is misleading when used in this restricted sense, for the pre-industrial era could be said to extend over the whole of human history, excluding the last two hundred years. Nevertheless, it has proved to be useful when referring to that chapter of the history of England and Wales which lies between the exit from medievalism and the onset of industrialization. Delimited in such general terms, the pre-industrial period has much to commend it as a framework for study, although it neither began nor ended abruptly, and the characteristics of life in this country during those years lingered on in certain regions for some time after the Industrial Revolution had shattered the relative tranquillity of others. Indeed, this essentially rurally-based, 'pre-modern' society persisted well into the nineteenth century: for example, as late as 1856 it was suggested that a virtue of the Rows in Chester was that they made shopping pleasant 'for old ladies of weak minds who quail at meeting cattle' in the streets.

Pre-industrial traits were not only perpetuated in this fundamentally negative sense, merely surviving and escaping the forces of change. One of the principal characteristics of the seventeenth and eighteenth centuries was the growing momentum of the drive for 'improvement' which was tidying, ordering, manicuring and ornamenting both country and town at the time when innovation of a different kind was starting to transform the nascent industrial regions. The continuing process of enclosure of both open field and waste, the building of country houses with their gardens, parks and associated model villages, and the creation of elegant towns all took place against the background of a society which, although it displayed growing energy and sophistication, had not yet undergone the momentous experience of industrialization. For this reason, and because of the nature of their consequences for the landscape, it is convenient to include these planned Georgian landscapes in the present chapter. Despite the fact that some of them extend beyond the stricter chronological confines of the pre-industrial period, they are nevertheless inseparable from the economic, social and aesthetic *milieu* of that age, in which the origins of the spirit of Improvement lay.

The Industrial Revolution, taken in its entirety, was a watershed separating present-day society from a pattern of life which in many respects was markedly different. It may seem strange to speak of Elizabethan and Georgian England in the same breath, but the basic framework of existence was directly comparable. It is important to grasp this essential continuity, for the period should be viewed – at least initially – in its own terms and not simply as one in which the prevailing forces were consciously paving the way for the economic developments to follow. In this sense the term pre-industrial must be used with care. There should be no implicit assumption that pre-industrial England was deliberately gearing itself for economic take-off: the retrospective search for the origins of industrialization, the identification of key sectors in the economy and the postulation of progressive waves of modernization which carried the country over the final hurdle and blasted it into self-sustained growth represent a particular (and inherently post-industrial) conceptualization inappropriate to many aspects of the age. Change there certainly was, but this was not always synonymous with growth. Frequently it amounted to quite the opposite, and it is just as important to examine the obstacles to progress as the stimuli which promoted it.

The society of pre-industrial England and Wales was a traditional one, and the economy, while far from being 'underdeveloped', was unsophisticated and vulnerable. Agriculture was the foundation of the economy, the focus of labour for nearly all those who worked, and the supplier of raw materials for related trades and manufactures. The harvest was the pivot of existence, and its success or failure meant the difference between prosperity and poverty, plenty and famine, and life and death. In an age when there were more sheep than people, few towns of any size, and no separate industrial sector, the rural character of life was all-permeating. Orchards and fields came right into the towns, the economies of which were inextricably bound up with the countryside. Few people were completely divorced from agriculture, for even in regions where farming did not provide a full-time occupation, the crafts which were practised as elements in a dual economy derived their dominantly organic raw materials from agriculture. Modern concepts of industry, based upon inorganic resources, advanced technology, huge power sources, fixed capital investment, mass production and permanent workforces, were completely alien. It is more appropriate to speak of 'manufacture' than of 'industry', for goods were literally made by pairs of hands, working up materials using human or animal muscle and the erratic forces of wind and water. Production in this 'hand-made' world was small-scale, geared to furnishing the necessities of life: food and drink, clothing and shelter. Labour was the central element in the economy, but large numbers of people produced or consumed very little. Manufacturing activity was widely spread across the countryside, coincident with the distribution of the population. It was essentially a rural rather than an urban phenomenon, its irregular and intermittent nature reflecting the regulating influence of the agricultural rhythm. At harvest time most operations ceased, and even the blast furnaces were blown out by the ironmasters in order to release labour for an all-out effort in the fields. The fire which destroyed Dorchester in Dorset in 1613 established its fatal hold during a summer afternoon when most of the inhabitants were out gathering in the harvest.

In many spheres of life nature exercised the upper hand. Agriculture was largely at the mercy of the weather, while extreme events caused great tribulation. Floods, droughts and blizzards can interrupt economic activity and bring transport to a standstill even in these advanced times, so it is easy to imagine the hardships they could inflict upon pre-industrial society. Floods drowned the fields and rendered the already wearisome roads impassable; droughts ruined crops, halted the operation of water-wheels and impeded river navigation; adverse winds interrupted the vital coastal trade, and gales such as the great storm of 1703 wrought havoc all over the country. The population had little means of insuring itself against the suffering occasioned by severe cold spells such as the bitter 'Lorna Doone' winter of 1684, or the terrible freeze of 1740. It is small wonder that pre-industrial attitudes to landscape reflected a love of fertile and productive districts and a dislike of untamed, uncultivated or wild places, whatever their romantic appeal to those later generations who belonged to a society which increasingly cushioned them from the discomforts of unrestrained nature. Contemporaries would have viewed their surroundings not as a rural paradise untainted by the disfiguring scars of heavy industry, but as a hostile and grudging environment from which – for the vast majority – sustenance had to be wrested by arduous toil amid unrelenting poverty and hardship.

In a less dramatic but more deep-seated manner the natural environment also influenced the spatial distribution of economic activity across the country, which in turn produced a set of distinctive cultural landscapes. There was no unified national economy in the modern sense, but a collection of contrasting regional ones, based upon the pattern of soils, vegetation, climate and resources produced by the complex arrangement of escarpment and vale, forest and down, heath and moor, fen and marsh. The varying combinations of these elements were reflected in occupational and social structures, particular links between agriculture and manufacture, and in a host of local cultures. In landscape terms this resulted in the creation, in association with natural landscapes, of regionally differentiated field systems, forms of land use, settlement patterns, and architectural styles. Until disturbed by the spread of new ideas, techniques and commodities promoted by improved transport networks and the evolution of an industrial structure, these regional landscapes formed a striking element in the geography of England and Wales. This kind of regionalism blossomed during the pre-industrial era, as traditional society attained its fullest development given the constraints imposed upon it. Industrialization complicated the pattern of individual districts, blurring and mixing them, and occasioning the emergence of new regions, but it by no means destroyed them completely, so deeply ingrained were they in the traditional scene. Indeed, the Industrial Revolution was itself not a national but a regional phenomenon, its roots embedded in particular geographical, economic and social contexts.

Agrarian landscapes

The regional dimension was especially significant for agriculture, which reflected the multiformity of both environmental conditions and local farming practice. The period was one of considerable importance in agrarian history, and although scholars will probably never agree on the precise nature or timing of the 'Agricultural Revolution', the significance of the seventeenth century is rarely denied even by those who place the Revolution conventionally between about 1750 and 1850. The traditional view, which maintained that Parliamentary enclosure was the spearhead of the Revolution, liberating agriculture from the fetters of the 'restrictive and conservative' open fields, has given way to a conception of longer-term change in which Parliamentary enclosure completed a wide-ranging process initiated some time before. Enclosure undoubtedly increased agricultural efficiency and facilitated the simplification of holdings, but in some respects it merely provided formal confirmation of functional changes which had taken place earlier by means of enclosure by agreement, or through a host of local arrangements made in the open fields themselves. The innovations which characterized the 'age of the improver' were adopted and integrated into agricultural practice before Parliamentary enclosure launched its steamroller campaign against the remaining open fields, many of which lay in the arable districts of the Midlands where pasture was often at a premium. By this time many other districts were partially or almost completely enclosed, either because they had never known open fields or because piecemeal enclosure had gradually converted them.

Agrarian change during the seventeenth and eighteenth centuries encompassed the introduction of new crops, advances in farming practice, and an increase in the total area of land brought into cultivation. The spread of root crops, sown grasses and clover enabled larger numbers of sheep to be kept (which in turn produced valuable manure) and improved soil fertility, particularly on the light lands. This, together with the greater measure of flexibility which these crops brought to rotational systems, raised yields and promoted a more efficient use of the land. The age-old mutual separation of permanent arable and permanent grass began to be replaced by less rigid arrangements. The alternation of grain and grass crops on the same piece of land (convertible or up-and-down husbandry) and the related practice of arable farming for fodder crops, involving the sowing of temporary grass and clover leys in the arable (alternate husbandry, also known as the Norfolk system), kept the soil in good heart and provided feed for the animals while at the same time obviating the need for fallow.

Another important development, particularly characteristic of southern and south-western England in the seventeenth century, was the creation of watermeadows. It had long been appreciated that meadows benefited from being inundated by river water, and eventually ways were found of flooding them artificially in order to stimulate the growth of grass. The extra fodder was of crucial value as a means of sustaining hungry animals through the lean weeks of late winter and early spring, while the extra sheep which could be kept as a consequence increased the amount of manure produced. The sheep were fed by day on the meadow and folded on the arable at night, thereby enriching it. Various methods of 'floating' the meadows were employed. One of the most elaborate involved a series of dams, sluices and artificial channels to carry the water along the contours of the valleyside and distribute it over the meadows before draining it off again. In some places, particularly along the Frome valley in Dorset (Figure 44), the systems of head mains, ridges and drains can still be seen. The blocks of ridges or water carriers often look remarkably similar to ridge-and-furrow, and care must be taken to distinguish between them.

Significant additions were made to the total acreage under cultivation by the reclamation of heathland (the infertile heathland soils of eastern England being improved by marling, turnip husbandry and the folding of sheep), the underdraining of the claylands, and the draining of the marshes. Several low-lying districts were the object of ambitious drainage

Figure 44. Watermeadows in the Frome valley east of Dorchester, Dorset (SY 7190); the area covered by the photograph is approximately one square mile

schemes, including the Somerset Levels (p. 238), but the most spectacular successes were achieved in the peatlands of the East Anglian Fens. Here the activities of the Dutch engineer Cornelius Vermuyden culminated in the triumphant declaration, in 1652, that the area now known as the Bedford Level had been well and truly drained. This achievement followed the construction of water courses, notably the two Bedford Rivers which dominate the landscape to this day, designed to carry the water of the 'upland' rivers across the fenlands to the sea. Despite the objections of those who lost their rights of common grazing, fishing, and turbary, the land was divided up into regular enclosures for the production of 'all sorts of corne and grasse' and a range of other crops besides. But the jubilation was premature. The transformation of the Fens triggered off a set of unforeseen physical consequences which contemporary technology was unable to counter. The river estuaries silted up, ponding back the water and flooding the fenlands, whose levels were progressively lowered during the later seventeenth century as the drying peat underwent substantial shrinkage. Hundreds of windmills were built over the next century, making a singular contribution to the fenland landscape, but their value as a solution to the flooding was limited. Not only were they at the mercy of the weather, but by a process of positive feedback they actually increased the flood hazard. By transferring water from the fields to the rivers (now flowing at a higher relative level) the windmills helped to drain the fen but caused in turn yet more shrinkage, thereby making the problem worse. Pre-industrial efforts at improvement had reached their limits, and only with the coming of the steam-driven pump in the nineteenth century were the obstacles to permanent control gradually overcome.

The study of these new agricultural landscapes emphasizes very strongly the importance of the regional dimension and the contrasting relationships which existed between agrarian change and landscape from place to place. At the same time it has to be stressed that many of the crucial developments in farming practice were not accompanied by alterations in the landscape, and that several of the major questions debated by agrarian historians, such as the processes governing the pattern of innovation diffusion, cannot be answered by examination of the formal landscape of field systems. Nevertheless, although it is impossible to reduce the role of enclosure in the general scheme of change to a simple formula, it was the enclosure movement which served to transform the landscapes of large areas of England and Wales.

In purely descriptive terms the basic kinds of enclosure are relatively easy to identify. Early enclosures took several forms but generally gave rise to patterns involving collections of irregularly shaped fields. Piecemeal enclosure of the open fields sometimes produced fields which preserved the boundaries of the old strips or furlongs, but even where these were disregarded the new fields varied considerably in size and shape. The conversion of formerly uncultivated areas to farmland also produced fields of this type. The edges of the old forests, heaths and moors can sometimes be detected by the presence of the small and intricate fields of squatter settlements which encroached upon the wasteland edge. This process was comparable to the assarting of the Middle Ages, and rep-resented the efforts of landless or unattached people to scratch a living by squatting on the peripheries of commons, often combining work on a smallholding with employment in manufacture or some extractive industry such as the quarrying of stone or the mining of coal, iron, tin or lead.

Diverse as these field systems are in terms of detail, their essential irregularity provides a common feature which distinguishes them from the landscape of Parliamentary enclosure. The practice of proceeding with enclosure through private Act of Parliament, despite the expense involved, enabled landowners to overcome local opposition to the loss of common rights, and to speed up what could otherwise be a frustrating and protracted process. Although the earlier Parliamentary enclosure acts date from the seventeenth and early eighteenth centuries, the vast majority were passed during the reign of George III. The peaks coincided with rising prices and the increased demand for wheat during the Napoleonic Wars (1793–1815), and much of the Parliamentary enclosure in England and most of that in Wales dates from those years. The enclosure awards embodied the recommendations of commissioners appointed to draw up plans and make judgements with regard to field boundaries, highways, drains and all the other details of the new landscapes. By this means the enthusiastic improving landlords replaced the remaining open fields (concentrated mainly in the Midlands), and also large tracts of waste, with neat landscapes of regular, geometrical fields bounded either by quickset hedges or, particularly in upland districts, by dry-stone walls. In most cases the hedges were constructed using only one or two shrub species, and as a result they present a quite different appearance from the botanically richer and more varied hedges marking older field boundaries. Nevertheless, the white blossom of the hawthorn makes a splendid show in early summer. The hedges were planted with trees, especially oak, ash and elm, which, together with the occasional spinney or gorse cover maintained for the purposes of fox-hunting, give the impression that the landscape is more wooded than is actually the case (Figures 11 and 45). In the Midlands the conversion to pasture fossilized the medieval ridge-and-furrow and produced a greener landscape than before. Elsewhere the change was in the opposite direction, particularly in East Anglia, where the heathlands were turned over to arable. The same was true of those upland margins ploughed up for a brief spell during the Napoleonic Wars, leaving patterns of low, closely spaced straight ridges known as 'narrow rig'. These were preserved, albeit faintly, after the fields were abandoned at the end of the Wars and the land reverted to pasture.

Parliamentary enclosure often swept away the old landscape almost completely, installing not only new field boundaries but new roads as well.

Figure 45. Parliamentary enclosure at Flecknoe, Warwickshire

These tended to be straight and wide, quite unlike the tortuous narrow lanes of the old enclosed districts. The width allowed for the inevitable ruts and potholes to be negotiated, but with improvements in road building detours for this purpose were no longer imperative, so that today only a narrow strip is metalled, leaving broad verges on one or both sides. Where they have not been poisoned or hacked about, these verges are crowded with grasses and familiar wayside plants. The cow parsley (*Anthriscus sylvestris*) delights in its restless sea of white-flowered umbels during the same enchanting spell of early summer which decks the hawthorn hedges with blossom. The classic landscape of Parliamentary enclosure is completed by the presence of Georgian or Victorian farmsteads set amidst the fields, names such as Quebec or Trafalgar betraying their date of foundation. However, in many instances the dispersion of farms from the village was either limited to the wealthier landowners or delayed until some time after the enclosure itself. Where the land was owned by a few large farmers, little change occurred in the existing arrangement of rural settlements, so the brick farmsteads typical of the Midland districts, set within a pattern of intercalated dispersion, are not to be found in all areas affected by Parliamentary enclosure.

Rarely, however, was the old landscape totally obliterated. Old hedges were incorporated into the new field systems, while the new roads some-times followed, in part, the lines of medieval tracks, their sudden right-angle bends marking the edges of the old furlongs. It was not unusual for a pre-existing path between two settlements to adopt a double kink in its course as a medieval clearing was made in the waste through which it ran, and features of this kind have persisted in the landscape to the present day, even when almost every other aspect of the scene has changed. Enclosures made from forests often incorporated isolated portions of woodland among the new fields. The former extent of those forests destroyed by Georgian improvers, such as Needwood Forest in Stafford-shire, can be reconstructed using these remnants in connection with the lines of parish boundaries and the distribution of the tiny fields of the squatters which encroached upon the periphery. The improved heaths and mosses of northern Salop, which account for nearly all the Parliamentary enclosure in that county – the open fields having been enclosed almost entirely by agreement – reveal themselves more subtly in the flora of the hedges. (However, care must be exercised in using hedge-dating techniques here, for it has long been the practice in Salop to plant mixed hedges: many of the Parliamentary enclosure hedges therefore contain approxi-mately the same number of shrub species as those planted much earlier.) Those medieval parks taken into cultivation at this time can be detected in a similar way. The fields around Chartley Castle in Staffordshire (SK 011285) furnish a good example of a disparked Georgian landscape. The tract north of the ruined thirteenth-century castle forms the residue of the park, the rest having been replaced by a spread of ordered, regular fields interspersed with occasional coverts and farmhouses. The contrast with the nearby old enclosed landscape around the village of Stowe, with its irregular fields and vernacular buildings, is unmistakable. Comparable differences can be observed in the field patterns of the reclaimed wetlands (p. 239).

Landscapes of wealth and poverty

Agricultural progress was not the only force promoting change in the countryside during this period. The wealth and prestige of the nobility and the greater landowners found visible expression in an institution which in social, economic and landscape terms was peculiarly English: the country house. The privately owned landed estate remained the focal point of English rural society for several centuries, and its effect on the landscape was profound. Its influence was not confined to the house itself but embraced the planned landscapes laid out around it, and even the agricultural land beyond. As a consequence, extensive areas of the rural landscape embody the changing fortunes, ideals and tastes of the upper echelons of a demonstrably hierarchical society, the foundations of which were firmly rooted in the ownership of land.

The traditional centrepiece of the estate was the house itself. The variety of architectural inspirations, regional styles and building materials, overlain by the whims and fancies of individual owners, have resulted in a bewildering diversity in appearance which contributes greatly to their appeal. The earliest ones developed out of the late medieval fortified houses, often incorporating original features into the new structures. With increasing political stability, the defensive functions were eliminated altogether and the country house came into its own. Nevertheless, the traditions of the Middle Ages lingered in an architectural if not in a military sense, the early Tudor houses such as Compton Wynyates in Warwickshire perpetuating the plan and appearance of the medieval house. As the sixteenth century progressed, a motley collection of half-digested classical motifs was grafted on to these medieval elements to produce an eclectic style which came into its own in the late years of the century. Rarely lacking in confidence or panache, it produced houses as individual as Bess of Hardwick's Hardwick Hall in Derbyshire, 'more glass than wall', Sir Walter Raleigh's romantic Sherborne Castle in Dorset, and the Elizabethan Renaissance extravaganza of Wollaton Hall in Nottinghamshire, built by the colourful Sir Francis Willoughby (in the words of Camden, 'upon a vaine ostentation of his wealth'). Some of the most elaborate of these Elizabethan houses, such as Burghley House in Cambridgeshire and Montacute House in Somerset, were built by high officers of state to advance their fame and to entertain royalty in a style likely to assist their personal preferment.

Although the number of large estates which developed entirely out of monastic lands was limited, the buoyant land market which resulted from the Dissolution and the subsequent sale of property by the Crown served to increase the membership of the secular landed establishment, with concomitant effects upon the landscape. Thus in 1540 John Thynne, son of a Shropshire farmer, bought sixty acres of land adjoining a tumbledown Wiltshire priory called 'Longlete'. This formed the nucleus of a new estate which was built up over the years around a house constructed in the Elizabethan hybrid style. Many country houses built on monastic property actually incorporated the ecclesiastical buildings into their fabric, or took their names from them, as at Rufford Abbey, Nottinghamshire, Wroxton Abbey, Oxfordshire, and Milton Abbey, Dorset (p. 245), begun in the sixteenth, seventeenth and eighteenth centuries respectively.

During the later seventeenth century the taste for classical styles gathered momentum and in the following century it erupted into a passion. The monumental Baroque edifices created by Vanbrugh and Hawksmoor in the early 1700s, notably Blenheim in Oxfordshire (designed more as a national monument than as a place to live), Castle Howard in North Yorkshire, and Seaton Delaval in Northumberland, are complex in their inspiration. Blenheim in particular recalls the bold romanticism of a great medieval castle and the exuberance of an Elizabethan mansion (Figure 46).

Figure 46. Blenheim, Oxfordshire: the grandiose prospect of palace, lake and landscaped park from the south

In the early Georgian period the quiet Palladianism of Lord Burlington superseded this monumental style, but it could still rise to the grand design, exemplified in Holkham Hall, Norfolk. Neo-classicism reached its peak of popularity in the late eighteenth century, when many new mansions were built and older ones altered. Much of the finest work, both exterior and interior, was associated with the designs of Robert Adam: Harewood House, West Yorkshire, and Kedleston Hall, Derbyshire, were partly built by him. Country houses almost everywhere were adorned with elegant neo-classical façades which partially or wholly conceal the older house forming the core of the new building, as at Saltram House, Devon, and Attingham Hall, Salop. But in spite of the craze for the classical, neo-gothicism was making its appearance even before the end of the century. Richard Payne Knight's Downton Castle in Hereford and Worcester, built in the 1770s, is a contrived castellated castle inspired not by English models, but by the semi-fortified houses depicted in the paintings of Claude and Poussin. (The interior, however, is the epitome of classical purity.)

Several factors contributed to the regional diversity apparent in the appearance of country houses. It is largely true that the leader of fashion was the Court in London, and that the various styles spread from this centre, but the diffusion process was complex. The arrival and acceptance of an innovation reflected ease of communication more than straight-line distance, and was conditioned by the social structure of a particular district, new architectural modes being adopted first by the nobility, and then percolating down to the lesser gentry. A special case was the north of England, where the stone-built fortified structures of the Middle Ages continued to serve an active role as a consequence of the isolation and insecurity of the region. The spread of more genteel country residences was long delayed, and the major phase in their construction did not take place until the growth of industry had produced the necessary wealth. In much of Wales the general absence of large landowners helped to restrict the number of mansions erected.

A major influence on the architecture of houses across the country was the suitability and distribution of building materials. The geological map (Figure 3) gives only a general idea of the variety of stone available, as both lithological changes within the conventional geological divisions and the presence of superficial deposits greatly complicate the overall picture. Brick and timber were used in stone-deficient districts, many builders of Queen Anne houses deliberately choosing red brick, but good stone (particularly from the Jurassic belt) was preferred, on account of its ornamental qualities and its connotations of wealth. Only really rich people could afford to transport large quantities of stone in the pre-industrial era. The Palladian mansion of Houghton Hall, on the drift-covered Chalk of northern Norfolk, was built in the 1720s for Sir Robert Walpole, who brought Jurassic sandstone for the facing by ship from Yorkshire. Stucco was widely used as an imitation of stone when the real thing lay beyond the owner's means.

Considered from the viewpoint of landscape as opposed to architecture *sensu stricto*, the setting of these houses was all-important. Some were designed and positioned with an eye to bold display; others were allowed to blend in with their surroundings. The country house's most extensive effect on the landscape came in the eighteenth century with the creation of large ornamental gardens and parks. In 1712 Joseph Addison suggested making a garden of a whole estate by means of frequent plantations, proposing that a man might make 'a pretty landskip' of his own possessions. Eventually the highly geometrical formal English gardens (p. 240) were replaced by the 'naturalistic' gardens of Kent, Brown, Repton and others, where trees, lakes, cascades, grottoes and ornamental buildings were carefully arranged in accordance with current taste and the preferences of the owner. Many fine parks have survived, notably Shugborough in Staffordshire, Stourhead in Wiltshire (p. 242 and Figure 53), and Rousham and Blenheim in Oxfordshire, the last two exemplifying the styles of Kent and Brown respectively. The effects of the movement were experienced over large areas of England, and the passion for planting spread beyond the confines of the parks themselves to embrace the rest of the estate, millions of trees, both native and exotic, being planted for posterity.

Again the significance of this development varied from region to region, according to prevailing social structures and the evolution of land-use patterns (a significant positive factor being the presence of medieval parks on the poorer soils). The landscape park was never so important in Wales as in England, partly owing to the different social hierarchy, but also because the grandeur of much of the scenery made it difficult to realize the aesthetic ideals of the English landscape garden. Not only were such gardens dwarfed in terms of scale, but the overpowering presence of real nature showed up their contrived and cosy ornamentation for what it was. Only when the gentle elegance of Brown and Repton was outmoded by the Picturesque of Knight and Price did the rugged uplands of Wales begin to find favour (p. 264). Knight's own particular preference for rough and wild nature found expression in his activities at Downton (SO 445748), on the Welsh border. For the building of his castle he chose a site adjacent to the scenic Downton Gorge, where the River Teme cuts through the Silurian escarpment. To achieve his effect Knight hardly had to alter the landscape at all: he simply left it alone.

But the conventional English landowner of the eighteenth century, wishing to surround his house with a landscape to suit his taste, had to contend not only with untamed nature but also with the existence, tiresome as it was, of the common man. Since nature and man were equally capable of interrupting his prospects and spoiling his view with undesirable elements, both had to be controlled and ordered. If a village interfered with the landscape it could be removed and the inhabitants resettled in a new village more conveniently located on the edge of the park. In some instances the decline of the village had begun prior to emparking, but the demolition of homes and the complete destruction of the settlement hardly counted as happy events for the occupants (p. 246). The best they could hope for would be a roof over their heads in the new village, which, having been erected by the lord primarily as a status symbol, might qualify as a 'model village' in aesthetic terms but was often less successful as a place to live. These planned villages can usually be easily identified, for they tend to consist of regularly spaced cottages of uniform design. Occasionally the lord would suffer one or two villagers to remain in the park to complete the landscape ideal by fulfilling the role of charming rustics (p. 247).

Only the privileged minority could indulge in grandiose designs such as these, but the lesser gentry also made a substantial contribution to the landscape. Land remained the principal means of translating new-found wealth into social status, and the squirearchy and *nouveaux riches* grasped at the opportunity. They might not be able to rival the great house, landscape garden, and deer park of their peers, but they were able to build smaller country houses, run minor estates and go fox-hunting, which became popular in the eighteenth century as a cheap alternative to deer-hunting. The contrived elements which needed to be incorporated into the landscape in order to preserve foxes and set up the ritual of the chase were markedly less expensive than those required for deer. As an organized sport, with its own etiquette and trappings, specially bred dogs and horses, fox-hunting is in fact a recent institution in England. It became widely popular in the later eighteenth century and enjoyed its 'golden age' early in the nineteenth. Socially it was inferior to deer-hunting, and a good deal of the money, then as now, came from the towns, much of it being spent on the creation, renting or preservation of the necessary landscape features, such as coverts and artificial earths (constructed in an endeavour to maintain numbers and avoid the use of bag foxes) and cut-and-laid hedges (for the horses to jump).

The more prosperous of the small farmers and artisans also built larger and better houses for themselves. The modernization and replacement of medieval dwellings were pursued with such energy that they seemed to embody a general movement, which, using local materials and displaying regional architectural styles and motifs, has come to be known as 'the great rebuilding'. Well-to-do farmers with secure tenures and fixed rents (enabling them to benefit from higher prices), together with lawyers and merchants, erected the beautiful houses which still grace many parts of England today. The small, stone-built manors or more substantial farmhouses of the late sixteenth and early seventeenth centuries, with their gables and mullioned windows (Figure 47), and the timber-framed buildings encountered outside the districts where good stone was available add immeasurably to the visual scene. Indeed, many villages took on their present appearances at this time, even though some of their basic lineaments were developed much earlier.

Figure 47. The manor house, Garsington, Oxfordshire. This beautiful house is a fine example of its style and period. The photograph shows the north front, flanked by high yew hedges which form a small courtyard closed by a low wall and stone gateway with ball finial gatepiers. (The ironwork is nineteenth-century.) The house is of two storeys, with a cupola, stone chimneys (incorporating brick shafts), three gabled attic dormers, mullioned windows, and a front doorway which has acquired a Georgian stone hood. Built in the sixteenth century and occupied by a 'yeoman farmer', the house was remodelled in the seventeenth century by the squires who resided there. The only evidence of its medieval forerunner derives from the presence of fishponds close by

The change was not limited to houses. As secular causes replaced religious institutions as the main recipients of benefactions, schools and almshouses sprang up in many villages and towns. In the richer farmlands imposing barns were erected, often magnificent in proportion and consisting of a nave and aisles (a feature which dates back to Anglo-Saxon times). Some of the finest examples are in the arable districts around the great market of London, notably in Essex.

The 'great rebuilding' was not, however, a straightforward event, limited in its essentials to the period 1570–1640, as was once thought. There is of course the regional dimension: the rebuilding of the north took place much later, at the time when the eighteenth-century improvers were making the most of the neglected landscapes of this formerly insecure and backward province. Over much of Wales, native traditions persisted, giving way before the new styles which entered the Principality from the east and gradually penetrated westwards. The diffusion process was complex spatially, temporally and socially, and the new styles were not simply adopted wholesale but were modified and absorbed into a new iconography intimately related to the geography of Wales. Thus the architectural landscape of the borderland suggests enthusiastic rebuilding in the seventeenth century (with the preservation of many earlier cruck-built timber-framed houses), while in west Wales the rebuilding took place in the nineteenth century. In architectural terms, as in many others, particular parts of Wales reflected the fashions and developments of the adjacent districts of England, the buildings of eastern Wales closely paralleling the English vernacular styles. In Wales, as in England, many buildings passed in later generations to new owners who were further down the social scale than the original occupants. This was especially common in the case of gentry houses, which subsequently became tenanted farms, a development reflected in the inferior quality of later alterations to the buildings.

The term 'great rebuilding' might perhaps be more realistically used to refer to the time when a particular locality was able to erect permanent homes for a substantial proportion of its inhabitants; the interest then concentrates upon the chronology and causes of the movement in different regions. The first wave of permanent vernacular buildings in the fifteenth century was succeeded by several phases of rebuilding in response to economic fortunes, investment preferences and the changing nature of the tenurial interest tied up in individual holdings. The building boom continued, with interruptions, through the seventeenth century, and the demand for houses was still active in the 1700s. Some idea of this complexity can be gained by careful examination of the buildings themselves, bearing in mind that many dated inscriptions record purchase (or the marriage of the occupants) rather than construction, and that the practice of dating itself declined as time went on. Many houses were subsequently altered, so that their histories are hard to unravel.

Despite these architectural puzzles, all the houses described above had one thing in common: they were built for and inhabited by people enjoying at least a measure of prosperity, founded upon a basis which afforded them some degree of security. Large numbers of those who lived and died in the pre-industrial period were not so fortunate, but it is easy to forget them because their apparent imprint on the landscape was not nearly so great. Indeed, it was the scale and resilience of the landscapes of wealth – the houses, gardens, parks, and new field systems – which inspired the once fashionable view that the English landscape was largely the man-made creation of the seventeenth and eighteenth centuries. Naturally, there is a multitude of reasons why this is quite untrue, but such an assertion at least serves, indirectly, to emphasize the very important factor of selective survival. The grand designs and substantial houses of the rich have not only lasted comparatively well but in many instances are being deliberately, and very properly, preserved. On the other hand it is extremely difficult to see concrete examples of several essential components of the pre-industrial scene, notably the transient houses of the poor. Almost all the older buildings in the landscape represent the homes of the better-off sectors of society; even the country cottages which are all the rage these days are rarely true cottages – however tiny they seem to modern eyes – but small farmhouses, and many are not, in their present form at least, very old. The prettified aspect presented by so many 'period houses' today is as far removed from the realities of any past period as are the tastes and occupations of their present occupants or weekenders.

The poor man's dwelling was neither built to last nor constructed by a craftsman. Most were squalid shelters or hovels erected by the occupant himself, using walls of earth or clay roofed with thatch and shored up inside with wooden posts to prevent the structure collapsing. Giraldus Cambrensis, writing in the late twelfth century, recorded that the Welsh lived in 'small huts made of the boughs of trees twisted together, constructed with little labour and expense, and sufficient to endure throughout the year', and Thomas Pennant described the 'houses of the common people' in strikingly similar terms nearly six hundred years later. It is likely that their form changed little over the centuries, and although almost none of the earlier ones exists today, their basic features are undoubtedly represented in the handful of later examples which do survive. Migrant workers made temporary abodes for themselves, such as the 'sorry "cote" pytched unto a nooke of a rock of stone' described in a document of 1604 relating to Charnwood Forest, Leicestershire. The writer goes on to state that the place 'hath been a dwelling house, upon the necessity and want of another house, of a poor man, a wisket [basket] maker, that for his own succour made the same of Stickes and turffes, but paid no rent or fine'. The antiquary William Stukeley, visiting the bleak marchland of Cumbria in 1725, found the houses of the cottagers 'mean beyond imagination; made of mud, and thatched with turf, without windows, only one story; the people almost naked'; in Longtown 'the piles of turf for firing are generally as large and as handsome as the houses'.

Conditions such as these were commonplace within a society where severe poverty was endemic. For thousands the so-called 'flowering of rural England' simply seemed to pass them by and signalled little change in fortune, while the 'age of the improver' actually marked a decline for those whose livelihood was ruined by the enclosure of the commons and the reclamation of the wastes for the benefit of the rich or up-and-coming. The landscapes of poverty are not immediate to the senses as are those of wealth. They are neither so obvious nor so striking, and were ignored by those topographical writers who sought to amuse their readers with antiquities, novelties and improvements. (Defoe referred to this omission in his own *Tour*, published between 1724 and 1727, most memorably in the passage describing his visit to the Giant's Tomb in the Peak District, where he 'miss'd the imaginary wonder, and found a real one', the poor woman who lived in a cave with her lead miner husband and their children. But, concluded the author, if any reader finds the tale 'too low and trifling for this work, they must be told, that I think quite otherwise; and especially considering what a noise is made of wonders in this country, which, I must needs say, have nothing in them curious, but much talked of, more trifling a great deal'.) But there are innumerable indirect clues which can help to reconstruct commonplace scenes. The details are unspectacular, perhaps, but they are essential to the understanding of the landscape as a synthetic whole. The displays of the self-important are only one element in such a conception; the others, in many ways more deep-seated, are furnished by the countless generations of ordinary people whose centuries of labour have contributed so much to the cultural landscape.

A cursory glance at any 'ordinary' piece of landscape will establish the fact of this contribution, but a more detailed examination is required if its full extent is to be revealed. Even those landscapes which appear recent in a morphological and material sense frequently reflect in their shapes and forms the outlines of much older features, such as routeways and boundaries which gradually evolved as a consequence of the activities of countless individuals long forgotten. In order to sense the atmosphere of the pre-industrial rural scene it is desirable to leave the beaten track (as far as this is still possible) and seek out those corners of England and Wales where odd vestiges of that vanished era can be glimpsed. Such places are usually quiet and sheltered, devoid of features likely to attract the attention of the compilers of guidebooks, and unremarkable in terms of architecture, scenery or historical and literary associations. For reasons of physical geography, land use, social structure or the pattern of communications, these districts have been to some degree protected from the winds of change, which, although they may have swept, have not in every case swept clean.

The traveller may come across them quite unexpectedly, struck by an indefinable change in the scale and quality of the landscape. One category comprises the squatter settlements referred to earlier. The chaotic morphology, with altered and patched-up cottages (originally made of turf and branches) linked by narrow lanes twisting between the irregular enclosures of the smallholdings, clearly reflects their haphazard origins. Patterns of life such as these, based upon dual economies, have shown themselves in some cases to be remarkably resistant to change. The traditional landscape forms associated with encroachments still persist in several districts around the country, bound up with distinctive local cultures. Their very locations – on the edges of heaths, moors or forests, beyond the limits of manorial control or the areas affected by enclosure – have aided their survival, except where the population has now declined altogether for want of employment. Even in instances where, although the cottages are still inhabited, occupations have changed, the remnants of the old economies refuse to pass away, as the landscapes themselves demonstrate (Figure 48). Some of the least prosperous local economies, which lingered long in the uplands of the insecure and poverty-ridden Scottish border country, were those associated with the practice of transhumance (shielding), whereby selected members of the farming

Figure 48. Plump Hill, Gloucestershire: an encroachment or squatters' settlement on the edge of the Forest of Dean. The cottages and tiny enclosures are interspersed with old quarries, iron mines and lime kilns

family took the animals up to the summer pastures (shieling grounds) for part of the year. This seasonal use of marginal land is recalled by the remains of stone or turf huts (shielings), stack stands (for the storage of fodder), enclosures of various kinds, and traces of cultivation such as 'lazy beds' (spade-built ridges for simple, small-scale cultivation).

Specialized or marginal areas are not, however, the only places to look. Visits to reputedly unexceptional pieces of countryside in most counties will bring their rewards, especially if one makes the effort to remove, in the mind's eye, such trappings of modernization as metalled roads and overhead wires. Venturing out at the dead time of the year, in January or February, when the landscape seems devoid of colour or life, it is still possible to imagine the dimly-lit scenes of rutted lanes, muddy fields and chill, damp habitations which, when both food and spirits reached their lowest ebb, represented for the great majority of the population the painful realities of life in the pre-industrial age (Figure 49).

Figure 49. February Fill Dyke by Benjamin William Leader (1881)

Towns

The juxtaposition of wealth and poverty was also apparent in the land-scapes of towns. In terms of urban history the pre-industrial period was one of transition between the establishment of the network of market towns during the Middle Ages and the explosive growth which ac-companied industrialization. But although the urban system, as a whole, exhibited a larger measure of qualitative change than of quantitative growth, the fortunes of individual towns fluctuated dramatically. The hierarchy gave the appearance of overall stability, but closer inspection provides many examples of sudden entries and exits, promotions and casualties, successes and failures. The pre-industrial town was small, simple and rurally based. The great majority of the population lived in the countryside, and the towns were intimately related to the agrarian economy. To modern eyes most pre-industrial towns would hardly have presented an urban aspect in the accepted sense of the word.

One of the most striking traits of the pre-industrial town was its vulnerability. Defoe noted in the 1720s that some towns 'are lately encreas'd in trade and navigation, wealth, and people, while their neighbours decay', and there are many accounts of towns which, although quite substantial by contemporary standards, fell into ruin. The causes were various. Catastrophic fires were commonplace, the Great Fire of London being the most spectacular only by merit of the exceptional size and singular importance of the metropolis. The often densely packed houses, with their primitive chimneys and oversailing (protruding) upper storeys, built of easily combustible materials such as plaster, timber and thatch, constituted an immense fire risk, and once alight usually defied the efforts of the inhabitants to extinguish the blaze until the greater portion of the town had been consumed. Major fires affected a large number of towns at least once, and in many cases several times: Wareham, Dorset, was largely destroyed in 1762 after some careless person had thrown out 'fiery Turf ashes on a Dunghil near ye center of ye Town and meeting of ye 4 principal streets'. Eventually these disasters prompted more careful rebuilding in stone, a movement which gave rise to the crop of elegant Georgian town houses to be seen today in provincial towns. Thus the brick houses of Marlborough, Wiltshire, erected after the fire of 1653, are late seventeenth- or eighteenth-century in their entirety, with no earlier timber-framing concealed behind their façades. At Blandford Forum, Dorset (p. 254), a whole new design for the town was executed after the conflagration of 1731. During most of the period, however, few effective precautions were taken against fire. It has been suggested that the attractive greens which are interspersed among the streets of Southwold, Suffolk, were deliberately created as firebreaks after the fire of 1659, but it seems that some of them at least were present before that date.

Physical changes such as the silting of estuaries or the erosion of coastlines could also adversely affect the lives of towns. Chester suffered from the silting of the Dee, while Dunwich on the Suffolk coast was progressively washed away by the sea, leaving only forlorn fragments on the shore. The debilitating effects of disease, exacerbated by insanitary living conditions, also contributed to the difficulties which beset nearly all towns during these centuries. Nor was prosperity in trade or manufacture sufficient to assure the future of an urban centre. There were, in any case, few specialized towns in the modern sense, founded upon the working of minerals or the mass production of textiles, although some possessed, on top of their basic functions, 'some particular trade or accident to trade', as Defoe put it. These trades were often bound up with one particular figure, for example the 'Rich Clothier', Thomas Spring III of Lavenham, or with some factor beyond the control of the town itself. Southampton flourished as an outport for London in the sixteenth century, but as the pattern of European trade shifted away from the Italian cities to Antwerp, direct dealings with the capital increased, to the discomfort of Southampton. By the end of the seventeenth century the town was, in the words of Celia Fiennes, 'almost forsooke and neglected'. Cases of towns which suffered from competition in this way are legion. Many of the quiet country towns of today, such as Stamford in Lincolnshire or Totnes in Devon, were once thriving places associated with particular manufactures, notably cloth. But new forms of economic organization and developments in the structure of trade, accompanied by spatial shifts in production, precipitated their eclipse. Some of the towns which lost their advantage literally fell down. Flint's ascendancy lasted only as long as its military significance, so that by the end of the seventeenth century Celia Fiennes saw 'a very ragged place many villages in England are better, the houses all thatched and stone walls but so decay'd that in many places ready to tumble down . . .' Middleton in Dorset was deliberately demolished by the self-styled Lord Milton simply because he was not greatly taken with the look of it (p. 245).

It is hard to grasp the scale of the pre-industrial town (Figure 50). Few county towns boasted populations of more than three or four thousand, and even those places regarded in 1600 as sizeable (such as Tiverton, Ipswich or Colchester) were only slightly larger. The top five towns at this time (London apart) were Norwich, York, Bristol, Newcastle and Exeter, but these were still small by modern standards, Norwich containing perhaps 15,000 people in 1600. Several of the towns which were in the upper part of the hierarchy are quite modest settlements today, and it is hard to imagine that they were places of importance, the image of the large town not yet being manifested in a Manchester or a Birmingham. But it would be quite wrong to think of the pre-industrial urban system as stagnant, even though there were losers in the struggles between individuals. Besides the developing market centres and, towards the

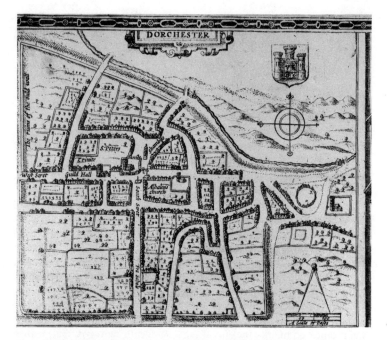

Figure 50. Dorchester, Dorset: a plan by John Speed, 1610. This map, although stylized –
Speed was not a surveyor – gives a fair impression of the scale, structure, principal buildings
and countrified aspect of a county town in pre-industrial England. It was compiled just before
the great fire of 1613. By this time most of the Roman defences had gone (although a good deal
had survived as late as the sixteenth century), but elements of the medieval street plan probably
reflect the configurations of the Roman town of *Durnovaria*, and the position of its gates. At
any rate, early seventeenth-century Dorchester lay entirely within the area delimited by the
lines of the Roman walls, and much of the town had not yet been built up

end of the period, the incipient industrial towns, where new modes of
manufacturing organization were shortly to emerge in association with
advances in technology and transport, several special kinds of town were
making their appearance. Among these were the ports, notably Bristol
and Liverpool. Some, like Falmouth, were new creations; Whitehaven in
Cumbria was laid out by Sir John Lowther in the late seventeenth century.
(Indeed, the very success of Whitehaven destroyed its original character:
most of the mansions which occupied blocks in the gridiron plan were
pulled down in the nineteenth century and replaced by rows of terraced
houses.) The dockyards formed a special category, in which Devonport
took pride of place. Established as a naval base in the late seventeenth

century it expanded greatly during the Napoleonic Wars, even outstripping for a time its venerable neighbour, Plymouth.

The seventeenth century also witnessed the emergence of the early spas. The towns which grew up around medicinal springs boomed in the Georgian era. They began as health resorts, attracting a fashionable clientele who were only moderately interested in taking the waters, as Cobbett observed later (1826) in his tirade against the watering places, 'to which East India plunderers, West India floggers, English tax-gorgers, together with gluttons, drunkards, and debauchees of all descriptions, female as well as male, resort, at the suggestion of silently laughing quacks, in the hope of getting rid of the bodily consequences of their manifold sins and iniquities'. Tunbridge Wells in Kent still displays some of the features which accompanied its success as a late seventeenth-century spa for the rich. The promenade known as The Pantiles, named after the original paving tiles employed there, preserves its arcade and shops, while local names such as Mount Ephraim and Mount Sion recall the Puritanical strain apparent in the patrons. Defoe declared that 'company and diversion is in short the main business of the place; and those people who have nothing to do any where else, seem to be the only people who have any thing to do at Tunbridge'. But the real flowering of the spa townscapes came in the eighteenth century, with the development of the watering places as desirable residential centres. In this respect Bath outshone all its rivals, totally outclassing even its nearest competitor, Buxton in Derbyshire, with its glittering social life and the architectural grandeur of crescent, square and circus (p. 256).

In terms of size, growth and dynamism London provided the exception to practically every rule regarding the pre-industrial town. A primate city *par excellence*, its population in 1600 exceeded that of Norwich, the second city of England, by approximately fifteen times, and before the end of the seventeenth century it had passed the half million mark, even the Plague and Fire causing merely momentary setbacks. Its demographic success was made possible only by in-migration, as the city was probably not self-replacing until about 1750. London was inseparably bound up with the rest of the country economically and socially as well as demographically, constituting as it did the greatest market, the centre of innovation, the seat of government and the hub of fashion. The spirit of James I's oft-quoted remark that 'soon London will be all England' was echoed many times and was borne out in a multitude of ways. Defoe wrote of 'new squares, and new streets rising up every day', but lamented the spreading out of the city 'in a most straggling, confus'd manner, out of all shape, uncompact, and unequal'. London was a colossus, a teeming hive of activity, crowded, insanitary and poverty-ridden; but it was also a catalyst of the modernization process which transformed the English pre-industrial economy.

In terms of urban landscapes, London played a crucial role as the trend-setter in architectural style and the testing ground for new concepts in planning and design. The ideas of Inigo Jones, inspired by the Italian Renaissance, first found expression in London (the Banqueting Hall of Whitehall Palace and the scheme for Covent Garden), but it was some time before their impact was felt elsewhere. Only with the popular tide of Palladianism a century later was the vernacular tradition severely displaced. The regional styles and local materials which gave English and Welsh towns such an individual stamp were supplanted by classical designs. Older buildings came to be hidden behind fashionable façades, and the obliteration by fire of large sectors of towns was used as an opportunity to plan afresh, as at Blandford Forum. The new fashions diffused hierarchically as well as spatially, appearing first in the 'society' towns such as Bath, where John Wood's Queen's Square was laid out following the success of the squares in London. The cathedral town of Lichfield was described by Defoe as 'a place of good conversation and good company', and its status as the social capital of Staffordshire is reflected to this day in its handsome seventeenth- and eighteenth-century houses. The atmosphere of the town was preserved by its subsequent relative stagnation and deliberate failure to attract industry.

The same tendencies were evident in civic and ecclesiastical building. The Georgian town halls, market halls and custom houses which grace many of the country's older towns are invaluable elements of the townscape. Some of the grandest monuments of the period can be seen in the university city of Oxford, where Gibbs's masterful Radcliffe Camera of 1737–49 concluded a memorable period of building associated with such distinguished names as Stone, Wren, Hawksmoor and Aldrich (Figure 51).

But whether one lingers amid the magnificence of exceptional cities like Bath or Oxford or wanders round the backstreets of less celebrated towns, trying to reconstruct in imagination the intricate townscapes which resulted from the complex patterns of occupational and social segregation characteristic of the pre-industrial urban scene, one conclusion remains inescapable. The era of explosive growth in towns, which was to transform a rural society into an urban one, changing almost out of all recognition the scale and nature of the townscape, was yet to come. The prime mover in this metamorphosis was the parcel of economic developments associated with the process of industrialization.

Figure 51. Oxford. This aerial photograph gives a splendid view over central Oxford from the south-south-west. The Saxon *burh* was established upon a gravel terrace above the floodplains of the Rivers Thames and Cherwell, both the site and the rectilinear street plan of the early settlement influencing the later development of the town. The principal streets intersected at Carfax ('the meeting of the four ways'), which can be seen near the middle of the left side of the picture. Cornmarket runs northwards from Carfax, while the High Street extends in a great sweep to the east (right) on its way to Magdalen Bridge. From the Middle Ages onward, the university buildings formed an increasingly prominent element in the townscape. The photograph demonstrates the contribution which the late seventeenth and earlier part of the eighteenth centuries made to the architectural heritage of Oxford. The climax came with the completion in 1749 of the Radcliffe Camera, the rotunda in the centre of the upper half of the picture. Immediately to the right is the North Quad of All Souls College, with its twin towers, built by Hawksmoor, who began work on it in 1716. Further still to the right, on the edge of the picture, is the Front Quad of The Queen's College, its screen with domed gatehouse (1734) fronting the north side of The High. The lower half of the photograph is dominated by the majestic spaciousness of Christ Church. West of the cathedral lies Tom Quad, the largest quad in Oxford, begun by Cardinal Wolsey in the 1520s but given its famous 'Gothic' tower by Wren in 1682. (The lower section of Tom Tower – the arched gateway with flanking turrets – is Wolsey's.) Above Tom Quad can be seen Peckwater Quad (completed in 1714), the work of the brilliant and versatile Henry Aldrich, who was Dean of Christ Church in the years around 1700

Sites

The Somerset Levels: the landscape of Improvement (O.S. 1:25,000 Sheets
ST 34 and 44)
The wave of enthusiasm for agricultural improvement which gathered
momentum in England and Wales during the eighteenth century encountered one of its greatest challenges in the marshlands. The particular
problems of these districts demanded more than the trial of new crop
combinations, husbandry practices and soil improvement techniques, or
a fashionable interest in innovation: the Levels had literally to be wrested
from nature by means of drainage schemes and protected from renewed
flooding before the new landscape could be created and put to profitable
use. This required not only energy and organization but the overcoming
of entrenched opposition on the part of the population, severe financial
obstacles, institutional inadequacies, and technological backwardness.
Although progress had been made in eastern England by this time,
producing the singular landscape of the Fenland with its drains and
windmills, these factors had conspired to frustrate large-scale attempts to
improve the Somerset Levels. The spirit of medieval improvement in the
Levels (p. 183) had languished in the depressed economic climate of
the fourteenth century, and with the eventual upturn came also the
Dissolution of the monasteries, which effectively removed the central
motivating force behind the progress made earlier. Even the renewed
concern of the seventeenth century,when the fashion for reclamation was
promoting change elsewhere, had few results. This was despite interest on
the part of Charles I, on the look-out (as ever) for any quick profit to
be gained, and the energy of Sir Cornelius Vermuyden, who, having
apparently succeeded with his Fenland operations, turned to Somerset
after the Civil War, only to have his plans blocked by the angry commoners. This opposition might seem to stem from nothing less than sheer
perversity, but reclamation was a very expensive business, paid for by a
levy on local inhabitants, and these costs, together with the loss of common
rights and the highly speculative nature of the drainage schemes, which
themselves carried no guarantee of success, tipped the balance away from
support to stubborn resistance.

In the last quarter of the eighteenth century came a notable change. A
period of energetic activity in the Levels was initiated through a combination of economic incentives consequent upon an increased national
demand for food, appeals by the commoners for a fairer distribution of
land in the face of intolerable levels of over-stocking, the emergence of a
class of wealthier farmers, and the improving zeal of a group of enthusiasts,

assisted by the institutional changes and legal advantages afforded by the Parliamentary Enclosure Acts. For the first time, a co-ordinated assault was made on the peat moors, so that by 1840 the Levels, although still liable to inundation and about to be subjected to another phase of insufficient maintenance and neglect, were at least drained in theory if not in reality. Furthermore, the years between 1770 and 1840 were of great significance in landscape terms, for they saw the creation of many of the present features of the 'landscape of improvement' in the Levels.

The biggest single project was the King's Sedgemoor Drain of 1791, which carried the waters of the River Cary along a new course from Henley Corner (ST 435327) to Dunball near the mouth of the River Parrett (310408), several miles below the original confluence of the Cary and Parrett at Burrow Bridge. The former channel had been sinuous and inefficient, and the disastrous submergence of King's Sedgemoor in times of flood spurred Arthur Young in 1771 to condemn the moor as nothing less than 'a disgrace to the whole nation'. The ten-mile-long Drain, although only partially successful in functional terms, formed a striking new element in the landscape of the southern Levels. At Dunball a new clyse was built; a clyse is a one-way tidal sluice which allows river water to flow into the sea at low tide, but at high tide, by closure of the gates, prevents penetration of sea water into the Levels. The success of the device depends upon the length of the high tide and the ability of the river channel to contain the water ponding up while the gates are shut; Dunball clyse was in fact built at too high a level, thus reducing the gradient of the drain and causing excessive siltation and renewed flooding. The faults associated with the King's Sedgemoor Drain were not rectified until the Second World War.

Other drainage works were less grandiose. The rhynes, which constitute the extremities of the drainage network, were increased in number, functioning not only as drainage ditches but as convenient sources of water in summer and as a cheap method of boundary marking. The resultant landscape is clearly represented on the O.S. 1:25,000 Sheets ST 34 and 44. Owing to the number and involved nature of competing claims, the pattern of eighteenth- and nineteenth-century enclosures is extremely intricate. A highly regular system of boundaries distinguishes these areas from the old reclamations, such as those on the coastal clay belt around Huntspill (ST 310455), where the winding natural drainage channels strongly influenced the shapes of the medieval fields. Tiny, narrow plots cover the districts where turbary (turf-cutting) rights complicated the division still further: good examples may be seen in the central Levels west of Glastonbury, especially at Catcott Grounds and Catcott, Shapwick and Meare Heaths (which lie in the south-west quarter of Sheet ST 44).

A certain degree of new building accompanied these enclosures, introducing unmistakable brick farmhouses (and distinctive place-names) into the previously sparsely settled Levels. (A clearly recognizable area of new settlement lies between East Huntspill and Highbridge on Sheet ST 34.) The opportunities were, however, limited, despite the improver John Billingsley's enthusiasm over the salutary effects of better drainage upon a district formerly cursed by 'agues, and low fevers, from the humidity of the air, impregnated with exhalations from the stagnant contents of the marshes' (*General view of the agriculture of the County of Somerset*, 1798). The maps also show the arrangement of new droveways created at this time for the movement of stock; many of them terminate abruptly in dead ends, and a large number are merely grassy tracks which have never been metalled.

In conclusion, the landscapes of the Somerset Levels, with their expanses of green pastures, meadows and warths divided by the network of rhynes and droveways, dissected by peat-digging trenches and interrupted by the lines of pollarded willows and osier beds, represent the visual manifestations of a fundamental change in the natural environment. The process of reclamation has profoundly altered not only the hydrology of the district but also the soils and vegetation and has created a landscape which at every turn records a delicate adjustment of human activities to natural constraints. As a wetland tamed from its natural state, it offers a remarkable comparison of the respective achievements of two principal phases of landscape development evident in the English countryside: the colonization of the waste, and the age of the improver.

Westbury Court Garden, Gloucestershire

The garden at Westbury Court (SO 718138) in the village of Westbury-on-Severn, Gloucestershire, is a very rare example of the formal style characteristic of the seventeenth-century English garden. The fact that such survivals are not numerous (Melbourne Hall in Derbyshire is one of the few others), together with their small size (five acres in the case of Westbury Court), might suggest that the English garden was of little importance in the landscape as a whole. Today this is certainly true, but before the 'naturalistic' landscaping of the eighteenth century superseded them and eventually swept them away, formal gardens were common, despite the expense and labour which their creation and upkeep demanded. Westbury Court (Figure 52) provides an invaluable picture of decorative landscape planning before the revolution in taste changed the face of the

Figure 52. Westbury Court Garden. This photograph shows the north-eastern end of the 'T' canal, with (from left to right), one of the *clairvoyées*, the gazebo, the walled garden (behind the white gate), and the statue of Neptune. It has been variously suggested that all these features were added to the garden by Maynard Colchester's nephew, Maynard II, shortly after he inherited the estate in 1715

landscape garden and destroyed very nearly all the formal layouts (p. 243). Westbury Court Garden was itself only saved by a whisker. A careful programme of restoration by the National Trust has transformed the garden from a state of decay, and it now equals the original meticulous standards of care. This restoration was made possible by the detailed notes left by its creator, Maynard Colchester, who laid out the garden between 1696 and 1705.

The formal English garden was inspired by continental models, particularly the French, and was rigidly geometrical, elaborately planned, and almost obsessively trim. Westbury Court is generally considered to be a classic example of a 'Dutch' garden, on account of its overall appearance, its details, and the style of its buildings. The sense of enclosure; the presence of regularly shaped lengths of water known in this context as canals, which reflect the lines of clipped holly and yew trees on their edges; the intricate topiary; the emphasis on bulbs and 'useful' plants; and the form of the *parterre* are all interpreted as Dutch characteristics. The tall red brick pavilion or summerhouse at the end of the Long Canal, supported on white pillars and surmounted by a glazed cupola, is accorded a Dutch inspiration by merit both of its style and of its height, affording a view over the flat garden with its canals. However, while a unifying framework has conveniently been created for all these features by means of the Dutch appellation, the lack of explicit Dutch connections or inspirations evidenced in the documents has led some specialists of garden history to doubt the reality of such an influence, and to suggest furthermore that in practice Dutch gardens were little different from French ones.

Whatever the truth, the matter does not affect the general significance of Westbury Court in the wider context of the English landscape. Here is a splendid example of a pre-naturalistic English garden, as faithfully restored in its details as finances and labour availability allow – Maynard Colchester after all had several 'weederwomen' working for him! It has been thoughtfully replanted with native species and an authentic selection of plants introduced into England before 1700; this careful use of 'old-fashioned' varieties instead of the often gaudy modern hybrids contributes a great deal to the atmosphere of the garden. The buildings have been restored and the canals dredged and repaired. Besides the pavilion and the straight canal, there is a small pavilion and a T-shaped canal (probably constructed slightly later, in the early eighteenth century), and the garden is separated from the road by two *clairvoyées* (screens of wrought-iron bars) flanked by pillars with, in one case, pineapple finials and, in the other, urns (Figure 52). The *clairvoyées* afford a glimpse of the garden sufficient to tempt one inside, but do not destroy the sense of seclusion once there. Three more have been added along the sidewall so that a view can be obtained from the nearby home for the elderly, which stands between the garden and the churchyard on the site of the sixteenth-century house occupied by Maynard Colchester.

Stourhead, Wiltshire

Stourhead is a unique planned landscape in which all the elements have been carefully selected, sited and integrated to provide a delicately staged aesthetic experience. It exemplifies the eighteenth-century vision of ordered nature, controlled yet enhanced by judicious improvements and subtly flavoured with symbolism, allusion and allegory to tempt the fancy, guide the steps and delight the eye of the informed visitor. Here is a landscape which expresses the philosophy of its creators as eloquently as any written document could.

The landscaping of the grounds at Stourhead (ST 7734) was begun in earnest during the 1740s by Henry Hoare II (1705–85), known as 'the Magnificent' to distinguish him from the other Henry Hoares, including his father who had replaced the old manor of Stourton with a new Palladian house twenty years earlier. The name Stourhead referred to the valley which contains one of the headwaters of the River Stour. The Upper Greensand-Gault junction throws out a series of springs to feed a small stream which by Hoare's day had already been ponded up to form a sequence of pools. Henry Hoare II constructed a full-scale dam in order to create a large triangular lake, whose level was allowed to rise as the various landscape features around it were completed. The lake provided the centrepiece for the whole design, which was developed by Hoare and modified by his successors before being placed in the wise and sympathetic custodianship of the National Trust.

The landscape around the lake was self-contained, the architectural pieces being carefully placed amid the scheme of planting to mark stages in a circuit walk. The buildings served several functions, recalling scenes and events of antiquity, encouraging the visitor to ruminate upon the march of human progress and to indulge his presumed love of the classics, and acting as foci within a deliberately manipulated visual scene. Similar enclosed and organized promenades were created at Stowe, Buckinghamshire (the Elysian Fields), and at Rousham, Oxfordshire, where the Venus Vale formed the central element in William Kent's design.

Kent's work at Rousham (1737–41) marked the first wholesale departure from the excessive geometrical formalism of the English garden, typified by Westbury Court (p. 240). Kent drew inspiration from the Palladianism which delighted his patron, the third Earl of Burlington; from the paintings of certain seventeenth-century artists, including Poussin and Claude, depicting idealized classical scenes amid 'natural' Italian landscapes dotted with ruins, which captured the imagination of those who made the Grand Tour; and from the writings of men like Joseph Addison and Kent's friend Alexander Pope, who lambasted the stiflingly unimaginative regularity of the English formal garden. Although the blazing Mediterranean sun which radiated from the canvases was noticeably absent from England, and despite the fact that Kent was no gardener – he once suggested planting dead trees for effect – he inaugurated a new era in garden design, smoothing out sharp lines and corners and introducing carefully contrived irregularities and sudden changes of scene. The rigid structure of the English garden had necessitated professional assistance for its creation, and a good deal of time, trouble and money for its maintenance. Now the amateur could experiment with his own curved and graded avenues, bodies of water, and mixtures of trees. The once clear distinction between the garden (an enclosure next to the house turned over to the cultivation of plants) and the park (a game preserve) became increasingly blurred. The garden was made more 'natural', and came to be integrated in a visual sense with the park beyond, from which it was no longer separated by a fence or wall which blocked the view, but by a sunken boundary invisible from a distance. This device was known as a ha-ha, allegedly because it surprised people who failed to notice this check to their walk until they suddenly came upon it, the discovery apparently doubling them up with laughter. The only traditional link between garden and park had been the 'wilderness', an intermediate area which contained an extended but not really 'natural' rambling walk amid trees, shrubs or hedges. This was continued into the park and made more irregular in order to produce the kind of involved circuit walk exemplified at Stourhead. The park ceased to be a hunting park in the medieval sense, and became a landscaped park instead. It attained its peak of popularity in the later eighteenth century when 'Capability' Brown abolished the garden altogether, extending the conception of idealized nature to embrace whole parks, sometimes designing on a huge scale (Blenheim, Figure 46), and finally setting the house directly in the park itself. Stourhead is important as a magnificent example of a landscape garden realized under the auspices of an amateur, who, having been to Italy and admired the scenery in the fashionable way with the help of Claude's paintings, expressed his own whims and fancies in a design intermediate between those of Kent (who died in 1748) and Brown.

The walk is of great variety, the diverse associations reflecting an eclectic background of inspiration. The pagan deities of rivers and springs are represented, together with heroes such as Aeneas, Hercules and King Alfred. This seemingly incongruous set is only one element in the complex iconography of the garden, which, like the paintings of Poussin, takes for granted a familiarity with classical myth and philosophy no longer current. Unlike Hoare, who was widely read – he was, it seems, particularly fond of Virgil – the vast majority of modern visitors to Stourhead are unable to interpret the elaborately constructed symbolism of the garden which its founder would have deemed central to its full appreciation. But the perambulation cannot fail to draw the wanderer into the pleasant dream world of eighteenth-century fancy, as he or she circumambulates the lake, admiring the rich collection of trees (the exotic species were added after Henry Hoare's time) and meeting or glimpsing the architectural adornments, such as the Bristol High Cross near the church (itself rendered part of the landscape composition), the Temples of Flora and Apollo, the Grotto, and the Pantheon (Figure 53).

Some commentators salute the Stourhead landscape as one of deep and tranquil beauty, in which idealized nature, contrived with rare skill and refinement, rises superior to real nature. Others find it absurdly mannered, and resent the assumption that nature could be so 'improved' to pander

Figure 53. Stourhead: the Palladian Bridge and the Pantheon

to the self-centred whims of the eighteenth-century aristocracy, who wished to have everything about them – man and nature – controlled and tamed. But gardens have always selected, tamed and coaxed nature, and the idea of the English landscape garden was to allow the fancies of the individual to roam upon the scene at will, gently prompted by the composition but free to play upon his or her personal fantasies. This surely remains one of the pleasures of such gardens, to be enjoyed and not taken too seriously. For as a garden Stourhead is undeniably beautiful, and it is an arresting thought that its creators designed it and planted it with an eye to future generations. Would that modern society displayed comparable concern for those to come.

Milton Abbas, Dorset
The destruction and displacement of villages by eighteenth-century land-owners were by no means uncommon. In order to realize their grandiose schemes for the parading of social and aesthetic pretensions, the aristocracy were as eager to remove those communities of their inferiors which impinged upon them too closely as they were to exclude those aspects of nature's handiwork which could not be similarly confined or manipulated. The villagers were often rehoused in a model village separate from the great house and its landscaped park, the cottage architecture embodying a style deemed appropriate to the station of the inhabitants.

Milton Abbas is of particular interest because the demolished settlement was not an already decayed village, but a small medieval market town which, although probably in decline by the eighteenth century, was still of a considerable size. The town of Middleton had grown initially as a result of the founding of a Benedictine monastery in the wooded chalkland valley, while the rich local agriculture and the town's markets and fairs had helped it to survive the Dissolution, when the townspeople were able to take over the magnificent fourteenth-century abbey for their parish church. The whole town, apart from the odd cottage, and all the monastic buildings except for the abbot's hall and the abbey itself were swept away in the late eighteenth century by Joseph Damer, M.P., Lord Milton and later first Earl of Dorchester, who bought Milton Abbey in 1752. He built a mansion beside the abbey (which he adopted as a distinctly oversized private chapel), and established a new village out of sight to the southeast; the park was landscaped by 'Capability' Brown.

Damer was described by his architect as an 'unmannerly and imperious lord'; it seems that his persecution complex was partly to blame for his destruction of a complete town simply because it irritated him. Perhaps some notion of Damer's self-importance can be formed from the monument to his wife placed in the Abbey, in which a reclining Lord Milton in full regalia gazes vapidly at his dead spouse. He may be trying to look affectedly grief-stricken here, but he cared little for the relatives of those whose headstones he deliberately broke up as a rebuke to sentiment when demolishing the old churchyard, or for the vulgar bones of the lower orders which kept appearing in a tiresome way when the gardens were being planned. He turned the nearby Norman chapel of St Catherine into a labourer's cottage, and built his mansion (condemned by its own architect as a 'vast ugly house') right next to the abbey. The style of ruination created by the demolition of Middleton was apparently not picturesque enough for Damer, so he erected his own 'ruin' to the southwest of the abbey, using materials obtained from the town! Nevertheless, the park south of the house (through which runs a public footpath from the west end of the abbey to the new village) preserves the plan of the old town as a series of banks and hollows, with the former garden plots of the houses especially clear on the eastern slopes.

Damer had to wait twenty years before all the leases in the town expired. One householder refused to sell, so Damer cut the dams which were ponding up water for his new lake, and flooded the offender's home. As Sir Frederic Eden reported in 1797, 'the town of Abbey Milton, which in the ancient times of abbatial grandeur was the central market of the county, is now converted into a fish-pond'. Many of the townspeople were no doubt poor enough, but those detailed to live in the prim new village must have found the tiny cottages intolerably cramped: not only was each box in the street designed to function as a pair of residences, but at one time was made to do for no fewer than four families. In the middle of one row is the church of 1786; opposite are the seventeenth-century almshouses, which were re-erected here in 1779. There is a certain irony in the fact that the 1950s council houses were built on the nearby windy heights in order to be away from the now desirable residences of the model village; Lord Dorchester would no doubt have approved of this twentieth-century extension of his own ideas concerning landscape aesthetics and social class.

Nuneham Courtenay, Oxfordshire

Nuneham Courtenay provides a perfect example of Georgian emparking; the removal and rebuilding of the village allegedly inspired Oliver Goldsmith's poem 'The Deserted Village'. In the 1750s Simon, first Earl Harcourt, decided to leave the ancient family seat of Stanton Harcourt to the west of Oxford and establish a new residence south of the city. The site chosen lay upon a tree-clad Lower Greensand bluff overlooking the River Thames, its infertile soils having been traditionally colonized by thick woods. The place was ideal for landscaping, affording a variety of potential vistas and a prospect of Oxford in the distance.

The scheme was begun by the first Earl (1714–77), who was, among other things, an antiquarian and amateur architect, and the work was continued by his son, George Simon Harcourt (1736–1809), patron of a group of writers, designers and painters and himself an artist. Between them they transformed the landscape at Nuneham Courtenay, removing the old church and village of Newnham (which spoilt the view from the new house) and building new cottages for the tenants on the edge of the park. The story goes that one old widow was unhappy about leaving her 'clay-built cot' and was allowed to stay until her death, residing in the gardens as a kind of 'Arcadian shepherdess'.

No detail was overlooked in the task of creating an ideal landscape which conformed to prevailing neo-classical tastes. The new house was designed as a Palladian villa, which goes a long way towards accounting for its deficiencies as a family seat and for the resultant extensions and alterations which rendered it unsatisfactory both in visual terms and as a place to live. In order to realize the views from the house, the glimpsed spires of Oxford were to be coaxed into recalling Claude's prospect of Rome from the Campagna – the village had to go. The church was pulled down and rebuilt in 1764 in the guise of a domed classical temple. The first Earl contributed to its design, which was inspired principally by aesthetic and ornamental considerations. (Not until the 1870s was a church provided in the village for the convenience of worshippers.)

The gardens were described by Horace Walpole in 1780 as among the most beautiful in the world, and it is a matter of great regret that they have suffered so much since 'Capability' Brown and others laid them out two hundred years ago. Little remains of the old flower garden, which represented an important stage in the evolution of garden design, although the Doric Temple of Flora survives. The paths, rustic bridge, thatched lock-keeper's cottage, busts, urns, inscriptions, shrubs, trees and lake formed an ensemble which epitomized contemporary taste. The poet William Whitehead lauded the improvements effected by his patron in a poem which functioned as a counter to Goldsmith's condemnation of the destruction of 'sweet Auburn':

> Dame Nature, the goddess, one very bright day,
> In strolling through Nuneham, met Brown in her way:
> 'And bless me,' she said, with an insolent sneer,
> 'I wonder that fellow will dare to come here.
> What more than I *did* has your impudence plann'd?
> The lawn, wood, and water, are all of my hand.' ...
> Brown:
> 'Who thinn'd, and who group'd, and who scattered those trees,
> Who bade the slopes fall with that delicate ease,
> Who cast them in shade, and who plac'd them in light,
> Who bade them divide, and who bade them unite?
> The ridges are melted, the boundaries gone:
> Observe all these changes, and candidly own
> I have cloath'd you when naked, and, when overdrest,
> I have stripp'd you again to your boddice and vest;
> Conceal'd ev'ry blemish, each beauty display'd,
> As Reynolds would picture some exquisite maid,
> Each spirited feature would happily place,
> And shed o'er the whole inexpressible grace.'

The new village was constructed on the Oxford-Henley turnpike, and consisted mainly of two rows of regularly spaced neat brick cottages, facing each other across the road (Figure 54).

Bradford-on-Avon, Wiltshire

Bradford-on-Avon embodies the last phase of the west of England's pre-industrial cloth manufacture, before the introduction of large factories in the north transformed the nature, structure and location of cloth-making.

Figure 54. Nuneham Courtenay: the new village

The site is an exciting one, with the streets climbing steeply up from the River Avon, which here begins its journey through the Jurassic upland, having cut through the Great Oolite to leave a vast amphitheatre in the northern valleyside slopes on its right bank. The terraces of stone houses and cottages rise above each other in tiers, looking down upon the intricate town centre, the convergence of streets at the bridge, and the winding course of the Avon itself (Figure 55).

Figure 55. Bradford-on-Avon: the bridge and town from the east

Although most of the fine buildings date from the late seventeenth and eighteenth centuries, there is an impressive heritage of earlier houses, which together with the monumental early fourteenth-century tithe barn at Barton (ST 824604) and the lengthened chancel of the same date in the church, serve to indicate that Bradford's prosperity was far from inconsiderable even in the centuries before its heyday. Leland recorded in his *Itinerary* (*c.* 1540) that 'Al the toune of Bradeford stondith by clooth making', and this early prestige, combined with the scenic splendour of the site, helped to distinguish Bradford as a town of superior taste in comparison with its neighbour Trowbridge, which was said to concentrate merely upon money-making, crude and simple. Although factories did establish themselves in Bradford in the early nineteenth century, Trowbridge was the only town in the district which succeeded in surviving the swing away from high-quality cloth such as broadcloths and medleys to cheaper, factory-made products. During the 1830s Bradford's population fell by a quarter, and although some of the mills were converted into rubber factories in the following decade, the town's fortunes never regained their former heights.

Since architecture is one of the main lines of evidence concerning the life styles and activities of the clothiers, a study of Bradford's houses is especially rewarding. Most of the town lies to the north of the bridge, which, although it presents a seventeenth-century aspect, still preserves two thirteenth-century arches south of the so-called chapel set on a cutwater (cf. St Ives, Cambridgeshire; Rotherham, South Yorkshire; and Wakefield, West Yorkshire). The chapel subsequently became a 'Blind House' or lockup. The domestic buildings of Bradford are of several types. The earlier clothiers' houses are represented by Old Church House in Church Street, built by Thomas Horton (d. 1530), and by the ruins of The Priory at the top of Market Street (near the junction with Newtown), hidden beyond the high, dark wall on the south-west side of the street. The family of Methuen (the original name of the house) lived here between the mid-seventeenth and mid-eighteenth centuries; Aubrey hailed Paul Methuen as 'the greatest cloathier of his time'. The Methuens attracted a number of Flemish weavers to Bradford, who in turn formed a community commemorated in the name 'Dutch Barton'.

The real building boom occurred in the late seventeenth and early eighteenth centuries, and left an impressive legacy of Georgian town houses. The wealth of the clothiers and the proximity of Bath and Bristol resulted in a good deal of swagger in the architectural details. Especially notable are Abbey House and Druce's Hill House (named after the Quaker clothiers) in Church Street, and a fine group (Lynchetts, Moxhams,

St Olave's) in Woolley Street (the extension of Silver Street). Finally, Westbury House, just to the south of the bridge, should not be missed. It was here, in 1791, that a mob of five hundred machine rioters besieged the then owner, the clothier Phelps, and demanded that he give up his scribbling machine. Eventually Phelps surrendered the offending object, which was burned on the bridge, but not before he and his supporters had fired on the crowd, wounding several and killing a man, a woman and a boy. It was a telling illustration of contemporary attitudes when the coroner's inquest returned a verdict of 'justifiable homicide'. Fifteen years later, a witness from Bradford was to state before the *Committee on the Woollen Manufacture of England* (1806) that if the machinery 'had not been instituted there would not be so many boys running about the streets without shoes or stockings on, and nearly half starved'.

A final example of a rich clothier's house is unique in that it was designed as a country house rather than as a town house. The Hall, reached by a lodge in Woolley Street, was built by the clothier John Hall in *c.* 1610, and is set in its own grounds. It offers a striking contrast with the terraces of cottages and weavers' houses which ascend the hillside above Newtown. Middle Rank and Tory furnish a real pre-industrial town atmosphere, where one can wander in front of the façades, admiring both them and the views which they afford over Bradford, before following the alleys behind the houses and climbing ever higher by means of narrow, steeply ascending stepped passages between the cottages and gardens.

Berwick-upon-Tweed, Northumberland
Frontiers are usually exciting and stimulating places, especially where the arrangement of natural features has played a part in shaping a zone of tension and separation through dramatic periods of history. Natural *frontiers*, however, rarely provide clear or precise lines for the drawing of political *boundaries*, while particular sections of a frontier may have been so open to cultural influences from both sides (notably at vital strategic points) that a true marchland landscape, heavily fortified and revealing a complex history involving the relative waxing and waning of the opposing groups, has resulted. A splendid example of such a landscape is found in Northumberland, that county of castles, pele towers, bastle houses and barmkins, occupying the northern part of the coastal sill of north-east England which commands the crucial route between the lowlands of England and Scotland (see p. 191). History's most eloquent testimony to the marchland nature of north Northumberland and the instability of any imposed boundary – not forgetting the use made of the Liddesdale-Cheviot-Tweed line by the Romans as an outpost frontier to the north of

Hadrian's Wall – is that enshrined in the fortunes of Berwick-upon-Tweed.

Situated on the north bank of the Tweed estuary, Berwick became one of the Four Royal Burghs of Scotland in the twelfth century. Although surrendered shortly afterwards to the English, the town changed hands more than a dozen times in the three violent centuries which followed, before becoming English for good in 1482. It then became a free town and a separate community with its own government, an autonomy which lasted in legal terms, rendering Berwick a county of itself, until long after it had ceased to have practical recognition or relevance. Nevertheless, its important strategic position and the continuing threat from the Scots (especially when assisted by those other traditional enemies of the English, the French) meant that Berwick's role as a defence against invasion continued very much in earnest. Edward I had built a castle and wall, but as late as the reign of Elizabeth I new fortifications were constructed. These are sufficiently well preserved to make Berwick one of the finest fortified towns in northern Europe, a place where the forces of geographical and historical momentum unite to impress upon the visitor the reality of the frontier (Figure 56).

Figure 56. Berwick-upon-Tweed from the north

The massive Elizabethan defences, unique in Britain, were begun in 1558 and represent one of the earliest and best-preserved examples in northern Europe of the new military architecture pioneered in Italy. This involved the construction of bastions, or pentagonal walled projections containing gun-platforms, which are connected to the massive walls by narrow collars, forming a sort of arrowhead shape (see Figure 57). Tucked in on either side of the collars, in the three-sided recesses between the collar walls, the main walls and the platforms, are the flankers, which were equipped with more guns, this time pointing across the spaces between the bastions, thus providing enfilade fire to protect every part of the walls. Today one may use the promenade on top of the walls to make a circuit of the old town, bearing in mind that the Elizabethan fortifications excluded the south-western and northern corners of the town. To the

Figure 57. Berwick-upon-Tweed

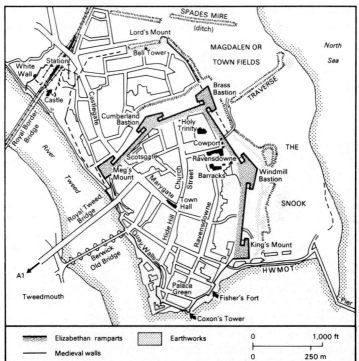

north-east lay the Town Fields or Magdalen Fields, which exhibit some good ridge-and-furrow. The fact that the walls were confined to the town itself and did not encompass the whole of the peninsula upon which Berwick is situated is one of the principal weaknesses of the Elizabethan scheme. Furthermore, the section along the river, between King's Mount and Meg's Mount, was never completed, thus leaving the medieval wall (unimproved until the eighteenth century) as Berwick's only defence to the river. After the scare of the Jacobite rising of 1745, the fortifications were repaired, taking on their present aspect, but since they were never completed in the first place they had exhibited major functional defects from the start.

The perambulation is full of interest, afforded not only by the fortifications, but also by the town itself. Inside the walls on the north-east lie the earliest barracks built in Britain (1717–21), and Holy Trinity, Wallace Green, one of the very few churches built during the Commonwealth. In the southern and eastern districts one finds evidence of the upsurge in prosperity which resulted from the Act of Union and the consequent extension of Berwick's hinterland. Pleasant houses of Carboniferous sandstone, with slate or red pantile roofs, can be enjoyed in Palace Green, Ravensdowne, and along Quay Walls; the impressive rise of Hide Hill, and the dominating cupola and belfry of the Town Hall and former gaol (built in the 1750s) characterize the town centre. Finally, the three bridges should on no account be missed; not only are they of individual interest, but the comparison is a telling one (see p. 314).

Blandford Forum, Dorset

The old town of Blandford, a route focus and market on the River Stour famed for its bonelace and glass-painting manufactures, was virtually destroyed by a great fire in 1731. The local architects John and William Bastard made the most of this opportunity to create a uniquely effective Georgian new town. The eighteenth-century buildings of Blandford can be enjoyed to the full to this day, since later development has largely been excluded from the town centre (Figure 58).

The best place to start is at John Bastard's fire monument, which stands outside the churchyard wall near the west end of the church, giving a good view of the market place. The circumstances of the fire vividly illustrate the precarious existence endured by pre-industrial towns and their inhabitants. The 1731 conflagration was the worst of many fires which ravaged Blandford. On this occasion nearly the whole town was burned to the ground in the course of a summer afternoon, leaving the inhabitants, many of them stricken with smallpox, homeless. The desperate efforts of

Figure 58. Blandford Forum: the market place and church

the population, aided only by primitive fire-fighting equipment, were all to no avail. The flames spread rapidly among the dangerously combustible thatched buildings, returning with a shift of the wind to consume the church. The monument not only acknowledges the Divine Mercy which raised Blandford 'like the PHÆNIX from it's Ashes to it's present beautiful and flourishing State', but was also designed to contain a head of water.

The church was built by the Bastard brothers in the 1730s. It presents an impressive neo-classical exterior, while the splendid interior contains Portland stone columns, a vaulted ceiling, and a wooden west gallery added in 1794. Two 'transepts' protrude on the north and south, midway along the aisles; it is a pity that these characteristic Georgian features have been interfered with. But tastes change: Sir Frederick Treves, in *Highways and Byways in Dorset* (1906), dismissed Blandford church as 'ugly, and only tolerable from a distance', and made no mention of the Georgian town buildings at all.

These are exceptionally fine, combining an overall uniformity with lively individualism, and benefiting from the imaginative use of coloured bricks with the Portland stone. The Bastards' plan involved more than visual aesthetics, however; it sought to establish a number of contrasting zones for the various classes or professions, differentiated by the architectural style deemed appropriate to each. No doubt Georgian preference would normally have dictated an axial alignment for church, monument and market place, but the constricted river valley site and former street plan did not facilitate such an arrangement. The market place contains some striking façades with pilasters and pediments, while in Church Lane, which climbs northwards from the fire monument, can be seen some of the best post-fire houses in the town. At the top, Church Lane meets The Plocks; by turning eastwards (right) here, and continuing through The Tabernacle and into The Close, The Old House is reached. This brick extravaganza probably dates from *c.* 1660 and stands as a notable survivor of the fire.

Bath, Avon

Despite the destruction caused by the Luftwaffe, the potentially even more damaging schemes of some of the post-war planners, and the insidious effects of the motor car, Bath remains the Georgian city *par excellence*. The magnificent succession of crescents, squares and terraces gracing the amphitheatre formed by the sweeping valley of the River Avon is unforgettable. Even at close quarters the perfection of the eighteenth-century landscape can leave one unaware of its two major forerunners: the Roman spa of *Aquae Sulis*, and a prosperous medieval market town and ecclesiastical centre. The present townscape is overwhelmingly the product of the golden age of Bath in the eighteenth century, when the spa, which had been revived following the Dissolution and the decline of the local weaving manufacture, overshadowed all others (Figure 59).

The credit for this transformation, which received considerable early impetus from a series of royal visits, culminating in those of Queen Anne in the first years of the eighteenth century, is generally given to a remarkable trio: Richard 'Beau' Nash, a gambler who became an energetic, bold and autocratic Master of Ceremonies; Ralph Allen, a businessman who bought and developed the Bath stone quarries at Combe Down; and John Wood, the surveyor and builder whose architectural vision inspired the physical realization of Georgian Bath. But the success of their ventures stemmed also from the rapidly changing and increasingly favourable social, institutional and economic context, both local and national, in which they worked. The creation of Bath was itself a sign of a new age, during which entrepreneurial activity and capital investment opportunities broke free from the restrictive structures and financial confines of the pre-industrial era. John Wood was able to solve his capital problems and begin building in Bath only by making a profitable

Figure 59. Bath: *Crescent and Lansdown*: an engraving by W. Watts (originally published in 1794)

arrangement with the owner of the Barton estate, one of the few areas not owned or controlled by the city corporation. Robert Gay leased forty acres to John Wood and his son, who in turn sublet the area to builders, controlling through a system of covenants the conditions and specifications of what was to be constructed, thereby preventing a chaotic explosion of speculative building. John Wood the elder was then in a position to realize his plans. Inspired by the aesthetic precepts of Palladianism, he wished to re-create the architecture of ancient Rome according to the style evolved by the sixteenth-century Italian architect Palladio. Queen Square was completed in 1736, North and South Parades in 1748; and in 1754 (the year of Wood's death) the King's Circus, based upon the Colosseum, was begun. John Wood the younger continued his father's work, his most famous achievement being the grand sweep of the Royal Crescent, built between 1767 and 1774. The principal building material was the beautiful but easily weathered Bath Stone, supplied by Allen from his quarries in the Great Oolite. By 1800 the classical city was more or less complete, and in terms of population was the ninth largest city in England, bigger than either Sheffield or Newcastle upon Tyne.

John Wood the elder was a complicated character. His artistic theories were derived from the belief that classical architecture constituted a divine inspiration, embodying the harmony, order and proportion of God's creation. Wood's urban landscape is more than a mere aesthetic exploration of neo-Roman styles: it is symbolic in a religious and philosophical sense, the geometrical patterns and combinations of artistic motifs being abstracted from an anthropocentric vision of man as the most perfect work of God. In at least three respects these grandiose theories seem contrived and incongruous in the context of Bath. Firstly, Wood's immediate use for them lay in the solution of a personal problem which stemmed from the fact that Palladianism had manifestly pagan rather than Christian roots. Wood needed to convince himself that the pagans had forgotten the divinity inherent in those forms which they had mistakenly claimed as their own invention, and he went to considerable lengths to prove this thesis in his book *The Origin of Building: or, the plagiarism of the heathens detected*, published in Bath in 1741. Secondly, Wood was a self-made man and, whatever his religious and theoretical ideas, he was concerned in practical terms to reap a profit. Finally, his desire to surround earthly man with a reminder of the place of humanity in God's ordered universe appears contradictory and hypocritical when one remembers that not only was Bath society motivated, to a deliberate and unique degree, by worldly pleasures, as well as by an eagerness on the part of its members to cultivate a high place in worldly society, but also that Wood and his fellow entrepreneurs promoted this hedonism and social obsession for their own profit and advancement.

By the time Wood's buildings were finished, Bath had already reached its peak as the premier city of fashion, a playground for the leisured classes governed by the conventions and ritual recorded for posterity in Sheridan's *The Rivals*. But the society has gone for ever, and only the buildings remain; it is all too easy today to regard Bath as the epitome of the 'Age of Elegance and Proportion' which is so often conjured up by modern rose-tinted conceptions of the eighteenth century. The elegance, which by and large comprised little more than affectation, frippery and trivial artistic taste, with a dose of condescension, spitefulness and arrogance thrown in, was indeed limited to a tiny proportion of the country's population, who were able to afford it by merit of owning a massive proportion of the wealth. Many contemporaries acknowledged the vacuous absurdities of Bath, and of the upper classes in general, but they tended to laugh at them rather than waste energy on indignation, pointing out that the city became even worse at the end of the eighteenth century, by which time the snobs, social climbers and the *nouveaux riches* – unpopular in every age – were in control; by Mr Pickwick's day the place had really gone to the dogs. Bath in its heyday was, according to Defoe, a city of 'raffling, gameing, visiting, and in a word, all sorts of gallantry and levity' – a real landscape of leisure. It was a unique, elitist landscape, beyond the reach of the vast majority. The problem today is to conserve the fabric without fossilizing the city: Bath was designed to be a living city, not a museum.

Monnow Bridge, Monmouth, Gwent, and Maud Heath's Causeway, Wiltshire

Given the primitive nature of medieval and pre-industrial roads, it is hardly surprising that their direct contribution to the modern visible landscape is limited. Generally speaking, only the more elaborate structures such as the stone bridges have survived. These were built where economic or military considerations demanded the safe and controlled crossing of a river by an important route, and where sufficient funds were available for their erection and maintenance. Money was forthcoming from a variety of sources, including charitable bequests or guild funds, but there was no organized or integrated system. Much of the construction stemmed from the commercial activities of towns, and the desire of boroughs to raise their standing in the eyes of visitors and traders. The lowest bridging or year-round fording points of rivers were major factors in the siting and growth of urban settlements. Many of the old bridges to be seen on the approaches to towns were constructed to supersede timber structures or simple fording places, and their presence furnishes clues regarding both the status of the roads which passed over them and the economic histories of the towns themselves. Occasionally the lanes leading down to the original ford are still there next to the bridge, as at Low Bridge, Knaresborough, North Yorkshire (SE 350565), although in this instance they are now blind.

Graceful or solid, well-proportioned or quaintly irregular, these bridges are invariably great visual assets. The different styles and the use of local stone ensure that in one way or another they are in keeping with their surroundings. They are notoriously difficult to date, because the structures tend to be composite, individual parts having been replaced or altered over the years. Furthermore, the forms changed little through the centuries once the basic principles had been mastered and had been shown to give good service, huge destructive lorries not yet having been invented. The picturesque clapper bridges of Dartmoor (for example, Postbridge, SX 648788), which consist of flat stone slabs laid across the tops of vertical piers, look ancient but can date from any time down to the eighteenth century. The low single-span packhorse bridges, common in the more rugged districts of the north, where goods were transported by packhorse rather than wagon, were still being built in the early nineteenth century, five hundred years after the earliest surviving examples were erected. Full-scale town bridges also perpetuated medieval designs. The early seventeenth-century bridge at Berwick-upon-Tweed (p. 251) displays several features characteristic of a medieval bridge, to its great advantage (Figure 60).

Figure 60. Berwick-upon-Tweed, Northumberland: Berwick Old Bridge (see p. 314 and Figure 57)

Nevertheless, medieval or early post-medieval bridges can sometimes be distinguished from later ones by studying their overall appearance together with certain details. They tend to have pointed cutwaters rather than the hydrodynamically more efficient rounded ones which later replaced them. Above the cutwaters are protrusions marking the road recesses which enabled pedestrians to take refuge from passing traffic. The arches often recall contemporary styles in church architecture. Bridges possessed considerable religious significance: all had crosses (mostly smashed during the sixteenth and seventeenth centuries), and some had chapels for the blessing of travellers and the collecting of funds for the bridge (cf. Bradford-on-Avon, Wiltshire, Figure 55). A further telling feature, best studied from a boat passing underneath, is the ribbed arch, which was favoured in order to save valuable building stone. Three medieval arches in the bridge over the Thames at Wallingford, Oxfordshire, can be detected by their ribbing.

Monnow Bridge, Monmouth (SO 505125), although greatly altered in the early nineteenth century, still presents a medieval aspect and is of unique interest on account of the fortified gatehouse on its crest (Figure 61). The bridge was built in the late thirteenth century and is situated at the end of the broad main street of Monmouth, linking the defended town with Overmonnow or Little Monmouth across the river, a suburb protected by the semi-circular Clawdd Du or Black Dyke, which acted as a kind of outer defence on the Welsh side. The Clawdd Du was spanned by its own bridge (aligned with Monnow Bridge), and it may have been possible to flood it using water from the river. Monnow Bridge comprises three broad arches, each with three wide ribs, separated by piers with pointed cutwaters. The medieval fortified gatehouse possessed only a single arch: the two outer passages were pierced when the bridge was widened in the last century. Originally the gatehouse had a portcullis operated from the room over the arch, together with three machicolations from which missiles could be dropped, and a garderobe discharging into the river. The guard house on the Monmouth side was removed when the gatehouse was altered.

Figure 61. The Monnow Bridge, Monmouth: the fortified gatehouse

In the days when fens, marshes and low-lying districts were still poorly drained and rivers were not confined and controlled as they are today, extensive areas of the country could prove difficult and dangerous to cross, especially in winter. A bridge over a river was of limited use if the neighbouring floodplain was impassable to travellers attempting to follow the line of the approach road. To overcome this hazard, some bridges stretched long distances over the wet ground on either side of the river (for example, Essex Bridge, Great Haywood, Staffordshire, SJ 995225). Sometimes causeways were built, particularly in the Fens, where roads ran along the tops of raised embankments. Aldreth and Stuntney causeways in Cambridgeshire date from the late eleventh or early twelfth centuries, and still carry traffic out across the fenlands from the Isle of Ely. At Huntingdon in the same county an arched causeway spans the floodplain of the River Ouse and conveys the road from nearby Godmanchester right up to the medieval bridge.

The financing of these structures was a haphazard affair. Maud Heath's Causeway in Wiltshire, erected *c*. 1475, provides an early example of a benefactor donating money to a civic project rather than to the Church. It is said that Maud Heath provided for the construction and maintenance of this handsome stone causeway having herself experienced the hazards of a journey across the River Avon floodplain when on her way to Chippenham market. This public-spirited gesture was undoubtedly of great assistance to the community, and the $4\frac{1}{2}$-mile-long causeway (distinguished by a set of sixty-four segmental arches at Kellaways) carries a path which is still a safe route for pedestrians when floods immobilize motor vehicles on the East Tytherton-Kellaways-Chippenham road. The causeway begins on the top of Wick Hill (ST 973737) and ends by St Paul's church in Chippenham, and represents an interesting but isolated instance of pre-industrial transport improvement. Apart from the infrequent causeways and the bridges, found only on major roads or in towns, the traveller in England and Wales had to make his way across country as best he could.

Princetown, Devon, and Tremadoc, Gwynedd
The early years of the nineteenth century, which witnessed such profound changes in the location, scale and organization of industrial activity, also encompassed a series of changes in the style of entrepreneurial activity and in the types of men who pioneered developments in business enterprise. The new class of self-made industrialists, the owners of coal mines, mills and factories, differed markedly from the philanthropic, paternalistic 'improvers' whose roots lay firmly embedded in the eighteenth century.

Naturally, in a process so all-embracing and complex as industrialization, it would be unwise to draw simplistic distinctions – some factory owners, like Wedgwood in the eighteenth century and Owen in the nineteenth, were also enlightened community builders – but the enthusiastic amateur, often from an established and respected family, who set out to transform a local economy by means of land improvement, new settlements, communications and manufactures was characteristic of a particular period. In general, such figures were only partially successful, confronted as they were by a host of difficulties – notably prevailing levels of technology and rigid financial structures – but the results of their labours can still be seen in several districts of the country.

Typical of these energetic promoters was Sir Thomas Tyrwhitt (1762–1833), who, having created the estate of Tor Royal on Dartmoor in the late eighteenth century, decided to establish a small working community nearby. The group of cottages named Prince's Town (Tyrwhitt was a friend of the Prince of Wales, whom he had met while up at Christ Church, Oxford) soon became known as Prince Town (SX 5873). But the new settlement was bleak and exposed, occupying a remote col up on the Moor at a height of over 1,350 feet, and it failed to prosper. Tyrwhitt realized that something besides agricultural improvement was required to make it flourish, and he proposed that a prisoner-of-war prison be established at Princetown to relieve the pressure on the hulks in Plymouth, which were being used to hold Frenchmen captured in the Napoleonic Wars. The prison was duly built and in turn encouraged the growth of Princetown, but the uplift was temporary. When the war ended and the last prisoners left in 1816 grass grew in the street, and it was clear that a more permanent basis to the local economy was required if Tyrwhitt was to fulfil his dreams of reclaiming a barren wilderness and clothing it with grain, of establishing a thriving community of industrious labourers, and of promoting trade with Plymouth. He therefore set about improving communications, in the hope that this would link his community more successfully to the outside world and persuade the authorities to put the now empty prison buildings to some use. A narrow-gauge railway was completed between Plymouth and Princetown which he hoped would carry two-way traffic, the horse-drawn wagons bringing up building materials, fertilizers and supplies, and returning with granite, minerals, peat, flax and hemp from the Moor.

Tyrwhitt, eminently successful in public life as Lord Warden of the Stannaries, local M.P. and Gentleman Usher of the Black Rod, never saw his visions transformed into realities. Neither the physical nor the economic environment was conducive. But one can still see his enclosures, trace sections of the sinuous course of the railway across the moor to Yelverton and on to Plymouth, and wander up the main street of Princetown itself with its granite houses, dominated by the grim mass of the prison (whose present appearance reflects the renovations of *c.* 1850, when Tyrwhitt's suggestion was at last taken up and the premises were made into a convict settlement). It is a wild and desolate place; the original French prisoners no doubt had their own opinions regarding Tyrwhitt's public-spiritedness. For them it was a 'vraie Sibérie', and the prison doctor wrote of 'that great tomb of the living ... embosomed as it is in a desert and desolate waste of wild, and in the winter time terrible scenery, exhibiting the sublimity and grandeur occasionally of elemental strife, but never partaking of the beautiful of nature ...' The Dartmoor poet Carrington, in his eulogy of Tyrwhitt, was surely premature in saluting the day when 'The wilderness,/ No longer rock-strew'd, blossoms as the rose'.

But sublimity and grandeur, as a backdrop for an attempt to combine Improvement with an appreciation of the Picturesque, were all-important for William Madocks (1773–1828), whose enterprises in North Wales offer an interesting comparison with Tyrwhitt's almost exactly contemporary activities. Madocks came from an ancient Clwyd family and, like Tyrwhitt, completed his education at Christ Church. Even in his early youth he was eager to realize his grandiose ideas in the fields of landscape planning, regional communication, architecture, and agricultural improvement, and before very long he found just the place to indulge them. In 1798 he acquired land near Penmorfa (SH 548406) on the north side of the River Glaslyn where it discharged into Cardigan Bay. The tidal estuary comprised a great expanse of sand and marsh known as Traeth Mawr, which flooded at high tide almost as far as Aber Glaslyn bridge (594462), severely interrupting and diverting communications to the Lleyn peninsula and the rest of north-west Wales (Figure 62).

Madocks reclaimed an area on the north side by constructing an embankment, then built a completely new town, Tremadoc, on the new land. Telford had not yet built his road (the present A5) through Snowdonia to Holyhead via the Menai Bridge, and Madocks had high hopes that the main route to Ireland would run to Porthdinllaen in Lleyn (2741) instead, using Tremadoc as a staging point.

The plan of Tremadoc was T-shaped, with a market place at the road junction. It contained public buildings including a classical town hall-cum-theatre, shops, inns, a church and a chapel, and survives today more or less intact as a celebrated example of contemporary town planning. For Madocks, appearances were everything – he gave orders to erect a gothic town privy and to 'sprinkle a few large larches' – but the basic

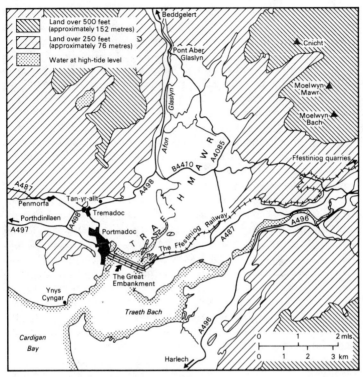

Figure 62. Traeth Mawr and its regional setting

purpose of the town (enshrined in the naming of the main streets London
Street and Dublin Street) was not forgotten. Its prosperity depended on
local enterprise (such as the woollen mill, in a style which was the very
opposite of satanic), and above all on the conquest of the Traeth. By a
monumental effort Madocks, without the assistance of a qualified engineer, completed a great embankment, nearly a mile long, which was
designed to seal off the estuary and carry the Porthdinllaen road across.
Although breached by a gale in 1812, it was repaired and stabilized, and
now carries the main coast road and the Ffestiniog Railway. Though the
railway was built after Madocks's death, it was an important element in
his solution to the problem of facilitating the movement of Ffestiniog
slate from the quarries to the markets. The River Glaslyn, having been
diverted when the Traeth Mawr embankment was built, had scoured out
a good harbour at the west end of the Cob. Madocks founded Portmadoc

as a slate out-port, and, unlike the subsequently isolated Tremadoc, it grew with the rise in trade. Without Madocks's guiding hand, however, it became an ill-planned settlement in comparison with its neighbour.

Like Tyrwhitt, Madocks enjoyed only limited success in realizing his aims, but, perhaps thanks to his greater panache, more of his individual spirit remains in the landscape. His own peculiar eclecticism, combining philanthropy with enterprise, social pleasures with commercial success, manifested in a settlement which was to be prosperous but small-scale, set within an integrated and improved regional economy, made him very much a man of his time. His craving for Improvement, his taste for the Picturesque, and the awe he felt at the contemplation of the Sublime, which provided the stupendous scenic backcloth for his drama, are all reflected in the townscape and setting of Tremadoc, and in Madocks's own house and garden at Tan-yr-allt nearby. He would have been upset by the suggestion that Tremadoc was a mere showpiece, and that the estuary in its natural state was infinitely preferable to a partially reclaimed tract of not particularly valuable land. Madocks possessed a genuine love for Welsh scenery at a time when Wales, in the eyes of the English leisured classes, had only recently ceased to be as remote, wild and uncivilized as the Alps (Defoe dismissed even the inoffensive ridges of Monmouthshire as 'those horrid mountains'). But Madocks the improver was not content with the untamed, indefinable, romantic melancholy of rocks, water and light. In his zest for aesthetic appearance, human betterment and the happiness of his town he had grasped several key principles of landscape design and community building which seem to have eluded many modern planners.

CHAPTER 6

Landscapes of the Industrial Revolution
and the Victorian Era

The manufacturing activities of pre-industrial England and Wales exerted, in general, only a limited and localized impact upon the landscape. This could hardly be otherwise given their restricted scale, limited capitalization and unsophisticated technology. The rural basis of the great majority of crafts, and the close association of home and workplace, spread manufacturing operations such as the making of cloth across the country-side in a multitude of small units which were readily absorbed into the landscape. Other important occupations such as salt-making and even quarrying for building stone left only minor imprints. The salterns of the Lincolnshire coast can be identified by the remains of enclosures and the heaps of debris found at such places as Marsh Chapel (T F 3699). Small overgrown quarries are common in the stone districts; even the famous medieval quarries at Barnack in Cambridgeshire created only the 'hills and holes' (T F 076046) next to the village, which, for all its trade in stone, was not particularly large.

Neither mines nor metals figured prominently in the pre-industrial scene, and the tainted air and 'coale pitts' described by Celia Fiennes on her visit to Newcastle in 1698 impressed her as something out of the ordinary: coal mines were generally small, being worked either as part of a dual economy or in a casual manner under the aegis of landowners who regarded them merely as fashionable sidelines on the estate. In either case their size was limited by the technology of the day, as deep mining was rendered almost impossible by the problems presented by accumulations of water, which arose as soon as mining progressed beyond the excavation of shallow bell-pits. These pits consisted of shafts sunk from the surface and extended underground laterally to produce bell-shaped chambers. Some groups can still be detected on the surface in the form of spoil heaps and depressions, as at Catherton Common, Salop (SO 6378). Similar pockmarking of the ground resulted from the winning of metallic minerals (the iron mines at Bentley Grange, West Yorkshire, SE 267131), an activity which also produced the gravel ridges of the tin-streaming districts (South Tawton, Devon, SX 628916) and the scars and trenches following the veins of lead in the Peak District (Dirtlow Rake, SK 151819). Even the iron industry, which in many respects was atypical, being subject to strong locational constraints on account of its technology and raw-material requirements, and requiring an unusual concentration of fixed capital, only disturbed a handful of districts with the hammering which so impressed Camden during his tour of Sussex in the 1580s. John Byng, travelling down the Wye valley two centuries later, recorded that the 'incessant thump' of furnace hammers terrified his dog Jock 'most exceedingly', but even at this late stage the forges could still be viewed in a rustic fashion as part of the traditional landscape (Figure 63).

Figure 63. Iron forge at Tintern, Gwent: an etching by B. T. Pouncy after a drawing by Thomas Hearne (1798)

Nevertheless, although there were no industrial landscapes in the modern sense, both countryside and town were exhibiting a growing bustle and activity. In his travels during the 1720s Daniel Defoe, who of course took a special interest in change and innovation, saw 'new discoveries in metals, mines, minerals; new undertakings in trade; inventions, engines, manufactures, in a nation, pushing and improving as we are: These things open new scenes every day, and make England especially shew a new and differing face in many places, on every occasion of surveying it'. Naturally enough, this positive picture reflected the state of affairs in some regions more accurately than others. Especially animated were those of the dual economy districts in which surplus labour was becoming more and more bound up with mining and manufacturing. Camden had discovered the country around Birmingham 'swarming with inhabitants, and echoing with the noise of Anvils, (for here are great numbers of *Smiths*)', although the busyness of the late-sixteenth-century scene he described was undoubtedly more reminiscent of a Brueghel painting than of the Descent into Nibelheim. But over the course of the seventeenth and early eighteenth centuries the west Midlands increasingly displayed the characteristics of a countryside undergoing the early stages of the change to industrialization. Iron-working villages, composed of cottages in which domestic industry flourished, formed a complex and seemingly chaotic pattern interwoven with communities of miners working shallow pits on the edges of heaths and commons. Elsewhere comparable developments were occurring in relation to textile manufacture. Approaching Halifax from Blackstone Edge, Defoe saw the slopes spread with houses and small enclosures, the 'whole country, however mountainous' being 'yet infinitely full of people; those people all full of business'. This business was the clothing trade, which, as Defoe noted, was able to flourish and support such a large population in 'this otherwise frightful country' only on account of the 'coals and running water' encountered there. He 'found the country, in short, one continued village, tho' mountainous every way ... hardly a house standing out of a speaking distance from another'. Most of the weavers kept a cow or two and worked small enclosures next to the house, while inside the cottages whole families occupied themselves, the women and children 'always busy carding, spinning, &c. so that no hands being unemploy'd, all can gain their bread'.

The seeds of industrial growth were not confined to the countryside, although the rural economies of prominently pastoral areas, subject to weak manorial control and exploiting their resources of common or thinly colonized land, were particularly conducive to the development of industries like iron, with its special locational requirements, and textiles, based upon the 'putting out' system. Sheffield was, according to Defoe, 'very populous and large, the streets narrow, and the houses dark and black, occasioned by the continued smoke of the forges, which are always at work: Here they make all sorts of cutlery-ware ...' Leicester, like Nottingham and Derby, had a 'considerable manufacture ... for weaving of stockings by frames; and one would scarce think it possible so small an article of trade could employ such multitudes of people as it does'. In general the manufacturing bases of the towns were more diverse, and the processes more complex, than those enterprises which used the surplus labour of the countryside. The towns were also active as central places, providing their hinterlands with a basic range of services, while some of them produced a particular commodity for the national or even the international market.

To contemporaries these busy scenes which distinguished 'the most flourishing and opulent country in the world', as it was hailed by Defoe, were quite naturally taken at face value and considered in their own terms. Few conceived mines and manufactures to be qualitatively different from other ways of gaining a living, or recognized them as developments laden with any kind of momentous significance. Defoe's account of Newcastle begins with the coal pits, which are of interest to Londoners who 'see the prodigious fleets of ships which come constantly in with coals' but who are 'apt to wonder whence they come, and that they do not bring the whole country away'. But almost in the same breath he is talking of 'Newcastle salmon' which are also sent to London, and is surprised to find – and anxious to record – that they come not from Newcastle at all, but from the Tweed. The manufacture of hardware or wrought iron, on the other hand, is only briefly mentioned as an introduction 'which is very helpful for employing the poor'. There is no mention here of key sectors or proto-industrialization; and how could there be when Britain was undergoing the early stages of an upheaval the like of which had never been seen in the whole span of human history? It is only with hindsight that attempts have been made to conceptualize the process of industrial transformation. But even the sustained efforts of modern scholarship have produced only a partial understanding of the immensely complex set of changes embraced by the Industrial Revolution: the use of the term itself is not universally accepted.

Industrialization and the landscape

The rise of industry involved more than the wave of inventions popularly identified with it. Industrialization was bound up with a number of other developments, notably demographic and agrarian advances, which played a considerable role in the accumulation of capital, the extension of trade, and the creation of labour force and market. The apparent co-ordination of population change with economic progress was one of the most remarkable achievements of eighteenth-century England, resulting in a rise in numbers which for the first time was not abruptly cut off by negative feedbacks manifested in high death rates or partially controlled birth rates. The traditional economic structure underwent a series of major alterations involving the use of different resources and the emergence of new modes of social organization and interaction. These upheavals in the relationship between man and environment, and within society itself, were such that in certain districts the cultural landscapes produced were quite unlike anything hitherto experienced.

The increasing use of inorganic raw materials focused economic activity upon distinct locations, for minerals are not ubiquitous in their distribution, but are found in discrete bodies. Their recovery was no longer a small-scale, casual, part-time affair, but involved the sinking of deep mines and the excavation of large quarries. Raw materials needed to be taken through several stages of refining and manufacturing before finished goods could be turned out; they had to be combined and processed in various ways, and this necessitated an improvement in transport. The unreliable, seasonal and expensive movement of goods in the pre-industrial period was superseded by new methods of moving bulky items. Improvement in river navigation led, by a series of logical stages, to the construction of artificial waterways; roads were improved; the extension of tramways and wagonways culminated in the construction of railways, with their attendant cuttings, embankments, tunnels and viaducts. In order to minimize the transport of heavy commodities, industrial concerns evolved linkages with each other, using each other's products as sources of raw material for their own particular processes.

The availability of power acted as a critical incentive to spatial concentration, particularly when coal came into its own as one of the great foundations of industrialization. Britain's reserves of coal were crucial to her success, and the distribution of the coalfields and their geological characteristics exerted a huge influence on the pattern of industrial activity. Some of them had exerted a pull even in the days before coal came to be used for raising steam or smelting iron, on account of their reserves of iron ore (either in the Coal Measures themselves or in the Carboniferous Limestone below), or their plentiful woods, which furnished charcoal for fuel. Others possessed streams which provided water power. Situated on the boundary of Highland and Lowland Britain, the generally poor soils of the coalfields had contributed to their haphazard settlement by squatters engaged in dual economies rather than leading to systematic colonization by tightly controlled manorial agriculture. Now they produced their own landscapes of mining and power generation, drawing other enterprises to them. All these activities required capital and labour. The accumulation and investment of capital by entrepreneurs, and their use of both machinery and organized labour to remove bottlenecks in production and increase output, were among the most dramatic changes affecting contemporary society.

The centralization of production had startling consequences. Technology and the division of labour dictated the layout of the plant, and for the first time large numbers of people were assembled in one place and rigorously controlled. The factory system, despite its identifiable antecedents, was something new, and it necessitated the organization of the workforce into strict routines, under the tight supervision of the master. This gathering together of materials, machines and people stimulated the growth of settlements, from the mining villages to the large towns with their densely packed areas of workers' housing. The momentum of nineteenth-century urbanization created immense social problems, and townscapes of squalor and poverty spread like some oily scum around the new industries. In these localities pollution reached unprecedented levels. The delving for minerals produced a blasted landscape of subsidence, spoil heaps, stark machinery and pools of filthy water; the industrial processes themselves left quantities of waste strewn across the derelict land, filled the air with smoke, and stripped the vegetation. In the towns, basic services of water supply and sanitation lagged far behind the rate of urban expansion. Such tortured landscapes influenced not just the lives of people but their ideas and attitudes as well. Both the appearance of the landscapes and what they stood for deeply affected political and social thought, painting and literature. The industrial landscapes of Britain were of immense significance, not only as the visible manifestations of a new order but as a formative element in the country's heritage.

In the light of this it is all the more surprising that the landscapes of the Industrial Revolution have suffered from a general lack of interest on the part of scholars. The reasons for this are complex, but social class, taste and fashion account for some of the neglect. The leanings of that part of the academic community concerned with landscape, however conceived, have tended more to the bucolic and the charming than to the urban and the squalid. Furthermore, a patronizing dismissal of anything Victorian has, until recently, tended to preclude objective assessment of that remarkable era. But in this respect, as in certain others, public interest has been in advance of educated inclination. The immediacy of the artefacts of industrialization, and the tremendous impact they exert upon those who readily relate to the trials and tribulations of ordinary working people, render the surviving monuments of the Industrial Revolution far more meaningful than faint humps and bumps in fields or the absurd posturing of some affected country squire. The landscapes of industry may be grimy and dismal, but they can also be monumental and sublime (Figure 64). They are rarely pretty, but they are often arresting, and their hold upon the imagination is all the deeper for it. What is more, they are unique: Britain was the first country to industrialize, and even now the achievement is not fully comprehended. However much one may hanker, in this automated, synthetic and mass-produced age, after the simple life, the

Figure 64. Stockport Viaduct, London and North Western Railway, by A. F. Tait (1848). This dramatic picture was painted shortly after Friedrich Engels had noted, in *The Condition of the Working-class in England in 1844*, that 'Stockport is renowned throughout the entire district as one of the duskiest, smokiest holes, and looks, indeed, especially when viewed from the viaduct, excessively repellent'. But despite the ugly cotton mills and the miserable cottages and cellar dwellings which were to Engels the most repulsive features of this forbidding town, the mighty arches of the great viaduct, built to carry the recently opened Manchester and Birmingham Railway over the Mersey valley, lend a certain epic quality to the enveloping malignity of the scene

image of a rural paradise of happy country dwellers being rudely shattered by the vulgar eruption of industry is just not tenable. The question who was worse off – the urban proletariat or the toilers in the fields who preceded them (and who existed alongside them) – makes for an interesting but inconclusive debate. But it is clear that both played their part in the overall process of development, and that for the majority, the country was no more romantic than the town. The fabric of industry constituted the surroundings and working places of millions of people whose labour provided the basis of modern prosperity, including the wealth and leisure which has allowed subsequent generations the luxury of taking a detached view of these scenes of travail. For it should be understood that industrial landscapes involve more than odd bits of machinery: the imaginative achievement involves the reconstruction of the scenes in their entirety, both as visible landscapes and as repositories of the aspirations, sufferings and failures of those who were associated with them.

Landscapes of mining

The scale of mining for both metallic ores and non-metallic raw materials increased out of all proportion during this period, especially after technological innovation paved the way for larger operations. Much of the activity took place in upland districts, away from the traditionally well-populated Lowland zone, for it is the older rocks of Highland Britain which contain most of the country's mineral resources. The pattern of distribution has found expression in the economic and cultural geography of these islands in a way which is apparent to this day, despite the subsequent use of imported raw materials and the greatly diminished local pull of individual energy sources.

The most familiar mining landscapes are those of the coalfields. Not only was the use of coal basic to industrialization, but, in the earlier stages at least, sources of power were among the prime locational factors. As Arthur Young commented in 1791, at a time when water-power was still widespread, 'all the activity and industry of this kingdom is fast concentrating where there are coal pits'. Each coalfield exhibited characteristics peculiar to itself, reflecting physical landscape, geological conditions or cultural traits. All three contribute to the striking contrast between, say, the landscape of the South Wales valleys and that of the Potteries coalfield. In addition, the areas of old workings, exploiting the seams which outcrop at the surface, present a different prospect from the later 'concealed' coalfields, where the Coal Measures are covered by younger rocks. But the basic landscape features associated with coal mining were common to all fields, certainly by the time when technological progress had initiated the movement to deeper and fewer pits. The pithead buildings and winding gear, the stores, offices, stock and timber yards, railway sidings and waste heaps dominated the scenery of the coal-mining districts (Figure 65).

The modernization and closure programmes of the twentieth century have removed many of these familiar elements. Coal mining can leave remarkably few substantive remains once the machinery has been removed, the buildings demolished and the rails lifted. Sometimes it is only the spoil heaps which survive, partially colonized by vegetation, or the mining settlements themselves, as in parts of the Somerset coalfield. Even the pit villages, with their stark terraces of brick or Coal Measures sandstone, are being demolished in some regions. With their departure a whole way of life vanishes for ever, and a new generation of deserted villages is created.

Some older casualties recall a grimmer story. The shrunken village of Shraleybrook, near Halmer End (SJ 781499) on the north-western edge of the North Staffordshire coalfield, housed a flourishing community until 1918, when the worst colliery disaster in the history of the field killed over 150 men and boys at the nearby Podmorehall colliery. The largest group came from Shraleybrook, and little remains there today except the public house. Examination of the broader settlement pattern of a coalfield can reveal much of its history (p. 297). Nineteenth-century pit villages were often planted in open country as new, productive mines were opened, and because of their situation they tended to be designed as self-contained settlements. West Cramlington in Northumberland (NZ 266758) was typical of these planned villages, with its terraces of miners' cottages set on three sides of a square, accompanied by the inn, Primitive Methodist chapel, and mechanics' institute. The colliery works and railway sidings were situated in the centre. Even the names of the terraces were in keeping with both the function and the atmosphere of West Cramlington, among them Smoky Row, Brick Row and Foreman Row.

For the remains of the mining itself one often has to look more carefully, but there is no mistaking the scarred appearance of a coalfield landscape, with its vegetation, soils and hydrology disrupted by the delving, dumping and transporting. Remains of railways and bits of machinery often survive for the determined explorer to piece together in the imagination, but the working landscapes of the late eighteenth and nineteenth centuries have largely disappeared. Some remain hidden underground like great forgotten cities, flooded by chill, unclean water or outlined only by the weird growth of honey agaric (*Armillaria mellea*), a luminous fungus covering the abandoned wooden pit props which litter the shafts and roadways. In order to bring these scenes to life one must turn to contemporary accounts and to pictures, such as the magnificent drawings of the Great Northern coalfield made by T. H. Hair, issued as a complete set in 1844 as *A series of views of the collieries in the counties of Northumberland and Durham*. These remarkable etchings bring to life the mining landscapes of the leading coalfield of the day with almost painful clarity. Within generally rigorous limits of artistic licence – the drawings can be taken as objective records – Hair conveys an atmosphere of unearthly horror in his depictions of pitheads, staithes, underground workings, railroads and early locomotives (Figure 65). The unsophisticated installations and the desolate surroundings conjure up images of endless labour amid the dark of night, the smoky gloom of day, and the blackness of the mines, where it was all the same. The eerie light issuing from the firebox of the old locomotive engine at Wylam Colliery, or the chasms and tunnels in which toiling men, women, children and animals risked flooding, firedamp, chokedamp and the prospect of being buried alive appear no less forbidding than the

Figure 65. Percy Pit, Percy Main Colliery, Northumberland, by T. H. Hair (1839)

apocalyptic visions of John Martin, who drew inspiration from industrial scenes for his prophetic panoramas of despair. Indeed, M. Ross, who contributed an introductory essay to Hair's drawings, witnessed scenes 'as wild and fearful as a painter or a poet could wish to see'. According to his description,

> The face of the country is thickly studded with engine-houses and coal-heaps attached to the respective pits, from which, at night, the sky is irradiated with a ruddy glow visible for miles around, and inducing the idea of some mighty conflagration, or, where the flaming heaps themselves are seen, appearing like the 'baleful watch-fires' of an immense army.

The mining operations which attended the extraction of metallic ores, although more localized, also caused drastic changes in the landscape. Some of these were referred to in Chapter 1, where the geological contexts of these minerals were outlined. Lead, which was used in the building and glassmaking industries, and in the manufacture of pewter, printer's type, shot, and paints, was worked in several areas of the Carboniferous Limestone outcrop. The lead dales of the Pennines are characterized by extensive areas of churned-up ground and disrupted drainage, although much of the evidence for lead mining lies underground. Copper and tin were obtained from the mineral zones of south-west England, where the mining became associated with a windswept landscape of disturbed surface features, waste tips, engine houses with tall chimneys, ore-dressing floors and small railways. One of the most famous sites in Cornwall is Botallack (SW 3633), near St Just, where the gaunt remains of the lower engine house cling to the precipitous cliffs in a seemingly impossible position above the seething Atlantic. This mine reached its peak in the mid-nineteenth century, with galleries extending far out under the sea, the whole enterprise demonstrating the determination of Cornishmen to mine ores even in the most difficult places.

Some of these sites possess a special interest on account of their connections with the history of the steam engine. This invention, which played such a key role in the Industrial Revolution, was particularly important in Cornwall, where there was both a lack of coal and a great need to increase the productivity of the tin and copper mines by exploiting the deeper, richer ore bodies. The Boulton-Watt engines which, by means of a patent, dominated the last quarter of the eighteenth century represented a considerable advance on the atmospheric engines of Savery and Newcomen. The Newcomen engine was inefficient but continued to be widely used in the coalfields where fuel was cheap, while the more economical Boulton-Watt engines could profitably be installed elsewhere. The Cornishmen nevertheless fiercely resented the monopoly, and when the Boulton-Watt patent ran out in 1800, a great flurry of activity on the part of men like Trevithick produced the much improved Cornish engine. These formed the basis of mining prosperity in the region during the nineteenth century, and made a considerable contribution to the mining landscape. Steam engines were ponderous pieces of equipment which had to be enclosed by engine houses stout enough not to be shaken to bits by the operation of the machines. This strength has contributed to their widespread survival; occasionally a whole group of buildings remains, as at Wheal Busy (SW 741448), north-east of Redruth.

The other major source of copper was discovered in Anglesey, where the huge deposits of Parys Mountain (SH 4490) were much more easily recoverable than those in Cornwall, and could be worked opencast. During the late eighteenth century Parys Mountain, which claimed to be the most famous copper-mining centre in the world, was transformed into a desolate 'lunar' landscape, in which the only relief was provided by the buildings and settling pits. Today, more than a century after the main period of activity ceased, the multi-coloured, poisoned landscape created by the exposure, weathering and processing of the ore demonstrates forcefully the enduring nature of the undesirable ecological effects of metalliferous mining.

Finally, the mining and quarrying of various other minerals and rocks were of considerable significance locally and regionally. Among the most important in terms of the landscape were (and are) the china clay works of Devon and Cornwall; the clay-pits associated with the manufacture of bricks; the meres, flashes and other subsidence features caused by rocksalt mining and brine pumping in the Cheshire saltfield; and the many kinds of stone quarries in England and Wales. Stone has been and is still quarried in large amounts either for ornamental and building purposes, or for use in engineering projects, road construction and industry. The effect on the landscape varies with the rock type, the quantities required, the method of working, and the purpose for which the stone is to be put. These factors determine whether the rock is carefully cut for use in buildings, as in the case of freestone, or crushed into fragments for railway ballast or road metal, like the harder limestones or certain igneous and metamorphic rocks. Where the demand has been considerable over a prolonged period, large areas have literally been quarried away, as on the Isle of Portland in Dorset or in the slate districts of North Wales and at Delabole in Cornwall (SX 075840). Quarries are found all over the country, excavated in a wealth of different rocks, and nearly every one has a unique atmosphere determined by its geology and history. Dramatic or forbidding, mournful or peacefully enclosed, an abandoned quarry is rarely devoid of interest, particularly if it has been left long enough to develop a rich flora and has not been used for the dumping of rubbish. Indeed, careful study of mines and quarries in all their aspects serves to deepen one's appreciation and understanding of the multifarious role of geology in both the natural and cultural landscape.

Landscapes of manufacturing

The organic products of agriculture and the inorganic raw materials described above were worked up into finished goods by an array of refining and manufacturing activities, each broad group of which made its own contribution to the landscape. This came about as a consequence of the particular operations involved, and the technology and patterns of labour organization associated with them. The input of raw materials, the type of power used, the waste produced (gaseous, liquid and solid), and the nature and transportability of the final product were all basic to the location and layout of the plant, and the appearance of its buildings and immediate surroundings. In some instances the technological aspect was all-important, as with the application of heat to raw materials, giving rise to the furnaces and kilns characteristic of a number of industries, while in others the system of labour was equally crucial, as in the early textile mills, geared to streamlined, mass production. Generally speaking, the degree of integration increased with time, intensifying the local effect of the industry upon the landscape.

Some raw materials required special treatment before they could pass on to the manufacturing stage. Thus, after winning, metallic ores had to be separated from the stone. This process of dressing could take several forms, some involving the use of running water or crushing mechanisms. Outside Odin lead mine, near Castleton in Derbyshire (SK 135835), are the remains of an early nineteenth-century horse-driven crushing circle, with an iron track and a gritstone wheel nearly six feet in diameter. After dressing, other treatments might follow, depending on the type of ore, before the next major stage, the smelting, was reached. Smelting, which took place in a furnace, involved the conversion of the ore (the sulphide or oxide of the metal) to the native metal. For example, haematite, one of the oxides of iron, was reduced to pig iron by heating with carbon in the form of charcoal or coke. The impurities were drawn off as slag by the addition of a flux, usually lime. Furnaces became larger and more integrated, and their remains can be impressive, for example those at Blaenavon, Gwent (SO 248093), or in the Forest of Dean in Gloucestershire (p. 304 and Figure 66). In some areas the smelting process came close to devastating the entire landscape, the most extreme case being the copper

Figure 66. Whitecliff coke blast furnace, Coleford, Gloucestershire, erected *c.* 1800

industry of the Swansea district (p. 300). Finally, the metals were refined. The cast iron produced by a blast furnace was too brittle to be worked by a smith, and until methods were devised of speeding up the process it had to be converted into wrought iron in the finery (to remove the carbon) before being hammered into bars in the chafery. These two hearths together made up the forge. Before the use of steam, the power for all these operations was provided by water; the hammer ponds formed by the damming of streams survive as some of the most obvious landscape features of iron-producing districts.

The greatest impact of the iron industry on the landscape came with the locational shifts which followed the technological breakthroughs of Abraham Darby (1709) and Henry Cort (1784), who devised ways of using coke in place of charcoal in the furnace and forge respectively. Freed from its dependence on charcoal, the iron industry concentrated on those coalfields where its main raw materials – iron ore, coking coal, and limestone – lay close at hand. The greatly increased output and larger scale of the coke blast furnace, the preparation of the materials (the calcining of ore, the conversion of coal to coke, and the burning of lime), their transport by tramway and railway, and the increasing use of steam engines for power all contributed to the creation of densely packed industrial scenes. Coalbrookdale in Salop was the first of these new landscapes to be produced by the marriage of coal and iron. Artists, writers and sightseers recorded their impressions of the iron bridge and the roaring furnaces – 'horribly sublime', in the words of Arthur Young – and ruminated upon the significance of the new relationships which were emerging between man and nature.

As time progressed, however, the new industrial landscapes could no longer be treated, particularly by those toiling in them day and night, merely as visual representations of the infernal regions of classical antiquity or some other pictorial or literary association, to be visited as sources of enjoyable horror or imaginative stimulus. The dismal terror of the scenes became a reality. That Dickens's lurid and impassioned vision of the Black Country recorded in Chapter 45 of *The Old Curiosity Shop* (1841) was by no means exaggerated can be demonstrated by turning to documentary sources such as the *First Report, Midland Mining Commission, South Staffordshire* (1843). The landscape was one 'interminable village', wrote Thomas Tancred in the *Report*; the houses 'for the most part, are not arranged in continuous streets, but are interspersed with blazing furnaces, heaps of burning coal in process of coking, piles of ironstone calcining, forges, pit-banks, and engine chimneys'. Refuse and waste were heaped up so high as to hide the roads which wound between them and past the subsiding buildings of this 'vast rabbit warren', a nebulous mass of filth and blackness. Most of the early industrial landscapes of the Black Country have since been obliterated or cleared away, leaving trails of dereliction in their wake, now interspersed with soulless modern factories built of concrete, metal and glass. Willingsworth (SO 9794), a mile west of the old centre of Wednesbury, is one such district; the colliery which once exploited the rich Thick Coal seam of the Middle Coal Measures, together with the ironworks and associated enterprises, have all passed away, leaving the visitor to gaze upon the decay and ponder the transience of the works of man and the ruination resulting from the rush to convert mineral riches into human wealth.

The decline of the traditional industries of the Black Country became evident at a relatively early stage. As the nineteenth century progressed, the magnetic attraction of the coalfields for the iron industry weakened, as other locations, particularly coastal ones, became more advantageous. By the middle of the century the most easily obtainable Coal Measures ores were being worked out while rich Jurassic ironstones began to be extracted in North Yorkshire. Meanwhile, technological advance was reducing the amount of coal relative to ore required in the iron-making process. The rise of Tees-side as an iron-smelting district was stimulated by the use of Cleveland ores, together with the proximity of excellent coking coal from Durham, limestone from the Carboniferous Limestone of Weardale, dolomite from the Magnesian Limestone of east Durham, and the coastal location itself, which facilitated the export of the bulky products and, later, the import of rich Spanish ores for steel-making. Gradually the dominance of the traditional districts declined, notably the heads of the valleys in the north-eastern part of the South Wales coalfield, and the South Staffordshire field (the Black Country). In their place new industrial centres gathered momentum, and with their greater scale in terms of plant they created new and even more imposing iron and steel landscapes in places like Middlesbrough, Scunthorpe and the portion of the South Wales coalfield adjacent to the coast.

The processes associated with the secondary metal trades and manufactures were many and varied. Some districts, such as those focused upon Sheffield and Birmingham, had long been active in the field of specialized metal products. Their townscapes comprised intricate mazes of courts, alleys, workshops and foundries. Industrialization itself created an increased demand for machinery and tools, and the engineering industries developed rapidly. One of the most important branches was marine engineering, and with the change from wooden to iron vessels the ship-building industry became concentrated upon the estuaries of the Tyne and Mersey, drawing on local iron and coal and developing its own pools of labour. The great shipyards dominated these rivers, and other engineering concerns, such as the manufacture of steam engines and locomotives, also gave a distinctive character to particular locations. The growth and character of Crewe and Swindon were inextricably linked to the establishment there of locomotive and railway repair works.

A wide range of manufactures were based upon non-metallic inorganic raw materials. Clay was used to make bricks, tiles and pottery, the traditional, semi-domestic manufacture being converted by Josiah Wedgwood into a thriving industry characterized by a unique landscape (p.309). In their turn, some of its products exerted a major influence on the visual scene, millions of bricks being used to build factories, chimneys, railway tunnels and viaducts, and great expanses of new housing. Especially striking were the tough blue bricks known as 'engineering bricks', produced principally in Staffordshire where both coal and suitable clays were readily available. Other industries made similarly distinctive contributions, among them the terrifying scenes of the gas works, where gas was made from coal brought to red heat in banks of retorts, or the brick cones which housed the furnaces and related working areas of the glass works.

The chemical industry, on the other hand, created little of distinction in either buildings or machinery; rather, its effect was one of singular devastation, emphasizing the point that those enterprises responsible for the greatest impact on the landscape were not necessarily those which employed the largest numbers of people or bequeathed the most interesting legacy in terms of industrial archaeology. The growth of the heavy chemical industry was stimulated by the demands of other concerns for large quantities of acids and alkalis. Locational ties were strengthened by the fact that the waste products of the alkali-consuming soap, bleach, textile and glass industries were rich in salt, one of the primary raw materials of the chemical industry. Before the Salt Duty was lifted in 1825, these plants were an important source of duty-free salt. In the early nineteenth century the manufacture of chemicals became concentrated in the mid-Mersey district around Widnes and Runcorn, its growth reflecting the proximity of the Lancashire coalfield and the Cheshire saltfield, and the existence of good inland water transport facilities. The manufacture of soda by the Leblanc process had a catastrophic influence on the landscape. This method involved the treating of sodium chloride (common salt) with sulphuric acid, giving sodium sulphate and liberating hydrogen chloride. The sodium sulphate was then roasted with limestone and coal, to produce sodium carbonate (washing soda) and calcium sulphide.

The vast quantities of choking gas (hydrogen chloride) caused terrible atmospheric pollution before the 'Gossage tower' was invented, in which the rising gas, being very soluble, was dissolved in a descending stream of water. The solution ran out of the bottom of the tower as hydrochloric acid. But until a use was found for it as a source of chlorine bleach for the paper industry, the acid was discharged wholesale into local streams, contaminating the water and killing all the life. The Leblanc process left solid as well as gaseous and liquid wastes. The large amounts of useless calcium sulphide which remained at the end were simply piled up in great heaps of black, immensely hard, evil-smelling sulphurous debris.

The final broad group of manufactures were those which used organic raw materials. These were, by tradition, extremely varied and widely distributed, but as demand increased and mechanization gathered momentum, some became sufficiently concentrated in spatial terms to dominate local and regional economies. Burton-on-Trent, formerly a decayed borough, became a prosperous town as a result of the expansion of the brewing industry (p. 55). Brewing involves several related processes, and these were reflected in conglomerations of buildings of various shapes and sizes, the use of gravity prompting the construction of tall brick edifices.

The greatest changes were those associated with the textile industries. While both the cotton industry of Lancashire and the Yorkshire woollen and worsted trades underwent a massive upheaval during the Industrial Revolution, the transformation was more sudden and took place earlier in the case of the former. Technological innovation emanated from Lancashire, cotton being more amenable to mechanization than wool, although the West Riding worsted industry was more adaptable to mechanical handling than the woollen branch. In terms of capitalization and organization, the worsted trade was more advanced than its partner, becoming an urban factory industry in such towns as Bradford and Halifax. The manufacture of woollens on the other hand retained its domestic character until the nineteenth century was well advanced, and even then became associated with smaller mills in industrial villages rather than with true factories in large urban centres.

The cotton industry was the first branch of the textile trade to attract the energies of entrepreneurs and inventors, to streamline its manufacturing processes and gather them together under one roof, applying mechanical power and a rigid division of labour to the mass production of cheap goods. Its pronounced degree of spatial concentration came about through the provision in Lancashire of practically everything the industry required as it developed, the locational advantages encompassing far more than soft water and Flemish weavers. The port of Liverpool traded with the New

World colonies which furnished the imported raw material for the cotton trade, and chemicals, power and transport facilities were close at hand. Water power was used at first, the Pennine valleys providing the sites for early factories such as Richard Arkwright's first cotton mill at Cromford, Derbyshire, erected in 1771. Business acumen, industrial organization and control of the workforce were crucial ingredients in Arkwright's success. A whole community was established around his mill, and Cromford soon attracted visitors to admire Arkwright's achievement and watch him at work as both shrewd employer and bountiful squire. Later on, Arkwright built a country house nearby, although he died before he could move in. The days when capitalists dropped the last vestiges of pretence at benevolent paternalism and turned their backs upon the squalor and poverty which they created had not yet arrived: Arkwright's scheme at Cromford may be compared with that of Wedgwood at Etruria, where the pottery factory, workers' cottages and country house had been laid out just a year or two before. Other similar projects followed, including further mills by Arkwright himself (Masson Mill, Cromford, and Cressbrook Mill, Miller's Dale, Derbyshire; Tutbury Mill, Rocester, Staffordshire); Jedediah Strutt (mills at Belper, Derbyshire); and Samuel Greg (Quarry Bank Mill, Styal, Cheshire). Some at least of the original buildings survive at all these sites, and are of interest not only for their significance in the annals of industrial history, but as embodiments of contemporary concepts in community planning and architectural taste: several of the mills, with their red brick façades, white-framed Venetian windows (Masson Mill) and pediments (Styal), drew inspiration from country house styles. The characteristic cupola was not, however, added merely for decorative purposes; it contained a bell to signal the working hours. Functionalism dominated in every sphere, and architectural pretension was not permitted to compromise it.

The real growth of the cotton industry came with the shift to the Lancashire coalfield consequent upon the substitution of steam for water power. Life for those working in the mills of Arkwright, Strutt, Greg and others like them was, generally speaking, unrelentingly hard – and dangerous – with ruthless routines, poor wages and insufficient food, but the housing was clearly superior to the terrible slums of nineteenth-century Manchester. The appearance of the factories changed too, the coal-fired steam engines being accommodated in large engine houses attached to the factory building proper. Both were dwarfed by the massive chimneys, many of which were deliberately designed on a huge scale as a kind of status symbol. The townscapes of the textile centres – Oldham, Rochdale, Bolton, Bury, Burnley, Blackburn and the rest – with their mills and terraced housing wreathed in smoke, displayed an unremitting dreariness (Figure 67). The landscapes associated with textile manufacture had indeed changed out of all recognition since the days of the great clothiers of East Anglia and the west of England, although even during the Industrial Revolution the Cotswolds managed to maintain its high standards of architectural quality. In the district around Stroud scores of cloth mills were erected at this time, but the visual effect is hardly suggestive of an industrial landscape. However, the centre of gravity of the textile trade, together with other manufactures, had shifted from Metropolitan to Industrial England, a move which had profound consequences for the economic and cultural geography of the country.

Figure 67. Preston, Lancashire, in the 1930s: nineteenth-century cotton mills and terraced housing

It would be wrong to view this process simply in terms of such factors as technological change or the discovery of new power sources, or to give the impression that every industrial scene can be recognized as the unmistakable creation of one particular industry. Many landscapes derive their character not from a single branch of mining or manufacturing but from the successive or coincidental effects of several. Indeed, even in their earlier days, major industrial regions by their very nature possessed complex economic structures, in which interconnected enterprises relied on each other for their raw materials and operated together in association with transport arteries, pools of labour, and nearby markets for their products. As a result, the phenomenon of industrial agglomeration is bound up with two key forces for change in the landscape, which require scrutiny for their own sakes: transport development and urbanization.

Transport

Transport in pre-industrial England was slow, inflexible, erratic, seasonal and expensive. By 1850 this state of affairs had undergone a dramatic change, the economic and social consequences of which were immense. Not forgetting the continuing importance of coastwise shipping, the developments in transport which were of greatest significance in terms of the landscape were threefold: the improvement of roads and the creation of canals and railways.

Pre-industrial roads often amounted to no more than wide, rutted strips of land, whose condition provoked bitter complaint. One eighteenth-century commentator wrote of 'these horrible, hilly, stony, deep, miry, uncomfortable, dreary roads' which looked 'more like the retreat[s] of wild beasts and reptiles, than the footsteps of men', while Sydney Smith claimed to have received between ten and twelve thousand 'severe contusions' while travelling from Taunton to Bath. But although many roads, particularly the ones in the claylands or those which were heavily used, were undoubtedly in a deplorable state, especially in winter, the idea that all was mud and gloom before the coming of the turnpikes has probably been overstated. Furthermore, the turnpike trusts represented an institutional rather than a technological innovation, and did not necessarily produce an advance in the standard of road maintenance upon that associated with the parish system, which they supplemented but did not replace. The trusts, whose boom period occupied the third quarter of the eighteenth century, were set up with the intention of raising money for road upkeep by charging tolls. Much of the money, however, went into the pockets of the trustees, so that users protested that nothing was left for the public like a road except 'the name and cost of it'. Nevertheless, significant progress was made, in some regions at least, in the early nineteenth century, following the development of the new methods of road construction and surfacing pioneered by Thomas Telford, John

Loudon McAdam and others. The techniques of McAdam, unlike those of Telford, proved sufficiently cheap to be used on turnpikes, and new as well as remade roads appeared. In many cases all that can be seen today are the routes themselves, but other reminders of the turnpiking days include mileposts and, where they have not been removed by road-widening schemes, tollhouses. These buildings came in many shapes and styles, but all were designed to give a clear view up and down the road (Figure 68). Some of the most elaborate road structures were those built not with private capital but with government money. Telford's strategic roads were financed in this way, and his superb Menai Bridge on the Holyhead route, opened in 1826, is one of the greatest civil engineering achievements of its day.

Figure 68. Early nineteenth-century toll-keeper's cottage on the Oxford to Henley turnpike at Dorchester, Oxfordshire

Despite these improvements, the road system in the years around 1800 was simply not equal to the demands of industry, however romantic the old coaching days might appear to later generations of Christmas card and table mat designers. The roads failed to cope in several respects, most notably in the conveyance of bulky goods. During this crucial phase of industrialization the burden of this kind of traffic was borne not by the roads but by the canals, which carried large quantities of weighty goods, particularly coal and manufactures, at much cheaper rates than the roads could offer. The importance of the canals may be judged by studying their distribution. The three principal foci were the industrial regions of the Black Country, South Lancashire and the West Riding of Yorkshire, where the canals performed a vital role in linking the sources of raw materials, the various manufacturing centres, and the existing river navigations. This achievement was especially significant in districts which had grown up on watersheds and were poorly endowed with river outlets. In turn the canals stimulated their own industrial growth, exemplified in the spectacular rise of the Potteries in association with the Grand Trunk from Trent to Mersey, promoted by Josiah Wedgwood, who wanted his fragile products to be carried in bulk but not in pieces. The scenery of these areas was greatly affected by the canals, particularly when the engineers became more confident and experienced, erecting grand structures and devising daring routes instead of simply following the lines of the contours in sinuous curves. Right at the very start of the canal era, in 1761, the Duke of Bridgewater's canal, designed by James Brindley to link the Duke's Worsley colliery with Manchester, astonished contemporaries not only on account of the immediate reduction in the price of the coal which followed its completion, but also because of the mark it made on the landscape. The Barton Aqueduct which carried the canal over the River Irwell provided observers with food for thought when they saw barges pulled by a single horse gliding apparently effortlessly through the treetops overhead while groups of boatmen struggled with their vessels in the river below.

Canals evolved their own styles of engineering and architecture, and these, together with the innumerable details recalling the all but vanished life of the bargees, and the fact that the canals pass from the countryside right through the very hearts of several of Britain's industrial regions, help to account for the recent surge of interest in inland waterways. A further attraction these days is the gentle pace of travel. Canal scenery is nothing if not varied, reflecting as it does a range of geographical and economic influences. Sometimes a physical obstacle was overcome with spectacular confidence, the most famous example being the Pontcysyllte Aqueduct over the River Dee near Llangollen, where the Ellesmere Canal is carried across the valley in an iron trough set on stone piers (SJ 270420). The Lancaster Canal passes over the River Lune by means of a fine classical aqueduct designed by John Rennie (SD 485639). Many tunnels were equally ambitious, such as the two-mile-long Sapperton Tunnel (SO 944033) at the summit of the Thames and Severn. Locks were sometimes built in 'flights' or 'staircases'. (In a staircase the locks empty directly into each other, the top gate of one forming the bottom of the next.) A remarkable flight of twenty-nine locks was constructed at Devizes in

Wiltshire (ST 9961), and a staircase known as Bingley Five Rise can be seen on the Leeds and Liverpool in West Yorkshire (SE 107400). Sometimes boats were hauled up to a higher level by means of inclined planes, such as the one at Morwellham, Devon (SX 445698), built in 1817 to connect the Tavistock Canal terminus with the quay situated on the River Tamar below. Apart from these large-scale triumphs of engineering, many minor features – bridges, reservoirs, pumping stations, loading-points, lock-keepers' cottages – grace the scenery of the canals with a pleasing diversity.

The canals were run in a manner comparable with that of turnpike trusts, the peak of investment coming in the years of canal mania in the 1790s. The indiscriminate construction of canals, resulting in their creation even where the economic need for them was slight, the early date of their initiation, when techniques were still being pioneered, and even their very success contributed variously to their subsequent demise. In terms of both inherent characteristics and the nature of the network, canals proved to be inflexible. Slow and narrow, they could not be widened once they were lined with buildings, while droughts in summer and frosts in winter, subsidence in mining districts, and inadequate water supplies on water-sheds all made for difficulties and delays. In the final analysis, the physique of England and Wales was not sufficiently conducive to the building and maintenance of canals, or to the creation of an integrated system, and with the coming of the railways they were forced to yield up much of their business. But their replacement was neither immediate nor total, and many continued, in their quiet way, to provide that service which had been of such value to the country during their heyday.

The railways evolved out of the tramways which had long been used to transport minerals (especially coal from the pitheads) or to provide feeders for canals and connecting links between separate stretches of waterway. Tramways took several forms, trucks or wagons being moved along various kinds of track under the influence of gravity or through power provided by horses or stationary engines. The development of the steam locomotive as a means of traction, which took place in the early nineteenth century, marked the beginning of the railway era. Railways were regarded by the existing vested interests as dangerous innovations, and as a consequence were hampered from the start by excessive costs. But like the canals they enjoyed a great boom (which after an initial spurt in 1836–7 culminated in the railway mania of the 1840s), and followed a similar pattern of haphazard and uncontrolled growth stimulated by the competi-tive activities of private concerns. Their effects upon industrial progress, urbanization and society itself were outstanding. The age of the engineer had well and truly arrived, and it was a sign of the times that one of the most famous tributes paid to it, J. M. W. Turner's extraordinary *Rain, Steam and Speed: the Great Western Railway* (1844), should itself strike contemporaries as something quite outside their experience. In painting this picture, which brilliantly juxtaposes the power of human invention with the dramatic forces of nature, Turner flagrantly defied artistic convention; according to the possibly apocryphal story, he also broke the first rule of the railway by gaining part of his inspiration through leaning out of the window of a train as it crossed Maidenhead Bridge on Brunel's Great Western during a storm.

It is hardly surprising that the early days of the railway provoked a mixed response. The constructional work caused unparalleled upheavals in the landscape, the turmoil being described with horror by Dickens in Chapter 6 of *Dombey and Son* (1847–8), which contains an account of the digging of the Camden Town cutting on the London and Birmingham Railway. But for others the image was not of deepening chaos, but of order emerging out of confusion. John Cooke Bourne, one of the greatest of the railway artists, saw in the frenetic scenes of railway building an organized plan and a pleasing achievement, in which the certainty and confidence of rational progress was combined with visual elegance and proportion (Figure 69). In time many of the gashes the railways had cut through the landscape were either absorbed and softened or accepted as making their own contributions to the scenery.

Figure 69.   Box tunnel: west front, drawn from nature and on stone by J. C. Bourne (1846)

The imagination and skill of the engineers, and the enthusiastic grasping of the architectural opportunities go a long way towards accounting for the railways' successes in these respects. In addition, anxieties concerning safety resulted in solid construction and careful routing, as the early engineers feared that trains would only run on near-level gradients. Much trouble was taken to create the most perfect and gentle permanent ways possible. The legacy of this approach is the tremendous collection of civil engineering monuments embodied in the railway system. A range of devices was employed to enable the lines to negotiate physical obstacles, especially on those routes which cut across the 'grain' of the country at right angles to the strike of the rocks. The results, particularly on such epic lines as the Settle to Carlisle route, and the views which the train affords are stupendous. But many of these works, built in conditions of difficulty and danger with the labour of thousands of navvies and horses, flash by in a moment, and the fruits of toil are apparent only in the smooth passage of the train through cuttings and tunnels, over bridges and viaducts, and along embankments. To appreciate these features fully, it is best to study them not only from the line but also, wherever possible, on foot (Figure 82).

This is particularly helpful with regard to the decorative aspects of railway architecture, which were not confined merely to the stations. The Great Western from London to Bristol begins at Paddington Station, the design of which was influenced by the Crystal Palace, and ended originally at the mock Tudor station at Temple Meads, Bristol; but in between are several other memorable features, notably the 'Egyptian' Wharncliffe Viaduct above the River Brent at Hanwell; the flat-arched bridge over the Thames at Maidenhead; Chippenham Viaduct; and Box Tunnel with its ornate classical portal (Figure 69). The architecture of the stations displayed a succession of different inspirations with increasing distance from London, passing through Classical and Tudor styles to culminate in full-blooded Gothic at the western end of the line. In this way new architectural elements and settlement forms were brought to hitherto sheltered rural districts, while the paraphernalia of railway transport – the signal boxes, sidings and engine-sheds – sprang up beside the tracks.

The significance of the railway for the landscape extended beyond these direct changes and additions. The movement of goods of all kinds, including mass-produced, standardized building materials, was reflected in the cultural landscapes of the districts into which the railways penetrated. It was said, with some justification, that Brunel's Royal Albert Bridge at Saltash heralded the 'second English invasion of Cornwall'. It is interesting to compare his broad-gauge South Wales railway from

Paddington via Gloucester, which adopted the route taken by the Norman armies, with Stephenson's standard-gauge North Wales line from Euston via Chester, which followed that of the Plantagenet conquerors. The construction of these very different railways perpetuated the historic contrast between the two parts of Wales, which for many purposes had long been connected more intimately with the adjacent regions of England than with each other. But one major effect of the railways was apparent in all regions of the country, and that was the stimulus they gave to the growth of towns.

Urban landscapes

Rates of urban growth in the early nineteenth century were prodigious. The populations of Manchester, Liverpool, Birmingham, Leeds and Sheffield all increased by more than 40 per cent in the decade 1821–31. In 1801 not a single provincial city contained as many as 100,000 inhabitants, but by 1851 there were seven – the above-mentioned five, together with Bristol and Bradford. Manchester and Liverpool had by this time almost reached the third-of-a-million mark. The rise of the great cities was an integral part of the process of economic development, in which both industry itself and successive advances in transport played principal roles. Not only were there mining and cotton towns, given their individual stamp by the nature and organization of the industries concerned, but also canal and railway towns, which prospered as a consequence of their strategic location upon a transport artery or at a route focus. In time the functional complexities of the mushrooming urban centres grew to embrace whole spreads of activities within individual towns and, most spectacularly, in the conurbations. The imprint on the landscape left by this early specialization and the subsequent, often more diversified growth was apparent on several levels: the internal structure and layout of the towns, the degree of co-ordination or planning discernible in their development, the style and standard of the buildings, and the image the townscapes conveyed to inhabitants and visitors.

Urban morphology was subject to a range of influences. The economic basis of a particular town was naturally a prime determinant, although this could alter over time. Widnes and Middlesbrough started out as railway towns, but like many such places their townscapes were soon being moulded by a surge of secondary industrial growth, which in these instances took the form of chemicals and iron respectively. Rising ports like Liverpool attracted their own particular assemblages of industries to the docklands. The overall pattern of growth was conditioned by a set of constraints which included physical geography and the system of landownership. The ribbon townships of South Wales evolved as a consequence of the physique of the long, narrow valleys which constricted the growth of the mining settlements within them. In the Rhondda the urban form is made up of terraces of houses aligned one above the other on the slopes, following the curve of the valley. The elongated townscape which resulted is quite different from the tentacular sprawl of some of the northern industrial towns. Existing land divisions could also direct or control even the most runaway urban spreads. The classic case is that of Nottingham, where the survival until 1845 of the open fields around the town prevented its outward expansion and caused terrible slum conditions in its densely packed courts and alleys. Only with the enclosure was it possible to obtain land for building, and since the parcels were developed individually by the new private owners, an unco-ordinated system of streets and houses resulted, their pattern reflecting the layout of the open fields themselves. In a similar way, the small size of the building plots in Leeds had much to do with the piecemeal development of the town.

Despite these influences rooted in the past, which continued to affect the details of urban form, the majority of towns grew in an uncontrolled fashion (Figure 70). The lack of a coherent structure reflected the incredible speed at which they grew and the eagerness of the speculative builder to realize a profit. Planning on the part of civic bodies or employers was rare:

Figure 70. London going out of Town or The March of Bricks and Mortar by George Cruikshank (1829)

neither felt responsible for housing the urban masses. Even the attempts which were made to design new towns were often swamped by speculators, whose activities spoilt the Furness Railway Company's project at Barrow-in-Furness. The dignified and carefully planned redevelopment of the centre of Newcastle carried out by John Dobson and Richard Grainger in the 1820s and 30s was a rare achievement indeed. In most instances open spaces were infilled and the built-up area extended by cramming together the maximum number of dwellings erected in the shortest possible time. The layouts rarely progressed beyond simple grids of streets. In many mining and manufacturing towns, shafts, spoil heaps, factories, houses, canals and railways were in close proximity, and the competition for space became ever more ruthless. Railways, which stimulated so much of the expansion, were also associated with a good deal of demolition as the companies sought to bring their lines to the very hearts of towns, and to build large stations at the termini. The railways thrust their way through existing housing, or were carried above it by viaducts (Figure 71), choosing routes which passed through the poorer areas where costs were lower and opposition less concerted than elsewhere. The construction of the tracks,

Figure 71. *Over London – by Rail* by Gustave Doré (1872)

stations and yards all affected the urban morphology, and contributed to the internal social and functional zoning of the cities by raising land values in central business districts, altering the pattern of land use, and realigning internal routes of communication.

The popular conception of the Victorian city undoubtedly draws much of its imagery from the conditions of life of the urban working classes. The principal factors governing the types of houses erected were, firstly, economy in terms of space, materials and cost; secondly, the need for speed in response to mass demand; and thirdly, the ability of speculators to find loopholes in the half-hearted legislation which was intended to prevent the worst abuses. As a result, jerry-built houses were hastily thrown up on the cheapest land – often flat and ill-drained – and various devices were employed in order to pack as many people as possible on to each site. Damp cellars, sunless courts and back-to-backs achieved this object at enormous cost in terms of health and welfare. Some urban quarters, like Little Ireland in Manchester, became notorious through the writings of Friedrich Engels and others, and the claims made by contemporary apologists that these terrible places were specially selected by the reformers to lend weight to their arguments cannot obscure the fact that, for all their individual differences, many large towns contained appalling squalor.

Not that squalor was something new in the landscape, but it had never been experienced on this scale before, or in such concentration, and even the well-to-do were eventually compelled to take notice. The social and political disquiet of the 1840s fed the growing measure of disillusion which clouded the optimism exhibited by the early industrial age. Visitors and travellers of half a century before had admired Etruria, Cromford and Coalbrookdale, but now, gazing on the filth and slums of Manchester, Liverpool and Leeds, their expansive style of reporting deserted them in favour of a less ebullient assessment. But the social segregation of the classes and the continued profitability of keeping the labouring classes poor impeded the progress of social reform. The employers, pushing the factory system as far as it would indecently go, insisted that poverty was an unavoidable concomitant of economic progress, and blamed the state of the lower orders on drink, immorality and an incurable lack of responsibility. The conditions of life in the mean districts of the great cities could thus be conveniently ignored by averting the eyes and concentrating the mind elsewhere.

But there were some who refused to be party to a lie of such enormity. Among them was the Frenchman Gustave Doré, who arrived in England in 1869 to start work on a series of drawings of London. Doré was a caricaturist and humorist by trade, but what he saw in the capital soon sobered him (Figure 71). His illustrations have a kind of intense, frenzied relentlessness about them, in which the individual is swallowed up in scenes of obsessive and inescapable misery. The costs of man's conquest of nature and his faith in technology were becoming apparent not only in the undesirable side effects of interference in the environment (p. 302) but also in the strife and deprivation which racked a society unable to check its own momentum.

But for the more fortunate at least, social status could continue to be expressed in personal property, and civic pride made to flourish. The consequences of this were reflected in two developments which, now that so much substandard Victorian housing has been cleared away, survive as reminders of the immense importance of the nineteenth century with respect to the creation of the country's urban fabric. The first was the growth of suburbia, as the middle classes escaped to create pleasant environments for themselves away from the discomforts of the inner city. The early suburbs took a variety of forms, but were usually spaciously and informally laid out. Some remain more or less unchanged to this day, notably Bedford Park in Chiswick, or the fine mid-Victorian suburb of north Oxford, containing both detached villas and model artisan housing. While these changes were taking place on the urban periphery, the city centres were also receiving attention from fashionable architects. The enthusiasm for public buildings and monuments bequeathed a legacy which in its enterprise and swagger has proved to be of great value in modern townscapes. Many towns acquired their clock towers, commemorative statues, town halls, exchanges, and art galleries during the Victorian era, and with the jungle of concrete growing daily, it is now less fashionable to sneer at their weighty Gothic than once it was. London was especially favoured with new streets, bridges, embankments and museums. It is important to remember that nineteenth-century towns contained elements such as railway termini which were appearing for the first time, and in these constructions the Victorians rose to the occasion with unparalleled flair. In their designs for the railway stations they combined modernism and revivalism to create an imposing and powerful style, the iron and glass of the train sheds being fronted with façades inspired by traditional modes. The most extraordinary of these is George Gilbert Scott's hotel at St Pancras, the monumental High Victorian Gothic mounting a tour de force which almost dares the observer to scoff (Figure 72).

The Industrial Revolution and the Victorian age embodied a curious mixture of socioeconomic convulsions and seeming paradoxes in matters

Figure 72. St Pancras Hotel and Station from Pentonville Road: Sunset by John O'Connor (1884)

of thought and belief. Many aspects of the period are reflected in the landscape, both in tangible forms and in symbolic images of social and aesthetic values. There is an urgent need to study these remnants, because, strange though it may seem, they are in some respects in greater danger of destruction than rarer or more ancient elements of the country's heritage. If we do not try to understand the Victorian era it is unlikely that we shall ever comprehend our own. The visual record is of crucial importance not only for the information it can give regarding contemporary events, but also because modern attitudes to landscape owe a great deal to the twin experiences of industrialization and urbanization.

Sites

Settlements of the Durham coalfield

The popular image of north-east England epitomizes the Victorian apogee of Britain's industrial greatness. The region's fame stemmed from its concentration of heavy industries (coal mining, iron and steel, shipbuilding, chemicals and engineering), the growth and subsequent decline of which established the north-east as a centre of mining and manufacturing in the nineteenth century and a microcosm of the British regional problem in the twentieth. The industrial landscapes of the district are in reality surprisingly diverse. Far from being the monotonous product of one brief, frenetic episode which submerged all previous periods beneath the grimy spread of town, factory and mine, the scenery of the coalfield bears the stamp of several phases.

Coal mining began in the Middle Ages, and in the eighteenth century the rivers Tyne and Wear, in recognition of the proximity of the coalfield to the sea, became centres of wagonway networks. Coal was transported in horse-drawn wagons running on wooden (and later, iron) rails from the pits to the staithes or coal wharves, whence the coal was shipped along the coast, mainly to London. By *c.* 1800 the increased demand led to the extension of mining operations to other parts of the coalfield. It is important to remember, however, that most local economies, even in coal-mining districts, were still predominantly rural – industry and agriculture, far from being opposites, had been partners for centuries – and there is evidence that in some areas early industrialization, by increasing the population, actually stimulated agricultural innovation and progress. Certainly the rural landscapes persisted between the mining settlements which grew up in their midst.

The pattern of nineteenth-century exploitation of the coalfield was strongly influenced by geological factors. The strata dip eastwards, so that in the west the seams are much nearer the surface than in the coastal zone, where the Coal Measures are concealed beneath a cover of Permian rocks (Figure 73). Consequently, mining operations began with simple adits driven into the valleysides of west Durham and, when these outcrops were exhausted, progressed down dip as deep mining technology became more sophisticated. Major problems were caused by the presence at the

Figure 73. Simplified geological section through the Durham coalfield

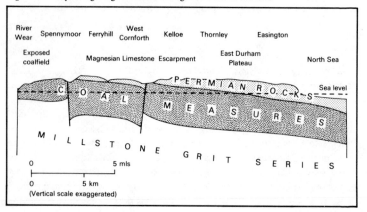

base of the Permian, under the Magnesian Limestone, of the water-bearing Yellow Sands, which threatened to flood shafts driven through them into the Coal Measures beneath. Nevertheless, as reserves of the famous coking coals of south-west Durham, which were of such value to the iron and steel industries, began to run out, the east Durham plateau on the edge of the concealed coalfield was opened up. Soon after 1900 a method was discovered of freezing the Basal Permian Sands during the sinking of shafts, and the final extension of the coal-mining area took place on the Durham coast just before the field reached its peak of production (56 million tons) on the eve of the First World War.

The changing fortunes of different parts of the coalfield are reflected in the distribution of the various settlement types. There is a fundamental distinction between the exposed and concealed portions of the field. The working of the numerous old, shallow pits of west Durham was accompanied by the growth of scattered, sprawling pit villages, originally with rows of cottages and later with terraces, which exaggerated an already dispersed settlement pattern. In east Durham, on the other hand, colliery settlements are compact, distinct, and more widely spaced, reflecting the change to deeper, larger collieries worked from a single pithead.

A second set of contrasts may be drawn with respect to the relationship of the mining villages and towns to the old rural settlements. The early pit villages tended to merge more closely with their forerunners, although the two landscapes can usually be easily separated in the field or on maps. At Ferryhill (NZ 2832) nineteenth-century mining development attached itself to a 'green' village. Sometimes the new settlement derived its name from a nearby village, as did Esh Winning (190420), hailed as a model colliery village when it sprang up south of Esh (197440) after 1859, or New Brancepeth (225415), north of the ancient village of Brancepeth (222380) with its church, castle and Georgian terraces. The site of Spennymoor (2533) was merely a thorny waste before the nineteenth century. Completely new settlements were characteristic of the concealed coalfield, where new locational factors, unrelated to those which inspired the original pattern, created unmistakable 'colliery towns' at the very pitheads with little regard to site or situation. A vivid description of the miners and the mining landscapes of the south Durham coalfield was included in the *Appendix to First Report of Commissioners, Children's Employment Commission (Mines)* of 1842:

> Within the last ten or twelve years an entirely new population has been produced. Where formerly was not a single hut of a shepherd, the lofty steam-engine chimneys of a colliery now send their volumes of smoke into the sky, and in the vicinity is a town called, as if by enchantment, into immediate existence.

Typical of the large, deep pits of the coast which now extract coal from seams extending far out under the North Sea is Easington Colliery, next to the village of Easington with its medieval church. The North Shaft (438442), sunk in the early years of the present century, passes through 500 feet of Permian strata (including 100 feet of the notorious Basal Sands) before reaching the Coal Measures, a technological achievement which would have amazed the early miners scratching at the exposed seams in the then remote valleys of west Durham.

The Lower Swansea Valley, West Glamorgan

Here, in all its desolation, is a true man-made landscape. So triumphant has been the society, so all-pervasive the force of its technology and so single-minded its desire for short-term gain, that the term 'man-made' must be applied to this landscape in a negative rather than a positive sense. What is immediately apparent in the case of the Swansea district is that a crucial portion of the natural landscape has actually been removed, including most of the soil and vegetation. A whole set of environmental systems has been destroyed to leave a scene for which man can take a larger share of the credit than in other, happier cases where, by merely adding a set of human artefacts to the enduring elements of nature, he is more willing but less entitled to do so.

In the middle of the nineteenth century the Lower Swansea Valley was the largest copper-smelting region in the world. At least thirteen works were established here between 1717 and 1850, the presence of which, together with a pool of labour and a tradition of particular skills, attracted related enterprises by a cumulative process of industrial concentration. Zinc smelting, tinplate and steel manufacture, and a range of subsidiary concerns completed the dense industrial scene focused upon the flat, marshy valley bottom of the River Tawe, which spreads out north of the river mouth to form a rough triangle (Figure 74). The high concentration of the smelting industry here may be explained by an involved set of factors operating at more than one spatial scale, some of which came into play successively as time went on, confirming rather than causing the original pattern. A consideration of central importance was the balance between the quantities of coal and ore required in the smelting process. In the nineteenth century, it took eighteen tons of coal to smelt thirteen tons of ore in order to make a single ton of copper by the Welsh process, so that the economic advantage fell to the coalfields, particularly one so conveniently situated between the sources of ore in south-west England and the principal market, the English Midlands. Furthermore, the semi-anthracitic steam coals, cheaply and easily accessible in large amounts in

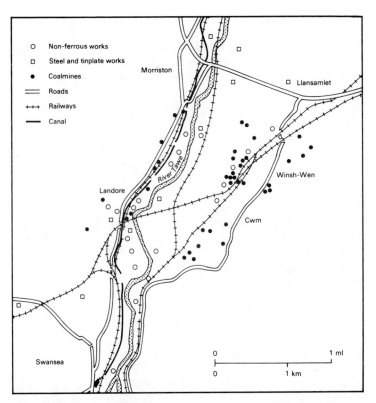

Figure 74. The Lower Swansea Valley

parts of the western end of the South Wales coalfield, were ideal for use in reverberatory smelting furnaces, burning with a bright flame and producing high temperatures with little smoke or ash. The port, advantageously located in Swansea Bay, was served by a navigable river which, besides operating as an artery for the import of copper ore from southwest England (and later from Central and South America), also functioned as a source of water and power. The Swansea Canal and a system of railways transported coal to the port, where it was used as a return cargo by the ore ships. Refractory fireclays suitable for furnace linings were also available nearby. Finally, the local acceptance, through familiarity, of heavy levels of atmospheric pollution also assisted the entrepreneurs who took up the well-placed sites in the valley for their industries.

In spite of these advantages the region's supremacy did not last.

The scale of demand outpaced Swansea's ability to maintain either its monopoly or the domination of its increasingly outdated technology in the face of overseas competitors, who began to introduce smelting at their own rich orefields in order both to reduce the weight involved in transport and to sidestep the efforts of the Swansea concerns to minimize ore prices and maximize the prices paid by manufacturers for the copper metal supplied. Copper smelting at Swansea declined, and it ceased altogether shortly after the First World War, although the fall was partly offset by the rise of spelter or zinc smelting.

Although several decades have since elapsed, the environmental legacy of copper smelting clings tenaciously to the landscape. There are few activities so damaging to the biosphere as the smelting of toxic metals, which leaves not merely the imprint of buildings and installations but poisons the very ground itself. In the 1960s a study was undertaken to find ways of bringing the Lower Swansea Valley back to life and restoring some of the hundreds of blighted acres. The smelters (Figure 75) had polluted the air with vast quantities of fume, made up largely of sulphur dioxide, and sulphuric and sulphurous acid in particulate form, produced by the roasting process which drove off the sulphur contained in the ore.

Figure 75. Copper-smelting works in the Lower Swansea Valley, *c.* 1860

In the words of Richard Ayton, who visited Swansea in 1813, the fume 'acts as a deadly blight upon all vegetation', and there was 'not a blade of grass, a green bush, nor any form of vegetation: volumes of smoke, thick and pestilential, are seen crawling up the sides of the hills, which are as bare as a turnpike-road'. Once the vegetation had been removed, the soil was exposed to erosion by wind and water, leaving a bare landscape scarred by gullies. Upon these barren surfaces were piled bleak tips of noxious waste, notably slag and furnace ash, together with colliery shale, which were joined later by heaps of rubble from the partly demolished buildings. Many of these piles of refuse spewed forth from the copper smelters were honeycombed with cavities produced by old cellars or kilns buried beneath them. In short, the land surface presented a tortured picture of convulsion and ruination.

Contemporaries were equally appalled by the human scene. Some of the employers made attempts to provide housing for their workers, such as John Morris's model gridiron town of Morriston (SS 669978), built in the 1790s, but these failed to keep pace with the demands exerted by uncontrolled industrial development. The fearful appearance of the inhabitants of the crowded stone and slag block terraces horrified travellers such as Ayton who, at the beginning of the nineteenth century, still expected industrial landscapes to be peopled by the bucolic labourers of honest toil, suitably deferential and happy in their lot. Ayton, describing the women coal-breakers in the Swansea Valley, showed less concern for their wretched living conditions than for the low standards of morals and manners which the growth of manufactures seemed to be instilling into the lower orders. Apparently the spread of misery and squalor in the cause of an individual's profits could not excuse the failure of the working classes to conform to appropriate standards of behaviour. Nor, in Ayton's eyes, should they be permitted to offend the sensibilities of their betters simply because, dressed in filthy rags, they spent their dreary lives on the banks of the canal preparing coal for the belching furnaces nearby. He even complained that the women all dressed alike!

These figures, and the industries which dictated their unhealthy existence, have now vanished from the scene, but it would perhaps be unfortunate if, in our eagerness to cure the ills wrought by the past, every vestige of the old landscape were to be erased. The fragments of the buildings, strangely coloured by the deposits of copper, symbolize a period in the history of this country, and an aspect of its life, which modern society has no more right to disregard than any other. In years to come these and other remnants of industrialization may be of more interest, on a number of levels, than those standardized and synthetic landscapes which are replacing them nowadays, with their levelled and grassed-over surfaces accompanied by monotonous expanses of characterless modern factories and insipid housing estates. The creation of man-made landscapes which in the eyes of posterity reflect credit on the society that inspired them is indeed a daunting task.

Soudley Ironworks, Forest of Dean, Gloucestershire
One of the best examples of a 'post-industrial' landscape is furnished by
the Forest of Dean, which now, after a distinguished and varied industrial
past, conceals its scarred and pitted coalfield under a restored sylvan
canopy.

One of Dean's most important industries was the smelting of iron. Iron
ore has been mined here since Roman times (p. 110), and ancient open iron
workings survive as eerie, dark and cavernous excavations. These 'scowles'
follow the Carboniferous Limestone rim of the Dean basin (p. 51),
colonized by lush ferns and mosses and overshadowed by gnarled yews
and other trees, whose great roots thrust their way into the joints and
crevices in the rock. The intricate and weird system of pits at Puzzle Wood,
Lower Perrygrove Farm (SO 579094) is particularly rewarding.

Three technological phases marked the development of the iron industry. From Roman times until the end of the sixteenth century, iron
production in Dean was carried on by means of the 'bloomery' process.
Itinerant bloomeries made a small mass of malleable iron (the 'bloom')
which was then reheated and hammered by the smith. This method was
capable of furnishing high-quality iron, but only in limited quantities.
The charcoal blast furnace, introduced into Dean *c.* 1590 (a whole century
later than in the Weald), produced a greater output, but the impure
charcoal pig iron had to be decarburized by oxidation in the finery before
going to the chafery for shaping (p. 280). This introduced an extra stage in
the process, which as a consequence came to be termed 'indirect', in
contrast to the 'direct' bloomery. It was a much larger and more expensive
enterprise than its predecessor, requiring a set of buildings and separate
water-wheels for the furnace (to power the bellows for the blast), the
finery, the chafery and the hammer. Ponds were often constructed nearby
to ensure a regulated flow of water; the presence of suitable streams for
damming even superseded the availability of ore and charcoal as the prime
locational factor. It is important to remember that the concentration of
charcoal blast furnaces in Dean was a response to these considerations,
not to the existence there of coal, which at this time was used only in
smithying.

It was not until after Abraham Darby's successful use of coal instead
of charcoal in the furnace, a development pioneered at Coalbrookdale in
1709, that the third period in the history of iron smelting began. But only
certain kinds of coal were found to be suitable, and it took most of the
eighteenth century to solve the technical problems associated with the
new process, which in any case, far from being a liberating breakthrough
rescuing the iron industry from an allegedly chronic charcoal shortage,
was adopted only gradually. The demand for charcoal was only one of a

number of pressures exerted upon the woods, and it seems that in many districts the widespread practice of coppicing ensured adequate supplies of wood. The greatest destruction in Dean in the seventeenth century was caused not by the iron furnaces but by Sir John Winter, to whom in 1640 the impecunious Charles I sold most of the Forest, including the minerals, for £106,000 plus a fee-farm rent. Winter, opposed by the inhabitants but in search of a quick profit for himself, promptly set about chopping down this 'wonderfull thicke Forrest'. (Incidentally, there is little doubt that the modern drive – so far, at the time of writing, successfully blocked – to sell off the Dean, in common with other forests, to private interests would have similarly disastrous results.)

The inherently conservative Forest of Dean, hampered by its relative isolation, problems of transport, and the comparatively small-scale and fragmented nature of its iron industry, was especially slow to adopt the coke blast furnace – the first was built only in 1795 – and to profit from technological innovation generally. Such factors contributed greatly to the demise of the industry there in the face of external competition, particularly as Dean was poorly endowed with accessible coking coal, and the once valued iron ores, with their low phosphorus content, no longer conferred an advantage upon the region after a means was found of using the ordinary and low-grade ores common elsewhere. Nevertheless, widespread evidence of all three phases in iron manufacture can be found in Dean. Especially rewarding are the remains at Soudley (SO 6510–6610; Figure 76).

Figure 76. Soudley: principal industrial sites

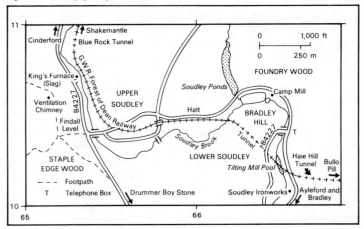

The sinuous Soudley Brook cuts through the double escarpment on the eastern side of the Forest of Dean by means of a deeply incised valley. Small open iron workings of early date can be seen in places, and there is documentary evidence of bloomeries at Soudley in 1228, at about the time that *Sudle* as a place-name (meaning 'the south forest-clearing') was first recorded. Beside the minor road which runs south from Upper Soudley towards Blackpool Bridge, one mile from its junction with the B4227, is the curious artefact known as the Drummer Boy Stone (65450895). It is thought to be a primitive smithing hearth probably dating from the bloomery period. Iron wire was being made at Soudley as early as 1565, but the next enterprise which has left a mark on the landscape is the King's Furnace of 1612–13. This was probably situated between the Brook and the modern B4227 road north of Upper Soudley, not far from the southern portal of Blue Rock Tunnel. The furnace was sold for demolition in 1674, at a time when the Crown was sufficiently well off to announce grandly that conservation of Dean's woods for ship-timber was a wiser policy than their sale to entrepreneurs. All that remains today of this charcoal blast furnace and its various buildings is a deposit of slag believed to be associated with it, which lies on the north side of the track which leads down to the stream from the B4227 (653107). (Slag produced by the various smelting and refining processes of the three periods can be distinguished in hand specimen by its density and colour. The deposit at Soudley is typical charcoal blast furnace slag, being glassy in appearance and bottle-green in colour. The original flow structures are strikingly preserved.) A related forge, destroyed during the Civil War, lay downstream by the site of Camp Mill (a later appellation), a building which has been put to a variety of uses and is now a museum (664106). During the eighteenth century several enterprises flourished for a time in the vicinity of Soudley, particularly at Bradley (666095) and Ayleford (666085), including wireworks, tilting mills and forges, which created a complex of buildings, millponds, dams and sluices. The precise location of these is now uncertain.

Soudley's last iron-smelting enterprise dates from the era of the coke blast furnace, when the Lower Soudley Ironworks enjoyed a brief but impressive life. The nineteenth century witnessed a new scale of activity in mining, industrial and transport operations in Dean. In the Soudley district, the Shakemantle iron mines (652113), following the almost vertical beds of the Carboniferous Limestone to depths attaining 900 feet, yielded 1,650,000 tons of ore between 1841 and their closure in 1899 (Figure 77). The smaller Findall mine in Upper Soudley supplied the Soudley Ironworks. Ventilation in this, as in most mines, was a considerable problem. In Staple Edge Wood a superb hot-air ventilation furnace

(65131058), recently restored, soars skywards amidst the trees. Probably dating from the years around 1800, it consists of a firebox surmounted by a masonry chimney over 40 feet high. The sucking effect of the fire, created by the updraught in the chimney, was conducted underground by a flume and in turn caused fresh air to enter Findall mine below. It is built near to a sizeable scowle hole, covered by ferns and mosses, which provides a memorable setting.

Figure 77. Shakemantle iron mine, *c.* 1900, after its closure

Meanwhile, in the first years of the nineteenth century, a tilting mill was in operation next to Tilting Mill Pool (665102). This lay at the mouth of the Haie Hill Tunnel (1809), on the new tramroad to Bullo Pill by the Severn. This transport artery was designed to bring to market 'the valuable productions of the Forest ... with a feasibility hitherto unknown', and was converted to a railway in 1854. By this time Lower Soudley had been transformed by the erection, in 1837, of coke blast furnaces. These were served by the railway, which, continuing into the Forest, emerged from a second tunnel (Bradley Hill) to arrive at Upper Soudley Halt (659105) on its way past Findall iron level siding to Shakemantle iron mines and dolomite quarries. The blast furnaces, which had a rather erratic history, were constructed where the valleyside afforded a natural charging point, and steam engines rather than water-wheels were used for power. In 1866 only one was in blast, using Dean iron and South Wales coke; the works then employed eighty hands. By 1877 the site was idle, and in 1891 it was reported that the rooks were the only sign of life. The stacks were felled *c.* 1900.

It is interesting to compare Lower Soudley today with the years when the works were at their peak (Figures 78 and 79). The transformation of

Figure 79. Lower Soudley Ironworks: the remains. A modern photograph of the scene depicted in Figure 78. The camera was pointing north-north-west from SO 666100 (see Figure 76), towards Bradley Hill. The outline of the spur, together with the house near the right-hand margins of the two pictures, provide the clearest points of reference. The south-eastern portal of Bradley Hill tunnel, visible in the centre of Figure 78, is obscured by trees in this picture, but some of the remaining stonework of the furnaces can be seen

this once compelling industrial scene seems at first sight well-nigh complete, but several details remain near the ruined walls of the furnaces. Sections of the tramroad and railway lines can be followed with profit, both in Lower Soudley and in the squatter-type settlement of Upper Soudley (Figure 76). Finally, in Foundry Wood and Sutton Bottom the tranquil nineteenth-century ponds, surrounded by magnificent stands of trees, provide one of the modern scenic attractions of Dean.

Longton, Stoke-on-Trent, Staffordshire

The majority of people would hardly expect to derive aesthetic satisfaction from the traditional industrial landscape of Stoke-on-Trent. But appreciation of the visual scene is not limited to the rural and the pre-industrial, while many landscapes which were deliberately planned in order to please the eye merely create an impression of a contrived and rather superficial charm. Much more compelling intellectually, and moving emotionally, are those landscapes whose distinctiveness and sheer impact evoke the spirit of a particular *period* and embody the character of a unique *place*. These landscapes, conveying a depth of meaning in their patterns and symbols, may furnish an experience which overwhelms the more self-conscious and restricted conventions of current taste with a power capable of creating its own kind of beauty. The North Staffordshire Potteries is such a landscape, immortalized in the novels of Arnold Bennett:

the singular scenery of coaldust, potsherds, flame and steam ... It was squalid ugliness, but it was squalid ugliness on a scale so vast and overpowering that it became sublime. Great furnaces gleamed red in the twilight, and their fires were reflected in horrible black canals; processions of heavy vapour drifted in all directions across the sky, over what acres of mean and miserable brown architecture! ... I do not think the Five Towns will ever be described: Dante lived too soon.

(*The Death of Simon Fuge*, in *The Grim Smile of the Five Towns*, 1907)

The 'Five Towns' which inspired Bennett are really six: Longton, Fenton, Stoke, Hanley, Burslem and Tunstall. They are inextricably linked so that the visitor, if not the native, finds it hard to identify precisely either the local centres or the core of the whole. Pottery manufacture here dates back to medieval times, and remained a domestic occupation linked to agriculture in a dual economy until the third quarter of the eighteenth century, when several factors combined to transform it. Predominant among these was a burst of entrepreneurial activity, notably that of Josiah Wedgwood, who set up his factory at Etruria (Hanley) in 1769 and who was responsible for technical innovations and crucial improvements in transport. Although the industry had originally relied upon local clays from the Coal Measures of the Potteries coalfield, Tertiary ball clays from

Dorset and Devon had begun to be imported earlier in the eighteenth century. They were used together with calcined flint to produce a whiter-bodied ware, but were costly to transport, relying on a cumbersome combination of coastal traffic, river shipment and packhorse. Road improvements resulting from the creation of turnpikes greatly assisted the local economy, but the problems associated with the import of clays and the export of the delicate finished goods were only solved by the completion of Brindley's Grand Trunk (Trent and Mersey) Canal in 1777, which slashed freight rates overnight. Although clays (including Cornish china clays) were now brought by the new canal, the large quantities of coal required relative to clay kept the industry firmly located in its original position on the coalfield, constituting a remarkable case of inertia. The distinctive spatial pattern and morphological structure of the Potteries are largely the product of these factors, the lines of settlement being influenced both by the outcrops of the 'long-flame' coals (fortuitously occurring near the junction of the Middle and Upper Coal Measures, next to the finest pot clays) and by the system of turnpike roads which carried coal at specially reduced rates.

These developments confirmed the pre-eminence of the district in pottery manufacture and laid the basis for great expansion in the next century. The cultural landscape created was quite unlike any other in Britain. Far from producing a monotonous scene, the very complexity and diversity of the industrial processes resulted in the construction of intricate sets of generally low buildings clustered around small yards on cramped sites, the apparent disorder of which disguised a high degree of organization. The most characteristic features were the bottle ovens, aptly named bottle-shaped structures made of brick and bound with iron strips or bonts, in which the pottery was fired. There were several types, reflecting the various products and processes, the individual shapes and details varying with each potbank owner. It was these which produced the vast quantities of dense smoke. Nearby were the 'shraff heaps' or dumps of waste materials and broken pots, the collieries and slag tips, the great pits in the Etruria Marl Group of the Upper Coal Measures (from which clays were extracted for use in the manufacture of bricks and tiles), the insanitary terraces of workers' houses and the even more wretched cottages and hovels.

Technological progress and social change have rendered many elements of this scene things of the past. The greatest visual loss was the abandonment of the bottle ovens for gas-fired and electric kilns, a process which began after the war and is now complete. These weird objects are now rarities in a new, almost smoke-free Stoke-on-Trent, and one has to seek them out. Some have been preserved in Longton, which in many ways is the best place to study the Potteries landscape. Being the poorest and most squalid of the six towns (paradoxically specializing in the production of delicate bone-china), it has been less affected by redevelopment, although the worst slums have been demolished. In 1845 Longton was distinguished by 'small houses, very bad open privies; refuse in heaps; puddles; no channels', while in 1864 the Factory Inspectors reported appalling living and working conditions. Pneumonoconiosis (caused by the pulverized flint) and lead poisoning (contracted by the dippers) were rife, while long hours of running in and out of the stiflingly hot premises with heavy loads ruined the health of the ill-fed children, who were often badly treated by the men in the 'small, dirty, dilapidated' rooms of the potbanks. The owners, greedy for higher profits with which to ape the manners of the country gentlemen, often forced the men to collect the pots from the ovens before they were cool, and conveniently attributed the misery and poverty of their employees to an excess of alcohol and a deficiency of morality and religion. The street frontages of the works attempted a level of architectural grandeur deemed to be suggestive of commercial success and social status. The popular design of a two- or three-storeyed brick range, with a central arched entrance, a Venetian window over, and a tripartite lunette window and pediment above that, is exemplified in the Boundary Works of 1819 in King Street. The style persisted long after the Georgian era, and may be seen at the Aynsley Pottery (1861) in Sutherland Road.

The most interesting site in Longton today is undoubtedly the former Gladstone china works, Uttoxeter Road, now a working museum where the social and economic history of the Potteries and the industrial processes themselves are brilliantly kept alive for posterity (Figure 80). The site, with its various buildings (including several bottle ovens), was recently saved from certain destruction, and now, inspired by a pioneering vision of what a museum can achieve, it embodies the rapidly vanishing Potteries landscape in microcosm and forms an island amid the new generation of industrial buildings in Stoke-on-Trent, which have lost all distinction.

Figure 80. Gladstone Pottery, Longton: the potbank yard

Gloucester Docks and the Gloucester and Sharpness Canal

Gloucester is a classic example of an ancient city sited just above the floodplain upon low ground at the head of a tidal estuary, functioning as an inland port and route focus at the lowest bridging point (until 1966) of a major river. But as long ago as medieval times the difficulties of navigation on the River Severn below Gloucester began to affect the life of the port adversely. The sinuous channel, scoured by complex and vigorous currents, was difficult if not impossible for seagoing vessels and hazardous in the extreme for inland craft. No solution was found until the canal era, when the creation of an artificial waterway linking the port directly with the lower Severn, bypassing the tortuous section above Berkeley, seemed the obvious answer to the problem.

The promoters of the canal scheme were confident that once the project, together with the system of docks at the canal terminus on the south-west side of Gloucester, was finished, the city would prosper as an inland port of importance. For not only would the canal afford easy access to the Bristol Channel, but it also stood to gain from connections, at Gloucester, with routes linking the city to the industrial Midlands. In the event, however, the construction of the canal was a long-drawn-out affair, mainly because of financial problems. It was authorized in 1793 as the Gloucester and Berkeley Canal, but the planned length of $17\frac{3}{4}$ miles was shortened when a decision was taken to end the canal at Sharpness, a mile upstream from Berkeley Pill. The years of canal mania had long passed when the chequered history of building was at last brought to a successful conclusion by the opening of the canal in 1827. By this time a new transport boom, that of the railways, was imminent.

But the coming of the railways did not, in the case of the Gloucester and Sharpness, carry the unhappy consequences which sealed the fate of many artificial waterways. For the Gloucester and Sharpness was a ship canal and not a barge canal, carrying imports and exports and coastal traffic rather than transporting goods cross-country. Therefore the more tramway feeders and railway connections which it could attract the better. Far from being its enemy, the railways helped the canal by linking it to places inland and supplying the ships with export cargoes, saving them from returning to sea in ballast. Moreover, the Gloucester and Sharpness was, at the date of opening, the largest ship canal in the country. (The Manchester Ship Canal was not completed until 1894.) Finally, by the time the canal was completed, Gloucester docks had already been in operation for some years, having been opened in 1812. Trade built up well, so extensions to the docks were made, and the canal was improved to accommodate larger vessels. By the early years of this century the annual tonnage figure had reached the million mark, inward traffic making up the major portion.

The extent of this prosperity can be judged by a study of the landscape today. As is often the case with canals, many of the most interesting features of the Gloucester and Sharpness are to be found at its termini, although there are pleasing little classical houses remaining by some of the bridges (replacements of the originals) spaced out along its length. The docks at Sharpness (SO 6702) retain some original buildings and installations, although the famous Severn Railway Bridge of 1879 is no more. The Dean coal which it carried direct to Sharpness served as return cargo for those larger ships which were unable to pass up the canal to Gloucester and so discharged at Sharpness instead.

Of the docks at Gloucester a good deal remains, including an outstanding array of nineteenth-century warehouses and other buildings (Figure 81). They are arranged on a 24¼-acre site centred upon the Main Basin, situated at the end of the canal, and the adjoining Victoria Dock, built in 1849. The water frontages comprise some 10,400 feet of wharves. The brick warehouses are excellent examples of their kind, the regular horizontal arrangements of the windows giving way periodically to the vertical lines of the loading bays and hoists. The oldest surviving warehouses are the two semi-detached units known as the North Warehouse (1826–7), finished just before the opening of the canal. Consisting of four floors and

Figure 81. Gloucester Docks: mid-nineteenth-century corn warehouses lining the Main Basin

a vaulted cellar, the North Warehouse stands at the northern end of the Main Basin near the junction of The Quay with Commercial Road (SO 827184). In the nineteenth century it was used by the corn trade. Despite the changes which have taken place over the last hundred years, including the disappearance of the various kinds of Victorian trading vessel, enough remains to convey the atmosphere of this once bustling inland port, with its crowded complex of docks, wharves and railway sidings.

The Royal Border Bridge, Northumberland

Three bridges span the River Tweed at Berwick (Figure 57). The oldest dates from the first half of the seventeenth century, and still carries traffic (Figure 60). Built of local red sandstone, it took nearly a quarter of a century to complete. The bridge's overall asymmetry – the gradient is a response to the cross-sectional shape of the river channel – together with the varying spans of the fifteen arches, separated by handsome cutwaters surmounted by busts and recesses for pedestrians, make an entirely appropriate and aesthetically satisfying approach to the historic town. The Royal Border Bridge is a worthy successor, and a lasting testimony to the architectural achievements of the railway age. It was designed by Robert Stephenson and built between 1847 and 1850, when it was formally opened by Queen Victoria. Two thousand men, using nearly one and three quarter million bricks, were employed in the construction of this last section of the London to Edinburgh East Coast line. Towering to a height of 126 feet, its twenty-eight stone-faced brick arches extend in a stately curve for over two fifths of a mile across the valley, the sensitively tapering stone piers creating an effect reminiscent of a Roman aqueduct (Figure 82). The only regret is that Berwick Castle was effectively demolished in order to make way for the railway station, which lies at the end of the bridge. (The platform marks the site of the castle hall in which Edward I declared in favour of John de Baliol as King of Scotland in 1292.)

Nevertheless, the third (Royal Tweed) bridge has had a more generally detrimental effect on Berwick by thrusting into Marygate a busy road which pours a heavy stream of intrusive traffic through the heart of the town. Furthermore, the Royal Tweed Bridge, built in the 1920s to cater for the motor age, looks a depressing companion for its infinitely more successful forerunners on either side. It was the work of engineers bent upon making their mark in naked concrete at a time when the material had not yet been revealed as the disaster it so often proves to be. (Since then the discovery has been emphatically and repeatedly made, but architects continue to use the stuff, demonstrating at every turn new ways

Figure 82. The Royal Border Bridge, Berwick-upon-Tweed

in which it repels.) At Berwick the now dirty, clammy texture of the concrete is downright dispiriting, the four progressively lengthening spans of the bridge constituting a heavy, rigid and lifeless structure which seems totally out of place. The new river crossing which the bypass (now under construction) requires will add a fourth bridge: can it be worse than the last one?

Bournemouth, Dorset
The first stirrings of interest in the ritual of sea bathing as opposed to that of taking the waters became apparent while the craze for inland spas was still at its height. In the first half of the nineteenth century the coastal resorts grew faster than any other group of towns in England and Wales, superseding the spas as the centres of fashion. The transition took place at Scarborough, where the seaside potential of the spa was at first developed as a sideline, and as the eighteenth century progressed other towns chanced a precarious existence in this new and fickle market. The decayed medieval towns of Melcombe Regis and Weymouth in Dorset took on such a new lease of life that they coalesced and became one, although Melcombe, capitalizing on the patronage of George III, was always more select than Weymouth. Even at this early stage the various resorts were assuming their individual characters and specializing with respect to their clientele. Margate, for example, was already exploiting its proximity to London by catering for those with modest incomes, who

travelled from the metropolis by hoy while the upper classes used the more expensive coach service. The classic seaside resort, however, which served as a model for those which followed, was Brighton. Patronized by the Prince Regent, its sumptuous Regency architecture and lavish arrangement of terraces, squares and crescents were the inspiration for features which soon became standard components of seaside townscapes.

The heyday of the resorts, when promenades and piers, terraces and parades, villas and boarding houses sprang up with astonishing rapidity in places which had until that time been small fishing villages or nothing but a cottage or two, came with the railway. But even this crucial development, which played such a significant part in creating perhaps the first landscapes of popular as opposed to exclusive leisure, was no guarantee of success for an ambitious resort. The potential for growth was only realized when landowners grasped an opportunity, shrewdly established a promising basis for expansion, and then promoted the town. Blackpool, for example, with its beautiful beaches, only took off in the late nineteenth century after advertising itself as a resort specially geared to the industrial working masses; Eastbourne's prosperity owed much to the energy of the seventh Duke of Devonshire. Saltburn-by-the-Sea, on the Cleveland coast, never did gain the necessary momentum, in spite of possessing both a railway link and a promoter, and it remains an incomplete but nicely preserved monument to Victorian seaside speculation and contemporary visions of coastal resort planning.

Bournemouth was one of the most enduring successes. Its rise during the course of the nineteenth century transformed a wild expanse of sandy heathland with gorse and pines into a high-class and populous resort. It grew up between Poole and Christchurch, where a little valley cut in the soft cliffs of gravel-capped Bagshot and Bracklesham Beds (Eocene) carries the River Bourne to the sea; today the urban mass has extended westwards and eastwards to engulf both these towns. The first house was built by Lewis Tregonwell in 1811 and now forms part of the Royal Exeter Hotel. In the 1830s a 'marine Village' was conceived nearby, composed of detached villas carefully situated within a deliberately maintained wooded landscape. Every effort was made to cultivate an informal plan, avoiding the straight avenues and terraces which so often dominated the new seaside towns. Only in those resorts where the land was owned by an individual or family who controlled the development, as at Torquay, were the consequences of unrestrained speculative building avoided. At Bournemouth, however, the looseness of the settlement's structure proved to be a mixed blessing when growth began in earnest after the arrival of the railway.

In certain respects the qualities of the site were cleverly exploited to Bournemouth's advantage. Even today the pines are inescapable, having been planted to fill every open space and to line the principal avenues. The resinous perfume, the melancholy sighing of the branches, blending with the whispering of the sea, and the thick carpets of needles which cover the sandy soils – all are as inseparable from the image of Bournemouth as the chines, those narrow, steep-sided clefts cut into broader valley floors by streams left hanging as a consequence of cliff recession. (Marine erosion of the slumped cliffs eventually became such a hazard that measures were taken to protect them, creating a new problem in the shape of diminished sand supply to the beach.) The hilliness of Bournemouth was used in conjunction with the informal pattern of streets to produce a pleasing variety in the layout of this 'Mediterranean lounging-place on the English Channel', as Hardy described his 'Sandbourne' in *Tess of the d'Urbervilles*.

But Bournemouth was spoilt by two factors, which detracted from the merits of the site and contributed to the failure of the informal plan. The first was the pattern of growth itself, which turned the already loose structure into an amorphous sprawl; the second was the indifference of the buildings. The character of Bournemouth was established during the 1860s and 70s, when the Surveyor to the Town Commissioners was C. C. Creeke, an undistinguished architect. Nothing has been done since to redeem the situation, and some of the creations that one passes in an attempt to find Victorian Bournemouth are nothing short of horrendous.

CONCLUSION

The Modern Landscape

A description of the modern landscape of England and Wales, even in broad outline, would fill a second volume devoted entirely to it, so extensive have been the changes experienced in the course of this century. It might also require a different approach from that adopted so far here, for the subject would not be a set of selectively preserved historical remnants, studied in order to pursue the related objectives of re-creating former landscapes and unravelling the contribution of the past to the complex totality of the present scene. Instead, an attempt would have to be made to assess whole new landscapes in the making. In some respects this should be an easier task, for the observer is set within the complete, accessible and living present; but in other ways it would be harder, not only because of the difficulties of understanding contemporary society, but also because of the need to distinguish those elements which will prove to be formative or long-lasting from those which are merely transient.

Nevertheless, some account must be given of the principal forces currently moulding the landscape, in order to complete the historical account and to place both the present and the past in perspective. Furthermore, the landscape is not to be viewed simply as a repository of antiquities and relics of mere academic interest, but as the tangible expression of many processes affecting the environment of modern society. This present phase in the history of the landscape is the most important of all in a practical sense, for the developments now taking place are the responsibility of those alive today.

A pivotal concept in the assessment of the twentieth-century landscape is that of change, which has of course been an implicit theme throughout this book. It is very tempting and convenient to suggest that, because landscape has always been subject to changes of all kinds, the questioning of current developments and the attempts made to conserve the past artificially are misguided because they stem from a delusion about the nature of landscape evolution. On the other hand, while accepting that the landscape cannot be fossilized as a museum-piece, it could be said that by no means all changes have proved beneficial to nature or man. A related issue stems from the proposition that very often innovations which are opposed on first appearance are, sooner or later, taken up and accepted. The fact that some artists, writers and composers were ridiculed in their own day but acclaimed later as geniuses – the opposite is also true – joins neatly with the human tendency to dislike being thought unprogressive, and makes possible the gigantic frauds perpetrated by some modern music, art and architecture. Uncritical acceptance of change is as reactionary and irrational in its way as blind opposition. The individual reader must be left to decide whether the twentieth century's contribution to the landscape of England and Wales will be hailed by posterity or not.

There is, however, a more concrete point to be made concerning the inevitability of change. It is true that the landscape has been influenced over thousands of years by man; but the sheer power of his technology, his ability to promote sudden and all-embracing change, is now vastly greater than at any time in the past. Although certain recent studies have emphasized the impact of human societies upon their environments in historic or prehistoric times, and despite the tendency of men to conceive of the achievements of their particular age as unique in history, it is undeniably the case that our power for change is unparalleled.

A prime example of rapid and widespread change is provided by that reputedly conservative sector, agriculture. The most significant influence upon the rural landscape during the twentieth century has been the rise of capital-intensive modern farming. The activities of the big farmers have been promoted by a high degree of mechanization (giving rise to extensive drainage, the ploughing of downland and moorland, the creation of large fields at the expense of copses, 'waste' ground and hedges, and the erection of silos and other plant); assisted by new strains of crop and ever-greater quantities of pesticides and fertilizers (permitting the cultivation of fragile marginal environments, increasing short-term yields, removing plants and animals detrimental to cultures of a single crop, keeping at bay the diseases which appear in highly artificial ecosystems such as these, and attempting to stave off diminishing returns); and supported by an extensive range of financial advantages and by a planning system favourable to the agricultural interest. In the present context, the concern centres upon the wholesale removal of older agricultural landscapes, of earthworks, buildings, hedges, woods, lanes and footpaths – the accumulated shapes, forms and artefacts of millennia.

Most people regret this trend, but many accept it as an economic necessity. In truth, it is precisely the economic aspects which constitute the roots of the problem, for the agricultural pricing system to which the farmers are responding encourages over-production, excludes cheaper food, keeps consumer prices artificially high and uses taxpayers' money to actively destroy landscapes and communities. Farmers cannot be expected to bear the cost of maintaining a romanticized portrait of the landscape; but it is sometimes concluded rather too glibly that an attractive countryside is justified only by sentimentality, and must by definition make economic nonsense. The nation is lamentably distant from an integrated policy which operates in the interests of the whole agricultural community, the needs of the population fed as a result of the farmers' labours, and the ultimate basis of support, the environment, the significance of which is by no means limited to aesthetics.

Agricultural land is itself continually being lost in the face of urban expansion. Over the first half of the twentieth century the percentage of the surface of England and Wales taken up by urban land doubled, the growth of towns in the form of ribbon development and suburban sprawl giving rise to formless and loosely structured urban landscapes comprising monotonous seas of red-roofed bungalows or seemingly endless estates of drab houses. Even the consciously planned urban developments have had a conspicuous struggle to establish any kind of individuality. The garden city movement, originating at the turn of the century with Letchworth in Hertfordshire, attempted to depart from the depressing conditions of the industrial towns by combining rural and urban elements in a carefully laid-out city exhibiting marked functional zoning. As in the late nineteenth-century model settlements built for the employees of Cadbury (Bourneville, West Midlands) and Lever (Port Sunlight, Merseyside), the living environment was designed to be green and pleasant. Spacious middle-class garden suburbs (notably Hampstead) followed in similar vein, although they were purely residential and the illusion of semi-rurality failed to convince.

After the Second World War a positive attempt was made to contain urban spread, particularly that of London, which was provided with a ring of New Towns beyond the Green Belt. These towns were planned to be complete entities in their own right, achieving decentralization by providing overspill populations with homes and jobs. But the tendency of New Town dwellers to commute to work was assisted both by the Towns' proximity to the capital and by the ability of development to drive through or leap over the Green Belt. In addition, the difficulties experienced in building pleasing, distinguished, yet economically prosperous towns enjoying a sense of community have proved considerable. Planned townscapes, which are designed, built and then lived in, are especially revealing landscapes for the study of contemporary societies, and the conceptions of mass-culture urban man embodied in certain British New Town landscapes speak volumes.

The vision of the New Towns as a solution to the country's urban problems has faded with the realization that while the peripheries of the traditional cities continue to extend themselves, the centres require rejuvenation. Dramatic changes have been taking place since the Second World War as a result of plans for the redevelopment of the inner cities, the clearance of slum, derelict or war-damaged sectors, the construction of new transport arteries, the erection of high-rise buildings for both residential and business purposes, the laying out of new shopping centres and car parks, and the modernization and standardization of paving, lighting and other amenities. Urban skylines have altered almost out of recognition in a matter of years, notably during the property boom of the 1960s, when the high land values in city centres were spectacularly exploited to produce clusters of tower blocks. Frequently, the 'change' philosophy referred to at the start of this chapter was given a further twist and pressed into service as the idea that towns must 'develop or decline', and that development necessarily entails drastic or rapid alterations to the plan, structure and fabric. The realization that scale, ensemble and materials are crucial in townscapes came too late to prevent the destruction of some historic urban centres. Even Bath suffered, being subjected to a policy which set out to conserve the highlights and set-pieces while demolishing two thousand of the 'lesser' Georgian buildings.

The key determinant of the urban landscape of the present century, creating prosperity and ruination by turns, has undoubtedly been that 'maker and destroyer of cities', the internal combustion engine. The vastly increased movement of people and goods, the separation of home and workplace, and the building of new roads have extended the limits of towns, congested their centres, and radically altered urban structures. Part of the problem with motor vehicles is again the way in which the economics of the case operate and are presented. Road transport is generally hailed as a flexible alternative to rail transport. But while the railways have to internalize their costs, putting them at a disadvantage despite their speed and more efficient use of power in terms of goods and passengers carried, motor vehicles (especially the large and frequently overloaded lorries) externalize many of theirs, so that they are borne by the community at large. These costs include the financing and maintenance of roads, and the very considerable environmental and social costs (death, injury, noise, pollution, damage to buildings, congestion, and land taken up by roads and services). Unlike the railways, the tendency of large roads (Figure 83) is to become more prominent as traffic increases. Feeder links and additional roads are constructed, and services and ribbon development sprawl along them. Motorways, with their concrete engineering, slash mercilessly through the sinews of the landscape and rarely make any pretence of rising above the strictly functional.

This greatly increased ease of movement, combined with the related shift to tertiary (service) industries from primary occupations (such as agriculture and mining) and secondary industries (particularly heavy manufacturing), has given rise to new patterns of economic activity. Primary and secondary industries are still important in landscape terms, the increased scale of individual operations often creating a huge impact at the local scale. Opencast coalmining and excavations for sand and gravel can completely alter the soil, vegetation and hydrology of an area, while modern quarries are capable of changing the very contours of the land. (Opencast mineral workings are increasing by over 5,000 acres a

Figure 83. An aerial view of the outskirts of Sheffield. When William Cobbett travelled through this district in 1830, he reported that 'all the way along ... it is coal and iron, and iron and coal'. With the locality's 'horrible splendour' now replaced by decay and dereliction, the twentieth-century landscape appears as a tortured and frightening battlefield through which the M1 motorway, carried by the Tinsley Viaduct, sweeps on its way seemingly regardless. This photograph, taken looking approximately north (SK 3990–3991), shows the River Don and the associated Sheffield and South Yorkshire Navigation winding wearily past sewage works, power station, railway yards and, on the left, the doomed East Hecla Steelworks

year.) Some modern manufacturing and resource processing plants, such as steelworks (Scunthorpe and Middlesbrough), oil refineries (Fawley and Milford Haven) and chemical plants (Merseyside and Tees-side), almost completely dominate their respective localities (especially coastal sites and deep-water estuaries) with their buildings and installations. The waste and pollution associated with the processes and products are often more widespread, exacerbated by the 'built-in obsolescence' which is a feature of consumer society. Refuse deposits, polluted and poisoned ground, and other forms of derelict and despoiled land occupy a frightening proportion of the country's land surface (more than a third of a million acres), and the total is being added to all the time, despite reclamation work (Figure 83). The landscapes of modern tertiary industry seem to be all but ubiquitous, as a large proportion of light manufacturing and service industries are reputedly footloose, erecting standardized factories and offices in locations spread throughout the country.

The dispersal of industry was facilitated by the establishment of the national electricity grid. Changes in the balance between different sources of energy have made their mark on the landscape. The huge thermal power stations, particularly those with clusters of cooling towers, are inescapable features of the scene for miles around. Power stations have become increasingly obtrusive with the move from locations close to urban centres, consequent upon the need for large plots of land, extensive transport facilities and the use of new sources of fuel, while pylons and transmission lines are the most prominent features in many a rural view. Nearly all the nuclear power stations have been built at coastal locations away from centres of population, for reasons of safety and in order to provide the enormous amounts of water required for cooling.

A controversial alteration to the scenery of certain upland valleys has been the creation of reservoirs for water supply. The national water requirement has grown very rapidly in recent decades and the authorities have been hard put to it to expand capacity at a commensurate rate. It may seem strange that this country should experience a water supply problem, given its climate, but although the amount and seasonal distribution of rainfall is adequate, annual and monthly departures from the mean can be considerable. While the bulk of the demand comes from the densely populated districts of Lowland Britain, the sparsely settled Highland zone experiences the highest rainfall totals and lowest evaporation rates. Also, the levels of water in the underground reservoirs of lowland England have fallen substantially, while the dry-weather flow of certain heavily used rivers such as the Trent is largely made up of effluent.

One solution to this pressing problem is the retention and storage of water in modified lakes or man-made reservoirs in the uplands, whence it can be piped to the cities. (In this sense, the water requirement is just another way in which urban demands for space and resources are threatening the countryside.) Many valleys in upland regions are well suited to this purpose in view of the nature of their catchments, which are underlain by generally impermeable rocks, voluminous, amply supplied and easily impounded. Indeed, some were glacially enlarged or blocked by glacial debris during the Pleistocene and transformed into natural lakes. The creation of artificial reservoirs is, however, fraught with controversy. The land use of the whole catchment has to be controlled in order to maintain water quality, which can restrict other activities, such as leisure pursuits, which prove to be incompatible with the main objective even in a carefully planned multi-purpose scheme. The slopes of reservoirs tend to plunge artificially, suffer from wave action, and be scarred with unsightly 'high-water' marks when the level drops. It is felt in some quarters that the flooding of valleys, particularly in National Parks (all of which are situated in Highland Britain), constitutes a violation of 'natural' scenery which cannot be justified. This argument is perhaps rather ironic when used in attempts to prevent reservoirs being constructed on Dartmoor simply because bodies of water are held to be alien ingredients in the landscape. Had it been glaciated, Dartmoor would probably now be admired by the very same people for its beautiful lakes.

Land use conflicts of this kind have proved increasingly hard to resolve as the inhabitants of England and Wales have become not only more numerous (very few countries in the world have higher population densities) but also generally wealthier, more mobile, and possessed of greater leisure time. In some places true 'landscapes of leisure' have been created. Some of these are comparatively small-scale, such as the 'honeypots' originally founded upon the site of a scenic or historic attraction but now dominated by shops, services and car parks. Others are much larger, notably those which extend for miles along parts of the coast in the form of holiday camps, seaside resorts, and amorphous towns composed almost entirely of residences occupied by retired people.

The examination of these familiar landscapes reveals the extent of the problems posed by new patterns of leisure in a country whose limited land reserves are subject to intense pressures of multiple use. There are no true 'wilderness' areas, excluded from economic exploitation, and few places are even remotely difficult of access by motor or distant from centres of population. Much of the landscape relies for its scenic qualities upon balance and composition; some of its most beautiful features are deceptively small-scale. Profound changes often result from the pressure of visitors, the spread of contrivances such as caravans which enable the paraphernalia of urban mass culture to be transported bodily into the countryside, and the installation of 'attractions' which are then promoted by the commercial manipulation of tastes, expectations and behaviour. In no time at all the tourists destroy what they originally came to enjoy, although in most cases this fact by no means precipitates a diminution in their numbers. Indeed, the very concentration of visitors at certain sites seems to be part of the appeal for some.

Elsewhere, the weight of numbers may be less, but new fashions in leisure still leave their marks. Especially significant have been the changes experienced by those rural districts where shifts have taken place in the socio-economic composition of the settlements. These movements followed the rise of the second home and weekend cottage, the practice of retiring to the country or coast, and the growth of adventitious populations in general, combined with the severing of links binding rural communities with the land consequent upon the spread of new farming methods. Whatever the ethics of the case, revolving around the trade-off between inflated social tensions and the local reversal of the decline apparent in many rural settlements, appearances have often altered radically. Some places have simply taken on the aspect of a new form of closed village, rigorously preserved by wealthy inhabitants in a state primarily reflecting their very particular tastes and backgrounds. Others, especially commuter villages, continue to grow rapidly through the creation of new estates and the remodelling of existing houses in the latest neo-style, regardless of the original character of the property. But while certain districts are receiving an influx of people, albeit with external economic affiliations, others are experiencing a net loss, particularly of younger people, as employment opportunities decrease, services are withdrawn, and the attractions of city life exert a migratory pull. The continued viability of hundreds of villages must be in question, although it is possible that at some time in the future a diminished or decimated population may be forced to return to a life on the land.

There is therefore plenty of evidence which demonstrates the potency of the forces currently promoting change in the landscape. Landscapes which have evolved gradually can now be suddenly obliterated, or removed more insidiously by a process of cumulative change: once the general aspect has been altered by a violent intrusion, landscapes often become more susceptible to progressive incursions. This is one reason why piecemeal planning has often enjoyed strictly limited success. Another has been the belated realization that the removal of particular features or the insertion of others can have an unexpectedly disproportionate effect upon the whole. The need is clearly for integrated research into the complex totality. From this could be evolved a planning system creating an informed, balanced and long-term landscape policy. It may be objected that the landscape of England and Wales is largely the product of the *un*planned passage of history and the unrestrained operation of human activities, and that the beauty we admire today is the legacy of chance (while much of the ugliness is the fault of planners). But deliberate moulding and the subtle interweaving of countless minor modifications have also played their part, while the disruption of recent decades has been partly caused by the unco-ordinated actions of a pressurized society wielding powerful tools, and demanding an ever greater range of resources. The economic system is inadequate as a regulator, on account of its inability to take the total costs of an activity into account. Many so-called intangibles, like scenery itself, which affect the quality of life but are not necessarily manifested directly in the current material standard of living (although they are often indirectly very important), are not reflected in price terms despite the fact that their value to man (and possibly to themselves and to plants and animals) is very great. Some resources which are essential to life are not represented at all in this way because until they are found to be in short supply or can be turned into a source of profit they are treated as free commodities and are abused accordingly. Air and water are examples, and so is landscape, which is one of the most priceless resources of all.

Landscape also has a reciprocal effect upon society itself. A particularly regrettable trend is the loss of the sense of place. The ability to relate to a particular *locale*, or possess a feeling of belonging, is a human need, and one to which the incredibly diverse landscape of Britain makes a vital contribution. But the sale of mass-produced goods, the diffusion of mawkish architecture, the appearance in every major town of identical shops, car parks and offices, and the spread of service industries have all contributed to a sameness in which each place is beginning to look like every other. The tendency is strengthened by the standardization of tastes and ideas in a society whose very complacency about its respect for individuality and its capacity for discriminating choice renders it vulnerable to subtle and effective manipulation of its attitudes and beliefs.

But there are opposing forces too. A good deal of regional culture has shown itself to be remarkably resilient. There is a growing body of informed and articulate people who care about their environment and their society. Although it is tempting, glancing back over the span of history, to identify inequality as somehow necessary to the creation of beauty, and to conceive of the more even distribution of wealth as contributing to the spread of mediocrity, there is another side to the coin. Concentration of wealth (which has of course by no means disappeared) may have been directly responsible for systems of patronage and some inspired use of money, but many members of the old elites could hardly be described as cultured, knowledgeable or creative, while true artistic genius has always manifested itself regardless. With the growth of equality of opportunity, many people today are far more broadly educated, critical and concerned than before, and while they are currently obliged to look mainly to the past for fulfilment of their enthusiasm for civilized values, they are also seeking to improve the present. With a tremendous slice of luck we may even yet save some of the achievements of the past and make a worthwhile contribution to the future; but the landscape of England and Wales is surely too precious to be chanced to mere fortune.

INDEXES

Items appearing in illustrations or their captions are indicated in italic, e.g. *43*.
  The Index of Subjects and Persons is followed by a Geographic Index listing places, sites, buildings etc.

INDEX OF SUBJECTS AND PERSONS

GEOGRAPHIC INDEX

MORE ABOUT PENGUINS, PELICANS, PEREGRINES AND PUFFINS

For further information about books available from Penguins please write to Dept EP, Penguin Books Ltd, Harmondsworth, Middlesex UB8 0DA.

In the U.S.A.: For a complete list of books available from Penguins in the United States write to Dept DG, Penguin Books, 299 Murray Hill Parkway, East Rutherford, New Jersey 07073.

In Canada: For a complete list of books available from Penguins in Canada write to Penguin Books Canada Ltd, 2801 John Street, Markham, Ontario L3R 1B4.

In Australia: For a complete list of books available from Penguins in Australia write to the Marketing Department, Penguin Books Australia Ltd, P.O. Box 257, Ringwood, Victoria 3134.

In New Zealand: For a complete list of books available from Penguins in New Zealand write to the Marketing Department, Penguin Books (N.Z.) Ltd, Private Bag, Takapuna, Auckland 9.

In India: For a complete list of books available from Penguins in India write to Penguin Overseas Ltd, 706 Eros Apartments, 56 Nehru Place, New Delhi 110019.

PENGUIN TRAVEL BOOKS

☐ *Arabian Sands* **Wilfred Thesiger** £3.95

'In the tradition of Burton, Doughty, Lawrence, Philby and Thomas, it is, very likely, the book about Arabia to end all books about Arabia' – *Daily Telegraph*

☐ *The Flight of Ikaros* **Kevin Andrews** £3.50

'He also is in love with the country . . . but he sees the other side of that dazzling medal or moon . . . If you want some truth about Greece, here it is' – Louis MacNeice in the *Observer*

☐ *D. H. Lawrence and Italy* £4.95

In *Twilight in Italy, Sea and Sardinia* and *Etruscan Places,* Lawrence recorded his impressions while living, writing and travelling in 'one of the most beautiful countries in the world'.

☐ *Maiden Voyage* **Denton Welch** £3.95

Opening during his last term at public school, from which the author absconded, *Maiden Voyage* turns into a brilliantly idiosyncratic account of China in the 1930s.

☐ *The Grand Irish Tour* **Peter Somerville-Large** £4.95

The account of a year's journey round Ireland. 'Marvellous . . . describes to me afresh a landscape I thought I knew' – Edna O'Brien in the *Observer*

☐ *Slow Boats to China* **Gavin Young** £3.95

On an ancient steamer, a cargo dhow, a Filipino kumpit and twenty more agreeably cranky boats, Gavin Young sailed from Piraeus to Canton in seven crowded and colourful months. 'A pleasure to read' – Paul Theroux

PENGUIN TRAVEL BOOKS

☐ *The Kingdom by the Sea* **Paul Theroux**   £2.50

1982, the year of the Falklands War and the Royal Baby, was the ideal time, Theroux found, to travel round the coast of Britain and surprise the British into talking about themselves. 'He describes it all brilliantly and honestly' – Anthony Burgess

☐ *One's Company* **Peter Fleming**   £3.50

His journey to China as special correspondent to *The Times* in 1933. 'One reads him for literary delight . . . But, he is also an observer of penetrating intellect' – Vita Sackville West

☐ *The Traveller's Tree* **Patrick Leigh Fermor**   £3.95

'A picture of the Indies more penetrating and original than any that has been presented before' – *Observer*

☐ *The Path to Rome* **Hilaire Belloc**   £3.95

'The only book I ever wrote for love,' is how Belloc described the wonderful blend of anecdote, humour and reflection that makes up the story of his pilgrimage to Rome.

☐ *The Light Garden of the Angel King* **Peter Levi**   £2.95

Afghanistan has been a wild rocky highway for nomads and merchants, Alexander the Great, Buddhist monks, great Moghul conquerors and the armies of the Raj. Here, quite brilliantly, Levi writes about their journeys and his own.

☐ *Among the Russians* **Colin Thubron**   £3.95

'The Thubron approach to travelling has an integrity that belongs to another age' – Dervla Murphy in the *Irish Times*. 'A magnificent achievement' – Nikolai Tolstoy

PENGUIN REFERENCE BOOKS

☐ *The Penguin Map of the World*   £2.95

Clear, colourful, crammed with information and fully up-to-date, this is a useful map to stick on your wall at home, at school or in the office.

☐ *The Penguin Map of Europe*   £2.95

Covers all land eastwards to the Urals, southwards to North Africa and up to Syria, Iraq and Iran * Scale = 1:5,500,000 * 4-colour artwork * Features main roads, railways, oil and gas pipelines, plus extra information including national flags, currencies and populations.

☐ *The Penguin Map of the British Isles*   £2.95

Including the Orkneys, the Shetlands, the Channel Islands and much of Normandy, this excellent map is ideal for planning routes and touring holidays, or as a study aid.

☐ *The Penguin Dictionary of Quotations*   £3.95

A treasure-trove of over 12,000 new gems and old favourites, from Aesop and Matthew Arnold to Xenophon and Zola.

☐ *The Penguin Dictionary of Art and Artists*   £3.95

Fifth Edition. 'A vast amount of information intelligently presented, carefully detailed, abreast of current thought and scholarship and easy to read' – *The Times Literary Supplement*

☐ *The Penguin Pocket Thesaurus*   £2.50

A pocket-sized version of Roget's classic, and an essential companion for all commuters, crossword addicts, students, journalists and the stuck-for-words.